PRAISE FOR THE FRACTURED [...]

"The Europe sequence is some of my fav[...]
and *Europe in Winte[...]* exce[...]
human, with espionag[...] wrapped up in a reality-altering
[...] [...], [...] here
was literary justice, catch the attention of prize after prize. I love
these books. I want more. Now."

Patrick Ness on *Europe in Winter*

"As rich and as relevant as its predecessor. It's funny, fantastical,
readable and remarkable regardless of your prior experience of the
series. Which just goes to show that, no matter how well you think
you know something—or someone, or somewhere, or somewhen—
there's almost always more to the story."

Tor.com on *Europe at Midnight*

"*Europe in Autumn* is one of the most sophisticated science fiction
novels of the decade: a tour-de-force debut, pacey, startlingly
prescient, and possessed of a lively wit. When approaching its
follow-up, I felt both nervous and excited. Would Hutchinson
be able to pull off the same magic a second time? The answer is
undoubtedly yes. *Europe at Midnight* is pitch-perfect, bursting with
the same charisma and intricate world-building as its predecessor."

LA Review of Books on *Europe at Midnight*

"In a way, what is most striking about *Europe at Midnight* is not
the hard edge of its politics, or even the casual brilliance of its
science fictional reworking of the political thriller, but Hutchinson's
thrillingly assured control of his material. He writes wonderfully,
his prose animated not just by a keen eye for character, but by a
blackly witty sense of humor."

Locus Magazine on *Europe at Midnight*

"The author's authoritative prose, intimate knowledge of eastern
Europe, and his fusion of Kafka with Len Deighton, combine to
create a spellbinding novel of intrigue and paranoia."

The Guardian on *Europe in Autumn*

EUR
IN
WIN

OPE

DAVE
HUTCHINSON

TER

First published 2016 by Solaris
an imprint of Rebellion Publishing Ltd,
Riverside House, Osney Mead,
Oxford, OX2 0ES, UK

www.solarisbooks.com

ISBN: 978 1 78108 463 2

10 9 8 7 6 5 4 3 2 1

A CIP catalogue record for this book is available from
the British Library.

Designed & typeset by Rebellion Publishing

Printed in Danmark by Nørhaven

The Fractured Europe Sequence

Europe in Autumn
Europe at Midnight
Europe in Winter

PART ONE

DESIRE
PATHS

TRANS-EUROPE EXPRESS

1.

THEY ALMOST MISSED the train. They had always planned to arrive close to departure time, so that Amanda had to spend as little time as possible on her feet, but there was a flash mob on the Place de la Concorde and all the streets leading into it were blocked.

"What the hell is this?" muttered William, who was driving.

"Anti-Union protesters," Kenneth said, reading the placards being carried by the crowds boiling between the traffic.

"Well, God has a sense of irony, anyway," muttered Amanda, shifting uncomfortably on the back seat.

William looked back at her. "How are you feeling?"

"I'm all right," she said. "Don't worry about me. Can we go another way?"

They were in a make of vehicle nicknamed *La Rage* by the French, basically a looming black mediaeval fortress festooned with bullbars and lights and antitheft devices. Kenneth had wanted something more anonymous, but William said the only thing Parisian drivers understood was force. It had one obvious drawback; although its defensive systems could cause epileptic fits and rectal bleeding in anyone stupid enough to try to steal or attack it, it was too large to go down many of Paris's lesser thoroughfares.

"We're stuck," William said, twisting left and right to look out of the windows and hovering his finger over the icon on the dash display which triggered a 10,000 volt charge through the skin of the car, as protesters bumped and pushed by between the line of vehicles.

"Don't hurt anybody," Kenneth said. "We'll be all right." He looked at his watch, then at Amanda. "We'll be all right," he told her.

"Fucking stupid car," she said with a little smile.

He shrugged helplessly and turned back in his seat to look out through the windscreen. From this vantage point, he could see a street filled with the roofs of lesser vehicles, the spaces in between them choked with protesters blowing whistles and waving animated banners. Most of the protesters were wearing gas masks or scarves around their faces, the traditional garb of the political mob; some were more self-consciously retro, sporting Guy Fawkes masks.

"Well," he said, to nobody in particular.

Unable to use the car's more proactive weaponry – the horn had a mode which, when activated, produced a note that could shatter shop windows – William had to amuse himself by depressing the throttle pedal every now and again; the low, rumbling throb of the engine was enough to make protesters shy away momentarily. But even that palled after a while; William really wanted to electrocute or nerve gas or incinerate or just simply drive up and over the wall of cars and people standing between them and their destination, and none of these options were available to him, so he just settled into a long loop of swearwords in French and English.

Eventually, the *gendarmerie* arrived. Kenneth, William and Amanda were treated to brief views of large grey vehicles driving back and forth across the Place, spraying the crowds of protesters, journalists and rubbernecking tourists with riot foam, at which point many people fell down fast asleep and were subsequently scooped up by other vehicles and deposited none-too-gently on the edges of the open space. There would be broken bones and damaged camera equipment and probably some deaths, and later many lawsuits and insurance claims and scandals uncovered by the news organisations, but for the moment the traffic could move again. Which pleased William.

"*Now* we're late," Kenneth observed.

"We'll be fine." William touched an icon on the dash and the car did his favourite trick apart from killing people – filling the windscreen with a head-up display which showed a GPS map of the surrounding streets, directions to their destination, and the location of anything the vehicle's expert system judged to be a possible threat. A green carpet seemed to appear before them, stretching away into the distance, curving around the obelisk in the centre of the Place and fading out of sight. William depressed the car's accelerator and it moved smoothly forward with the stream of traffic, passing police vehicles and straggling protesters alike.

The early part of their route had been something of a bone of contention. Kenneth had maintained that it would have been preferable to head directly north from the flat in the 8th and pick up the ring road. William had pooh-poohed that idea, saying it added miles to their journey and that it would be best to head almost directly south towards Savigny. In the end, the thing which decided the matter was the fact that William was the only one of them who could drive and could, basically, do whatever he wanted once he was behind the wheel of *La Rage*.

Once they were out of the traffic in the centre of town, William set the car into cruise mode and the note of the engine dropped to an almost subliminal vibration that pushed them gently back into the upholstery. Beyond the windscreen, the green carpet unrolled before them.

Kenneth looked at his watch, and from the back seat Amanda said, "We can always take another train."

He shook his head. Travel on the Line was not like any other kind of rail travel. One did not, for example, normally have to take out temporary citizenship in the company which ran the Channel Tunnel rail route. If they missed this train, they might not be able to travel again until the Spring, and he couldn't put her through all this again. He glanced across at William, who nodded at the little numbers at the bottom of the windscreen to indicate that they were already at the speed limit for this road. The French had a particularly bloody-minded band of traffic policemen, known as *guêpes* after their black and yellow ballistic armour, who rode ferocious 3,000 cc BMW motorcycles and carried assault rifles. Nobody in their right mind wanted to tangle with them. Kenneth shrugged.

The Line itself did not pass anywhere near Paris; the amount of demolition needed to accommodate it would have been ruinous. Its track gauge was unlike any other in Europe, to prevent other rail companies using it, but this also meant that everywhere the Line wanted to go, dedicated track had to be laid; it could not share the rail infrastructure of the nations and polities and duchies and sanjaks and earldoms and principalities and communes it passed through. In the case of Paris, a long consultation period had accompanied the negotiations for a Line Embassy. There had been protests and riots and sit-ins wherever the government proposed granting a site, and in the end Savigny-sur-Orge had been chosen simply because the level of civil unrest had been slightly lower there than elsewhere. There was a general feeling in France that Savigny had wound up with the country's Line Embassy because the Saviniens had just not tried quite hard enough.

France was an unusual proposition for the Line. Everywhere else it passed, cities and polities clamoured for branch lines and Consulates and Embassies; there was a certain – unfounded – cachet in having a connection with the Line. But in France there was, on the whole, very little welcome, and the Line Company had found itself having to deal with militant architects, conservationists, eco-terrorists, political terrorists of many stripes, politicians, heavily-armed farmers, the French Army and Air Force, and hundreds of thousands of annoyed property owners. The Line solved the problem the way it solved all the problems it encountered during its decades-long plod across the Continent. It just kept going and eventually the opposition gave up. The Line stitched its way from one side of France to the other, and in time a branch curled away towards what, in a gesture of capitulation, the French began to call Paris-Savigny.

The Line recommended that all passengers arrive at least two hours before departure, to allow time for security and document checks. In practice, this always resulted in a last-minute rush before the boarding gates were opened, and by the time Kenneth, Amanda and William arrived at the Embassy compound there was a long line of people waiting to pass through.

They had to park outside the compound – the Line allowed no foreign vehicles onto its territory – and find a concierge who could come up with a motorised wheelchair for Amanda, but after that everything went to plan.

William had no visa, so they had to part at the gate to the compound, and all of a sudden the events of the morning seemed to melt away and they stood there awkwardly, unable to think of anything to say to each other. They settled for hugs, and then William turned away and headed towards the car park without looking back.

Kenneth looked at his wife. She was sitting uncomfortably in the wheelchair, cradling the bulge of her pregnancy, her face pale. "We'll soon be on board," he told her.

"It takes ten minutes to process each passenger," she said with a weak smile. "Baggage check-in, security, documents, more security. They can process a hundred passengers at a time. Each train has a maximum capacity of fifteen hundred passengers."

He reached down and squeezed her shoulder affectionately. "I know," he said. "I know."

"Two and a half hours to completely board each train," she went on calmly. "And that's if everything goes smoothly, which it never does because passengers forget their documents or their phones set off the security scanners or their perfume sets off the explosive sniffers or they just decide to argue with the officials about any damn little thing that occurs to them."

"We're in a priority queue," he reminded her.

"More expense," she said. "This is costing a fortune."

"Just a few more minutes," he said.

She reached up and took his hand. "I love you," she said.

He squeezed her hand and looked around at the lines of people waiting to pass through the boarding checks. These were not, it occurred to him, people who were normally used to queuing for anything. Very few of them – none at all, in fact, he decided as he scanned the crowds – presented as working class, or even upper middle class. There were furs and Louis Vuitton carry-ons and cashmere overcoats draped capelike over shoulders, and children with sunglasses worth more than your average Renault factory worker's annual salary. One small group – beefy shaven-headed father with expensive wrist jewellery, slim mother with a pushchair designed by the same people who designed Formula One racing cars, and three large neckless men who were almost certainly bodyguards – he tagged as *mafiye*. He thought he caught a glimpse, at the core of another knot of passengers, of a German actress of a certain notoriety. The Line was not so much a mode of transport, more a lifestyle choice. He and Amanda looked the part, but their clothes were all cheap copies, their luggage bootlegs of Swaine Adeney Brigg classics.

The Line did not care what its passengers were wearing. Its French Embassy was a forbidding four-storey grey cube at the heart of the compound, its upper three floors lined with tall slit windows and its flat roof festooned with dishes and antennas. To one side stood a building which looked like a small out-of-town motel, and it was through this, shepherded by liveried and armed Line security personnel, that the queues of passengers were disappearing.

Amanda was speaking on her phone. "Yes," she was saying. "We're just waiting to get on board now. Very, yes. Some time the day after tomorrow. In the evening, I think."

They had been living in Paris for five years now. Amanda had her own design business, producing limited-edition silk-screen T-shirts for film and theatre premieres. They had been here long enough, Kenneth thought, to get a sense of the city's moods and rhythms. He had thought that apart from the obvious signifiers of architecture and weather and language, all European cities were much the same, but Paris had proved him wrong. It was quite unlike anywhere else he had ever lived.

"What are you thinking about?" asked Amanda. She had finished her call and returned her phone to her pocket.

He smiled and shook his head. "Nothing much. Who was on the phone?"

"The office." She was worried about how the business would cope without her, even though Marie-France, her assistant, was more than capable of taking care of things in her absence. "The Luhansk stuff."

Despite their name, Luhansk were a middle-aged stadium rock band from Leicester in the English Midlands. Amanda was trying to branch the business out into high-end concert merchandising. Kenneth said, "I thought all that was wrapped up."

She shrugged. "It's nothing. A couple of last-minute details. I'll conference with Marie-France and their merchandising manager when we're on the train."

"You're not supposed to exert yourself," he told her.

She waved it away. "Fifteen minutes in a conference space. I won't even have to stand up. Half an hour at the most."

The queue moved forward a few metres, then stalled again. They were just outside the open glass doors of the departure building.

"Do you think William will be all right?" Amanda said. "On his own?"

"Yes," he replied. He had gone over things with William over and over again; he was as sure as he could be that everything would run smoothly. Homicidal driving tendencies apart, William was a solid, reliable fellow. He was a credit to the group.

"I shouldn't worry about him, I suppose," said Amanda. "But still."

The line moved again and they passed into the departures building, and then there was a smartly-dressed young Moroccan, with a pad under his arm and a little badge on the breast pocket of his blazer identifying him as 'Etienne,' standing beside them, murmuring apologies in almost accentless English.

"Mrs Pennington, Mr Pennington," he said, "I'm so dreadfully sorry. You were never meant to queue here. Please accept my most abject apologies on behalf of the Trans-Europe Rail Company."

"We expected to queue," Kenneth said equably. "Everyone else has to."

"But Mrs Pennington's condition..." Etienne shook his head. "Unforgivable. I promise you the staff members responsible will be disciplined."

"We don't want to get anybody in trouble," Amanda said.

Etienne shook his head again. "Madame," he said with a solemnity deeper than his years, "we do not treat our citizens like this."

The exchange was carried out in quiet voices, but even so it was starting to attract the attention of other passengers around them. Kenneth said, "So what can we do?"

"Please," Etienne said. "Please, come with me."

"Oh, there's no need for that," Amanda said. "Look, we're almost at the head of the queue now."

"Mrs Pennington," Etienne said, holding out his hands. "I insist. It's the least I can do."

Amanda and Kenneth exchanged glances, and he nodded fractionally.

"Lead the way, then, Etienne," she said, loudly enough for her voice to carry as she steered her wheelchair out of the queue and followed the Moroccan, the chair's tyres hissing softly on the hardwearing carpet.

Etienne led them up to the line of Security desks and then turned off sharply and opened a door at the edge of the room. Beyond was a stark, utilitarian corridor ending in another door, and when they went through that they found that they had passed beyond the security and document checks. Etienne took them to a small side-room, where a young woman in a blue and silver uniform sat waiting beside a portable scanner.

"You understand," Etienne said. "You must still undergo the usual procedures."

"Of course," Kenneth said, suddenly feeling trapped. The plan had been to go through Security with all the other passengers. It was late; the staff would be under pressure to process everyone quickly, they would be able to see the line stretching back to the doors of the departure building and know that they still had a lot to do. They would hurry, be sloppy. Here it was just them and Etienne and the young woman in her smart uniform, and all the time in the world. He looked down at Amanda and said, "Ladies first?"

If Amanda was at all nervous, she didn't show it. She rolled the chair up to the scanner and waited patiently while the young woman – whose nametag identified her as 'Claudine' – set things up. Claudine was just as apologetically efficient as Etienne, but she and Amanda exchanged a few words – her English was almost as good as Etienne's – and at one point Amanda reached out and rested her hand on the girl's forearm, and Kenneth knew everything would be all right.

At one point during the procedure, Claudine looked up from the scanner's readout and said, "Madame, there is a..." She touched her stomach.

"It's a remote foetal heart monitor," Amanda told her. "There were some problems early on. It lets my doctor keep an eye on things."

"But no problems now?" asked the girl sincerely.

Amanda shook her head. "We decided to leave the monitor where it is, though, until after the baby's born."

Claudine nodded. "My sister, she was the same," she said.

"Her baby, it's okay, though?"

"Him? He's just started school. Strong as a horse."

Etienne, standing quietly in the corner using his pad to process their documents, glanced up momentarily, but said nothing.

"That's good," Amanda said with a smile. "I'm glad."

Claudine beamed and patted her on the shoulder. "There," she said. "You're done." She looked at Kenneth. "Now you, if you please, sir?"

Kenneth also passed the security scan, as did their luggage, and as Claudine packed up the scanner Etienne took over again, showing the couple out of the room and down another corridor and through another door and suddenly they were on the platform and there it was in front of them, the sleek blue and silver Paris-Novosibirsk Express, all seventy carriages of it, sleeping in the lunchtime sunshine.

"I have taken the liberty," Etienne announced, beckoning a liveried porter over to help with their luggage, "of upgrading your berth."

"There was no need to do that," Kenneth said. "Really."

Amanda reached up and touched him on the arm. "Darling." She said to Etienne, "That's very kind of you, Etienne. I'm sorry that we've caused you so much trouble."

"You have caused us no trouble at all," Etienne assured them, handing their documents back to Kenneth. "It has been a pleasure to meet you, and I hope you have a safe and comfortable journey."

He turned and walked back along the platform, no doubt to firefight some other small problem. Kenneth watched him go, knowing that the young man's life was about to become interesting in ways he could never possibly have imagined. Then he followed Amanda and the porter along the train, where a ramp had been fitted to allow Amanda's wheelchair to board.

The upgrade Etienne had told them about turned out to be roughly the equivalent of upgrading from a Sopwith Camel to Concorde. They had booked the cheapest sleeper they could afford, a cramped berth with bunks and many space-saving features. The berth they were shown to was more of a stateroom.

"It's got a bed," Amanda said with a big smile.

They were obviously in oligarch territory. Kenneth had spotted the *mafiye* family a little further down the corridor, entering their own stateroom. "And a shower," he said, peeking in through an open door.

"Oh, thank God," she said, levering herself out of the wheelchair. "I really need the loo." She went into the bathroom and closed the door, leaving Kenneth to tip the porter, who collapsed the wheelchair, stowed it in a cupboard, and left.

Kenneth wandered around the stateroom. It seemed unbelievable that they had been upgraded quite so far, and if it was unbelievable it was suspect. He took his phone from his jacket pocket, opened an app that would sweep the room for bugging devices, and left it on the bedside table. There were baskets of fruit, chocolates and complimentary toiletries on the bed, along with a bottle of a nice-looking Cabernet and two shrink-wrapped wineglasses. He picked them up, turned them over, put them back.

The room was in fact four regular-sized berths knocked together. At one end was a little kitchenette-diner area; in the middle was a living area with an entertainment set and a coffee table and a small sofa. He looked in the cupboards in the kitchenette, found basic cooking equipment. One cupboard hid a little fridge with some wrapped cheeses and sliced meats. In one of the drawers he found a corkscrew, and he took it back to the bedroom and opened the bottle of wine, set it on the bedside table to breathe. The phone was still scanning, but it hadn't found anything yet.

The door of the bathroom opened. Amanda came out, saw him sitting on the bed, and came over and sat beside him. She took his hand and held it against her cheek. Neither of them said a word.

THE LINE HAD been decades in the building. It had originally aspired to being a straight line drawn across Europe and Asia, from the Atlantic coast of Spain to Cape Dezhnev, facing Alaska across the Bering Strait. Geography and simple pragmatism meant that this was never achievable, and the Line crossed the continent in a series of meanders and doglegs. Only one train a year ever made the entire journey – popular with tourists and gap-year students with wealthy parents and train buffs who had spent the previous decade saving for their tickets. The rest of the scheduled services ran on a weekly or monthly basis, vast trains crossing the continent at up to two hundred and fifty kilometres an hour and peeling off down branches from the main Line to reach their destinations.

The Paris-Novosibirsk Express ran twice a month, in each direction. The capital of the Republic of Sibir had reconfigured itself into a financial powerhouse to rival Shanghai, a genuine global player, and according to Kenneth and Amanda's temporary Line citizenship application they were travelling there to meet with a group of hedge fund managers who had shown some interest in investing in Amanda's business. Siberian businessmen were big on physical presence; for important meetings they preferred face-to-face, in-the-flesh stuff rather than teleconferencing. It was a nine-hour flight from Paris, which Amanda's doctor had advised against, and driving was out of the question. Which left either a journey on various national railways made almost impossible by interminable border delays, or a three-day trip on the Line.

The train left Savigny on time on a quiet vibration of motors. It was said, although no one had yet been able to prove it, that Line trains were powered by fusion generators, notwithstanding that fusion power was still in its infancy. The train made its way down the branch line from Savigny at a steady seventy kph, leaned into a long curve as it joined the main West-East Line, and accelerated smoothly up to full speed.

Before they were even out of France Amanda put on her glasses, dialled some numbers on her pad, and settled into a long and apparently very dull conference with Marie-France in Paris, Luhansk's merchandising manager in London, and at least two members of the band themselves, probably in some Caribbean tax haven. Kenneth could only hear her side of the conversation. Glancing at her pad, on the living room coffee table, he saw a two-dimensional representation of the conference space she and the other participants were using. It was a generic boardroom with the avis of the others gathered at the end of a narrow conference table; the perspective looked odd because Amanda was seeing it in fully-rendered three-d through her glasses.

He left her to it, went over to the window. Not that there was much to see. The twin tracks of the Line ran across Europe between high fences, about a kilometre apart. The space between the fences was a rushing wasteland of gravel broken by the occasional siding and repair depot. Any scenery was a long way away. He went and had a shower.

Amanda was still at it when he came out, sketching notes in a text editor on her pad while she carried on her conversation via the conference space. Kenneth poured himself a glass of wine and stretched out on the bed.

He woke some time later, the empty glass on the table by the bed and Amanda sitting beside him.

"Sorry," he said, struggling upright against the headboard. "Nodded off."

"It's the rhythm of the wheels on the tracks," she said. She stroked his hair. "It always makes me sleepy."

"Where are we?"

She looked across the stateroom to the little paperscreen pasted to the far wall beside the kitchenette. It was showing, in a constantly-scrolling series of measurements and languages, their speed and present position.

"Still in Greater Germany, by the look of it," she said.

He picked up his phone and checked the time. The bug-scanning app had finished its job and found nothing objectionable, but that didn't rule out all forms of surveillance. "How was the conference?"

She shrugged. "It's always the same. Last-minute tweaking, last-minute panics. They just need an adult to hold their hand and tell them everything will be fine. You know how it is."

He sighed. "Do you want to go out for dinner or get room service?" he asked.

"Maybe we can eat out tomorrow," she said with a smile. "I'm tired."

"All right," he said. He got up and went over to the entertainment centre and waved up the onboard menu.

Room service turned out to be excellent.

OLIGARCH STATUS OR not, it was still, after all, a train journey, and the next day dragged as the express crossed Poland, skirted the northern borders of Ukraine, and passed teasingly close to Moscow before angling away eastward. Amanda took care of some more work, Kenneth tried to read a novel. They sat and watched a film, and then spent an hour or so arguing about it.

In the evening, they took the wheelchair out of its cupboard, unfolded it, and headed for the dining car in the next carriage. Few of the passengers had decided to take advantage of the early sitting for dinner, and the car was nearly deserted. Most of the other diners seemed to be travelling alone. Kenneth ordered Kobe beef with dauphinoise potatoes and a green salad. Amanda chose red snapper. They ate in silence, apart from a few comments about how good the food was.

Afterward, they went back to their stateroom and lay on the bed, holding each other, while the paperscreen on the wall ate up the kilometres and the train reached the edge of the European Plain – the edge of Europe itself, as some saw it – and began to negotiate the Ural Mountains.

Just before eleven o'clock in the evening, Kenneth's phone rang a discreet little chime. He sat up unwillingly and checked the screen on the wall, found that his calculations had only been a few tens of kilometres out, and he leaned over and kissed his wife. There was no need to say anything.

They didn't bother with the wheelchair. Kenneth began to take it out of its cupboard, but she put her hand on his shoulder and shook her head, and he understood that this was something she wanted to do under her own steam.

As they stepped out into the corridor, Kenneth felt the train slow and lean into a curve in the track; the approach to the Ufa Tunnel, cutting beneath a number of problematical mountains in the Southern Urals which it had been uneconomical or geographically impossible to go around. At twenty-four kilometres, it was the longest of the Line's many tunnels.

Kenneth and Amanda walked unhurriedly. Few people were about at this time of the night; they saw a couple of white-jacketed stewards carrying trays of late snacks to other sleeper berths, nodded hello as they passed. Just an ordinary couple stretching their legs before retiring for the night.

They walked three carriages towards the front of the train. At the end of the third, they came to a dead end, a blank wall. On the other side of the wall was the carriage containing the train's power unit, whatever it was. As they reached it, there was a concussion through the train, the shockwave as it entered the tunnel at a little over ninety kilometres an hour. At that speed, they had about eight minutes until it reached the midpoint. Kenneth triggered the stopwatch countdown on his phone and looked into Amanda's eyes. There was nothing to say, really. She put her arms around him, buried her face in his neck, hugged him tightly.

Everything had, in the end, gone all right. Kenneth thought of William, hopefully by now out of France and on his way home. He thought of Etienne, probably sleeping the sleep of the innocent in a flat somewhere in the Paris suburbs. He had liked Etienne. He thought of the *mafiye* family, all the other families on the train, all the children. *We are not evil people*, he thought.

He held his phone so he could see it over Amanda's shoulder – she was a little taller than he was – and dialled a number, touched *call* to arm the device implanted in her belly. She'd carried it for so long, so stoically. She had never faltered. His heart swelled with love and pride for her.

The alarm on his phone started to beep. He dialled another number, hovered his thumb over *call*.

He said, "I love you so much."

She hugged him tighter. "Oh, sweetheart…"

He touched *call*.

For a fraction of a second, before the top of the mountain blew off in an explosion which was heard in Kyiv and detected by a college seismology experiment in Vermont, both ends of the tunnel jetted a plume of plasma as hot as the corona of the Sun.

AT PLAY IN THE FIELDS OF THE LORD

1.

THE HUNGARIANS CAME into the restaurant around nine in the evening, eight large men with gorgeously-tailored suits and hand-stitched Italian shoes and hundred-złoty haircuts. Michał, the maitre d', tried to tell them that there were no tables free unless they had a reservation, but they walked over to one of the large tables and sat down. One of them plucked the *Reserved* card from the middle of the tablecloth and sailed it out across the restaurant, causing other diners to duck.

Instead of calling the police – which would at very least have resulted in a brawl and massive property damage – Max, the owner, seized a notepad and set off across the restaurant to take the Hungarians' orders. This show of confidence did not prevent a number of diners signalling frantically for their bills.

The Hungarians were already boisterous, and shouted and laughed at Max while he tried to take their orders, changing their minds frequently and causing Max to start all over again. Finally, he walked back from the table to the bar, where Gosia was standing frozen with fear.

"Six bottles of Żubrówka, on the house," he murmured calmly to the girl as he went by towards the kitchen. "And try to be nimble on your feet."

Rudi, who had been standing in the kitchen doorway watching events with interest, said, "Something awful is going to happen, Max."

"Cook," Max replied, handing him the order. "Cook quickly."

By ten o'clock the Hungarians had loosened their ties and taken off their jackets and were singing and yelling at each other and laughing at impenetrable jokes. They had completed three courses of their five-course order. They were alone in the restaurant. With most of the meal completed, Rudi told the kitchen crew they could go home.

At one point, one of the Hungarians, an immense man with a face the colour of barszcz, began shouting at the others. He stood up, swaying gently, and yelled at his compatriots, who goodnaturedly yelled at him to sit down again. Sweat pouring down his face, he turned, grasped the back of a chair from the next table, and in one easy movement pivoted and flung it across the room. It crashed into the wall and smashed a sconce and brought down a mirror.

There was a moment's silence. The Hungarian stood looking at the dent in the wallpaper, frowning. Then he sat down and one of his friends poured him a drink and slapped him on the back and Max served the next course.

As the hour grew late the Hungarians became maudlin. They put their arms around each others' shoulders and began to sing songs that waxed increasingly sad as midnight approached.

Rudi, his cooking finished for the night and the kitchen tidied up and cleaned, stood in the doorway listening to their songs. The Hungarians had beautiful voices. He didn't understand the words, but the melodies were heart-achingly lonely.

One of the Hungarians saw him standing there and started to beckon urgently. The others turned to see what was going on, and they too started to beckon.

"Go on," Max said from his post by the bar.

"You're joking," said Rudi.

"I am not," Max told him. "Go and see what they want."

"And if they want to beat me up?"

"They'll soon get bored."

"Thank you, Max," Rudi said, setting off across the restaurant.

The Hungarians' table looked as if someone had dropped a five-course meal onto it from ceiling height. The floor around it was crunchy with broken glass and smashed crockery, the carpet sticky with sauces and bits of trodden-in food.

"You cook?" said one in appalling Polish as Rudi approached.

"Yes," said Rudi, balancing his weight on the balls of his feet just in case he had to move in a hurry.

The Polish-speaker looked like a side of beef sewn into an Armani Revival suit. His face was pale and sweaty. He crooked a forefinger the size of a sausage. Rudi bent down until their faces were only a couple of centimetres apart.

"Respect!" the Hungarian bellowed. Rudi flinched at the meaty spicy alcohol-and-tobacco gale of his breath. "Everywhere we go, this fuck city, not respect!"

This statement seemed to require a reply, so Rudi said, "Oh?"

"Not respect," the Hungarian said, shaking his head sadly. His expression suddenly brightened. "Here, Restaurant Max, we got respect!"

"We always respect our customers," Max murmured, moving soundlessly up beside Rudi.

"Fuck right!" the Hungarian said loudly. "Fuck right. Restaurant Max more respect."

"And your meal?" Max inquired, smiling.

"Good fuck meal," the Hungarian said. There was a general nodding of heads around the table. He looked at Rudi and belched. "Good fuck cook. Polish food for fuck pigs, but good fuck cook."

Rudi smiled. "Thank you," he said.

The Hungarian's eyes suddenly came into focus. "Good," he said. "We gone." He snapped a few words and the others around the table stood up, all save the one who had thrown the chair, who was slumped over with his cheek pressed to the tablecloth, snoring gently. Two of his friends grasped him by the shoulders and elbows and lifted him up. Bits of food adhered to the side of his face.

"Food good," the Polish-speaker told Rudi. He took his jacket from the back of his chair and shrugged into it. He dipped a hand into his breast pocket and came up with a business card held between his first two fingers. "You need working, you call."

Rudi took the card. "Thank you," he said again.

"Okay." He put both hands to his face and swept them up and back in a movement that magically rearranged his hair and seemed to sober him up at the same time. "We gone." He looked at Max. "Clever fuck Pole." He reached into an inside jacket pocket and brought out a wallet the size and shape of a housebrick. "What is?"

"On the house," Max said. "A gift."

Rudi looked at his boss and wondered what went on underneath that shaved scalp.

The Hungarian regarded the restaurant. "We break much."

Max shrugged carelessly.

"Okay." The Hungarian removed a centimetre-thick wad of złotys from the wallet and held it out. "You take," he said. Max smiled and bowed slightly and took the money, then the Hungarians were moving towards the exit. A last burst of raucous singing, one last bar stool hurled across the restaurant, a puff of cold air through the open door, and they were gone. Rudi heard Max locking the doors behind them.

"Well," Max said, coming back down the stairs. "*That* was an interesting evening."

Rudi picked up an overturned stool, righted it, and sat at the bar. He had, he discovered, sweated entirely through his chef's whites.

"Anyway, no one was hurt." Max went behind the bar. He bent down and started to search the shelves, straightened up holding half a bottle of Starka and two glasses.

Rudi took his lighter and a tin of small cigars from his pocket. He lit one and looked at the restaurant. If he was objective about it, there was actually very little damage. Just a lot of mess for the cleaners to tackle, and they'd had wedding receptions that had been messier.

Max filled the two glasses with vodka and held one up in a toast. "Good fuck meal," he said.

Rudi looked at him for a moment. Then he picked up the other glass, returned the toast, and drained it in one go. Then they both started to laugh.

"What if they come back?" Rudi asked.

But Max was still laughing. "Good fuck meal," he repeated, shaking his head and refilling the glasses.

* * *

THE NEXT MORNING, Rudi got up before dawn, pulled on a pair of shorts and a T-shirt, and went out for a run. He liked the early-morning streets of Poland's old capital, before the shoppers arrived. It was a landscape of beautiful old buildings and delivery drivers and early-morning workers huddled sleepily in trams. On the Market Square, three *Straż miejska*, civilian City Guards, were standing looking at a naked man who had been handcuffed to a rubbish bin. The naked man was looking up in fuddled incomprehension while two of the *Straż* shouted at him in Polish. The guardsmen didn't seem in any great hurry to help him, or even tase him. Shouting, for the moment, appeared quite satisfactory. It was hardly the worst outcome of a stag weekend they'd ever seen.

He veered off across the square, along the front of the Sukiennice, the mediaeval Cloth Hall in the middle, and out towards the river. He skirted Wawel Hill, the Castle all spotlit high above on its crag, and through the riverside gardens at its feet. The Poles had recently repaired the statue of *Smok Wawelski*, the dragon supposedly slain – by feeding it a dead sheep stuffed with sulphur, which Rudi had always found a quintessentially *Polish* story – by Krak, the city's legendary founder, and now it breathed a jet of flame every five minutes or so, via a hidden gas-pipe which emerged in its mouth. A series of unfortunate incidents involving the light toasting of drunken revellers and one small child had led to a large area in front of the statue being fenced off. Krakowians, because they were Krakowians, kept pulling the fence down, and the city authorities kept putting it back up; the whole thing had turned into a minor sport, with neither side prepared to back down.

Rudi liked the Poles for a lot of things like that; it was one of the reasons he stayed rather than moving on to another city and another restaurant. There was a building near the Mogilskie Roundabout whose construction, begun way back in the 1970s, had been permanently interrupted by lack of money and Martial Law in the '80s. Once upon a time it had been the tallest building in Kraków. It had never been finished, but instead of knocking it down the Poles had turned it into a huge billboard display. They called it

'Szkieletor,' after a children's cartoon character. Nobody now knew who owned it.

He did a threequarter-circuit of Wawel Hill, then back along Grodzka into the Market Square. The drunken tourist was still there, still being goodnaturedly yelled at by the guardsmen. There were more people about now; some of them had gathered to watch and make helpful suggestions. Others were walking across the Square, heading for work. As Rudi rounded the Mariacki Church, he saw from the corner of his eye someone standing on the opposite corner, watching him, and for a confusing moment there was something so familiar about their body language that he almost stumbled. By the time he regained his footing and managed to look properly, the figure was gone.

At the restaurant, there was much activity following the previous night's excitement. One of Max's many relatives was standing on a stepladder replacing the smashed sconce, and a small team of professional cleaners was using a machine which resembled a stunted Dalek to clean the trodden-in mess of food and broken glass and crockery from the carpet. Max was standing near the bar, dolefully regarding a broken chair.

"Can't find one to match it," he said when Rudi arrived, freshly-showered and ready for the day. "The firm that made them went bust two years ago."

"And you didn't know?" asked Rudi.

Max looked at him. "Do I look like a man who pays attention to every furniture manufacturer who goes out of business?"

"So we're down one place setting now."

"I'll find something similar," said Max. "Put it at one of the tables over in that corner. No one will ever notice. And if they do, no one will ever mention it."

Rudi thought this was somehow emblematic of Max's attitude to the restaurant business; he had a laudable faith in the power of good food cooked well to bring in customers, but everything else was a struggle for him. It was at times like this – and really only at times like this – that Rudi missed the presence of the sainted Pani Stasia, the restaurant's former chef and Max's mother.

He said, "At least we have replacements for all the broken tableware."

Max looked at the chair again and shrugged. Tableware was constantly having to be replaced; there were boxes of plates and cups and saucers and cutlery in one of the storerooms, bought cheap in large quantities at a bankruptcy sale a couple of years ago. Eventually, that was going to start running out too, Max would equivocate about replacing it, and then another bankruptcy sale would come along and solve the problem. You never had to wait long for a bankruptcy sale in the catering business, these days.

Rudi left Max to puzzle out the chair problem. It would, as these things usually did, become his problem soon enough. He went into the kitchen, where the crew were prepping for the day's service.

THE DAY PASSED as they always did. There were minor crises and minor triumphs. Out in the restaurant, a child, unwillingly dining with his parents, enacted a spectacular temper-tantrum which Max defused with nothing more sophisticated than native charm and a lollipop. Max found the nuts and bolts of being a restaurateur a bit of a chore, but he was wonderful with people, particularly children.

As the afternoon diners were gradually replaced by the evening crowd, most of them coming in for an early dinner before going on to the theatre or a club, Rudi went out to the loading bay in the courtyard behind the building for a smoke. The courtyard was small and narrow, just wide enough for a van to reverse through the archway at the other end for deliveries. It was surrounded by tall, old buildings, and on rainy days he felt as if he was standing at the bottom of a chimney lined with windows.

Stubbing out his cigar in the bucket of damp sand beside the back door of the restaurant, he had the strangest sense of being watched. He looked across the courtyard and thought he caught the barest scrap of movement, but it was gone so quickly that he couldn't be sure. He walked across to the archway, stepped through into the street, and looked left and right, but there was nothing out of the ordinary. Just another day when you think people are looking at you; everyone has them, now and again.

There was a brief lull in custom around seven. Rudi had a quick dinner of *kotlet schabowy* and potatoes with pickled red cabbage and apple at the private table by the kitchen door, and when he got up to take his plate back into the kitchen he looked across the restaurant and found himself looking at himself.

For a few moments he stood there, completely flatfooted, all manner of scenarios running through his head. Then the person sitting at the table on the other side of the restaurant smiled and beckoned cheerily, and he felt as if a trapdoor had opened beneath his feet but he hadn't yet quite fallen through it.

He shouldered the kitchen door open, put his plate and coffee mug on the worktop just inside, and walked across the restaurant and stood beside the newcomer's table.

And it really was him. Or rather an older, slightly more worn-out him, with wrinkles at the corners of his eyes and grey in his hair. There was a cane propped against the table beside him, and he was partway through a bowl of *flaczki*. Rudi felt that sense of standing on thin air even more acutely.

"Oh, sit down," said the older him in an avuncular manner. He indicated the bowl of tripe stew in front of him. "This is really good, but you've got to stop putting so much pepper in it; not even the Poles like it with this much pepper." He smiled. "Sit."

Rudi sat. "Who are you?"

The older Rudi was buttering a slice of rye bread. "I'm you," he said, "obviously."

"No you're not." It was the only thing he could think of to say.

"Yes I am. A version of you, at any rate."

Rudi shook his head. "No, I'm sorry," he said, "this doesn't make any sense." He made to stand, but the older Rudi waved him down.

"Some of what I'm about to tell you will be quite hard to believe," he said, laying the slice of bread down on a side plate and picking up his wineglass. He took a sip of wine. "Actually, pretty much everything I'm about to tell you will be hard to believe."

"Is this some kind of joke?" Rudi glanced around the restaurant, hoping to spot a couple of hidden cameras and a group of friends waiting to spring a late birthday surprise.

"I suppose the easiest way to start is to say that this is like *The Matrix*. Do you have *The Matrix* here?" He saw the look of incomprehension on Rudi's face and shook his head. "Keanu

Reeves? Laurence Fishburne?" He blinked. "How can there be a world without *Laurence Fishburne*?"

Rudi stood up. "I'm going to call the police," he said. "I'll give you two minutes' head start, but I'm going to call the police."

Elder Rudi looked up at him, not at all concerned. "You, and your entire world, are very, very sophisticated computer programs," he said. He added brightly, "And in fact, so am I."

Rudi turned for the kitchen. "You've had your two minutes' head start," he said.

"You've got a scar on your arm where you fell over on a paring knife in the Turk's kitchen," Elder Rudi called. "How do I know that? Because I have one too. Look."

Rudi turned back, saw that Elder Rudi had rolled up his sleeve and was showing him a familiar-looking scar. Then Elder Rudi unbuttoned his shirt and exposed another scar that started on his chest and disappeared from view. "Skinheads," he said. "Warnemünde." He cocked an eyebrow. "Come and sit down," he said reasonably. "I don't mean you any harm. I just have some things to ask you."

Rudi went back to the table and sat.

"The best way I can explain it is that there is a place in Germany," Elder Rudi said. "It's called the Republic of Dresden-Neustadt. You've never heard of it, because it doesn't exist here, but that doesn't matter. Basically it's a little walled city-state and it contains the densest concentration of computing power on Earth. The people who built it meant it to be a data haven for oligarchs, a place to keep all their dirty little digital secrets, but that stuff only occupies a tiny percentage of the Republic's capacity and a number of people have been wondering what else goes on in there."

Rudi sat staring.

Elder Rudi took a mouthful of *flaczki,* chewed, shook his head, swallowed. "Too much pepper," he said again sadly. "Anyway. Yes, the Republic. After a lot of hard work and chicanery and not a little derring-do, it was possible to install a number of *software agents* on the Republic's systems." He tapped himself on the chest. "Autonomous programs designed to adapt to the system, scrape data about what's going on inside, and report back."

"This is fucking crazy," Rudi murmured.

"Now, I can't speak for the other servers in the Republic," Elder Rudi went on briskly, "but this one seems to be running exquisitely detailed simulations of Europe." He looked about him. "It really is wonderful work." He smiled at Rudi. "Oh, incidentally, I'm not nearly this sophisticated usually; I'm borrowing a lot of processing power from the server running this simulation, and I look like you because I copied the server's rendering of you. With a few *somatic* changes." He beamed. "There," he said. "I knew you'd take this well. I've always congratulated myself on being adaptable, if nothing else."

"I'm not taking this well," Rudi said. "I'm not taking it at all."

Elder Rudi said, "They run the simulations in batches of about a thousand at a time, at really high speed, compressing a year of elapsed time into a few hundredths of a second. And all the simulations are ever so slightly different. If they're using *all* their spare capacity to run simulations that's an *insane* amount of computation. Whole worlds."

"Why?" Rudi couldn't help himself.

Elder Rudi grinned. "I have no idea. I'm a computer program; I'm tasked to observe and record, not to come to conclusions. I'm not AI."

Rudi felt himself starting to fall through the trapdoor. "You said you had some questions."

"Yes, yes I do." Elder Rudi leaned forward slightly. "Have you ever," he asked, "heard of *Les Coureurs des Bois*?"

"What?"

"I'll take that as a no. Does the European Union still exist?"

"Of course it does."

"Have you heard of the *Community*?"

"What community?"

"Has there been a flu pandemic in Europe in the past forty years?"

"No. What kind of questions are these?"

"Does the name *Mundt* mean anything to you? No? How about *Andrew Molson*?"

Rudi shook his head.

"Where does your father work?"

"I'm not going to answer any more of these questions. Why do you want to know these things?"

Elder Rudi smiled and shrugged. "It's what I do. I collect data and return it to my creator. A bit like V'ger." He sat back. "No!" he said. "You don't have *Star Trek*? What kind of monsters programmed this place?"

"Nobody." Rudi stood up. "Nobody programmed this place. I don't know who you are or what you think you're doing, but I'm going to call the police now. The real police, not the *Stráž*."

"Of course," said Elder Rudi, sitting back in his chair and grinning – did he *ever* stop smiling? "Go right ahead. I should warn you, though, this... interaction might have some effect on the simulation. It might skew the data. They might let it run to the end, or they might abandon it and start again. I'd say I was sorry about that, but I don't feel compassion, and it doesn't matter anyway because none of this is real."

Rudi strode back across the restaurant and pushed through the kitchen door. But he didn't call the police. He stood where he was for a couple of minutes, then he looked back through the door, but the man who had claimed to be him was gone. He'd left a big tip, though.

2.

"It's a PREDICTION engine," said Lev.

"A what?" asked Rupert.

"It's a machine for predicting the future."

"I'm sorry, Professor," Rupert said, shifting in his chair, "but you're going to have to do better than that." He didn't trust the Russian; there was something ever so slightly *broken* about him, although he seemed, on the surface at least, to be doing all right. His flat, in one of the more upscale neighbourhoods of Novosibirsk, was tastefully austere in a way that only moderately successful people can achieve.

"They're running all possible scenarios of European history, over and over again," Lev explained with a happy smile. "Can you imagine the processing power they must have in there?"

Rupert, who was content to use computers without having the slightest idea how they worked, nodded. "It is rather wonderful," he said.

"No, you don't understand, obviously," Lev said eagerly. "These are full-scale simulations. Virtual worlds, populated by virtual people who have no idea that they're software agents. This... thing is probably capable of artificial intelligence. There is nothing else like it anywhere in the world. And there is nothing else like it anywhere in the world because it is impossible."

Rupert raised an eyebrow. It had taken him, Rudi, Seth, and all of Rudi's resources, almost four years to infiltrate Dresden-Neustadt. There had been threats, bribery, corruption, blackmail, one brief kidnapping that he knew about, and enough adrenaline to last him a lifetime, to get information about what the machines there were doing, and all they'd come back with was a *computer game*. He found it difficult to understand what Lev – a very recent acquaintance whom Rudi seemed to regard with great nostalgic fondness – found so exciting about it.

"This kind of sophistication, it's *unheard of*," Lev said patiently. "Whoever's done this, they've made unimaginable leaps in computing." He looked at Rupert, realised he was getting nowhere, and sighed. "I should speak with him about this. Face to face."

"He's busy." Although in truth, Rupert had no idea where Rudi was at the moment, or what he was doing. He'd set up this liaison with the Professor and then gone off to parts unknown; they hadn't been in touch in months.

Lev got up from his chair and went to the window, looked down into the bustling streets of the Siberian capital. "Advances like this don't just appear out of nowhere," he said to the view. "They always flow from earlier work, stuff which doesn't seem very important in the beginning. It doesn't matter how restricted or secret the final result is, you can always trace it back to research that's in the public domain. And I can't find it anywhere. And that's impossible."

Rupert thought it might be perfectly possible, if the research had taken place in another universe, particularly if that universe had subsequently been bombed out of existence. He said, "Is there any mention, anywhere, of the name *Mundt*?"

Lev shook his head and turned from the window. "No. There is a *lot* of topological calculation being done in there, though. *Very* out-there stuff. Or maybe not so out-there, these days, I don't know. I'd need to show it to an expert."

"No," said Rupert. "No more experts. We don't know who we can trust. What about the owners? Is there any way to find out who built the Neustadt?"

"I'm working on that separately," Lev said. "I've identified about a dozen financial institutions who put money into the project, but really all I've managed to do so far is scratch the surface. I need more time if I'm to do it properly, without raising any alarms."

If this were some kind of entertainment, this would be roughly the point where Rupert said, "We don't have any more time, Professor; you must complete your research as soon as possible," but there was no great sense of urgency, no sense that it even *mattered*. It was just something Rudi was interested in, for his own reasons. They could be working on this for years and still not understand it, and it wouldn't make a blind bit of difference.

He said, "Look, Professor, a lot of effort went into getting you that information. We'd be grateful if you could make *some* kind of sense of it reasonably soon."

"There is one thing I can tell you right now," Lev said, going over to a table in the corner and pouring himself a glass of vodka. "Whoever is running this thing, they're *really* interested in railways."

AND, WELL, WHO wasn't, these days? When Sibir had declared its independence from European Russia twenty years ago, there had been some discussion about what to call its capital. Novosibirsk had originally been named Novonikolayevsk, in honour of both St Nicholas and the Tsar Nicholas II, and it was here basically because here was where the Trans-Siberian Railway had built a bridge over the River Ob. Back then, the Trans-Siberian Railway had seemed one of the greatest engineering projects the world had ever seen, but these days it looked a bit like a formerly major road running beside a brand-new six-lane highway. Except the highway was closed.

Eight months after the Ufa explosion, nobody was any the wiser about its cause. The Line was in virtual lockdown, bombarding the media with denials about fusion power which no one believed. It had even managed to knock the Community off the top of the news for the first time in almost half a decade.

In the wake of the explosion, the Trans-Siberian was enjoying something of a resurgence after years of neglect, but it had taken Rupert, who refused to fly anywhere, more than a week of rackety trains and twelve-hour waits for connections to reach Novosibirsk for his meeting with Rudi's pet mathematician, and it took him twelve days to get back to what he considered familiar territory.

In Prague, he checked into the Hastal in the Old Town and had a long shower to wash off the journey's grime. Snow was starting to drift down from the low clouds as he left the hotel that evening and used his phone to navigate to a Brazilian restaurant on Malá Štupartská, a narrow, traffic-choked street not far from the Market Square.

"I ordered churrasco," Rudi told him after they'd sat down at a corner table. "It comes with fries, because of course it does."

The fries arrived, served in what appeared to be small cowboy hats, which Rudi regarded sourly. Also side salads. A waiter came to their table with metre-long skewers of barbecued meat, which he sliced with great ceremony onto octagonal slabs of wood before departing again.

"So," Rudi said when they were alone and the rather irritating samba from the restaurant's music system drowned out their conversation from nearby diners.

Rupert gave him a potted version of what Lev had told him in Novosibirsk. By the time he had finished, their platters were empty and another waiter had visited the table with a dessert menu, which Rudi had waved away after a moment's consideration.

"Well," he said. "That's interesting."

"Is it?" asked Rupert.

"These are interesting times. Someone who could predict even the dozen or so most likely outcomes of an action would have something of an advantage over the rest of us. *I* could certainly use something like that. Thank you." This last to yet another waiter, who served coffee.

"He said there's a lot of topological research going on there, too," Rupert said. "Which means Mundt."

"Not necessarily. Although it may involve the work Mundt was doing before you jumped him out of the Neustadt."

"Anyway." Rupert took a little hard drive from his pocket and passed it across the table. "He says everything he's learned so far is in here. He's nowhere near finished, though."

"No," Rudi said. "We got a lot of data back. It's going to take a while." He pocketed the hard drive. "Did you hear the UN are offering the Community a seat on the Security Council, by the way?"

"I haven't seen the news in almost a fortnight," Rupert said.

"Have they been in touch?"

"The Directorate? They'd have had to move fairly smartly to find me."

"Hm. Fair point." Rudi sat back and looked towards a corner of the ceiling. Rupert thought he looked tired and grumpy.

"From what I understand, a seat on the Security Council is hardly a badge of honour," Rupert said.

"Oh, not these days, no." Rudi smiled wearily at him. "I just think it's interesting. Everything is interesting; the hard part is working out how it all fits together."

"Where have you been?"

"Me?" Rudi shrugged. "Ah, talking to people. Asking questions. Not getting many answers."

"Are you asking the right questions?"

Rudi chuckled. "Well, now, that *is* a question."

They paid for their meal and left the restaurant. Outside, the snowfall had thickened. A breeze, funnelled by the street, carried it in swirls and whorls, brushing against car windscreens and making pedestrians hunch their shoulders. Rupert wondered just *where* Rudi had been asking his questions; there were alleyways in Prague which led over the border into the Community, crossings which everyone seemed to have forgotten about, although he knew the Directorate, the Community's security service, better than that.

"What next?" he asked, turning up the collar of his jacket.

"We'll let Lev continue his research," Rudi said, stirring the tip of his cane in the millimetre or so of dry snow which had settled on the pavement just beyond the restaurant's canopy. "I'll keep asking questions. Something will turn up; it always does."

"What if it doesn't?"

Rudi looked out into the street, the snow dancing through the car headlights. "It will," he said. "Eventually we'll just start to annoy the wrong people. Then something will happen."

3.

RUDI WOKE FROM a troubled sleep, stumbled out of bed and into the bathroom, used the lavatory, had a quick wash, and breakfasted on toast and cereal and coffee. He dressed in his running kit and went downstairs to the street door. And stopped.

It was foggy outside. This was not entirely unusual for Kraków, but this was different. It was unseasonable, for one thing. And it was so thick that he couldn't see across the street. It deadened all sound; he couldn't hear anything. No people, no traffic, no trams. Nothing.

Standing on the step, holding the door open behind him, he craned his neck left and right, but he could only see a few metres in either direction along the pavement before the world vanished into an impenetrable grey wall. It was as if he and his building were the only real, solid things on Earth. He thought about what the man who looked like him had said last night.

Thinking about that made him angry. He shook his head and stepped out onto the pavement, and as he did the building behind him calmly vanished.

A TOWN CALLED PEACEFUL

1.

ONE MORNING IN November, Spencer experienced a moment when he didn't know where he was.

He was on his way into town, changing trains at Euston Underground station, riding the escalator up from the Victoria Line platforms, and as he neared the top everything was suddenly unfamiliar. It was as if he had not only never been in this place before, but in this *situation*. What was this moving staircase? What were these tunnels? What did all these signs mean? Which language were they in? He felt a sense of fear so profound that he stopped at the top of the escalator and several people coming up behind him bumped into him and almost knocked him over.

The jostling was enough to snap him out of whatever had happened to him, but it didn't happen all at once; understanding faded back in like something from a film. That was a sign for the Northern Line; this was an escalator vestibule; he was at Euston.

It only lasted a moment or so, but it was unnerving enough for him to turn and take the down escalator back to the Victoria Line, get a train to Victoria, and go to see his ex, Bethan.

Bethan lived in Peckham, just beyond the southern edge of the London Control Zone. To the north and west and east the Zone stretched out beyond the M25, but the River was a useful border, and the boroughs immediately to the south had always had a raw deal from whoever was making the big decisions for London and the country in general. From some streets in Peckham you could see the Shard and other buildings of the City, tantalisingly close but on the other side of several security checkpoints.

They went to a pub across the road from Rye Common and Spencer told Bethan what had happened at Euston, and Bethan shook her head sadly.

"Have you been taking your meds, Spence?" she asked.

"Of course I have," he said.

"Are you sure?"

Well, of course, now he thought about it, Spencer *wasn't* sure. He had an image in his mind of taking his tablet, but he couldn't have sworn that it was from this morning. Or yesterday morning. Or the day before, for that matter. *Yesterday* and *the day before* were slippery concepts for Spencer, anyway, like *tomorrow* and *the day after*.

Bethan sighed again and took out a small plastic container. "Here," she said, "take one of mine."

"Are you sure?" asked Spencer.

She rattled the container. "I've got plenty."

"But suppose I *did* take one this morning."

"Suppose you *didn't*. Do you want to have another episode on the way home?" Bethan popped the top off the container with her thumb, tipped a white tablet, not much larger than an artificial sweetener, into her palm, and held it out to him. "You can't overdose on this stuff, anyway. It'll plateau you out."

Spencer took the tablet and put it in his mouth, where it dissolved into a gritty bitterness that he washed down with a mouthful of beer.

"There you go," Bethan said approvingly. She was a tall woman with close-cropped red hair and a penchant for vintage T-shirts. Spencer had several powerfully erotic memories of their brief time together, but he couldn't remember how they had met, or quite why they had split up. Dr Cragoe, his therapist, considered it a form of post-traumatic stress and had prescribed yet more medication and a monthly mindfulness session which Spencer, mixing the dates up, kept forgetting to attend.

"How've you been?" he asked, while he waited for the medication to come on.

She shrugged. "Up and down. Work's been a sod lately."

Bethan worked for one of the American news aggregators. Spencer tried to remember if something newsworthy had happened in the past few days, but came up blank. He said, "You need a holiday."

She snorted. "Everybody needs a holiday. I need another job."

Spencer thought things were starting to settle down; the vague sense of anxiety he'd been feeling since this morning was dissipating, objects around him were beginning to make sense. He said, "Me too."

Bethan looked around the bar. There was a fashion, these days, to convert gastropubs back into old-style boozers, and this one was a dreary lino-floored space with uncomfortable wooden seats and dull mass-produced beer. The closest thing it had to food was pork scratchings. The clientele, which hadn't changed, appeared as content with this as they had been when the pub had been serving quinoa salads, but Spencer hated places like this. All he really wanted was a cup of coffee, and the nearest cup of halfway decent coffee was a walk away in East Dulwich.

Bethan said, "Short of cash?"

He nodded. "A bit."

"You've got the rent and the bills covered, though, right?"

He shrugged.

"Oh, Spence," she sighed, and though he couldn't quite remember the final days of their relationship, that falling, disappointed tone of voice was crushingly familiar. He felt himself shrivel inside.

There was a silence. Bethan sat looking at him, while he sat watching the traffic go by outside, remembering other times like this.

Finally, she said, "I know someone who's got a job going."

BETHAN LIVED IN one of the streets off Bellenden Road, a name which always made Spencer snigger. The house seemed perpetually full of furniture from other homes. Passing through the living room, he noticed stuff that seemed to have washed up here since his last visit – most notably a large elephant's foot umbrella stand, several intact turtle shells that were probably two hundred years old, and a glass-fronted case containing what appeared to be a meerkat stuffed by a taxidermist in the throes of a powerful breakdown. Any of these could have got her arrested for possession of the products of endangered species, but Bethan didn't care. It was just Stuff. She picked it up here and there, sold some of it, kept some of it, periodically threw the rest away.

A previous owner of the house had built a small extension on the back, probably in defiance of planning regulations. It wasn't much more than a spare room, into which Bethan had installed the servers and monitors and other assorted hardware of her job. The walls were white and the lights were bright and it was always too warm for Spencer's tastes in there. It was also fantastically well soundproofed. When the four-inch-thick door was closed there was a sense of dead air, a sense of being sealed off from the rest of the world

Bethan sat him down in front of one of the monitors and waved up an interface. She stood behind him, air-typing through menus and submenus and diallers and anonymisers and it all got a bit confusing for Spencer so he asked for another of her tablets and washed it down with a bottle of water while she talked and talked and talked calmly and quietly and then there was an image on the monitor and another voice was talking, slowly and soothingly, and Spencer felt his eyelids grow heavy and his head loll forward and it seemed such a very, very long time since he had slept properly.

2.

AIR TRAVEL IN Western and Central Europe could be tricky these days. If there was an appreciable lag between booking your ticket and actually taking your flight, there was an outside chance you'd discover that your destination airport was no longer actually in the country you wanted to go to. Most polities which sprang into being with a national or – the great prize – international airport were smart enough to realise that a large machine for making revenue had fallen into their laps, and swiftly renegotiated fees and timetables with the major carriers. Some, though, were bloody-minded, and Europe was dotted, here and there, with ultramodern airport architecture falling slowly into disuse and disrepair because the airlines had grown tired of various micronations' demands and simply told them to fuck off and gone to land elsewhere.

The situation was, if anything, even worse the further East you went. Beyond Rus – European Russia – and Sibir was a patchwork of republics and statelets and nations and kingdoms and khanates and 'stans which had been crushed out of existence by History, reconstituted, fragmented, reinvented, fragmented again, absorbed, reabsorbed and recreated. The situation was not helped by a tradition of short-lived and frankly catastrophic regional airlines, some of them flying aircraft more than a century old, many of them with a cheerfully cavalier attitude to irksome expenses like basic maintenance. Air travel east of Nizhny Novgorod, say, had always been a bit of an adventure – there had been times when getting on a flight travelling east of *Moscow* had been an act of considerable bravery – but airspace beyond the Urals had turned into an enterprise on a par with the early days of the Oregon Trail.

Spencer flew from Heathrow to Moscow, where he had five hours to wait for a connecting flight. He took a cab into the city and spent the time shopping for cold-weather clothing, was back at Domodedovo in time to board the UralAir flight to Yekaterinburg.

At Yekaterinburg, Koltsovo Airport was still over-run with old 787 cargo conversions belonging to international aid charities working on the relief effort two hundred kilometres or so to the south. Looking out of the window as his flight taxied to the terminal, he could see ranks of heavy-lift airships tethered to the tarmac. The humanitarian catastrophe following the Ufa explosion still hadn't eased noticeably. Tens of thousands of refugees from the surrounding countryside had upped sticks and marched on Chelyabinsk, where they had set up camp at the city's airport. They called it 'Putingrad' and started to farm between the runways. Nobody could move them, not even the army. Even if they left tomorrow, the airport would be next to useless for years.

The next two legs of the journey took him to Novosibirsk and then on to Krasnoyarsk, at the eastern edge of Sibir. Looking from the window as the rackety old turboprop made its descent, he saw a snowbound city nestling beside a river surrounded by deep forests.

He saw, in the final light of the sunset, tall industrial chimneys expelling solid plumes of vapour or smoke. The plane made a steep turn to line itself up with the runway at Yemelyanovo airport, and he found himself looking almost straight down into the amphitheatre of a football stadium, all lit up and full of people.

That was, it turned out, all he saw of the old Russian border city. Yemelyanovo was some distance outside town, and he was booked into one of a complex of grim-looking budget hotels beside the airport. He stomped into the foyer in thermal boots, quilted coldsuit and fur-lined parka, to find that the temperature in the hotel had been cranked up to tropical levels.

Five floors up, he waved his phone at the door of Room 502 and stepped inside. The room was small, stark, utilitarian, the only decoration a single replica ikon on the wall over the bed. The window looked down into a courtyard calf-deep in snow. Two figures, bulky as Kodiak bears in their cold-weather gear, were enthusiastically throwing snowballs at each other in the light of the hotel's many windows.

Spencer closed the curtains, put his overnight bag on the floor, and sat on the bed for a few moments, trying to let himself catch up with the journey. He took a container from his pocket, shook out a couple of tablets, dry-swallowed them, and closed his eyes until the fog went away.

He had a shower, ordered a steak and fries and a green salad from room service, sat eating in front of the entertainment centre watching a local news feed that seemed to consist mainly of stories about football and nationalist marches. Later, he went to the room's cheap little wardrobe, opened it, and took out the package on the shelf inside. Then he went to bed.

THE NEXT DAY was a series of hops in prop-driven aircraft of varying decrepitude, to cities with names like Bratsk and Ust-Ilimsk and Erbogachen, like places out of a fantasy novel. The landscape below was a dense carpet of snowy forest divided by winding rivers and the white lines of roads and spotted with frozen lakes. It seemed to go on to the misty uncertain edges of the world.

There was an hour's layover at Erbogachen Airport – the last stopover before the Sakha Republic – and the coffee shop where he had a late lunch seemed to be mostly full of ethnic Yakuts with industrial quantities of luggage, many of whom packed themselves on his flight.

The sun was setting, here in what had once been the Russian Far East, when the plane descended from the cloudbase for its final approach to Mirny. Looking down, Spencer saw a now-familiar scene – dense larch taiga forest, a sprawl of housing blocks festooned with balconies and every kind of aerial created by humanity, a main road running through it all, industrial chimneys pumping out clouds of smoke and vapour, lakes, open-cast mine workings, everything blanketed with snow. Just beyond the city rose an enormous tessellated blister, a startling dome that shone with a green-tinged interior illumination in the dusk.

Once upon a time, mineral-rich Sakha had produced more than a quarter of the world's diamonds, and the majority of them had come from here, the great terraced open-cast pit of the Mir Diamond Mine, a hole in the earth almost a mile across and so deep that it caused air currents strong enough to suck helicopters out of the sky overhead.

The mine had closed in the early years of the century, and after a number of false starts a company had come in – no one knew quite from where, although they were notable, in those cash-strapped days, for having seemingly limitless money – and proceeded to roof over the pit and 'terraform' the interior. This was something of a misnomer, as the mine was already on Earth, but it looked good in the corporate materials, and if any of the existing inhabitants of the town were at all disgruntled about the area being compared to an alien world, their sensitivities were soothed by several philanthropic improvements to their infrastructure, including a new hospital and football stadium.

A courtesy bus took passengers from the airport to what was now the Mirny EcoState. For those who couldn't be bothered to wipe the condensation off the windows and look out at the grim town which had been built to service the mine, there were paperscreens showing a cheerful documentary about how the world's second-deepest man-made hole had been transformed into an arcology which was the byword for sustainability. Spencer watched the documentary, with its lively animations about spray-insulation and injection-polymer permafrost stabilisation, and found his mind wandering. He took a tablet.

The bus pulled up outside a large featureless cube of a building, considerably cleaner and in a better state of repair than the rest of the town, a few metres from the dome. The passengers disembarked and shuffled through the stinging cold to the doors.

Inside, all was quiet and warm, a big airy foyer laid out like the departure gates of an airport. A few people were already queuing to pass through scanners and metal detectors and progress further into the building. Most of the new arrivals, Spencer among them, headed for a set of gates marked 'Residents,' although in truth residents and visitors were treated more or less the same – both went through the same document and security checks.

On the other side of the gates, Spencer stepped into a gents' restroom, locked himself into a cubicle, stripped naked, and put his clothes into a bag. He took from his overnight bag the package from the hotel room in Krasnoyarsk and peeled back the outer layer. Inside was a pair of polymer gloves. He put them on, then undid the inner layer of the package. Inside were two bags. One was about the size of a large padded envelope. He tore it open carefully and shook out what appeared to be a very large surgical glove. He stretched the neck and stepped into it, and there followed a couple of minutes of contortions made more complicated by the fact that he was trying not to make contact with the outer surface, but finally he was wearing a sort of skin-tight transparent onesie. He pulled the hood over his head; the edges sealed themselves against his face, leaving only his nose and mouth and eyes exposed.

Quickly now, he opened the other bag – jeans, trainers, a T-shirt and hoodie – dressed, put everything in his overnight bag, pulled the hood up, and left the restroom.

There was no sense that he was in a foreign country, a pocket nation carved out of the permafrost of the Sakha Republic. He walked down wide corridors floored with hard-wearing carpet and the occasional door marked *AUTHORISED ACCESS ONLY* in half a dozen obscure languages. It was like being in a very large but rather disappointing office building.

Finally, though, he emerged from one corridor into a vestibule the size of a tennis court. It was open on one side, and when Spencer stepped out and stood at the railing which ran along the edge he found himself looking across a space so huge that its far side was almost lost in a mist of humidity.

Craning his neck, he could barely see the great panes of the dome through the glare of the lights strung from it. They hung over an enormous steep-sided amphitheatre, its sides scored with a spiral of broad terraces paved with broad walkways and festooned with hanging plants. Spencer could see crowds of people and bicycles moving along the terraces. The walls of the amphitheatre were set with tens of thousands of windows. The air was warm and humid and it smelled like a jungle. Far below, cupped in the base of the great bowl, was an elliptical lake with a small island in the middle.

In theory, the Mirny EcoState had been quite a simple proposition. Take a colossal stepped hole in the ground, roof it over with a fullerdome, build apartments and shops and cinemas and theatres into the walls of the hole, landscape the terraces, and install a closed-loop biosphere. Everything is simple, in theory. Before anything could be done, specialised equipment had to be brought in. The single road connecting Mirny with Almazny and Chernyshevsky, the two nearest cities, was useless for the Mirny EcoCompany's needs, so the airport had to be rebuilt to handle wide-bodied cargo freighters, in temperatures so low that metal tools shattered like glass and the ground had to be thawed with jet engines before any work could be carried out. After that, things only got more difficult.

Spencer leaned on the railing. A delta-winged microlight was whining like a mosquito across the great open space of the arcology a hundred feet or so below him, navigating the slowly roiling air currents in big slow spirals. A dozen or so parakeets flew past the balcony, squawking loudly.

He walked down a set of broad steps leading down to the nearest terrace, and walked unhurriedly, stopping to look in shop windows and examine the menus of cafés and restaurants, until he reached a bank of lifts. He took a lift down to the next terrace, walked some more, took another lift.

The terrace this one opened onto was mostly residential, the walls lined with doors and windowboxes and broad shallow concrete planters full of vegetation. Pausing to make sure he wasn't being observed, he dumped his overnight bag in one of the planters, hiding it among the foliage. A few metres further on, he stopped at one door, and slipped a mask over the exposed parts of his face. It sealed itself to the material of the isolation suit, trapping skin flakes and all kinds of forensic evidence inside. He waved his phone at the door, and there was a click as it unlocked.

Inside was cooler, a quiet draft of aircon – the EcoState was so efficiently insulated from the permafrost it was excavated from, mainly to stop it melting its way to the centre of the Earth, that without some kind of cooling system the apartments would have eventually become uninhabitable – and smelled of eco-friendly cleaning materials and floor polish.

The front door opened into a small receiving room with cupboards and a rack of coats. This led to a flight of stairs up to a large airy living room, sparsely-furnished. He walked through the apartment carefully, looking for signs that someone had carried out a search. The people who had prepared the apartment had left tells – fine layers of dust, hairs spit-glued across door-jambs; basically stuff from twentieth century espionage novels because frankly no one did this kind of thing any more and nobody would notice them – to mark the passage of the unwary, and he was carrying an itemised list of them in his head without quite realising it. He checked the three bedrooms, kitchen, dining room, utility room, and bathroom, and none of the tells seemed to have been disturbed. Only then did he go back downstairs and take the tools from one of the cupboards in the reception room.

The tools were in two cases, each about large enough to hold a big power drill. He took them upstairs and opened them on the living room coffee table. Inside, nested in foam, were items which at first glance would have seemed more or less incomprehensible to a casual observer.

Spencer went over to the window and looked out. On this floor, he was above head-height of residents passing by on the terrace. He knelt down until his head was more or less level with the top of the coffee table and looked again. The terraces wound around the inside of the old pit in a huge gentle spiral, covered in vegetation. From where he was kneeling, Spencer could see all the way across the great open space to the other side of the spiral, maybe ten or fifteen metres lower than his position. He took a monocular from one of the cases and focused on a certain spot along the opposite terrace, where a number of people seemed to be congregating. He took out his phone and checked the time. He was on schedule, to within a minute or so. A lot of time and effort had been taken to make sure he was here, in this place, at this time, but the things in his head, the things he had been told in London, didn't allow him to think about that. He wasn't even aware that he had *been* told anything. This was this and that was that, and he was doing it because he was doing it.

He went back to the table and started to remove the tools from their cases, laying them out on the coffee table and making sure everything was there because once he had gone on a job and a certain component had been missing and he'd had to pull the entire operation. Not his fault, of course, and he didn't even think about the consequences for anyone else, because he wasn't wired for it.

And it wasn't going to happen this time. Everything was here. He started unhurriedly snapping components together, making sure each piece fitted and functioned before moving on to the next one. As he worked, a rifle took shape on the coffee table.

Although only bits of it looked like a rifle. It had a barrel almost two metres long, wound in a mathematically-precise spiral with three kilometres of fine wire and studded with connector blocks. The breech was the size of a cigarette packet and there was no butt, just a pistol grip. Mounted on top of the breech was a sniperscope the size of a restaurant peppergrinder, the big ones that waiters pester you with when you're trying to eat your pasta. The whole thing was connected to a hydrogen-cell car battery and set on a small bipod.

Spencer checked his phone again, went to the window, unlocked it, and slid it sideways a fraction. He went back to the rifle and sighted through the scope, went back to the window and slid it open a fraction more, checked again.

He knelt down at the end of the coffee table, took hold of the pistol grip, and lifted the rifle until it balanced perfectly on the bipod. The scope was a beautiful thing, right at the limit of modern non-digital optics. Looking through it, he could see the little crowd of people on the opposite terrace as if they were standing just outside the window. There were what appeared to be dignitaries in formal suits, and larger, stouter men and women who could only have been security operatives of some kind. Some of the people in the group were wearing indefinably old-fashioned clothing – tweeds, knitted ties, waistcoats – and looking about them with the air of Third Worlders visiting New York or a Westerner seeing Shinjuku at night for the first time. Spencer's heartbeat and breathing began to slow. The view through the scope became the entire world. A great calm suffused him, the only real calm he ever experienced.

He saw, in the crowd, a face he recognised, and his brain performed a calculation, based on the flocks of parakeets and the microlight flying past the window and the air currents he had felt on his face as he stood outside the apartment, which would have taken a supercomputer a week to complete. He channelled pure force, felt it rising from the floor and flowing through him. He ceased even to exist on a sentient level.

He squeezed the trigger.

The coilgun accelerated the round, a fragment of depleted uranium the size of a kernel of corn enclosed in a treated fibre sabot, to a muzzle velocity three times the speed of sound. Venting and suppressors rendered the report no louder than a sneeze. Through the scope, he saw the face he recognised contort suddenly, then drop out of view.

Then he was moving. He had no instructions to clean up after himself; someone else would do that, if it was necessary. He closed the window, went back downstairs, out of the front door, locked it behind him. Back along the terrace to the lift, collecting his bag as he went, no sign of alarm on this side of the arcology, the scene on the other side too far away for any sound to reach him.

In the lift, he plucked the mask from his face and put it in his pocket.

Next level, still no alarms. Nor on the next. Spencer went back through the security checks on a different set of documents to the ones he had entered with. It was five minutes since the shot; he felt no hurry or agitation, even when he had to queue to get through the gate.

Everything had been timed exquisitely. There was an airport bus waiting outside. He was one of the last to get on, and moments later the doors closed and the vehicle moved off.

At the airport, he had just enough time to lock himself in one of the toilets and strip off his outer clothes and the isolation suit. He bundled the suit up and put it in the toilet, cracked an ampoule of enzyme over it and watched it dissolve. When it was gone – it only took a minute – he flushed the toilet, dressed in his travelling clothes, put the clothes he'd worn in the arcology in his bag, and was in time to board his flight.

There followed an increasing blur of airport arrival and departure lounges. At some point he disposed of the clothes he'd worn in Mirny.

Changing planes at Krasnoyarsk, he felt things start to slip away and then reassemble themselves into a long, tiring and not very successful business trip. He was going to get paid anyway, but he worried what his employers would think.

Preoccupied with this thought, he failed to pay any attention to the person who stepped right up to him in the middle of the departure lounge and shone a tiny, very bright light in his eyes. The light stuttered; he could almost hear it, a rapid irregular clicking somewhere deep down inside his head, and he suddenly didn't feel like doing anything but standing still.

The person with the light was all out of focus. He felt someone rummaging in his coat pocket, then the light flashed in his eyes again and he heard a man's voice saying something and a distant corner of his mind found it quite remarkable that someone with such a broad West Country accent was speaking to him in an airport in Sibir, then the light flashed again and he realised he was late for his flight and he began to run.

SECRET SQUIRRELS

1.

LEWIS WANTED HER to fly from Stansted. Lewis said that she'd be able to lose herself in the crowds at Stansted, particularly at this time of year and if she timed her flight properly. Lewis could fuck off. It was all very well if, like Lewis, you lived in Bishop's Stortford, practically at the end of one of Stansted's runways. It was another thing entirely if, like Gwen, you lived in Greenwich. Faced with a two-hour commute to Stansted and Lewis's endless prattling about *operational security*, Gwen booked herself on the midmorning Luxair flight out of City Airport.

Which she ended up missing by fifteen minutes, due to one of those conjunctions of roadworks, Underground signal failures, double-decker buses hitting low bridges, bomb scares and street markets which only ever happens when you need to be in a certain place at a certain time.

"How was the trip?" Lewis asked that evening over the phone.

"It was fine," Gwen said, desperately scrolling through last-minute tickets to Luxembourg on her pad. "Stansted was busy."

"What's the hotel like?"

Gwen glanced around her flat. "*Pension*," she said. "It's not a hotel, it's a *pension*. An *auberge* maybe, at a pinch." She wondered whether she'd turned off the location data option on her phone. She thought she had, but she couldn't remember. Did it make a difference that Lewis had called her, rather than the other way round?

"What's it like?" Lewis asked again patiently.

"It's all right. It's a chain. These places all look alike."

"How's the weather?"

How was the flight? What's the hotel like? How's the weather? Was Lewis just trying to make conversation, or did he suspect something? Fortunately, Gwen had had the foresight to open a cam window on her pad; at the moment it was showing the view from one of Lëtzebuerg's many, many traffic cameras. "Raining," she said. "Chucking it down."

"Okay," said Lewis. "Well, get some sleep. You've got a busy day tomorrow."

You have no idea. "Yes, okay."

"Let me know when it's done."

"Sure," said Gwen, heart sinking as she saw the only flight tomorrow with any seats available. "Sure."

THERE WERE THOSE, supposed to know about these things, who said that Luxembourg was the most stable nation in Europe. Roughly translated, the Grand Duchy's national motto was, 'We want to stay the way we are,' and it had certainly shown no signs of breaking up into smaller and crazier polities like other Continental nations. It had the highest GDP per head of population of anywhere on Earth, and the Luxembourgers were not about to do anything to jeopardise that. Gwen's first impression, staggering out of Arrivals at Luxembourg Findel at six o'clock in the morning having had hardly any sleep the previous night, was of a rank of taxis emerging from a drizzly sunrise which could have been anywhere in Northern Europe.

One of the taxis drove her the short distance to the *pension*. There was no telling where she was. It could have been Germany, it could have been France. It could, at a pinch, have been Wallonia. The streets were full of coffee chains and burger franchises, and the people making their way to work through the drizzle were mostly conservatively-dressed. Her flight had lasted barely an hour; it seemed ridiculous to feel jetlagged after such a short journey.

The *pension* was just outside town, beside what appeared to be a brand-new ring road. Gwen supposed that at one time the building might have sat in the middle of acres of landscaped grounds, maybe out in a forest. Now it looked as if the Luxembourgers were building an industrial park next door and were eyeing the land the *pension* occupied with some covetousness.

It turned out not to be part of a chain. Or if it was, it was a chain which held back demolishing modernity with *fin de siècle* furnishings, wood-panelled walls, and the horns of what must once have been a magnificent twelve-point stag adorning the wall above the fireplace in the lobby. At the front desk, Gwen filled in an actual registration card and then paid for her stay by waving her phone at a contactless reader set discreetly into the desktop. The *concierge*, a young woman in a smart black business suit, loaded the room's key-code into the phone with a swipe of a stylus and summoned a liveried porter to carry Gwen's overnight bag up the deeply-carpeted stairs to the second floor.

Alone in the room, Gwen went through the time-honoured routine of the international business traveller. She jumped up and down and found the floor to be solid. She rapped on the walls and found that they, too, were of more than satisfactory thickness. She'd stayed in hotels where her room had been separated from the adjoining one by not much more than a plywood partition and someone walking across the room above her had made the ceiling bow. She sat on the bed and bounced up and down, went to the window and looked out on the expectant scrubland of the nascent industrial park, looked in the bathroom and noted that the shower was free of mould and that there was a small selection of complimentary bathroom goods, examined the entertainment set and was disappointed to discover that it only had a touchscreen interface. The wardrobe disclosed a rack of wooden hangers and half a dozen mysterious objects comprising two small shaped wooden blocks connected by a length of springy metal. After ten minutes' consideration, she still had no idea what the objects were, so she took a photo of one with her phone and image-searched it, and a few moments later was informed that it was a *shoe-tree*. She read the description, shrugged, and put the shoe-trees back in the wardrobe.

Less mysterious were the room's refreshment facilities. Everything – kettle, cups, tea and coffee sachets, spoons, milk pods, packets of biscuits – was shrink-wrapped for her hygiene and convenience. In one corner there was a small ironing board with a disposable catalytic iron clipped to it, and beside that was a trouser press. There was always a trouser press, no matter where she stayed. She had never used one. She wondered if anyone had, ever.

A check of the drawers in the bedside tables revealed a Gideon Bible, a Qur'an, a Book of Mormon, and a leather-bound two-volume biography of L. Ron Hubbard. None of these books – *actual books* – appeared ever to have been opened, let alone read. She sat on the bed and riffled through the Bible. Then she held it upside down by the spine and shook it over the bed, and a leaf of tissue-thin paper no larger than a Rizla fluttered down from between the pages and settled on the duvet.

Covert.

She didn't pick it up, not right away. She sat where she was on the bed, looking at it. Lucky, she thought, that the room had not been rebooked when she didn't turn up yesterday. The piece of paper had fallen face-down, but she thought she could see the shadows of lettering from the other side. She had thought that her arrival in Luxembourg had been the first step, but it wasn't. This was. This was the key that opened the mystery, something that had fallen, not from the pages of a Bible, but from the pages of an espionage novel. She felt a delicious thrill at putting off reading whatever was on the other side of the slip of paper. Once she looked at it there would no going back; she would have to keep moving forward. *Drink me*.

She reached forward and delicately took one edge of the piece of paper between thumb and forefinger, turned it over and laid it back on the bed. There, in tiny printing, was a date, an address, and a time, and the words *Are you the guide? No, I'm an engineer.*

Spy stuff. Her first reaction was a dizzying sense of relief; the date was today and the time two hours from now. She'd made it. Yesterday's fuckup didn't matter any more; Lewis need never know.

Her second reaction was a wave of excitement that felt almost exactly like fear.

Gwen sat back and took a deep breath. All right. So, *tradecraft*. At her final briefing, in a pub not far from Waterloo Station a couple of days ago, Lewis had drilled into her the importance of remaining covert. She had to assume that she was under some kind of surveillance, because that was just what national intelligence agencies did, it was axiomatic. The most common form of surveillance – because it was the least labour-intensive – was monitoring of communications and internet usage, algorithms ceaselessly winnowing a torrent of content for hotphrases and keywords. So, no Googling of the address. She read it again. She had crammed mercilessly with information about the city before leaving London, but the address only rang a faint bell. She read it one more time, closed her eyes, recited it under her breath, opened her eyes to make sure she had it right, then she picked up the slip of paper and put it in her mouth. It melted on her tongue. It tasted faintly of cinnamon.

Okay. She checked the clock on her phone. Enough time for a shower and a change of clothes. Wherever she was going, she hoped it had a café. She'd been too nervous to eat anything at Stansted and there had been no time on the flight. She was starving.

AT HER REQUEST, the *concierge* summoned a taxi to take her into town. She asked to be dropped off, as Lewis had instructed, at the Luxembourg headquarters of Deutsche Bank, a forty-storey wedge of glass and steel and carbon composites balanced improbably and alarmingly on its thin end. There was a piazza in front of the building, busy with street vendors' carts and businessmen and tourists, all of whom appeared oblivious to the possibility of the bank toppling over on them. At one edge of the piazza was a row of public information kiosks. Gwen stooped into one and called up a tourist map of the city. She found the address almost at once, without even having to search the map. Park Dräi Eechelen was in Clausen, a district about a kilometre from where she was standing. She left the kiosk and walked out into the piazza, bought a bunch of white roses at a florist's cart, and set out for the rendezvous.

The walk took her through a district of modern office buildings, onto a busy road, then over a bridge which crossed high over a broad wooded river gorge. The sky was grey and cloudy and it was windy on the bridge; she had to hold the flowers close to her body to stop them blowing away. On the other side, she crossed the road into the Parc des Trois Glands. The footpaths and cycleways through the wooded park were signposted, and she headed for the Museum Dräi Eechelen.

She came upon the museum suddenly, emerging from the trees and discovering herself standing beside a small mediaeval castle or fortification which seemed to have grown out of a much larger and much more modern glass and steel building.

Gwen wandered around to the front of the fortification, where an animated banner proclaimed an exhibition about Luxembourg's history. A short bridge had been built across the structure's moat, and in front of this were parked two police cars.

Her heart performed a single colossal *thud* in her chest. They couldn't be here because of her. Could they? She forced himself to keep moving forward, because turning and running would only have looked suspicious.

As she approached the cars, four policemen emerged from the entrance to the fortification. Between them was a short man with a florid, anxious face. The short man took in Gwen and the bunch of roses in one glance, and for a moment their eyes met and Gwen *knew*.

All of a sudden, the short man stomped to a halt and began arguing loudly with the policeman nearest to him. The others stopped and turned to see what was going on, and Gwen walked past them, past the cars, and around the other side of the museum. She was out of sight of the little group when a wave of dizziness overtook her, and she realised that she had been holding her breath ever since she had seen the police cars. She stopped for a moment, breathed out shakily, and inhaled slowly. Her heart was racing and little black spots danced in front of her eyes. She simultaneously wanted to throw up and to curl up and lose consciousness until this mess went away.

The sound of engines startled her. She looked around as casually as she could manage, and saw the police cars coming towards her along the block-paved drive that circled the museum. Her heart seemed to pause for a moment, then the driver of the lead car waved her away and she stepped to one side to let them pass. As they went by, she saw the short man sitting in the back of the second car, his head bowed. Gwen watched them disappear around a curve in the driveway, then she turned off the drive and into the large glass building, which turned out to be a museum of modern art.

She walked straight through the building and out the other side, onto a bleak, windy plaza between tall buildings. On the other side of the plaza was a main road. She dumped the roses in a litter bin, walked to the side of the road, and hailed a taxi.

THERE WERE MORE police cars at the *pension*. A line of four of them, parked at the front of the building. Gwen had asked the taxi driver to drop her at a motel she'd noticed on the ring road this morning, and walked the rest of the way. From the embankment the road ran along, she could look down and see the police from a couple of hundred yards away. Again, she kept going as casually as she could. Just an ordinary pedestrian out for a stroll alongside a busy three-carriageway road. Yes, officer, I wanted to take a look at this building site where the industrial park's going to be. What of it? The *pension*? Not me, officer. I am not the droid you're looking for. Nobody raised an alarm, nobody chased her.

Half an hour later, she found a bar and went in and sat in the darkest corner staring at a glass of beer. After a while she took a long, shaky drink.

THIS WAS, ON the face of it, a rich season for conspiracists. On top of the hardy perennials like the death of Princess Di, and the Other Gunman, there was the explosion of the Line train in the Urals, and looming over everything else was the Union with the Community.

Although in truth, the Community had already had its fans, even before it had revealed its existence. Intensely paranoid groups of conspiracy theorists, shunning the internet and its inherent surveillance, meeting – if they met at all – in suburban front rooms and noisy pubs, fans of espionage fiction passing photocopied documents and theories via dead drops. They combed obscure texts in private libraries, parsing them for any mention of a lost land. They were so artless, so extemporaneous, that they had managed to keep their existence out of the eyes of the authorities for decades as they carried on a long distributed conversation about a fabled landscape which had been written over Continental Europe by a family of eighteenth century English landowners. *The Community*. Its name was spoken in hushed tones, as if its shy inhabitants might be listening. It was a place of wonders, accessible only if one had certain maps. Shangri-La, Utopia, Lyonesse. There were those who theorised that it was the location of Avalon, that Arthur lay sleeping there. Others believed it was the origin of flying saucers, that the Nazis had founded a Fourth Reich there, that Hendrix and Morrison and Elvis still lived there, hugely aged but still hale.

Imagine their disappointment, then, to discover that the Community was *dull*. The first travellers to return after certain border crossings were opened reported a single Europe-spanning nation which seemed to have been laid out by English landscape gardeners, its people stolid and polite, its society contentedly stalled in an approximation of the 1950s, as if an Ealing comedy had been set in an alternate world. No Hendrix, no Nazis, no flying saucers, no unicorns.

In the wake of what was being spoken of as the *Emergence*, several Community conspiracists had retooled themselves as media pundits. You saw them most days on the rolling news channels, giving their opinions – and they were, without exception, extremely opinionated – on the latest treaty or arrangement negotiated between the Community's government and this or that European nation or polity or sovereign state.

Lewis, de facto leader of the little group of Community fans to which Gwen belonged – they shunned the term 'conspiracist' in much the same way as they shunned the term 'nut' – turned his nose up at these new media stars, the way he turned his nose up at the flood of Community commentators who had suddenly, as if out of nowhere, appeared on social media. Most of them, he opined, were Johnny-come-latelies. The ones who had kept the faith during the long covert years and then suddenly emerged into the spotlight of the news cycle had, he said, betrayed the purity of the Cause.

Here, as on a number of other important points, Gwen's opinion diverged quite sharply from Lewis's. Gwen was delighted to discover that the Community really did exist, was reassured that it seemed to be so ordinary, and if somebody wanted to make themselves famous on the back of it, she was fine with that.

In the first heady days of the Emergence, when it seemed as if there was nothing else happening in the world but the discovery that there was a parallel universe and it had been settled by the English, the group had met several times and discussed what the repercussions would be for the world – although what they were really discussing, between the lines, was what the repercussions were for them. In the end, as more and more detail of the Community emerged, the group ceased to meet. There was nothing left to do.

People began to drift off, some no doubt to other conspiracies, others to more mundane concerns. This seemed to provoke a fury in Lewis which expressed itself as a deep and sarcastic politeness. For Gwen, it was simply a matter of work pressure. The Emergence had coincided with a general election in England and a change of government. The MP for whom she worked as a researcher found herself elevated to the post of Junior Minister at the Home Office, and all of a sudden she needed Gwen's input at all hours of the day and night. It was hard enough to stay on top of the brief as it was, without worrying about parallel worlds, and Gwen had, ever so gently, uncoupled herself from Lewis and his dwindling band of followers.

It turned out that the Home Office was *intensely* concerned about the Community. The government was being forced to make up policy towards the vast new European neighbour on the hoof. Ironically, Gwen found herself doing more Community research than she had ever done on Lewis's behalf. Most of it was crushingly dull, but there was the odd titbit of interest. Gwen was involved in organising a state visit of President Ruston and several Community officials, involving a banquet at Windsor Castle for the sake of the news organisations, and a number of quiet meetings with her Minister and others out of the public eye.

And so Lewis came back into her life.

* * *

"ARE YOU USING an unsecured phone?" Lewis asked incredulously. "I can't believe you're... are you using your *own* phone? Jesus fucking Christ, hang up."

"I am not going to fucking hang up and I don't give a flying fuck who can hear me," Gwen said.

"Have you been drinking? You'll get us both arrested." Lewis sounded on the verge of panic. Gwen could hear, at the other end of the connection, a background noise of traffic. Then Lewis hung up.

"Oh, you *twat*," Gwen muttered. She dialled Lewis's number again, but this time all she got was an *unavailable* tone.

She looked around the bar. This was not, she had sensed the moment she walked in, one of those bars popular with tourists or business people. It was dark and roughly-furnished. Most of the other patrons had the look of career drinkers. A lot of the older ones had tattoos and lots of bling, and attack dogs slumbering watchfully beside their tables. It was really not a place for a lone Englishwoman, and she suspected that if she hadn't been so obviously and monumentally pissed-off one of the other drinkers would have tried to hit on her.

Her phone buzzed. She looked at the screen and saw a text from an unfamiliar number. *Buy a disposable phone and call me on this number*, it read. *I've had to ditch my sim you stupid bitch.*

"Oh, do fuck off," Gwen muttered. But she finished her beer – her third in the past hour or so – and got up and wandered back into the street. There was a tobacconist's kiosk a little further along, its windows piled with sun-bleached packets of condoms and bubble-packs of porno HDs. She bought a pack of disposable phones and stood in the street while she took one out and went through the interminable setup process. The phone was about as thick as an old-style credit card, printed on cheap resin stock, and the screen was almost unreadable.

Finally, she got it up and running and dialled the number Lewis had texted her on. He answered almost immediately.

"Do you want to get me arrested?" Lewis demanded. He sounded a little breathless, as if he'd been running. He'd probably just done what Gwen had done, gone down to the newsagents on the corner and bought a pack of phones. Lewis was out of condition.

"I don't know what you've got me involved in, but I'm finished," Gwen said. "If I ever see you again I'll fucking punch you."

"What? What's happened?" The phone's speakers were fragile and tinny; Lewis's voice kept breaking up.

"My contact's been arrested and the police were at the hotel."

A long silence at the other end of the connection. So long that Gwen would have thought Lewis had hung up and thrown the phone away, if it weren't for the sound of cars and buses in the background.

Finally Lewis said, "What?"

Gwen looked around to make sure nobody was paying her undue attention. "I went to the meet," she said, "and as I got there the police were marching the contact away."

"How did you know it was him?" Lewis interrupted.

"Lewis, I *knew*. All right? I knew. I went back to the hotel and the police were there too."

Another long silence. "Where are you now?"

"Somewhere in Luxembourg City. I don't know where. Lewis, *all my stuff is at the hotel*. I can't go back there. I've got no clothes."

"Fuck your clothes," Lewis said in a sullen, distracted voice. "Did you see where they took the contact?"

"No, because I was going in the opposite direction," Gwen said with exaggerated patience. "Lewis, will you listen? Something's gone wrong. I'm *on the run from the police*."

"You don't know that."

"*What*? Okay, come on, Lewis, you tell me. You think about what I just told you and you tell me what's really going on." Gwen suddenly realised she was shouting. She glanced around, but she was still not attracting attention, which she thought was pretty good going, considering. She said quietly, "They'll be watching the airport and all the border crossings. I'm *stuck* here, Lewis."

"Did you leave any ID at the hotel?"

"No, but it doesn't matter. I booked the room in my own name."

"You did what?"

"How the fuck else was I supposed to do it?"

"You fucking *amateur*!" Lewis roared at the other end of the connection. Then the phone went dead. Gwen took it from her ear and looked gravely at it. Oddly enough, she found she felt rather better for having vented at Lewis. Of course, it hadn't improved her situation at all, but still. If there were going to have to be Famous Last Words, *fuck you* would have to do.

She snapped the phone in half, extracted its SIM, snapped that in half as well, and dumped both in a nearby bin. She looked around her. It was late afternoon, and the street was full of workers making their way home at the end of the day. Most of them were business-suited and carrying document cases. None of them paid her any attention at all. Gwen turned her collar up against a spit of cold rain, put her hands in her pockets, and started walking.

SHE WALKED FOR hours. Night fell and the temperature plummeted. Around eleven she found an all-night café. The bar from which she'd called Lewis had served food, and she had tucked into a local dish of smoked ham and chips, but she was hungry again and her blood sugar was low and her feet hurt, so she sat down in the café, ordered coffee and something described on the menu as *Judd mat Gaardebounen*, and tried, for the hundredth time that day, to work out what to do.

There was no way, she thought, that she was going to try to leave the country. The moment she tried to board a flight or cross the border she would have to offer up her passport, and that, she assumed, would be that. Ditto for booking into a hotel. She wondered whether there were any hostels which had a less-than-rigorous policy about registering foreigners. As just another face in the crowd, she thought she might be safe from surveillance cameras. Unless there were cameras at the *pension*, all the authorities had was her name, and facial recognition software only worked if you had an image to feed into it. Had there been a camera in the lobby? Had there been one in the taxi she'd taken into town? The *concierge* and the taxi driver would be working with the authorities to produce a likeness of her, but that was notoriously unreliable, just a guide, too vague for facial recognition.

She'd used her phone earlier to withdraw a thousand euros – Luxembourg was almost the only European nation to use them, these days – at a Bureau de Change, so at least she wasn't leaving an electronic trail when she paid for things, but that wasn't going to go very far. There were some places where a thousand euros would have let her live like a queen for a week or so, but Luxembourg was not one of them. Would it be possible, she wondered, to hike across the border into France or Greater Germany or Wallonia? Luxembourg was a small country but surely it wasn't possible to fence the whole thing off?

Her food arrived. Pork again, this time served with beans and potatoes. She wolfed it down.

While she was eating, someone came into the café and stood looking casually around. He was of medium height, and he was walking with a cane. Gwen watched with mounting horror as he smiled gently and began to walk over to her table.

Thoughts of fleeing, of fighting her way out, passed through Gwen's mind and were dismissed. There was nowhere to go. She sat, frozen, as the man with the cane limped up to the table, pulled out the other chair, and sat down opposite her.

"Hello," he said. "My name is Smith." His English was excellent, and almost – but not quite – accentless. He had a young face, but his brown hair was touched with grey and his eyes looked tired. "You seem to be in some trouble. May I help?"

Gwen sat where she was, speechless, fork in hand.

The waitress came over. Smith said to her, "I'll have what this lady is having – is it *Judd mat Gaardebounen*? Good. It looks excellent. And do you have any Polish beers? Tyskie, if you have it."

When the waitress had departed, Smith leaned his cane against the arm of his chair and said to Gwen, "I've been following you all day."

Gwen said nothing.

"I'm not the authorities," Smith said. "I don't even live here. I was due to meet somebody at the museum in the park earlier today."

Gwen stared at him.

"I'm making the assumption that you, too, were due to meet with this person. He'd scheduled his meeting with me after yours, but I got there early to scope the place out and I saw him being arrested and I saw you making a run for it." He smiled again. "Was that your hotel you went to? The one with the police cars outside?"

Gwen nodded.

"Then you need my help, I think," said Smith. "I'm renting a flat on the other side of the city; you can stay there tonight and tomorrow morning you can tell me your tale of woe. And no, that is not a pickup line."

"Why should I trust you?" They were the first words Gwen had said since she'd ordered her food, and her voice sounded scratchy and very, very tired.

Smith thought about it. "No reason at all," he said finally. "And in your place I would be asking the same question." He clasped his hands on the table in front of him. Gwen saw that his fingers and the backs of his hands were covered in scars from old burns and cuts. "I'll be honest; I have a selfish motive. Your interests and mine have intersected, and that intrigues me. I'd like to find out more, and in return I'm willing to help you leave Luxembourg. I might even be able to get you back into England without causing any unpleasantness, although you might give some serious thought to never going back."

"I have to go back," Gwen said. "I have a job."

"What do you do, if I may ask?"

Gwen told him, and Smith looked sad.

"Well," he said, "if you worked on a building site I'd say there was a better than even chance of your job being waiting for you when you got back. But government?" He shook his head. "It'll only take another day at most for word of this business to reach your Minister, and as far as he's concerned you're perfectly expendable."

"She."

"My apologies."

Gwen looked at her meal and suddenly felt sick.

Smith's food arrived and he tried a forkful. "This is terrific," he said, half to himself.

"Suppose I do go with you," Gwen said. "What happens then?"

"Well, let's not get ahead of ourselves. You need to get a good night's sleep, and then we need to talk. Now, finish your meal and let me eat this in peace. Then I have to have a quick word with the chef before we go."

* * *

SMITH'S FLAT WAS half an hour's drive across the city. About halfway there they drove into a hailstorm fierce enough to make it sound as if an entire armoured division was machinegunning the taxi. Two minutes later they had driven out the other side, and it was as if they were in another city altogether. The officescrapers and historic buildings were gone, and instead they were in a district of shabby apartment blocks with brightly-lit convenience stores at pavement level, their windows lined with anti-riot mesh.

Smith saw her looking out of the cab window and said, "Bad part of town. Took me ages to find it."

The taxi pulled in through an archway which led to a big dark space surrounded by flats. Some of the windows overlooking the space were illuminated, but not many. The taxi bumped along an uneven driveway at the bottom of one block, then abruptly came to a halt.

"This is us," Smith said calmly. He paid the driver – in cash; Gwen had begun to notice things like that – and led the way to a door and then up several flights of steps to a darkened landing, where he opened another door, stepped inside, switched on the light. Gwen stood where she was. There was still time to make a run for it.

Smith, standing in the brightly-lit hallway unbuttoning his coat and unwinding his scarf, saw her standing there and said, "There's a forecast of snow for tonight; you're not dressed for it. You might make it to morning by moving from café to café, and you might even survive another night, but I wouldn't bet on you seeing the weekend."

Ah, fuck it. Gwen stepped into the flat.

2.

IF THIS WAS a rich season for conspiracists, it was a decidedly thin one for Rudi. The Emergence had taken hold of the world and given it a good shake. His primary purpose, jumping citizens out of the Community, had blown away on the wind when the Presiding Authority selectively opened the borders and allowed anyone –

within reason – who wanted to travel to Europe to do so. For a while, he had actually taken it personally. It was as if, unable to stop him doing what he did, the Community had finally decided to neutralise him by taking away the need to do it.

Coureur business in general had taken a knock. Once, someone would find themselves having to retain Coureur Central in order to transport a package across Europe's constantly and trickily reconfiguring borders. These days there was a postal service which passed through the Community, neatly bypassing all those irritating little countries. True, there were still certain things – and people – which the Presiding Authority would not allow on their territory, but the bulk of Central's business had always been the movement of perfectly ordinary mail, and that had dried up almost completely. Again, if Rudi was of a paranoid frame of mind – and he found paranoia a perfectly rational worldview – he might think that this was a deliberate attempt on the Community's part to stifle Coureur Central.

The operation to infiltrate Dresden-Neustadt had really only been an attempt to satisfy a vague curiosity, to tie up some loose ends which nagged at him, to try to get a read on where Mundt might be and what his research might have entailed. There was no sense of any progress, and anyway, now it was over there was nothing much he could do but wait for Lev to come up with an analysis. In the meantime, all he could do was ask questions and poke and prod blindly, hoping something would happen, even if he didn't know quite *what*.

Lost for something to do, feeling weirdly adrift all of a sudden, he had stood down his networks and gone back to Kraków and the kitchen of Restauracja Max, where Max had been making do with a series of agency chefs, unable to quite work himself up to making a decision to appoint a full-time replacement. Late at night, after the restaurant closed, Rudi watched the news networks as the Community emerged blinking into the mellow sunlight of media attention. Like every other European, he scoured the magazines for articles about the Community's negotiations with various nations and polities, read interviews with the first citizens to be allowed free access to their neighbours. Unlike every other European, he wasn't reading to learn about the Community – a handful of years ago he had known more about it than almost anyone else in Europe – he was looking for *subtext*, trying to read the Community's body language, gauge its intentions.

He gave up in the end. His remaining contacts in the Community's small and embattled dissident groups – which had more or less evaporated as soon as they were able to leave – were as clueless as anyone else. No one knew why the Presiding Authority had chosen to make itself known to Europe. Nobody knew what they wanted. Nobody knew what they were going to do next.

Incredibly, even cooking, the safe space he had so often retreated to in the past, did not satisfy any more. He caught himself in the middle of preparing meals, *wondering*.

"You're bored," Rupert said to him one evening.

"Mid-life crisis," Seth said.

Seth was over from London, Rupert touching down from one of his long hungry tours of the Continent, so Rudi had taken them to Bunkier, over in Planty, where the food was basic but excellent and there was more beer than anyone could drink. Bunkier wasn't, on the whole, a tourist place. It was a locals' bar, really, for all its pretention, and he knew most of the faces in the crowd; students making use of the free wifi, people who had come to attend some evening presentation at the gallery, people meeting up with friends ahead of a performance at the theatre next door, people just out for a drink. And the three of them, sitting on Bunkier's uncomfortable wooden chairs, the remains of three suspiciously artisanal burgers on pieces of slate in the middle of the table and glasses of Okocim in front of them. Rudi looked around the café and wondered sourly what people saw when they looked at him and his friends. Not the truth, certainly, which was that two of them were former Coureurs and the third came from another universe.

He said, "There's something *wrong*. Do you not feel it?"

Seth shrugged. Rupert took a drink of his beer.

"It's like that old cartoon, the one with the wolf and the bird."

Rupert, who couldn't be expected to know what he was talking about, just sat there watching him. Seth looked mystified.

"The wolf and the bird," he said again. "The wolf's always chasing the bird and the bird always gets away because the wolf comes up with these *fantastically* complicated plans that always go wrong and it blows itself up or falls off a cliff or –"

"Road runner," Seth said. "Coyote and road runner."

"Whatever. But there's always a bit where the wolf – the *coyote* – chases the road runner and suddenly they run off a cliff. The road runner's going so fast that its momentum carries it across, but the coyote keeps on running on thin air until it realises what it's doing, and *that's* when gravity takes over. It's like that."

"What's like that?" asked Rupert.

"*This.*" Rudi made a gesture which was intended to encompass the entire world and all its madness but only succeeded in thumping a passing waitress on the hip. The waitress favoured him with the briefest of hard stares and a muttered *kurwa* under her breath, and was gone again between the tables. Rudi folded his hands in his lap and looked at his friends. "It's like running upstairs and finding that someone's forgotten to put the top step in."

"You have," Rupert suggested, "unfinished business."

"Damn right," said Seth.

"None of us has had *closure*," Rupert continued, pronouncing the word as if he'd only learned it recently and was pleased to be able to use it in conversation.

"Damn right," Seth said again and drained his glass. "Beer?"

Rudi and Rupert nodded and Seth twisted in his chair to begin the usually-extended process of catching a waitress's attention. All of Bunkier's waitresses were beautiful and very, very smart, and Rupert liked coming here because he was usually in love with one or other of them.

Rudi looked about him. The weather had turned chilly and the staff had rolled down the plastic sheeting that served as an outside wall for the bar, and turned on the catalytic heaters. He thought about *closure*. They were no closer to knowing who had killed Seth's flatmate and his flatmate's girlfriend and basically burned his life down to the ground than they were to understanding the presumed intelligence war which had taken over Rudi's. Of the three of them, Rupert – he still insisted on going by his chosen *nom de guerre*, Rupert of Hentzau – was closest to gaining closure. At least he knew who had destroyed his home and killed everyone he knew, and why, even if the prospect of exacting some kind of justice remained out of reach in a misty distance.

Rudi said, "Good trip?"

"Very interesting," Rupert said. "Azerbaijan. Baku. Extraordinary place."

"Dangerous place."

Rupert shrugged. "It's okay if you're careful."

"I've never been." Baku had declared itself an independent city-state a couple of years ago and was currently gorging itself on oil money. Once upon a time, Coureurs would have flocked there. Now it hardly registered.

"You should. It might take your mind off things for a while."

Rudi pulled a sour face. "It's my experience that no matter how long you take your mind off things, the things are always waiting for you when you come back."

Rupert sat back and looked at him. "You were busy for years," he said. "Running everywhere. Now there's no need to run any more, but you still feel as if you have to."

"I know." Rudi bent over the table and drew a line through a splash of beer.

"You need a white whale."

Rudi looked up. "A what?"

"A white whale. Like the captain in the book. Ahab."

"Ahab was crazy."

"Yes, but he was crazy with a *purpose*. A foolish and destructive purpose, but a purpose all the same."

"I'm a chef."

Rupert waved it away. "That's a job, not a purpose."

Rudi pictured himself walking out into the restaurant in the middle of service and announcing that it was a job, not a purpose. He said, "Any suggestions? Any particular *white whales*?"

Rupert spread his hands. "We should make more of an effort to find Mundt."

"Efforts are being made," Rudi said. "Believe me." Herr Professor Mundt had discovered a form of topology which the rulers of the Community believed would allow him to open border crossings between them and Europe, which clearly posed something of a security problem for them. He had also, unfortunately, been missing for the best part of a decade now, having been squirreled away with enormous efficiency by a Coureur named Leo. It was impossible to ask Leo where Mundt was because someone had subsequently cut off his head and left it in a luggage locker at Berlin-Zoo Station.

One of the waitresses came over finally, and Seth gave their order. "I'm going off shift in a minute," she told him. "You want to settle up now and another waitress will bring your beers?"

Seth, who wasn't used to table service in pubs, looked over at Rudi, who nodded and took out his phone and waved it at the waitress's credit terminal to pay their tab. He watched her head back towards the bar. He thought about white whales.

AFTER SETH HAD flown back to England and Rupert had taken off for the gods only knew where, the conversation kept coming back and nagging at him. He found it playing over and over again at the back of his mind through long days and nights at the restaurant. Unfinished business. Closure. Purpose.

Late at night, he found himself jotting things down – on paper, which was easier to destroy than notes on a pad. At first it was just scraps of ideas, half-remembered conversations, Situations, but at some point he realised that what he was doing was writing his own life, or at least the latter part of it, the part which had been taken over and used by Coureur Central and, quite probably, by others. He had no idea who these people were, or what they wanted. He had done what he had thought was right at the time, although to be honest now he looked back none of it seemed to have made any difference to anything. He'd jumped people out of the Community until the Presiding Authority opened the borders – really, in the great scheme of things he could only have been a minor irritation. He sat and thought about white whales again.

Which eventually brought him here, to this flat in one of the rougher parts of Lëtzebuerg, using his phone to trawl some of the wilder chat rooms and bulletin boards and blogs for word of one Dieter Wilhelm Berg, last seen being marched towards a police car this morning. *Yesterday* morning, it being three a.m. now. The

Englishwoman was snoring in the spare room. Rudi had done some discreet searches of her name, and found no mention of her. Which was interesting. The local police certainly knew her name – they'd raided her hotel – but they had chosen not to circulate a public bulletin, and there was nothing about her in the great undertow of rumour and hearsay which made up most of social media these days. Ditto for Berg, who had claimed to have information for Rudi and appeared to have been preparing to hand the same information to Gwen. Rudi felt a little disappointed with Berg for doing that.

Berg had found him, heard word that he was looking for something and made contact using a very old word-string on a microblogging site sometimes used by Coureurs. Rudi only saw it by chance, and was intrigued enough to set up a series of blinds and dummies and cut-outs via which to reply. And here he was. And Berg was... nowhere. Not a word of him anywhere, not even among the most paranoid discussion groups, who surprisingly often, and usually without realising it, stumbled across information that was actually of some use. Nothing.

Rudi shut down his phone and put it on the kitchen table in front of him and rubbed his eyes. Beyond his reflection, snow eddied in the light from the living room window. It had been snowing for a couple of hours, and the sound of the traffic in the street below had given way to a soft, snuggled silence.

He got up and went to the window. The snow turned the streetlights into great fuzzy spheres illuminating the occasional car or van picking its way carefully along a fat pair of tramlines cut into the pillowed white surface of the road. The shopfronts on the other side were blurry and indistinct. A couple of figures, bulky in cold-weather clothing, fought their way along the pavement, heads down against the wind.

Rudi turned and perched on the windowsill and looked around the flat. It was two years since anyone had tried to kill him. Something was wrong.

"It was supposed to be safe," Gwen said. "It wasn't even supposed to be illegal."

They were sitting at the dining table having breakfast. Rudi had made eggs Benedict, which Gwen had regarded with some initial suspicion.

"I don't understand," Rudi said. "If it wasn't illegal, why go to the trouble of all the cloak-and-dagger?"

"Lewis," Gwen answered, sitting back and picking up her cup of coffee. "Lewis thinks he's living in a spy novel."

"And you?" asked Rudi. "How do you feel about that?"

"It's a bit stupid, isn't it," said Gwen, and Rudi saw a hint of embarrassment in her body language, as if she'd been caught enjoying a game meant for toddlers. "Lewis said it was better if a woman came for the meeting because nobody would suspect a woman."

"If you'll excuse me for saying so," Rudi said, "Lewis sounds like a dick."

"I was the only woman in the group," she said. "The whole conspiracy scene's mostly blokes. Blokes without lives of their own."

"How did you get involved with them?" Rudi asked. "If it's not a rude question."

She shrugged. "Rob," she said. "My ex. He was at university with Lewis. Lewis invited him to one of the meetings, he took me along. We split up, he stopped going to the meetings, I didn't."

"You found Community conspiracy theories interesting?"

She tipped her head to one side and looked at him. "I really hope that wasn't a prelude to some sort of mysoginistic comment."

He shook his head. "That never occurred to me, in all seriousness," he said. "I'm just fascinated by the Community groups."

"It wasn't any weirder than the UFO nuts," she pointed out. "And it turned out to be true."

"Have you ever heard the name *Delahunty*?" he asked.

"No."

"*Rafe* Delahunty? Or possibly *Araminta*?"

"No."

Rudi shrugged. "A friend of mine knew them," he said. "They claimed to have been in touch with a Community group in London, people who had maps of border crossings."

"It wasn't us. Lewis would have multiple orgasms if he ever got his hands on a map like that. When was this?"

"Quite a while ago. Ten, maybe fifteen years."

"No," she said. "Not us. We've only been running for six years or so. And we weren't that serious." And she scowled to realise that she was still saying *we*. As if she was ever going to do anything but knock Lewis unconscious if she ever saw him again.

"Well, it seems to be fairly serious to me," Rudi said. "For Herr Berg, anyway. Although to be fair, we don't know what he was being arrested *for*, or whether he was released after questioning. For all we know, he might have failed to pay maintenance to his ex-wife. I presume you had no fallback procedure, no way of contacting him directly?"

Gwen took a drink of coffee. "Lewis," she said. "I didn't even know this bloke's name."

"And you have no idea what brought Berg into contact with your friend Lewis?"

Gwen shook her head. "What was he supposed to be giving you?"

Rudi got up from the table and started to gather up the breakfast things and carry them over to the kitchen area. "If it's something likely to bring you into conflict with the authorities, it's best you don't know," he said.

"Fucksake," Gwen muttered. "You and Lewis."

"So far, you haven't done anything wrong," Rudi said, bending over to put the breakfast plates into the little dishwasher. "From what you told me, Berg probably didn't know your name or even have a description by which to identify you."

"The police were at the hotel."

"Yes." He closed the dishwasher and stood up awkwardly. His leg was aching again. "Yes, that's interesting."

"You think Lewis grassed me up."

Rudi limped back to the table and sat down. "He knew when you were coming and where you were staying. As did whoever left the contact procedure at the hotel for you." He shrugged. "I have no idea. Things go wrong all the time; it might be no more suspicious than that."

Gwen scowled and drained her coffee. "So what do we do now?"

"The first thing we have to do is make sure you're safe."

"And safely out of the way."

Rudi tipped his head to one side and smiled.

"According to you I can't go back home. My job will be gone and I'll probably be arrested the moment I set foot in the office, if not before. My life's in ruins; I'm not going to let you just... *file* me somewhere. I want to know what's going on."

Rudi crossed his arms, came to a decision. "Herr Berg gave me to understand that he had information relating to *Les Coureurs des Bois*, something they were doing here in Luxembourg."

"It's not the same thing, then," Gwen said. "Lewis isn't interested in the Coureurs."

"That's been puzzling me," Rudi admitted. "What are the chances that Herr Berg would have two separate pieces of information to sell to two different people on the same day?"

"I have no idea," said Gwen, taking the coffeepot from its coaster in the middle of the table and refilling her cup. "Right about now I'm prepared to believe anything."

Rudi lit a cigar and frowned.

"Who is this Berg, anyway?" Gwen asked.

"He works for the Defence Ministry," Rudi said. "I looked him up. He's in Procurement."

Gwen thought about it. "Have you tried to find out what the Defence Ministry has been procuring recently?"

Rudi stared at her through a cloud of cigar smoke.

"I'M NOT A SPY," Rudi said. "I don't do espionage."

"It sounds like exactly what you do," Gwen told him.

"It's not the same."

Gwen shrugged. They were sitting in a little café, improbably named the Bouffy Hutch, near the centre of the city. The place was packed; mainly, it appeared, with people sheltering from the snow, which was still blowing past the windows like the carriages of a steam locomotive. The air inside was warm and smelled of coffee and food and damp clothing.

"What I mean is that it's not second nature for me," Rudi grumbled. "I have to think about it." He sighed. "I'm getting sloppy."

Gwen looked at the windows. "Is it ever going to sodding stop?" They had spent the past two days at the flat, digging stuff up from the internet and making phone calls, and the snow had not ceased once. In some places it was over a metre deep.

"Better pray it keeps up," Rudi told her, sipping his coffee. "There's nothing the police hate more than searching for a fugitive in a blizzard."

Gwen had found herself quite surprised by how easily she had taken to being a *fugitive*. The trick, it seemed, was simply not to *act* like one. So long as you looked as if you belonged somewhere and knew what you were doing, nobody noticed you. Stomping through the snow bundled up in cold-weather clothing, fur-lined hood pulled up over her head, she was perfectly anonymous. Sitting here, she was just another face in the crowd.

"Here's our man," Rudi said, and Gwen looked up to see a short, stout figure making its way through the café towards them, annoying diners on either side by shaking flakes of snow off its sleeves. Rudi waved – three friends meeting each other for lunch – and the figure came over, pulled up a chair, and sat down.

There were some awkward moments while they all stared at each other. The newcomer was in his early sixties, dressed in a leather jacket over a hoodie over a massively-thick knitted sweater, what seemed to be several metres of scarf wound round his neck. He had tiny, annoyed eyes under bristling badgery eyebrows, and an old-fashioned lumberjack-style hipster beard.

"Fritz," he said. "We spoke."

"Indeed we did," Rudi said. "Are you hungry? Can we get you anything? A pastry, perhaps?"

"You mentioned money," Fritz said. His English was heavily-accented.

"I did," Rudi agreed again. "If you'd care to check, you'll find a small addition to your bank balance."

Fritz took his phone out, thumbed a sequence of numbers, swept through a couple of menus, read the screen. He looked at Rudi and raised his eyebrows.

"For your time," Rudi told him. "I'll transfer the rest, if your story's interesting enough."

Fritz put his phone away. "Three weeks ago," he said. "Everything's puttering along nicely, then all of a sudden we get this order."

"Out of the blue," Rudi said. "Urgent."

Fritz nodded. He looked at Gwen.

"My friend can be trusted," Rudi assured him. "Although the money isn't hers."

Fritz pouted. "A kilometre of fencing," he said. "In ten-metre sections. Five metres tall."

"That's a lot of fencing," Rudi noted. "Did your employers have that much in stock?"

"Business has been slow lately," Fritz said. "We had a big contract, an office renovation, but they ran out of money and left us with the fencing we'd manufactured. My boss was sick of it; he wanted to sell it for scrap and start again, stupid bastard."

"There must have been a contract, though? Were you never paid?"

"The firm doing the renovations went bust; it's still in the courts."

"But you wouldn't need a kilometre of fencing for a building site," Rudi said, and Gwen got the sudden impression that the firm Fritz worked for must be teetering on the brink of disaster, mainly because his boss had made some very poor business decisions.

"Do you want to hear the story?" Fritz asked. "Or shall I call up a spreadsheet of our accounts?"

Rudi smiled and made an *after you* gesture.

"So we get the word," Fritz went on grumpily. "A kilometre of close-woven mesh, so-and-so tall, buyer to collect. Boss went wild, never seen him smile so much."

"But the buyer never collected?"

Fritz shook his head. "Got the word a couple of days later, there'd been some kind of fuckup and could we deliver for them."

"That's interesting. Did they say why?"

"No, but it was obvious later; they were just so fucking poorly organised, they didn't have enough transport of their own."

"And where were you to deliver it to?" Rudi asked nonchalantly.

Fritz sat and looked at him.

"You make me sad, Fritz," said Rudi. He took out his phone and thumb-typed quickly. "Here's another third."

Fritz checked his own phone and then stared at Rudi again.

"The rest when I've checked out your story," said Rudi. "I would hate to believe you think I'm an idiot."

Fritz sighed and took a slip of paper from his pocket. He put it on the table in front of him and pushed it across towards Rudi. "GPS coordinates," he said.

Rudi left the slip where it was. He leaned his elbows on the table and smiled. "So," he said. "To recap, this mysterious – and apparently quite wealthy – client failed to budget for sufficient transport and asked your firm to make the delivery. And you were one of the drivers?"

Fritz nodded. "The whole transport staff. We'd been sitting around drinking coffee for weeks, and then all of a sudden all six of us loaded up the trucks and took the fencing out there." He nodded at the slip of paper.

"And what did you find when you got to the coordinates?" Rudi asked.

"Soldiers," said Fritz. "The entire fucking Army, looked like. In the middle of a forest. Trucks, helicopters, those modular office things they use as barracks. Fucking arseholes."

"Trucks," Rudi noted.

Fritz leaned forward and said quietly, "Sir, I have never seen so much fencing in one place. They must have run out of their own supply and had to get the rest wherever they could. It was piled *everywhere*."

Rudi smiled again. "You must have developed quite an expert eye for fencing, during your career," he said.

Fritz glared at him. "Listen, son," he said, "I drive a fucking truck. It's what I do so I don't have to live in a hedge. It's not a fucking *career*."

Rudi tipped his head to one side.

"I don't know if I saw all of it," Fritz said. "What I *did* see, with the inventory we delivered, I reckon there was more than four kilometres of fencing."

Rudi thought about it. "Did you see any sign of building work? Clearance work?"

Fritz shook his head.

Rudi reached out and took the slip of paper, read the figures written on it, put it in his pocket. "How did the soldiers seem?" he asked.

"Seem?"

He shrugged. "Were they agitated? Angry? Bored?"

Fritz gave this some consideration. "The officers seemed agitated," he said finally. "But that lot always are, the pricks. That's how you get to be an officer, right?"

Rudi nodded enthusiastically.

"The squaddies..." Fritz shrugged. "They were just doing as they were told."

"Was..." and here Rudi sat back and looked up at the ceiling, as if casting about for the correct phrasing, before looking at Fritz again. "Was there anyone *else* there? *Civilians*, perhaps?"

Fritz's little eyes narrowed so much they almost disappeared.

"I'm just trying to picture the scene," Rudi told him. "I can imagine you and the soldiers and stacks of fencing lying around everywhere. It must have looked quite chaotic. I was just wondering if I have the picture right."

"There were some suits there, as it happens," Fritz said carefully. "Giving orders."

"There," Rudi said with a huge grin. "And that completes my picture."

"Five of them," Fritz said. "Older men. One was English."

"Oh?" Rudi sounded surprised. "You spoke with him?"

"Nah, never got close to him. He was dressed like an Englishman out of a nineteen-fifties movie. You know what I mean? All buttoned up in old-fashioned clothes."

"So you can't be sure he was an Englishman, then," Rudi pointed out. "He was just dressed that way."

Fritz narrowed his eyes again as if he was suspected of being caught out in a lie. "Yes," he said. "No."

3.

BEING INVISIBLE – PROPERLY invisible, not just the everyday invisibility of being a woman – was something of a novelty for Gwen. Rudi had left the flat and returned some hours later with two duffel bags which turned out to contain what seemed, at first sight, to be masses of haphazardly sewn-together rags.

"Stealth suits," Rudi told her. "For stealthing."

They'd tried the suits on in the flat, to test the fit and allow Gwen to get used to the fact that, with the suit and its weird mutilated helmet on, Rudi was reduced to a transparent patch of barely-roiling air which only resolved into a recognisable figure when they were almost toe-to-toe.

"It'll get warm," Rudi warned. "The suit traps your body heat so it doesn't show up on infrared. Don't worry about it; just find somewhere inconspicuous and loosen the collar and wait until you cool down."

"How warm?" Gwen asked.

"Quite warm."

'Quite warm' turned out to be 'uncomfortably hot'. In fact, there was a sense, as they crouched down behind this tree, that she was slowly cooking. She loosened the collar of her suit and a geyser of hot, slightly sweaty air fountained up around her face, condensing into a cloud of vapour which anyone nearby, if they were paying attention, could not fail to miss.

"Okay?" asked Rudi from a volume of thin air a couple of metres away.

"Quite warm," Gwen said.

"Told you."

"Yes. Yes, you did." Gwen experimented again with the head-up display of her visor, zooming her view in and out until she felt a little queasy. She was familiar – or at least she'd thought she was – with the Coureurs from films and thrillers, but she'd never thought she'd actually be using some of their kit, or that it would turn out to be quite so uncomfortable.

They were in a forest somewhere to the east of a village called Pintsch, close to the GPS coordinates Fritz had given them. Pintsch's tiny population had been swollen by a small temporary town of soldiers, many of them, judging by their associated equipment, combat engineering troops. Many of them also seemed to be leaving. She and Rudi had ventured as close to the village as Rudi thought prudent, and watched, invisible, from the side of the road as truck after truck passed by.

Rudi's opinion was that the engineers had already accomplished their task and were returning to base. "I suppose we could always try talking to one of them at some point," he said. "But you can never tell with the military. They have surprising attacks of patriotism."

From Pintsch, they had worked their way from tree to tree through the forest until Gwen spotted, in the distance, the dull grey metal shine of woven metal fencing. And here Rudi had elected to pause, waiting for who knew what.

Periodically, armed soldiers passed by, patrolling outside the fence, their faces bulky with image-amps, and it took Gwen a while to realise that Rudi was timing them. One went by, his boots sucking in the mixture of slush and leaf litter trodden in a path around the fence. He went off into the distance. There was a pause. Then Gwen caught a whisper of motion out of the corner of her eye and a moment later a shower of snow suddenly drifted down out of the lower branches of a nearby tree.

"What are you doing?" she whispered; she still hadn't got used to the subvocal mike which was part of the suit's suite of equipment.

"I'm climbing this tree," Rudi's voice said in her ear. "It used to be easier for me."

More snow fell out of the tree. As a covert move, Gwen thought, it left a lot to be desired.

"What did you do to your leg?"

"What?" Even subvocalising, Rudi sounded out of breath.

"Your leg. What happened?"

"Ballooning accident." The fall of snow stopped; a branch high in the tree bent all on its own, steadied. "Years ago. Just a moment, please."

Another soldier came along the fence. He was dressed in snow-cammo, mottled shades of white and grey, the hood of his combat suit pulled up. From inside the hood, the twin turrets of his image-amplifier protruded. He was carrying a short automatic rifle, and from his posture he would rather have been anywhere else than here, walking endlessly round and round a fence in a snowy forest. Gwen had tried to work out how many of them were on patrol, which might have allowed her to time them and get some idea how big the perimeter of the fence was, but they all looked alike.

He passed by, and a minute or two later there was a fall of snow, a creaking of branches, and a sudden thud to her right, accompanied by several muttered swearwords in her ear.

"You okay?" she asked.

"Yes," Rudi said. "Absolutely excellent. Never better, thank you."

BACK AT THE flat, Gwen showered to get rid of the sweaty feeling of the stealth suit, and when they were sitting at the kitchen table having coffee Rudi showed her what he had seen from the tree.

He'd managed to climb up far enough to look over the fence, and the video he'd taken with his phone showed... at first Gwen couldn't quite work it out. The forest was in an area of steep little hills and valleys, quite wild, considering this was after all Luxembourg. On the other side of the fence, however, the land was perfectly flat. It was as if the forest had been cleared and the entire site had been levelled and then given over to a rather quaint-looking vista of fields and hedges and little copses of trees. Gwen thought she could see, above one stand of trees, a drift of smoke, and in other places as Rudi panned the phone's camera she caught sight of solid-looking stone-built houses. In one shot, she could see in the distance the Luxembourg forest rising on the other side of the farmland, maybe a mile or so away.

There were people in there.

She couldn't make out their faces or even what they were doing, even with the image zoomed to maximum, but she could see them moving about.

When they had watched the video half a dozen times, Rudi got up stiffly and limped over to the worktop to make more coffee.

"I don't understand," Gwen said. One of them had to.

Rudi didn't say anything, just busied himself with the kettle and coffee grounds and the cafetière.

"Do you know what this is?" she asked.

He didn't answer straight away. He stood watching the kettle as the water started to drum inside and steam emerged from the spout. He seemed to be playing a weird game of chess with the cafetière, the mugs and the sugar bowl.

Finally, he said, "Not for sure, no."

"But you have an idea. Whatever it was, it happened all of a sudden. The authorities didn't have enough fencing in stock, then they didn't have enough trucks to transport it out there. It took them by surprise."

"There are stories," Rudi said, "and maybe your friend Lewis has heard them, of a holy grail, the Creation Myth of the Community."

Gwen shook her head.

"No one knows how the Community was created," he said. "It's common knowledge now that an English family named Whitton-Whyte did it, or had it done for them, but what's not so well-known is that they seem subsequently to have lost the knowledge of how to do it. Either it was lost, or stolen, or destroyed, no one knows, not here or in the Community. There are stories of a book of instructions, floating about somewhere, which tells how to map a new landscape over an old one."

"I've never heard of that," she said.

He shrugged. "People in the Community have been looking for it for a very long time. Maybe it exists, maybe it doesn't. I don't know." The kettle stopped boiling. Rudi let it settle for a few moments, then poured water into the cafetière. "We still haven't decided what to do with you," he said.

"What?"

He put the lid on the cafetière and turned to look at her. "We still haven't decided what to do with you."

"If you think you're just going to hide me away somewhere, you'd better think again," she told him. "I want to know what's going on."

"I'm not certain what it is."

"Then I want to know what you *think* it is. Otherwise I'm not going anywhere."

Rudi rubbed his face. "All right," he said. "I'll tell you on the way."

"On the way where?"

He turned back to the worktop, and pushed the cafetière's plunger down. "Have you ever," he asked, "visited Poland before?"

MR PASQUINEL'S HOLIDAY

1.

CHRISTMAS HAD COME and gone before any of them got a break, and it was another two months before the emergency leave rota rolled around to Mr Pasquinel's department, and even then he didn't feel that he could put his workload on everyone else's shoulders.

"There's just too much to do," he told his department head one day over lunch. "Too much we don't know yet."

His department head, an exhausted-looking Latvian named Grigorijs, sighed and looked at the remains of their meal. He said, "Don't be noble, Donatien. Everyone else has taken leave."

"You haven't," Mr Pasquinel pointed out.

"The captain is always last to leave the sinking ship," Grigorijs said.

"Is the ship sinking?" asked Mr Pasquinel.

Grigorijs thought about it. "A poor metaphor," he admitted after a few moments. "But you take my meaning."

Mr Pasquinel wondered if it hadn't been more of a Freudian slip, but he kept that to himself. He said, "I still have some live work to finish. I can't go away yet."

Grigorijs nodded. He knew the work Mr Pasquinel was talking about, a matter of some delicacy involving Greater Germany.

"How is that coming along, by the way?" he asked, even though Mr Pasquinel had memoed him a progress report the previous day.

Mr Pasquinel shrugged. "Germans," he said.

Grigorijs topped up their glasses. They'd left the Consulate compound and driven into Charleroi, to a little Belgian restaurant on the Avenue Paul Pastur. Grigorijs had ordered *stoverij*, and Mr Pasquinel had elected to try the entrecôte with *Stoemp*. They were both drinking a rough and robust house red. Grigorijs liked to take his senior staff out for lunch every couple of months, to discuss work and other things informally, but he'd had to suspend the custom while the Republic was in lockdown. It was only since January that he had been able to resume his unhurried expense-account exploration of the local Wallonian eateries.

He said, "Is it anything we should be worrying about?"

Mr Pasquinel picked his glass up and took a drink. "The past year or so," he said, "has rather reset the boundaries of *worry*."

"Quite," Grigorijs said. He looked at the window of the restaurant. Outside, flakes of snow were blowing in gusts down the street. "Do you have a sense that they'll come round to our way of thinking, then?"

Mr Pasquinel shook his head. "The best we can expect is a compromise. And they know that. They will make an offer, we will make a counter-offer, they will counter our counter-offer... And so on. They're pragmatists, and so are we. All we're really doing is exploring the parameters of the compromise."

"That's not so bad," Grigorijs mused. There were places, further to the East, where the Republic was finding compromise a much harder proposition.

"It's bad enough. I'd hoped to have this finished by the end of last year."

Grigorijs shook his head. "It's the times we live in. Once upon a time the only people we'd have had to negotiate with were the EU and the Russians."

Mr Pasquinel, who was something of a student of the unhappy history of the EU, grimaced. "I don't see how that would have been any better."

The little towns and cities of the *Sillon industriel*, the former heavy-industrial heartland of the former Belgium, had been spreading towards each other along the Sambre-Meuse Valley for centuries; now Charleroi and Liége were the two ends of a ribbon metropolis which some people with satirical intent called the *Dorsale Wallonne*. It was some considerable time since the area had been an industrial backbone, or much of an industrial anything. The steelworks along the Meuse had gone to their knees in one or other of the economic crashes of the first half of the century, been retooled, gone to their knees again during the Xian Flu, been retooled once more, and finally went bust in a spectacular flurry of union riots and corruption trials which had heralded the referendum that eventually broke the country up.

As metropoli went, the Dorsale Wallonne wasn't much to call home about, a belt of rusting industrial plants and shabby towns through which the Line passed as efficiently as possible, casting off a branch just outside Charleroi to connect the polity to what had been intended to be its Belgian Consulate. Unfortunately, a year after the branch line and Consulate were completed, Belgium split in two, and now they were just another bone of contention for the perpetually-squabbling Flemish and Walloons.

Officially, the Independent Trans-European Republic held no view on what happened to the various territories it ran through. As far as it was concerned, if a country broke up after an Embassy was established, that was too bad. Unofficially, that kind of thing caused all manner of problems for the diplomatic staff, but as Grigorijs was fond of saying, no one ever joined the Diplomatic Service expecting a quiet life. The Belgian Consulate had been tooled up to represent the Republic's interests in the whole of Western Europe, and following the Incident it had fallen to the staff there to smooth feathers among the nations under its purview through which the Line passed.

"Do you have a view on how long it will take?" he asked.

Mr Pasquinel shrugged. "Are you trying to get rid of me?"

"Human Resources have noticed a single glaring exception to our programme of leave."

"Oh." Mr Pasquinel sighed. "I'm sorry. Have there been memos?"

Grigorijs shrugged.

"I would just like to mention for the record that there was no sign of HR's presence a year ago, when we were all working eighteen and twenty hour days," said Mr Pasquinel, becoming irritated. "One of my staff worked three straight days without sleep; it was a miracle she didn't suffer some kind of breakdown. It's a miracle we *all* didn't. Human Resources. Pah."

"Even so."

Mr Pasquinel looked toward the windows again. "This is not efficient," he said finally. "Sending people away when there's still work to be done."

"We will *cope*, Donatien," Grigorijs said. "Go away. Have a rest. When you come back you'll be more *efficient*."

2.

THE SNOW WHICH blanketed Western Europe had come and mostly gone in England. From the train, he could see fields half-flooded with meltwater, little rivers swollen almost to overflowing, with narrow boats bobbing at their moorings. He wondered what would happen if those rivers did break their banks; would the boats slip away and drift across the waterlogged fields, or would they follow the channels still flowing beneath the surface?

The day was grey and cold, the trees and hedges like scribbles against the clouds. At one point, the train passed alongside some kind of industrial plant – all blocky concrete silos and angled conveyors and modular sheds – which turned out, judging by the trucks parked at one end of the complex, to be a cement works.

The train stopped often, at little stations, first in Essex, then in Suffolk. The station car parks were full of vehicles left for the day by commuters, and beyond them Mr Pasquinel could see little villages, small groups of old houses with newer estates grafted on to them, the square towers of Saxon churches rising above the rooftops. A spit of rain dabbed at the windows.

Almost an hour and a half out of London, Mr Pasquinel took his rucksack down from the overhead rack and left the train at a station which seemed to sit all alone out in the countryside. He was the only passenger to alight from the train, and as it pulled away out of sight around a curve in the track he could see no one on the opposite platform. No staff. No one. He turned the collar of his waterproof jacket up against the wind, shouldered his rucksack, and left the station.

The station did in fact serve a village, but for some reason it had been built almost two miles from the nearest houses. Mr Pasquinel did not turn towards the village, however. He set out along the road, occasionally stepping up onto the banked verge when a car passed by.

After a mile or so, he came to a little graveyard with an iron gate. He stepped inside and found himself among perhaps fifty gravestones, most of them dating from the middle of the previous century, some of them more recent. None of them dated from the years of the Xian Flu, and he found that momentarily confusing, until he remembered that by the time the pandemic had reached outlying areas such as this the victims were being taken to isolation centres and then to hurriedly-built crematoria.

A moss-covered wall ran along the back of the graveyard, broken down in a couple of places. He clambered over tumbled stones into a little wood carpeted with snowdrops and stubborn patches of ice. On the other side of the wood was another wall, this one even more dilapidated. He stepped over it, and there he was, in the churchyard of St John's.

Mr Pasquinel knew his hobby had, in the past, been the subject of much innocent humour among his staff and co-workers, but he didn't mind. No one had ever been cruel about it, and even if they had, it wasn't in his nature to take offence. Life was too short.

The church dated from 1346, just before the Black Death had reached England, although it was obvious that the Victorians had given it a thorough makeover. It was stout and no-nonsense, its walls covered with cemented flints the size of his fist, its tower and walls crennelated. Mr Pasquinel walked slowly around it with his phone held in front of him, taking photographs. There was a graveyard here, too, these stones far older than on the other side of the wood. They were mostly covered in moss, their inscriptions all but erased by wind and frost. He could make out a few dates from the seventeenth and eighteenth centuries on some stones, the name

Hezekiah on another. On one side of the graveyard, where a stone wall separated it from the road, was a line of eight stones all bearing the same surname, their dates fifteen, twenty, thirty years apart. An entire lineage spanning more than a century. Mr Pasquinel took more photographs.

Returning to the church, he stepped into the porch and tried the door, but it was locked. He went back outside and walked around the graveyard for a while longer, then he sat down on a bench and contemplated his holiday, far from home and the cares of work. Let his colleagues make their jokes; Mr Pasquinel never felt as at peace as he did when he sat in an English churchyard.

After fifteen minutes or so, he heard brittle undergrowth being crunched underfoot in the wood, and a few moments later a young man dressed in hiking gear and walking with a cane negotiated the broken-down wall and stepped into the churchyard.

The newcomer's interests seemed similar to Mr Pasquinel's. He took photographs of the church, examined the gravestones, took more photographs. Eventually he came over and sat on the bench and put his leg out in front of him, as if it pained him.

They sat there like that for a little while. A car passed by on the other side of the wall, the hiss of its hydrogen-cell engine fading away into silence as it drove away.

Finally, the newcomer said, "I understand this parish is where the last wild wolf in England was killed."

"Yes," Mr Pasquinel said. "I remember reading that somewhere."

RUDI LEANED BACK and looked into the sky. It was perfectly possible for a drone the size of his hand, hovering a kilometre above them, to hear everything they were saying. You could go mad trying to cover every eventuality of surveillance. "Shall we have a look inside?" he asked.

"I tried," said Mr Pasquinel. "It's locked."

Rudi smiled and took from his pocket something that looked like a little battery-powered screwdriver. "No it's not," he said.

The little device opened the door with a faint *click*, and they stepped inside. Mr Pasquinel looked around. A double line of pews led towards an altar on which stood a diptych showing what appeared to be an angel with a flaming sword defeating a dragon. He thought *that* might date from the Flu Year. The interior of the church smelled of incense, which was unusual for Suffolk Anglicans. He thought he might like to come back here one day, to see what a service was like.

Rudi was wandering around the church, taking small matt-black boxes from his rucksack and placing them on the pews, where they sat apparently not doing anything at all. Finally, he came back to Mr Pasquinel and they sat together.

"Thank you for coming," Rudi said. "It's good to meet you at last."

"And you," said Mr Pasquinel. Close up, he realised he had been wrong about the newcomer. He wasn't young; he had a young face, but there was grey in his hair.

"Did you have any trouble getting away?" asked Rudi.

Mr Pasquinel shook his head. "They forced me to go, in the end. Threatened me with Human Resources. I'm sorry it took so long."

"Please don't apologise," Rudi said. "I can guess how difficult things have been for you."

"It has been busy, it's true," Mr Pasquinel allowed.

"How are things in the Republic?"

"We're running a limited service through most of Western and Central Europe, as you know. Greater Germany is proving stubborn, but they will come round. Further East..." Mr Pasquinel shrugged. "The explosion severed the Republic; we could run an eastbound service from the Consulate in Chelyabinsk, but Sibir refuses to allow our trains to run across its territory."

"They can't stop you, can they?"

Mr Pasquinel scowled. "It's a complex thing. We are a sovereign nation which does not grow a single item of produce. Not one potato, not one orange. We could run out to Chukotka tomorrow, but the Siberians would embargo our supplies. We have a population to feed. Some nations were starting to squeeze us, even before the incident."

"Squeeze you?"

"You'd only see it if you had a regional overview. At a local level, suppliers have been putting their prices up, or even just ceasing to trade with us. Head Office suspects a cartel operation, which is an interesting development." Mr Pasquinel bent down and rummaged in his rucksack. "It seems the awe in which people held us is finally wearing off. Sandwich?"

Rudi looked at the shrink-wrapped package in Mr Pasquinel's hands. "What are they?"

"Chicken salad."

Rudi shook his head.

"I also have roast beef and horseradish," Mr Pasquinel offered. "I was going to save them for the return journey, but we could eat them now and I can have the chicken later."

Rudi chuckled. "I'm fine. Really." He looked around the church. "Why is this place deserted, by the way?"

"Church of England," Mr Pasquinel said, unwrapping his sandwiches. "Minority religion, these days."

"Really?"

"The congregation here is probably no more than ten or fifteen strong. Most English people are Catholic or Muslim or Jewish. The ones who're religious at all. Didn't you know this?"

Rudi shook his head. "It's not something I've thought very much about."

"There's talk of a resurgence. The Community is Church of England. Well, a variant, but close enough." Mr Pasquinel took a bite of sandwich and looked about him. "I hate to see these places unused; they're quite lovely." He washed the mouthful of sandwich down with a sip of water from a plastic bottle. "You should see some of the Saxon churches. All Saints at Brixworth is extraordinary. Over a thousand years old, imagine that." He put his sandwich and its wrapping carefully down on the pew beside him and took a little plastic envelope from a breast pocket of his jacket. "Here you are."

Rudi took the envelope and looked at the object it contained, a hard drive the size of his thumbnail.

"There's no way to be certain what happened," Mr Pasquinel said. "The site is under about a billion tonnes of rubble, telemetry tells us nothing useful, surveillance footage is inconclusive; we can't even establish for sure whether the explosion happened on the train or in the tunnel itself."

"But you have a theory."

"*Pennington*," said Mr Pasquinel. "Kenneth and Amanda.

Originally from London, lately resident in Paris. She had one of those T-shirt businesses, he did some media consulting." He picked up his sandwich again and started to eat.

"Are you sure?" asked Rudi.

"No, we're not. The list of possibilities is quite long; God only knows we get some shady characters taking out citizenship. But there's something..." He shrugged.

"They're too good to be true," Rudi suggested.

Mr Pasquinel shrugged again. "Their cover – if it *was* a cover – was exquisite. I've never seen anything like it." He sighed. "She was pregnant. Two of our staff processed them privately – it seemed inhumane to make her queue in her condition. There was an anomaly on the scan."

Rudi raised his eyebrows.

"She said it was a foetal heart monitor," Mr Pasquinel mused. "And examining the scan, it *could* be."

"But you're thinking a bomb."

"Something powerful enough to destroy one of our trains but small enough to present as a piece of implanted medical equipment. Is that possible?"

Rudi thought about it. "No, but it might have been a component of a larger device which didn't show up on your scan."

It was Mr Pasquinel's turn to raise his eyebrows. "That's... interesting," he said.

"You didn't hear that from me, obviously."

"Obviously."

"What have you done with them? Your staff?"

"Sequestered. Contemplating the error of their ways. Similarly with the Penningtons' staff. Extramural rendition. They don't know anything, though. We'll let them go. Eventually."

Rudi sat back in the pew and folded his hands in his lap. "Of course," he said after a while, "you have to say that. If it's a matter of your trains being unsafe, that's the end of the Line – you'll excuse the pun. Terrorism, on the other hand..."

"We're certainly not making this up," Mr Pasquinel protested mildly. "We don't go around arresting people for the exercise."

"Kidnapping," Rudi corrected. "It's called kidnapping."

Mr Pasquinel sighed.

"No fundamentalist tendencies?" Rudi asked. "The Penningtons?"

"No tendencies of any sort," Mr Pasquinel said. "No extremist connections of any kind. Their legends go back *decades* but they have no family, no long-term friends. No former neighbours in London remember them in any detail. For five years everything is concrete; before that it becomes vague. They both attended Brunel University in London, and their names are on record there, but no one remembers them. Classmates think they recognise photographs of them, but they can't swear to it." He looked at the stained glass windows. "Nothing you could take into court. It's all on the drive. Photos, video, documents. Everything I could gather. Perhaps you will have more luck with it."

"If we accept the premise that they caused the explosion, the question is who exactly they were, and who they were working for."

Mr Pasquinel was quiet for a while, breathing in the smell of incense and old Bibles and centuries of worship. "There is," he said finally, "going to be a piece of *sleight of hand*."

"You're going to blame somebody," Rudi said. "At random."

"Not *random*, precisely," said Mr Pasquinel. "Plausible candidates. As you say, terrorism is one thing. An accident is something much more far-reaching. And it's not as if they don't deserve it," he added. He thought about it. "Public relations."

"And meanwhile, the Penningtons."

"They seem our strongest candidates at the moment; if whoever they worked for thought we were going off in the wrong direction, that would be useful."

"They won't," Rudi said. "Think you're going off in the wrong direction. They wouldn't be so stupid as to assume you were blaming some half-arsed terrorist group."

"I know." Mr Pasquinel shrugged. "I don't make policy."

"Also they will have a source within the Republic."

Mr Pasquinel sighed. "I had an ancestor who was a Coureur, you know," he said.

"Oh?"

"One of the original Coureurs, the French-Canadian traders who explored New France. Jean-Baptiste Pasquinel, a contemporary of Pierre-Esprit Radisson. My family have moved around quite a lot, for various reasons." Mr Pasquinel started to gather together the wrappings from his lunch and put them back in his rucksack. "I'm old enough to remember a time when we thought there would be no borders in Europe."

"Happy days," Rudi said.

Mr Pasquinel looked at him and tried to gauge whether he was being sarcastic, but all he could detect was a certain tired wistfulness. He finished doing up his rucksack and said, "Well, it didn't last long, anyway. Barely long enough to enjoy it, really."

"It's what Europe does," Rudi said. "Borders." He didn't bother to add that the Trans-European Republic had the longest border in Europe. He got up and started to retrieve the little cubes – bafflers against electronic and sonic snooping – and put them back in his rucksack. "By the way," he said, "have you heard anything about Luxembourg?"

"The Republic does not run through Luxembourg," said Mr Pasquinel.

"Not even diplomatic gossip?"

"Luxembourg," Mr Pasquinel said, "is really not chief among my concerns right now."

"No," Rudi said. "No, of course not."

"So," said Mr Pasquinel, standing and shouldering his rucksack, "it was good to meet you."

"You too," Rudi said with a smile. "I hope you enjoy the rest of your holiday."

"I'm going to treat myself. A couple of days in London. Wren churches. Wren said he built for eternity."

"Doesn't everyone?"

They shook hands and Mr Pasquinel went back up the aisle to the door. He opened it, but instead of leaving he stood in the doorway looking at something outside. Rudi paused in picking up the last couple of bafflers, looked at him for a moment, and then went to join him in the doorway.

A tall woman was standing outside. She was wearing a rumpled three-piece suit, a long grey belted raincoat with its collar turned up, and a fedora. She appeared to have been beamed into rural Suffolk from a Raymond Chandler novel. She was standing looking at them, hands in pockets, smiling broadly. She seemed to be alone.

Rudi and Mr Pasquinel exchanged glances. Then Mr Pasquinel took a deep breath, stepped outside, walked past the woman, and without looking back went out through the gate, turned left, and passed out of sight down the road. Rudi was quite impressed that he managed to resist the urge to break into a run.

The stranger had not moved, not looked away from Rudi, not stopped smiling. They looked at each other for some time.

Curiosity won, in the end. Rudi closed and locked the church door behind him and walked over to the woman and said, "Hello."

She was in her mid-thirties, fair-haired. She dipped a hand into an inside jacket pocket, brought it out holding a laminated card. "Detective Chief Superintendent Sarah Smith," she said. "EU Police."

The phrase 'EU Police' was the punchline to any number of jokes, but Rudi just raised an eyebrow and said, "You're out of your jurisdiction, Chief Superintendent."

"Then it's fortunate I'm not here in an official capacity," Smith said. She pocketed the identity card. "Are you interested in churches?"

"All Saints at Brixworth is extraordinary," Rudi deadpanned.

Smith nodded and glanced in the direction Mr Pasquinel had taken. She said, "I used to date the Rokeby Venus," and she looked back to Rudi and beamed.

Rudi devoted a few moments to wondering how long that particular phrase was going to dog his footsteps. He sighed. "Chief Superintendent," he said.

"Will you walk with me?" Smith asked. "There's a rather nice pub just along the way."

Why not? "Lead on, Chief Superintendent."

THE PUB WAS called the Black Ben, and the sign outside was so frankly racist that Rudi wondered how it had not been burned down. Inside, though, it was Generic English Country Pub, all polished wood and horse brasses and carpeting and snug velour upholstery. Rudi glanced at the lunch menu while Smith bought them drinks, considered ordering *Crevettes en Croute* just to see how badly an English pub kitchen could abuse the dish, decided against it.

They took their pints over to a table in a quiet corner, away from the handful of locals standing drinking at the bar. Smith took off her overcoat and draped it over a neighbouring chair. She had not once stopped smiling, not for a moment. It was beginning to irritate Rudi.

Smith took a printed photograph from her pocket and put it on the table beside Rudi's pint. It was a full-face shot of a stocky, tousled and confused-looking man of about forty. Rudi gave it what he thought was due attention, then he looked at Smith and said, "I don't know this man."

She looked a little disappointed. "That's a shame, because you might have been able to help us tidy up a small mystery," she said.

"I'm sorry."

"Oh, please, don't apologise." Smith tried her beer, apparently found it to her satisfaction. She put her glass back down on the table. "He was arrested flying in to Warsaw-Chopin from Moscow a few months ago. Passport Control thought there was something not quite right about his papers so they detained him while they made checks. It turned out he was travelling on very good forgeries."

"Not *that* good, if they were spotted," Rudi pointed out, although Polish Border Security were famously savvy and well-trained, not to mention ill-tempered.

Smith admitted the point with a nod. "He had no luggage," she said. "No other identification. We've been able to trace his journey back to Krasnoyarsk, but before that..." She shrugged.

"Difficult liaison conditions?" Rudi asked.

"You know how it is." Smith didn't appear too upset about it. "He seems to be English. At least, that's the only language he appears to speak. He's foggy."

"'Foggy'?"

Smith sat back and crossed her arms. "Amnesiac. Doesn't know who he is, where he's from, where he's been, what he did there."

"Is he suspected of some crime?"

Smith shook her head. "We're at a loss, really."

Rudi took a swallow of beer. He looked down at the photograph again. "I genuinely don't recognise him, Chief Superintendent," he said.

"Then you wouldn't have any idea why the only other thing he was carrying was an envelope with your name, address and an identification phrase printed on it," Smith said.

Rudi gave the detective a long, level look. "No," he said finally. "No, I wouldn't."

"One theory we're working on – the obvious one, really – is that he was coming to deliver the envelope to you."

"That would follow," Rudi admitted while parsing the fact that Smith had approached him in England, where she had no powers of arrest, rather than in Kraków, where she did. "What are you playing at, Chief Superintendent?"

"Me? Oh, I suppose I'm playing the postman. This is what was in the envelope." She took another photograph from her pocket and placed it beside the first.

This one was in black and white, a grainy crowd scene of many gentlemen in old-fashioned formal dress, heavy overcoats, top hats, wing collars. At the back of the crowd was part of the façade of what appeared to be quite an imposing building. In the foreground were four men, one with his back to the camera.

"I'm sorry," Rudi said, "but I don't know any of these people either."

Smith laughed. "The gentleman on the left, the one with the rather impressive moustache, is Georges Clemenceau. The patrician chap next to him is President Woodrow Wilson. The man beside *him* – he's the one just peeking over the chap with his back turned – is Vittorio Orlando, the Italian Prime Minister. And the jolly gent on the right who's just putting on his top hat – or taking it off, I can't tell – is David Lloyd George."

Rudi looked at the photograph again. "I'm sorry," he admitted. "I'm lost."

Smith sat forward and became businesslike. "So what we have," she said, "is a chap travelling on forged documents, with apparently no idea who he is or what he's doing, carrying a photograph taken in 1919 during the Versailles peace conference, addressed to you." She drank some more beer. "You can't blame us for being intrigued."

"I get the feeling," Rudi said, "that you're rather enjoying yourself, Chief Superintendent."

"Well," Smith admitted, "this has certainly been an interesting little excursion. Would you, for instance, have any idea how my superiors knew you would be here, keeping in mind that you're travelling on a false passport yourself?"

"No, I would not. Would you?"

Smith shook her head. "I'll be honest with you, we'd find it an effort to care less about you entering England illegally. England is a constant pain in the arse; always whining, European only when it suits them. Let *them* worry about passport control. All I want to do is find out who this poor chap is."

"I can't help you with that," Rudi said. "I'm sorry."

"One last time?" Smith said. "Passing business acquaintance? Someone you know on social media? A customer at the restaurant?"

It occurred to Rudi – not for the first time since they had sat down in the pub – that he was actually being given two messages, neither of which he understood. He really didn't like that reference to the restaurant.

He looked at the photo again. "I don't do social media much," he said.

"Ah well," said Smith, "it was worth a try." She finished her beer and took her overcoat from the chair.

"May I keep this?" Rudi asked, nodding at the mugshot. "Just in case?"

"Of course, of course." Smith stood and started to put on her coat. "My contact details are on the back, if you think of anything. You can keep the other photo, too."

"Well, it *was* addressed to me."

"I'm afraid it's not the original. Evidence. Forensics and all that. You understand."

"The envelope?" Rudi asked, thoughts of microdots crossing his mind.

Smith shook her head. "Same thing. Even I'm not allowed to touch it." She settled the coat with a shrug of her shoulders, picked up her hat, patted her pockets to make sure she hadn't forgotten anything, and smiled. "It was good to meet you," she said.

Rudi inclined his head. "Chief Superintendent."

"Oh, and please don't travel in the EU on false papers. We really are quite strict about that."

"I'll keep it in mind."

She started to leave, but stopped at the door as if suddenly remembering something. For Rudi, who had grown up watching old episodes of *Columbo*, it was almost funny.

"Oh, I forgot," Smith said. "Have you ever visited Luxembourg?"

"Not to my knowledge," he said. "I would have remembered, I think."

She nodded. "Ever heard of a Gwendoline Katherine Craig?"

"Are you trying to tie up a lot of old cases here, Chief Superintendent?" What Rudi chiefly remembered about *Columbo* was that Peter Falk had simply *annoyed* his suspects into confessing. If they'd only managed to keep their heads his conviction record would have been a catastrophe.

"Name ring a bell, though?"

He shook his head.

She smiled. "Ah well," she said cheerfully. "Worth a try, though. You take care now."

After Smith had gone, Rudi sat for some minutes drinking his beer and looking at the two photographs and trying to work out what had just happened to him. One of the drinkers from the bar, an older man with a broken nose, came over and sat opposite him.

"I had to go back through the wood to get here ahead of you," Rupert said. "I tore my trousers."

This was Rupert's way of saying 'you're welcome,' so Rudi said, "Thank you. I appreciate the backup."

Rupert shrugged. "I thought this was just going to be a pleasant day out and a bit of babysitting."

"That was the plan, yes."

"What was it all about, anyway?"

Rudi picked up the black and white photo and looked at it. His life these days was rarely, if ever, conventional, but even by his standards this was unusual. "And here I was thinking that nothing could ever surprise me again."

THEY DROVE TO Bury St Edmunds, where Rudi visited a copy shop and had the two photographs digitised. He put the originals in a rubbish bin at the bus station. Two days later he was back in

Kraków – on his own documents – and Rupert had resumed his happy exploration of Europe.

There was no point bothering to scope out his flat or the restaurant. Passive surveillance devices, small enough to be all but invisible even without a mimetic coating, could be glued to buildings and just left to run almost for ever. If EUPol wanted to keep an eye on him close to home, they would, and there wasn't a lot he could do about it.

He did all the usual stuff with the photos. Facial recognition, pattern recognition, image searches. He quietly circulated the Versailles image through some boards and rooms frequented by Coureurs, looking for useful comments, but nothing turned up.

To his knowledge, only four people had ever used the Rokeby Venus contact string – himself, Seth, Rupert, and a Community intelligence officer named Molson. Process of elimination suggested that Molson, whom he had some time ago begun to suspect enjoyed his job far too much, had sent him the photograph. *Why* was anyone's guess, but he had stopped expecting *why* in his life a long time ago. Was he supposed to go to France? Was a French person about to approach him? The problem with some people who worked in Intelligence, he had discovered down the years, was that they took it too fucking seriously, bought into the whole le Carré thing of dead drops and honeytraps and one-time pads, whereas in reality it was just a case of continually winging it.

So that was the first part of the message. The second part, delivered mostly via body language and innuendo, was that EUPol knew who he was, what he did, and where they could find him, which was not, when all was said and done, much of a surprise. But they had known about his meet with Mr Pasquinel. Maybe Molson – or someone else – had told them about it. And that *was* a bit of a surprise, and also fucking irritating.

And, of course, there was the third part of the message.

"I don't know anyone called Smith," Gwen said, one evening in the restaurant. "Well, I mean, I do. Everyone knows *someone* called Smith. But I don't know any detectives called Smith."

Rudi shrugged. "I presume Berg sang his little heart out about arranging separate meetings with us. It's hardly a great stretch of the imagination to connect you and me."

"But they can't know we saw... whatever it was. Unless Fritz went to the police and told them."

"No." Actually, the thing which was bothering him was Berg's insistence that his information involved *Les Coureurs*. Had that been true? Had it been a lure to get him to Luxembourg for some purpose which he had, without realising it, evaded? One of the problems with his life the way it was lived now was that there were too many scenarios to consider. If he took all of them into account he'd never do anything.

"Have you had any more ideas about what to do with me?" Gwen asked. She was living in Bonarka, in an old Coureur safe-flat, and she was beginning to get cabin fever. Max let her do shifts at the restaurant, waitressing, just for something to do, while Rudi tried to work out what was going on and how to help her.

He looked around the kitchen, feeling suddenly claustrophobic and at the same time rather invigorated. At least he wasn't bored any more.

"Do you feel like taking a little trip?" he asked. "Nothing dangerous, just something to do."

"Sure." She had been in touch with a couple of people in England, just to let them know she was alive and well and... somewhere. She hadn't contacted her employers; there had seemed no point, her professional life was over. "Where?"

"I'm not sure yet. I'll let you know."

Gwen checked her watch. "I'd better get back out there," she said, heading for the door to the dining room. "Let me know, yes? Don't leave it too long."

After she'd gone, Rudi rubbed his eyes and considered what Mr Pasquinel had told him in Suffolk. Unless they were rather extraordinary, the Penningtons – if they *had* bombed the Line – hadn't acted alone. There was a lot of resentment about the Line, here and there in Europe, but Rudi didn't think anyone was quite *that* resentful. What was it? Business rivals? An insurance scam? A particularly spectacular and messy assassination?

He really didn't want to jump the dapper little Frenchman out of the Line, for any number of reasons, but equally he didn't want to see him arrested for espionage. He knew from personal experience that the Line's security services favoured an iron fist in an iron glove sort of approach when they were annoyed.

"Well nobody's *said* anything yet," Mr Pasquinel told him a few days later in a crash call using encrypted SIMs. "I finished my holiday and just went back."

"That was very brave," Rudi said.

"I have nowhere else to go." The encryption made it sound a little as if he was being voiced by Mel Blanc. "Who was that person outside the church?"

"So your feeling is that you'll stay?"

Mr Pasquinel paused, just to make Rudi aware he had noted that his own question had been ignored. "I really don't see why not."

The encryption was bouncing the call between frequencies and anonymisers, but even so they had less than a minute before being connected long enough for someone to detect it. Rudi said, "Stay in touch. If you get the slightest sense that something's wrong, let me know and I'll jump you out of there. Okay?"

"Will do. Is everything all right with you?"

"Everything's fine. Where are you?"

"In a restaurant. It's snowing here again." There was a moment of dead air at the other end of the connection. "You remember you asked something about Luxembourg?"

"Yes?"

"Someone said something, in a meeting a couple of days after I got back. A contractor, one of the security firms we employ to look after some of our outside interests. He said his company had taken a big new contract in Luxembourg, then he shut up about it."

"That could have been anything," Rudi said, relaxing again.

"It could have been, but he said it was connected to something he called the *Realm*."

Rudi sat back and looked up at the ceiling. "Are you sure that's what he said?"

"I was sitting right next to him. Tedious, self-important little man."

"If there were no tedious, self-important little men, there would be no Intelligence," Rudi told him. "What's the name of the firm?"

"Arabesque. Arabesque Security. Dreadful name."

Rudi made a note on the back of an old restaurant order slip. "Okay," he said. "Thank you. You take care of yourself. I'll be in touch."

He hung up and looked out of the window. It was snowing in Kraków, too.

THE JUSTIFIED ANCIENTS OF MUHU

1.

ACCORDING TO HIS father, once upon a time winters had been so cold that the Suur Strait regularly froze and it had been possible to build an ice road from the mainland to Muhu. That only happened about one year in five these days, and Rudi had never seen it.

In fact, he had only been here once before, and that had been at the height of summer. The Manor at Pädaste had had an international reputation for the quality of its cuisine since the early days of the century, legacy of a long line of quite extraordinary chefs who had passed through down the years. He'd come up here when he was working in the Turk's kitchen in Riga, saved up what amounted to a month's salary to stay for a couple of days and work his way through the menu. Back then, the chef had been a burly, taciturn Norwegian named Amund, and his food had been so good that Rudi had almost quit cooking on the spot because he realised he would never be half as talented.

"Oh, do fuck off," Amund told him one evening when service was finished and they were sitting in the Manor's bar, one chef to another. "I knew a guy once. Simeon. Worked in a kitchen in Hamburg." He shook his head in wonder at the memory. "I'm still trying to cook as well as he did."

"Fucking hell," Rudi said, trying to imagine that.

"He told me his mum did this *fantastic* salmon dish. He'd always wanted to try to replicate it, so he worked for *months*, trying out this and that, but he could never get it quite right, so finally he went to his mum and asked her what she did that made the dish so special, and she just said, 'Oh, I don't know, I buy it from the fishmonger.'"

They both laughed. It was an old story, one of those urban legends. Everyone 'knew' a chef that had happened to.

"There's always someone better than you," Amund said. "Sooner you get used to the idea, the better. Stop thinking about it, just try to do the best you can."

Leaning on the rail of the ferry, Rudi watched the red and white buildings clustering about Kuivastu harbour draw closer. Even at this time of year, the ferry was packed with tourists and their cars heading for the other side of Muhu and the causeway leading to Saaremaa. Kids were running about on deck, enjoying the twenty-five minute crossing, their parents promenading more quietly. At least it wasn't as busy as midsummer. Rudi remembered the last time he had done this trip; there had been a kilometre-long queue of cars waiting for the ferries at Virtsu.

His phone rang. "How are you?" asked Lev.

"I'm all right."

"Are you? Really? I was talking to the Community Man. He told me what happened." Lev refused point blank to call Rupert 'Rupert of Hentzau'. He said it was the stupidest workname he'd ever heard.

"I'm fine, Lev. But thanks. Is there a problem?"

"I've been looking for commonalities in some of the data we've been working with," Lev told him. "And I think I've found one."

Rudi flicked his cigar butt into the breeze. "Anything interesting?"

"Well, if you think about it, it's probably not *that* surprising, but most of the money to build Dresden-Neustadt came from some of the same places the money to build the Line came from."

"You've found out where the *Line*'s money came from?" As far as most people were concerned, the Line had been funded by pots of gold found at the end of rainbows. Journalists and conspiracy theorists had been trying to identify the Trans-European Republic's infamously shy founders for decades.

"Well, yes, some of it," said Lev. "I was working from the other end, though. I don't have any names yet, just a bunch of hedge funds and anonymous trusts and offshore accounts. As I said, it's not all that surprising; there's only a finite number of people with money like that."

"That's..." Rudi thought about it. "That's a *colossal* amount of money."

"Of course it is. You think they built the Line with coupons?"

Rudi looked out across the Strait. "Okay," he said. "Thanks for letting me know." He hung up and dropped the phone in his pocket. The ferry was starting to manoeuvre into the harbour at Kuivastu. He picked up his rucksack and started to head down to the exit doors.

A YOUNG MAN wearing the dark blue uniform of a Lahemaa park ranger was waiting at the bottom of the gangplank. Rudi entertained a brief notion of ignoring him and walking on by, but that was never going to solve anything, so he walked up to him.

"Hello," he said. "Are you waiting for me?"

The young man looked him up and down – quite possibly measuring him against his father, Rudi had seen that look before – and put out a hand. "Kustav."

They shook hands. "Can I help you with your bag?" Kustav asked.

"No, I'm fine," Rudi told him.

Kustav looked at him again – the cane, the careworn look, the nondescript clothes. Not for the first time, Rudi thought he ought to dress like an International Man of Mystery, just to confuse people. "Okay. Well, I'm parked over here."

'Over here' turned out to be a Park Hummer, looking somewhat out of place on this mostly flat, sparsely-populated, juniper-strewn island. It had also been scrupulously cleaned and waxed. "Where are you staying?" Kustav asked when they were strapped in.

"I'm booked into a guest-house in Soonda."

"Okay." Kustav started the engine and put the vehicle into gear. "That's not far."

* * *

"PERSONALLY, I THINK this is a disgrace," Kustav said when they had left Kuivastu and the line of cars and coaches waiting to board the ferry.

"What's that?"

Kustav waved a hand at the scenery going by outside the Hummer. "This."

Oh. "I hardly think he's going to mind."

"Fucking government," Kustav muttered.

"He did try to secede the Park from Estonia," Rudi pointed out. "You can sort of understand them being vindictive."

"It's not right."

"It is, however, in character."

Kustav glanced over and gave him a look which confirmed to Rudi that he had, indeed, bought heart and soul into the Cult of Toomas.

"He wouldn't listen," said Kustav. "Man his age, riding around the park on a quadbike. We told him and he wouldn't listen."

Rudi had found, down the years, that it was possible to judge how long someone had known his father by parsing statements like *we told him and he wouldn't listen*. Only people who had more or less only just met Toomas still thought there was any point in trying to tell him anything. And nobody who had known him for more than a couple of years could fail to acknowledge the essentially comic nature of his death.

"Who's running things now?" he asked.

"Priidu's Head Ranger."

"Will Priidu be coming?"

Kustav didn't answer, which told Rudi everything he needed to know. Of course Priidu wasn't coming. Nobody else was coming; they'd sent their most junior colleague, just to keep up appearances.

The guest house in Soonda, a little village near the centre of the island, was actually a farm. Kustav drove the Hummer into the farmyard, and from the bits and pieces of squeaky-clean agricultural equipment carefully arranged here and there it was obvious to Rudi that it had been a while since anyone had done any farming here. The outbuildings surrounding the yard had all been converted into comfy-looking cottages, and Rudi saw a sign pointing down a path towards a 'Children's Zoo'. Probably goats and sheep and rabbits. Maybe an alpaca or two, if the children were lucky. He stood beside the Hummer feeling sad and a little empty.

"I'll pick you up tomorrow morning at eleven," Kustav told him from inside the car.

"It's only down the road," Rudi said. "I can walk."

Kustav looked at him for a few moments, then he said, "Okay," and reversed back up the track towards the road. Rudi watched him go, and he stood looking up the track for a long time after the sound of the Hummer's engine had faded into the distance before turning and walking over to the farmhouse to check in.

IT SEEMED TO Rudi that the chief emotions he had felt for his father for almost his entire life were frustration and anger. And really, he thought that was fair enough. His father had been selfish and mean and whiny and manipulative and the only two things he had ever believed in wholeheartedly were Baltic folk songs and the Lahemaa National Park. He'd risen to the post of Head Ranger of the Park, and dug his evil little fingers into the place so deeply that even after what would normally have been regarded as retirement age, even after Rudi's brother Ivari had succeeded him, nobody could dismiss him.

All of that had changed when Toomas decided to turn the Park into a sovereign nation. Rudi had missed the violent end to that particular scheme, but he knew Toomas had been unceremoniously dumped out of Lahemaa in the aftermath. Some of his mates in the folk song community had crowdfunded a flat for him in Rakvere, and cobbled together a small stipend to replace the pension which the government stubbornly refused to pay him on the grounds that he was lucky not to have been jailed for treason. He still had fans among the Rangers, though, and in spite of an order banning him from ever setting foot in the Park again he spent most of his time there, happily doing the things he had been doing for almost thirty years. Including riding quadbikes all over the Park in spite of being in his eighties, until one day the throttle and steering of his bike had jammed and he had driven off a promontory into the Gulf of Finland. When he heard the news, Rudi had imagined his father clinging to the handlebars like grim death, afraid to jump in case he got hurt, and simply sailing into the void, and he had giggled.

It was less than half a kilometre's walk along the main road to Liiva and St Catherine's Church, a black and white building which looked like several pointy-roofed structures of varying size stuck together. A number of mourners were standing outside, and even from the other side of the church grounds Rudi could separate them into two groups. The really old people who were standing in a loose bunch near the door of the church were the folk song guys, and he wanted nothing to do with them because that would mean having to listen to their stories about how great his father had been. Everyone else was... well, just everyone else. He looked around the mourners, but he didn't see his brother's widow. Frances had had a complicated relationship with Toomas – everyone did – but her relationship with Rudi was more straightforward. She had never forgiven him for missing Ivari's funeral, and he had judged that telling her the truth – that he had been unable to attend because he had been kidnapped by English special forces and held prisoner in London – would be unproductive at best.

"Hey, boy."

Rudi turned and found himself looking at the deeply seamed and florid face of Juhan, infamous rocker, bass player with any number of catastrophically self-destructive bands, and his father's oldest friend. He felt his heart sink in his chest.

"Juhan," he said.

Juhan was wearing skinny black jeans, a black T-shirt, and a massive black leather jacket with jangly silver zippers, which hung from his shoulders like the wings of a pterodactyl. In appearance, it was as if Somerset Maugham had, in the final years of his life, decided to take up death metal.

"You came, then," Juhan said, peering myopically at him.

"Yes," Rudi said. "I came. I cannot deny that. Here I am."

Juhan tipped his head to one side; he looked so frail that Rudi wondered how he intended to return it to its upright position. "Don't be smart with me, boy," he snapped. Rudi waited for a follow-up along the lines of 'I was wrestling alligators when you were still soiling your nappy,' but none came.

He shrugged. "Okay."

"You hated the old bastard."

"Yes, I did." It was hardly confidential.

"So what are you doing here?"

"I wanted to check out Pädaste's new chef and I thought I'd kill two birds with one stone," Rudi deadpanned.

"Cheeky little cocksucker," said Juhan, who was at least a foot shorter than Rudi. "Don't you have a hug for your Uncle Juhan?"

"Firstly, you're not my uncle," said Rudi, "and secondly, I'd be afraid of snapping you like a dry twig," but he hugged the old man anyway, and discovered that Juhan was considerably stronger than he looked, and determined to prove it.

"So," Juhan said when he had finished compressing Rudi's ribs, "you're in Poland now?"

"Sometimes. I get about a lot." Rudi wondered if Juhan hadn't actually *broken* something. He squirmed discreetly to try and return some of his internal organs to their original positions. He looked over Juhan's head and saw someone walking towards them from the direction of the church, so out of context that for a moment he couldn't work out where he had seen her before. It was her hat he actually recognised first.

"Chief Superintendent," he said as she reached them. "Forgive me if I briefly comment on the surreal nature of meeting you here."

Smith beamed at him. "Aren't you going to introduce us?"

Rudi suppressed a scowl. "Chief Superintendent, this is Juhan Salumäe, an old friend of my father. Juhan, this is Detective Chief Superintendent Sarah Smith of the EU Police."

Juhan looked Smith up and down with undisguised lasciviousness. He nudged Rudi. "Been naughty, hey, boy?" and they all laughed except Rudi, who was staring at Smith.

Smith looked benignly at Juhan and smiled radiantly. "Mr Salumäe," she said. "Have you ever been back to the Savoy?"

All of a sudden, Juhan seemed to be two hundred years older. "I need to talk to somebody," he said, and he turned and walked away towards the church.

"Savoy?" Rudi asked when he was out of earshot.

"Misspent youth," Smith said. "He still owes them four hundred quid. How are you?"

"Oh, I'm super, thank you. What are you doing here?"

Smith pouted. "Everybody has to be *somewhere*."

Rudi leaned on his cane and said, "Did you know my father, Chief Superintendent? Because if you didn't, I have to admit I can't come up with a single reason why you should be here."

"Your father?" Smith looked thoughtful. "No."

"You do know this is his funeral." He waved at the church, the mourners, Juhan standing watching them.

"Yes," she said. "Yes. My condolences. Were you close?"

"There were times when I would cheerfully have killed him myself."

"Not close, then." Smith smiled. "We've identified the chap who was carrying the photograph."

"You've come to tell me *that*?"

"No, I may have come to arrest you."

Rudi rubbed his face. "All right, Chief Superintendent, you have my undivided attention."

"Robert James Spencer," said Smith, and this time she wasn't smiling at all. "Age thirty-eight, formerly of 22 Special Air Service Regiment. That's English Special Forces. He was invalided out four years ago; roadside bomb in Damascus."

"I told you, I don't know him."

"We've managed to reconstruct his movements in the week or so before he tried to enter Poland. He seems to have travelled a great deal on false passports."

Rudi sensed where this was going, and braced himself. "Yes?"

"It seems he was in the Sakha Republic at the same time that a member of a visiting Community delegation was assassinated."

Rudi frowned. "I hadn't heard about that."

"And you won't; there was a total blackout, witnesses sequestered, everything. We can't prove Spencer was responsible, but he was there and he had sniper training when he was with the SAS. It seems someone's been feeding him some very odd medication. He's in a terrible state."

"I still don't know him," Rudi said. "And if you're going down the road of assuming he's a Coureur, don't. They don't do assassination."

"That you know of."

"Chief Superintendent, there is no life on Pluto *that I know of*. Come on. Please." He looked over to the church; people were starting to go in. "I need to go."

Smith followed his gaze. "Yes, of course."

"Who died, by the way? In Sakha?"

"Ah," she said. "That's interesting. He was with the Community delegation visiting this biodome or whatever it is, but he wasn't from the Community. Turns out he was actually a citizen of Dresden-Neustadt."

Rudi had a good poker face. "Oh?"

"Chap named Mundt. Ring any bells?"

"No."

"*Former* citizen of the Neustadt, I should say," Smith corrected herself. "It's a very confused situation. Jurisdiction is a nightmare."

Rudi said, "I have nothing to do with this and I can't help you, Chief Superintendent. I don't know this man Spencer, I have no idea who he is or what he wants, and I have no idea why he was carrying that photo. It's as much a mystery to me as it is to you. More so, I suspect."

Smith was studying his face. He had not had any dealings with EUPol before, but it suddenly occurred to him that she had quite an unusual way of doing things. He said, "May I see your ID again, please?"

"Of course." She took the card out and held it in front of his face. They both knew how easy it was to forge pretty much any kind of document these days – certainly in terms of a visual examination – but he thought it was important to make the point.

"Thank you," he said, after what he thought was a reasonable interval. "I can't help you, Chief Superintendent," he said again. "I wish I could, if only to get you to leave me alone. Now, are you going to arrest me? Because if you're not, I should attend my father's funeral."

"I'm not going to arrest you," she said. "Today."

He sighed.

"Go," said Smith. "You've got my details if you think of anything to tell me. I'm staying at Pädaste Manor tonight, if you feel like having dinner."

"Your expense claims must be a thing to behold."

"That's the great thing about the EU," she said with a smile. "Lots of money, but hardly any members to spend it on these days." And with that she turned to go. "See you later."

Rudi watched her walk away, mentally cursing in several European languages. He'd been looking forward to trying out Pädaste's tasting menu. He looked towards the church, where several aged men were carrying what seemed to be a long laundry basket on their shoulders. His father had arrived.

NO ONE KNEW where Leo had put Mundt, which was unfortunate. A lot of people, so far as Rudi knew, had spent a lot of time and resources trying to find the Professor in the intervening years. He was among them. And now... what? He turned up as part of a Community delegation in Sakha – and what the hell had they been doing all the way out *there*? – and someone had assassinated him. There was just too much Story there to process all at once.

Rudi thought about all this while he stood at the back of the church and watched his father's funeral. Toomas had left only two instructions about what to do after his death, apparently. The first was that he was to have a Humanist funeral, and the second was that he wanted to be buried in Lahemaa.

The latter was never going to happen, not unless his mates wanted to bury him in secret at midnight. There was a surprising amount of paperwork involved with interring bodies, and the moment the authorities got the merest sniff that Toomas wanted to be buried in the Park they dusted down their rage at his abortive attempt at Independence and turned the application down flat. *This man committed treason and you want to bury him in the Park? Stick him in a bag and drop him in the Gulf of Finland instead. Fuck him.*

The folk song guys had cast around for alternate venues and come up with St Catherine's, it seemed, simply because the Lutheran pastor here had proven less resistant to a Humanist ceremony than anyone else they had approached.

Down at the front of the church, the wicker coffin containing the remains of his father – what remains had finally washed up some distance along the coast, anyway – stood on two trestles. The celebrant was standing beside it, talking about Toomas's invaluable contributions to the Estonian folk song community. Rudi tuned him out and looked around the church. Some of the folk singers were in national costume. Kustav was sitting a couple of rows behind them in his uniform, head bowed. Juhan was in a pew on the other side of the aisle. There was no one else there that Rudi recognised, even slightly.

It occurred to him that the last time he had visited the land of his birth had been for a funeral, too. Sergei Fedorovich, the chef who had first introduced him to restaurant cooking, had finally succumbed to an aneurysm in the middle of a spectacular rant at one of his waitresses. That funeral had been enormous fun; the food had been fantastic, there was a colossal amount of alcohol, chefs from kitchens up and down the Baltic had come to pay their respects, ethnic Estonians and Russians had put aside their differences for a while. Everyone called him 'Ruudi,' the proper form of his name, and it sounded strange to him. He'd long ago stopped trying to correct everyone else in Europe who mispronounced it. Anyway, in Estonian *rudi* meant *to bruise*, which he had found, down the years, that he rather liked. The wake had lasted for two days, his hangover for three. He suspected that wasn't going to be the case here; Toomas and his pals had an unnatural capacity for booze, but money was tight. He had no interest in seeing what the funeral meal was like. It was going to offend him professionally and he was going to wind up talking to strangers he couldn't care less about. He checked his watch, considering getting the next available ferry back to the mainland.

Some of the costumed figures at the front of the church began to shuffle along their pew into the aisle, and for a moment Rudi thought the service was already over, but the singers gathered around the coffin and composed themselves and Rudi stared in horror. *Oh, gods, they're actually going to sing.*

And after a moment or so, they did, these old men and women who looked as if they had stepped out of a kitsch tourist postcard, and it was beautiful. Rudi didn't know the song, didn't even think it was Estonian – he caught a few words that sounded Lithuanian, which had been one of his father's obsessions – but the old folk sang their hearts out, and Rudi suspected that, had he any feelings left for his father, it might have brought him to tears.

The song finished, the celebrant delivered one last homily, then the old chaps took up the coffin again and began to carry it down the aisle to the door. None of them was under seventy, but even in life Toomas had been virtually weightless, a figure composed mostly of gristle and sinew and spite, and they bore him easily. As the mourners in the church turned and started to follow the coffin, Rudi noticed a number of curious glances cast his way.

When everyone had gone outside, Rudi left the church and followed them along the path around the building to a little graveyard. A group of people was already standing around an open grave. Rudi stood at the back again while the celebrant said something the wind blew away, the coffin was lowered into the grave, and then everyone just spontaneously started to wander off.

As the other mourners were leaving, he saw a woman he thought he recognised, although he couldn't work out where from. She was very short and quite stout and rather beautiful, and moved with the rolling gait of someone with hip problems who was wearing a powered exoskeleton under her clothes to help her walk. He thought she must be in her seventies, her grey hair cut collar-length and her clothes sensible but not cheap, and she had on her face an expression of acute irritation.

She seemed to be unaccompanied, standing to one side of a small group of people, and as Rudi looked at her she turned her head slightly and their eyes met and with a single lurch of his heart he suddenly knew who she was.

He took a step towards her, stopped, and she turned away from the grave and walked back towards the trees at the edge of the church's property, and a moment later she had vanished from sight in the direction of the little line of parked vehicles on the road.

Rudi blinked and took a long, unsteady breath.

"Are you all right?" asked Juhan.

"Yes," said Rudi. "Yes, I am."

"DID YOUR FATHER ever tell you how we lost the Frenchmen?" Juhan asked.

"No," said Rudi.

They were sitting in Rudi's cottage back at the farm, Juhan having tagged along with him without being asked, a paper-wrapped package tucked under his arm. He had then produced from an inside pocket of his leather jacket a full bottle of a rather good whisky, put it on the table in the little living room, and found a couple of glasses in the kitchen. Rudi suddenly couldn't be bothered to argue.

"I should tell you the story of how your father was born in two places at once," Juhan mused.

"I should tell you that nothing about my father would surprise me," Rudi said, topping up their glasses.

Juhan picked up his glass, looked at it for a moment, then emptied it in one and put it back on the table for another refill. "We were in our twenties. That was a wild old time, you have no idea."

Rudi lit a small cigar, offered the tin to Juhan, who shook his head. "I have some idea," he said.

"You never lived under the Russians. It got pretty surreal. Once upon a time you had to get a permit from your workplace to buy a car, and the Party had to approve it, and when it arrived it would most likely be some piece of shit Lada that cost you three years' pay." He picked up his glass and waggled it above the table until Rudi refilled it. "But the *Finns* now, the Finns were having a wild old time, buying cars and just giving away the ones they didn't want any longer. And when we kicked the Soviets out everybody wanted a car, didn't matter how crappy it was. Me and your father, we went over the border this one time and we bought an old Saab from this bloke on the other side for three bottles of vodka." He drained his glass again. "Damn thing caught fire the moment we drove it back into Estonia."

"You were saying," Rudi murmured, refilling the glass again and wondering when exactly the old man would start getting drunk, "something about my father being born in two places."

Juhan nodded. "Your grandfather's family came from Parnu. Your grandmother's came from some godawful village out east, I can't remember where, but both families wanted Toomas to be born where they came from. It was important to them, the gods only know why. This caused a lot of friction between the two families, so your grandfather came up with this plan."

Rudi sat forward and leaned his elbows on the table.

"Your grandfather, he was an interesting man. Knew a lot of interesting people. Knew a lot of interesting *things* about a lot of interesting people. So he had a word, and called in some favours, and lo and behold, on the day of Toomas's birth there were two birth certificates. Both identical, apart from the place of birth. One in Parnu, the other in... wherever it was, somewhere near Räpina, I think. And your grandfather could show his parents one certificate, and his wife's parents the other one, and everyone was happy."

Rudi thought about it. "I can think of any number of ways that could go wrong," he said.

Juhan shrugged. "They got away with it. For years Toomas had two passports."

"What?"

"Two passports. You don't have an uncommon surname, the place of birth was different, all the forms were in order, the authorities never checked."

"So where was he born? Parnu or Räpina?"

Juhan chuckled. "Neither. He was born in Viljandi."

"So he had *three* birth certificates."

Juhan shook his head. "The birth was registered in Parnu and Räpina. Officially, he was born in two different places."

Rudi sat back and downed his vodka. "Jesus Maria," he muttered. "I come from a family of con artists."

"Anyway, he showed me the two birth certificates this one time, and are you going to top my glass up for me or do I have to do it myself? Thank you."

"You were going to tell me," Rudi said, putting the bottle back down on the table, "about Toomas and the Frenchmen."

"Mm," said Juhan. "Yes. The Frenchmen." He picked up his glass and, with miraculous self-control, managed to only half-empty it before looking thoughtful. "Toomas and I were working as guides at Kadriorg. The band had split up; I needed the money. One day Toomas turned up for work and told me he'd been contacted by this Frenchman who wanted to hire us as guides for him and his friends."

Because this seemed to require a response, Rudi said, "Why?"

"Why what?"

"Why you and Toomas, in particular?"

Juhan shook his head. "I never found out. Do you want to hear this or not?"

Not particularly, no. "Sure. Go on."

"I need a piss. Back in a minute." Juhan got up from the table, jacket zippers jingling, and walked to the bathroom without the slightest hint of a weave or stagger or stumble. Rudi looked at the bottle, which was threequarters empty – most of it now inside Juhan – and shook his head. Most of his father's friends had been legendary drinkers, but they always said it was just part of being an Estonian male.

He took out his phone and called up its news browser and flicked through the front page articles. Community, Community, Community. Reports about the ongoing talks at the UN, travelogues from writers who had visited the Community, recipe books, films, novels, fashions. Starbucks was opening another fifty franchise operations around the Community; an American firm was in discussions about providing new-generation coal mining machinery. The edges between the nations were beginning to blur. He wondered what the Presiding Authority thought about it all. He didn't bother Googling Mundt or murders in the Sakha Republic; if Smith had been telling the truth about a news blackout he wasn't going to find anything in the public record, and he didn't have any resources of his own that far east. He looked at the package Juhan had brought with him, sitting on the other side of the table. It was wrapped in somewhat aged brown paper and it was about the size of a box of chocolates. He reached out and picked it up speculatively. It was heavier than he'd expected. He put it back down.

"There were three of them," Juhan said, returning from the bathroom. "And they all had umbrellas."

Rudi put his phone away. "Umbrellas."

"Three of them." Juhan sat down and held out his glass and Rudi refilled it. "Weird. Twitchy. They wanted to go to Lahemaa."

Rudi sat back and looked at him. "Really?"

"Really." Juhan drank half his drink and put the glass down on the table. "The one in charge, he had maps of the Park. Said they were botanists and they'd heard of this really rare plant that was only found in this one place and they wanted to photograph it and take samples and stuff. I don't know; neither of us knew anything about plants."

Rudi poured himself a drink. "What happened?"

Juhan shrugged. "We took them out to the Park and we lost them."

"How can you lose three Frenchmen?"

The old man shook his head. "We were... oh, I don't know where, out in the wilds somewhere, kilometres from Palmse. The French bloke was dicking about with his maps and coordinates and stuff and all of a sudden they all just charged off down a track and your father followed them and he came back half an hour later and said they'd gone."

Rudi sat very still, an awful realisation beginning to dawn on him. "What happened then?"

"We looked for them for hours, but they were gone. Toomas said he thought they'd fallen into a bog and we'd better make a run for it or we'd be arrested." He picked up his glass and drained it. "So we left."

"Jesus Maria," said Rudi. "You just ran away?"

"We were young. The police would have thought we'd killed them. We didn't want to go to jail."

"What happened after that?"

"We watched the papers and the news for a while, in case they turned up. Or their bodies. But the years went by and nothing. I'd almost forgotten about it until I heard your Dad had died."

I'd almost forgotten about it... "Three men might have died and you just *ran away*."

Juhan shrugged. "We weren't supposed to be there." This time he reached out and filled his glass himself. "Fucking Frenchmen."

"I had no idea *Paps* had ever been to the Park before we moved there."

"It's not exactly something you tell your kids."

"Why are you telling *me*?"

Juhan sat back and looked sourly at him. "Toomas is gone, I won't last much longer. I just thought someone should know. In case the bodies turned up one day. At least you can tell the authorities who they were."

"You don't seriously think *I'm* going to get myself involved in this, do you? Gods, just telling me about it makes me an accessory."

"What you do with it is your business," Juhan told him. "I've done my bit."

"No, *your* bit was to contact the Park authorities and get them to search properly and take the consequences. Not just... Christ." Rudi rubbed his eyes. "I shouldn't blame you; this was probably all Toomas's idea," he said tiredly. "I know how his mind worked. Evil old bastard."

"What time is it?" Juhan asked.

Rudi looked at his watch and scowled. He looked at the window and discovered that somehow, while they had been exploring the surreal landscape of his father's life, night had fallen. He'd missed the last ferry back to Virtsu.

Juhan pushed the package across the table to him. "This is for you," he said.

Rudi looked at it. "What is it?"

"Your father told me to give it you if anything happened to him."

Rudi sighed. His father had had a great fondness, although when all was said and done very little flair, for the dramatic. "What is it?"

"I don't know."

"I don't want it, whatever it is."

"He gave it me a year or so after the Coup." *Coup*, Rudi presumed, being Toomas's word for the possibly government-sponsored riot which had put an end to his dreams of statehood for the Park. "Not long after we moved him into the flat in Rakvere. 'Anything happens to me, give it to the boy,' he said."

There was no need to ask *which* boy; his brother Ivari was dead by then, of injuries sustained during the riot. He poked the package with a finger. Then he pushed it back across the table. "I don't want anything from him, Juhan," he said. "He made our lives a misery, he drove my mother away – now I learn he was probably responsible for the deaths of three Frenchmen. If you think I'm taking this thing, you're crazier than he was."

Juhan regarded him levelly. Then he poured the last of the Scotch into his glass and knocked it back in one. "He said you'd say that."

"Well then."

Juhan reached into his jacket again, and, like a stage conjurer, produced another full bottle of Scotch. He snapped the seal on the bottle's cap, filled their glasses. "He wasn't a bad man, you know."

"He was a wizened little monster, Juhan; he damaged every life he ever touched."

"He did a lot for the Park. Don't you ever forget that." Juhan pushed the package back to Rudi. "He didn't leave a lot. Some books, old recordings. They all went to the Folk Song Society. This is for you." He sat back and drank his drink.

Rudi felt his shoulders slump. It had been an eventful day; if he had ever been unsure of what the word *infodump* meant, he wasn't now.

"Anyway," Juhan said. "Let's finish this bottle and then I'll get a cab back to my B&B and we can go our separate ways. Okay?"

As IT TURNED out, it took them – Juhan, really – somewhat longer to finish the second bottle than it had the first. The years seemed to finally be catching up on the old musician. By the time Rudi started to try and find Juhan a ride back to his lodgings on the other side of the island, it was past midnight and Muhu's only taxi service had gone to bed and so had the family who owned the farm.

"Well I'm not walking back," said Juhan, who finally seemed to be getting a little tipsy.

"Oh, for fuck's sake," said Rudi, who was not particularly drunk – he was too angry about too many things for that – but really, really tired. "You can have the sofa."

Juhan looked across the sitting room at the old-fashioned and somewhat overstuffed sofa and sniffed. "With *my* back?"

Rudi looked at him. "You old sod," he said.

Juhan blinked innocently at him. "One day you'll be my age," he warned sagely.

"I fucking hope not. Okay. You have the bed."

AFTER JUHAN HAD spent half an hour in the bathroom – and rendered it uninhabitable probably for the next century or so following what must have been a spectacularly catastrophic bowel movement – and gone to bed, Rudi sat in the living room staring into space, trying to fit bits and pieces of half a dozen things together. Juhan's story about the Frenchmen – assuming it was true; he didn't entirely trust any of Toomas's friends – cast a new light on his father's tenacious interest in Lahemaa. Had Toomas actually *killed* them for some reason? Once upon a time he would have said murder was about the one thing his father wasn't capable of, but now he wasn't sure. He was almost certain he was going to have to tell the authorities about this somehow.

He sighed and waved up the entertainment set's browser, pulled down a menu and did a search for Mundt and the Sakha Republic, was none the wiser after half an hour's surfing. Pointless. He was too tired to make sense of any of it. He sat for a while thinking of the short woman he had seen at the graveside and wondered why she wasn't crying. At around two, he rearranged the cushions on the sofa, curled up, and fell asleep.

HE WASN'T SURE, at first, what woke him. Or even, for a few moments, where he was. His mouth tasted awful, his head throbbed, his eyes were all gummy, and his neck ached because he had slept awkwardly. He spent so long dwelling on these things that it took him a while to notice that the room smelled of smoke.

He sat up on the sofa and his head spun a little. He waved a hand at the floor lamp in the corner and it came on, filling the room with a foggy nimbus of illumination. Smoke was drifting through the living room in slow billowing panes.

"Juhan!" Rudi stood up and went over to the bedroom door. "Juhan, we're on fire!" He put his hand on the door handle, snatched it away again. The handle was red hot. He put the fingers of his other hand on the door experimentally, then the flat of his hand. The door was hot too. Looking down, he saw smoke pouring out from under the door and around his feet. "Juhan!"

Rudi ran over to the front door, threw it open, and immediately tripped and fell headlong over something lying just outside. On his hands and knees, he took his phone out of his pocket and switched it on, and by the light of the screen he found himself looking at the body of a young woman lying almost on the threshold of the cottage. She was wearing black combat fatigues and a webbing harness festooned with knives and guns and grenades and other, more inscrutable, devices. She had been shot in the chest at least twice, maybe several more times, it was hard to tell.

Okay. Rudi looked left and right. Across the farmyard, the main building was burning fiercely, as was the only other occupied cottage. From behind the buildings, he could hear the panicked noises of the animals in the children's zoo.

He searched through the woman's webbing harness, came up with a small torch, switched it on. Checked the body quickly for ID and comms devices, came up empty. He took one of her pistols – something ludicrously light and ceramic – and got up and limped around to the back of the cottage.

The bedroom window was shattered; flames were roaring out of the hole. The room itself was full of flame; even the walls appeared to be alight. Rudi swore and ran back to the front, went back inside, grabbed his jacket and cane, and turned to leave again. Halfway to the door, he stopped and turned back, scooped the package from the table.

Near the junction of the track and the road, the beam of the torch caught something poking out from under a bush. When he looked closer he saw that it was a booted foot. He pushed the bush aside and saw that the foot belonged to a man's body, sprawled bonelessly face-down. The man was dressed and equipped identically to the woman. The back of his head shone wetly in the torchlight.

Rudi stood up and looked around him. The cottages were completely alight, the main house ablaze. He started to run as best he could.

IT TOOK HIM almost two hours to hike to Pädaste, staying in the rough country off to one side of the road. By the time he got there the sky was starting to lighten and his leg was in agony. He dithered at the end of the lane leading to the Manor, trying to decide what to do, then he turned away and loped down to the shore a kilometre or so away. He remembered a boathouse from his last visit, part of the Manor's facilities, but he had to walk along the shoreline for a little while before he found it.

He'd thought he would have to break into the boathouse, which would have caused more complications, but there was a little fishing boat tied up to the jetty, not much more than a dinghy with an outboard motor. He checked the motor, found a full can of petrol in the bottom of the boat along with a pair of oars and a grubby waxed jacket. He put the jacket on over his own. There was a weird knitted cap in one of the pockets, along with half a pack of cigarettes and a battered old Zippo. He put the cap on, cast off, and rowed the boat away from the shore.

Rudi rowed for about an hour before starting the engine. The boat was battered, but the engine, though an antique, was obviously well cared-for. He opened the throttle and put some distance between himself and Pädaste, going southwest along the coast. At the far southwest corner of the island, he struck out across the strait towards Saaremaa.

A few hours later, he pulled the boat up onto a beach east of Nasva, filled the engine's fuel tank from the petrol can, and set out again. Not far from Läbara, in the west of the big island, he beached the boat again. He dragged it up as far as he could from the waterline, broke branches off nearby trees to conceal it with, found some bushes a few hundred metres away, curled up in them and fell asleep, hoping that if anyone connected the theft of the boat with him they would assume he had headed east towards the Estonian mainland simply because that was the most rational thing to do.

The next morning, just after dawn, he topped up the boat's fuel tank one last time, briefly checked the GPS on his phone, and steered due south, the boat rocking and plunging alarmingly on the waves.

It took several hours to cross the Irbe Väin Strait. The pain in his leg, from yesterday's exertions and sleeping in a bush, was almost unbearable, and he hadn't eaten since breakfast the previous day. He slumped in the back of the boat, vaguely seasick, one arm draped over the engine's steering column, occasionally checking his phone to make sure he was still on course and not heading into the Gulf of Riga.

He fell asleep again, was woken by a jolt through the hull of the boat, jerked his eyes open terrified that he had struck something. But when he sat up he saw that it was okay. He'd only struck Latvia.

2.

"WELL, WE'VE ANNOYED *somebody*," Rupert said.

"Mm," said Rudi. "I hadn't quite anticipated a reaction like this."

They were sitting in the garden of a guest house not far from Biarritz, the destination of Rudi's month-long dustoff from Latvia, during which he had burned through six ready-made false identities and twenty or so disposable phones. Rudi had his leg, which was still giving him discomfort, up on a footstool. In response to his crash alert following his arrival in Latvia, Seth and Gwen had gone to ground somewhere outside Poland and Lev had packed up his computers and departed Sibir for points west.

"So, are we any closer to knowing *who*?" asked Rupert.

"No," Rudi grumped. The fire at Soonda, and its aftermath, had been on Estonian news sites for about a week, more interesting for what was left out than what was mentioned. Initially it had been ascribed to faulty wiring, then vandalism, then 'criminal activity'. Five people had died, according to the official account – the husband and wife who owned the farm and three guests, their bodies too burned for easy identification. Of the dead man and woman Rudi had found, not a word. Which was interesting. Eventually, the story had dropped down the news agenda and then disappeared altogether. His name was not mentioned once. "I hate being on the run," he said.

"Yes," said Rupert, who had also spent time on the run.

They sat for a while, side by side, in their deckchairs, looking out across the couple of hectares of garden. It was unseasonably warm and the high hedges surrounding the garden trapped the sun's warmth. The world, and all its cares and problems, seemed far away, but they both knew better.

"Do you at least have an idea what we *did*?" Rupert asked finally.

"I'm not totally certain we *did* anything," Rudi said after a moment's thought. "I have the awful feeling that this was coming anyway." He and Rupert looked at each other. "I don't know."

"What do you want me to do?"

Rudi smiled. "Well..."

LATER, AFTER RUPERT had left, Rudi took himself back to his room and sat on the bed. It had been a long time since his first encounter with *Les Coureurs*, since his first Situation. He had, he thought, become quite adept at certain things in the interim, and now he thought about it, that had made him lazy, complacent. He'd learned that he could cope, and coping wasn't enough.

Someone, it seemed, had tried to kill him at Soonda. Either the dead couple he had found outside the cottage had been sent to stop the assassin, and had failed, or they themselves were the assassins and had been killed by another party. That was a picture he might not ever understand.

Smith's presence on the island was, of course, suggestive, as was the news that he was somehow connected to Mundt's murder by the photograph the presumed killer had been carrying. Had someone tried to kill him in retaliation for that?

Reaching under the bed, he took out the package Juhan had given him, his inheritance. Stripped of its brown paper, it had proven to be a chocolate box – an unfamiliar English brand. He lifted the lid and looked inside. There was an ancient external hard drive, almost as big as the box itself, a single gigabyte of storage, a couple of cables to plug it in to a computer, and a little plastic bag of adaptors which spoke of many years of computer evolution. Beneath this were his father's two passports, and beneath those was a long envelope containing his father's two birth certificates.

He had found, taped to the inside of the lid of the box, a newer, smaller envelope containing two safety deposit keycards, a folded slip of paper with three names written on it in his father's spidery, near-illegible hand – *Roland Sarkisian*, *Jean-Yves Charpentier*, *François Tremblay* – and a black and white photograph.

He took out his phone and thumbed up the photograph Smith had given him in Suffolk. He held up the photograph he had found among his father's effects, and looked from one to the other and back again. They were, so far as he could tell, identical.

He closed the photo on his phone, called up a browser, Googled the three names, hoping that at least this time the internet might offer up some kind of explanation, but there was still only a brief wiki entry about Roland Sarkisian, born in Alençon in 1894 – *Le Parapluie*, as he'd apparently been known. A mathematician of some charisma, it seemed, because he had managed to draw around him a group of like-minded young men who styled themselves the 'Sarkisian Collective.' A search for mentions of the Collective only turned up half a dozen hits, all of them footnotes to various arcane-looking mathematical treatises.

He held up the photograph again and squinted at it. The background was crowded with people and it was hard to make out faces, but there was a little group of young men, eight of them, standing close together and staring solemnly towards the camera. They were all holding furled umbrellas.

Rudi put the photo down on the bed and took his father's birth certificates out of their envelope. He read the birthdates again, and he shook his head.

"You old fucker," he muttered.

PART TWO

THE FAR
DOMINIONS

ARGENTINIAN TANGO

1.

AFTERWARD, NO ONE was quite certain when Carey arrived in Szolnok. She claimed it was the end of September, but there was credible evidence that she'd been there since at least August. The country's various border agencies, squabbling like rival shopkeepers, were unable to come up with a name, a date, or a frontier crossing at which she had entered Hungary; all anyone was able to be sure of was that at some point she had started quietly filing lifestyle pieces – fashion, music, food – to a little-known online magazine. She was American, travelling on a Texas passport, and she was serious about her work. Later, in interrogation rooms at Police Headquarters, dozens of people she had interviewed all over the city were debriefed. It was generally agreed that she had been utterly professional about maintaining her legend. More than one member of the Intelligence services expressed a degree of admiration for her, although they also expressed a greater degree of annoyance that she had been in the country at all.

It was Carey's first time in Hungary; her beat usually took in France and Spain and all the little nations thereof. She was a tall, cheerful woman of a certain age who spoke seven languages, four of them fluently, and could swear convincingly in three more. She seemed particularly interested in a number of Avar burials unearthed by workmen building a new ring-road outside the town. The Avars buried their dead with their horses, and these were particularly splendid examples.

Carey made several visits to the site, talking to archaeologists from the University of Budapest who were excavating it, and it was later presumed that it was during one of these visits that she took receipt of the Package, although nobody could be entirely certain.

She next popped up on the official radar at one of the border crossings over the River Dráva between Hungary and Croatia. It was a rainy afternoon in mid-October, and the light was already starting to fail when she pulled her car in to the border station and joined the queue of private vehicles waiting to be processed.

The Hungarians had hardened their borders decades ago, even before the Xian Flu and the atomisation of the EU, against refugees fleeing the Middle East and North Africa, and the border station still bore the signs of hasty expansion; temporary buildings which had become permanent, piles of rubble and fencing material almost completely overgrown, a lorry park whose asphalt had cracked and sprouted weeds over the years here by the river.

The Ufa explosion had caused a spike in terrorist alerts across Europe; border guards had become particularly bloody-minded, and today there was a long line of cars and vans waiting to cross into Croatia, as well as maybe thirty lorries and half a dozen coaches. A little bar on the other side of the waiting area was doing a roaring trade in burgers and bottled beer and soft drinks, and there was a line of people outside the toilet block.

This much was normal, in fact comforting. This was a landscape Carey knew well, and nothing looked out of the ordinary. Border crossings, when you boiled off much of the local colour, were all pretty much the same. She put the car into Park, set the handbrake, and got out to stretch her legs. She'd done the trip from Szolnok in one go, and she felt a little stiff. The rain had tailed away to a fine mist of drizzle blowing in veils across the border station. From the direction of the road, she could hear cars and lorries going by on their way from Croatia.

She saw them coming from all the way across the compound, three soldiers in the Lincoln green uniform of Hungary's border guard. Two of them were women, in officers' uniforms; the third was a youth with a rash of acne in a corner of his mouth and a cap which was half a size too small.

"Madam," one of the officers said as they neared the car. "May we see your documents, please?"

This was far from unusual; you could never predict what border officers would do. Some were bored, some were preternaturally attentive, some hewed fetishistically to regulations, some were prepared to bend a little. Carey wasn't worried; her papers were all good, there was no reason why anyone should suspect her. This was a milk run.

She reached into the car and took her passport from the glove compartment, handed it over. The second officer waved the passport over her pad, looked at the displayed information, looked at Carey, looked at the information again. It suddenly occurred to Carey that the boy, who had a short assault rifle – something of German manufacture, she thought – slung over his shoulder, seemed unusually tense for what seemed on the face of it a perfectly routine document check. He caught her looking at him and made a spirited but ultimately rather poor attempt at staring defiantly back.

The two officers consulted briefly in whispers, then the first said, "Madam, would you accompany us, please? Leave the key in the car."

And even this was not outside operational limits. She didn't panic when she heard the car start up behind them. She turned and saw the second officer behind the wheel, reversing a little before she drove the car out of the queue and off towards a row of sheds on the other side of the compound. There were always spot checks.

The officer, whose nametag read SZILI, led her to a small concrete building. The young soldier stationed himself outside the front door without having to be told. Inside was a short, brightly-lit corridor that smelled of damp carpeting. At the far end was a door opening on to a little room with a table and two chairs. Szili showed her inside and asked her to sit.

"Your phone, please, madam," she said.

Carey turned over her phone – there was nothing operationally important on it – and Szili left the room. There was a quiet click of a lock, and then she was alone.

Well.

This was not the first time Carey had been detained at a border. There had been an occasion about five years ago, trying to get into one of the many short-lived little statelets which infested Greater Germany, when she had remained in a room not unlike this one for almost two days. When she was finally released, it was because the polity's ad hoc government had collapsed and a new, temporary, administration had voted to rejoin the Bundesrepublik as soon as humanly possible. The borders had come down and her Package had simply walked out. She looked around the room. At least then there had been a bed. And a lavatory.

Hours passed. At first they passed slowly. Then there was a point where she checked her watch and discovered that two hours had gone by without her consciously noticing.

She got up and went over and banged on the door with her fist. "Hey!" she shouted. "Hey! I need the bathroom!" Nothing happened. She walked back into the middle of the room and started to look around where the ceiling met the walls. She was damned if she was going to start feeling her way around the place looking for stealthed cameras, but it didn't hurt to look. "I need the bathroom!" she shouted again, with no more success.

Almost an hour later, the door clicked and swung open, and there was Szili. Her uniform was crumpled, and there was an oil stain on her sleeve. Carey stopped pacing and looked at her. She said, "I want to speak with the Texan Ambassador. And I want the bathroom."

"The Texan Embassy is in Budapest," Szili told her. "And the toilet is this way. Please, madam."

Outside, night had long fallen. The border post, lit up by blue-white lamps on ten-metre poles, sat in the still, silent heart of a huge darkness. There were no vehicles anywhere to be seen, and that was what finally made Carey start to worry.

Szili walked her across the compound to the toilet block, waited outside the cubicle, then marched her back outside and over to the sheds. The door of one had been rolled up, and inside was her car.

At least, it was all the bits of her car. It was hard to see if any of them were missing because none of them were connected to each other any longer. They were arranged all over the cement floor of the shed in a sort of rough sketch of a car. A couple of mechanics in filthy overalls were standing near the back of the shed. One was smoking a pipe; the other was wiping his hands on a rag. They were both looking at her as if she had done them a terrible personal wrong.

"Boys," Carey said to them, "you have some explaining to do to Hertz."

"Madam," Szili said, going over to a metal cupboard by one wall and opening one of its doors. "Can you please tell me what this is?" And she reached inside and turned back holding the Package. It was a little larger than a pack of playing cards.

"I never saw that before in my life," Carey said.

SHE WAS GETTING too old for this shit. Certainly too old to spend all night in a windowless room somewhere on the far edge of Hungary. Definitely too old to sleep in her clothes on a really uncomfortable folding bed in a windowless room on the far edge of Hungary.

They woke her before seven. Two soldiers she hadn't seen before; one to carry a tray and put it on the table, the other to hold a rifle at the ready in case she suddenly tried to incapacitate the first with a weapon cunningly fashioned out of... well, there was actually fuck-all in here to fashion a weapon *from*, and they knew, from last night's strip search, that she wasn't carrying anything lethal or even remotely annoying.

When the soldiers had left and the door was locked again, she got up stiffly from the bed and went over to the table. On the tray were a biodegradable Starbucks cup of unsweetened black coffee and a plate with a couple of small, sticky and slightly stale pastries. She wolfed the pastries down and drank the coffee in two swallows, and suddenly she really, really wanted a cigarette, even though she hadn't smoked in almost a decade.

A few minutes later, the door opened again, and Szili stepped into the room, accompanied by yet another soldier. Szili had slept and breakfasted well. She had showered. She was wearing a fresh uniform and discreet makeup. She looked smug.

"Madam," she said, "come with me, please."

"You could stop calling me 'madam,'" Carey said, going over

to the bed and collecting her overcoat. "In some places this would count as an engagement."

Szili smirked.

Outside was a grey, chilly morning. The border station had reopened and there were queues of cars and lorries and coaches. Carey turned up the collar of her coat. Some of the passengers in one of the nearest coaches looked down incuriously as Szili and the soldier accompanied her to a small grey van. The rear doors were open; Carey looked inside and saw wooden benches mounted on either side.

"Please, madam," Szili said.

Carey climbed inside and sat on one of the benches. "It's been a blast," she said.

Szili smirked again and closed the doors.

THEY DROVE FOR an hour and threequarters; Carey timed it. Not long enough to reach Szolnok, not nearly long enough for Budapest. More often than not, these fuckups ended with the authorities deporting the offending Coureur after varying periods of abuse and incarceration, and she entertained the possibility that she was being taken across the border, there to be either dumped at the side of the road or handed over to the Croatian authorities, who would have to let her go because she hadn't done anything wrong on their territory. Neither of these outcomes, to be honest, would be so bad. She entertained herself for a while by examining the lock on the rear doors; it would have been reasonably straightforward to spring it with the blade of a penknife and simply step out at the next set of traffic lights and walk away. But the border guards had taken her penknife.

The van finally slowed, made several sharp turns, and bumped over something before pulling to a stop. The doors opened, revealing a man dressed like an undertaker standing outside. He was tall and severe and completely bald, and he wore an old-fashioned suit and a long black coat. He motioned her to get out.

The van was parked in a cobbled courtyard at the heart of a tall old building with many windows and balconies; she didn't get a chance for a very good look, because the undertaker grasped her upper arm with a bony hand that felt like a bear trap and urged her, not terribly gently, across the cobbles, to a door.

The door led into an echoing stairwell, its walls painted lime green. The stairs were just wide enough for Carey and the undertaker to walk side by side, and he never relaxed his grip on her arm. They walked up seven flights, the undertaker led her through a door into a wood-floored corridor, and up to another door, where he knocked with his free hand. A voice inside said "Come," in Hungarian. So, not Croatia, then.

The room was large but sparsely-furnished. The heavy curtains were drawn, and the only illumination came from a green-shaded lamp on a desk. Behind the desk sat a small, neat, middle-aged man in a suit which had seen better days. He looked at her, standing there still in the undertaker's grasp, and he frowned.

"Oh, let her go," he said tiredly. "We're not savages."

The undertaker released her.

"And I think Ms Tews and I can manage a reasonable conversation without a chaperone."

Without a word, the undertaker turned and left the room. The door closed, but Carey didn't hear it lock.

The man behind the desk gestured at a chair over by the wall. "Please," he said, "bring that over here and sit down. You must be tired."

Carey picked up the chair, put it in front of the desk, and sat. The little neat man was maybe in his early fifties. He had a kind, weary face and collar-length brown hair that was still only touched with grey.

He clasped his hands on the desktop and said, "You may call me Martón."

Carey stared at him.

Martón sighed. "We have a problem, Ms Tews."

"I want to speak with the Texan Embassy," she said.

"I have been in touch with your Ambassador," Martón told her. "She has chosen, in the first instance, to leave this matter in our hands."

"Balless bitch."

"It's a matter of diplomacy," Martón suggested. "All we are required to do is make your Ambassador aware of the situation; it's up to her what she does with the information. Considering you are in Hungary on behalf of a non-state actor, she has chosen not to intervene at this point."

"'Non-state actor'?"

Martón reached down beside his chair, came up holding a cardboard folder. He put it on the desk in front of him, opened it, and took out four sheets of paper. In spite of the situation, Carey thought this was quaint. Paper. Seriously.

"The Hungarian government really does take a very dim view of *Les Coureurs des Bois*, Ms Tews," said Martón.

"Who?"

Martón regarded her levelly. Then he put the sheets of paper back in the folder and closed the flap. "Very well," he said. "Then perhaps you will do me the courtesy of listening to what I have to say."

"Do I have a choice?"

"Of course you do." Martón smiled. "You can listen to me, or you can be taken directly to a special court, where you will be tried on charges of espionage. You will not be granted representation, but you will be given an opportunity to state your case. In all likelihood, you will be given a mandatory sentence of ten years' imprisonment." He nodded to himself. "I think that would be a certainty, given the circumstances."

Carey gave him her very best hard stare.

"Now," he went on, "the item you were attempting to transport out of Hungary – and it was very well-hidden, I congratulate your associates on that – is not, in and of itself, illegal. Nor, as it turns out, is it illegal in Croatia, which I admit does confuse me slightly. However, Hungary operates a zero-tolerance policy when it comes to the activity of smugglers, and in particular the organisation of which you claim not to have heard. There are other nations, I am aware, which are more... um, *enlightened*, but we are not. We view the organisation of which you claim not to have heard as a hostile intelligence agency, and for many years we have dealt with them accordingly. This has not deterred them in the slightest. We find them quite tiresome and, if you'll forgive me, charmlessly amateur."

Carey sat where she was, hands folded in her lap.

"What we could do, here and now, you and I, is come to some kind of *accord*," Martón went on. "The situation is not unsalvageable, from your point of view. All you have to do is indicate the individual or organisation which retained your services."

Carey thought about this. She sighed. "I have no idea what you're talking about," she said. "I am a Texan citizen, visiting your country for the purposes of work. All my permits are in order."

"Yes," Martón agreed, "they certainly are. Your permits, your passport, your travel documents. Everything in order."

"I hired the car from the Hertz desk at Szolnok railway station," she went on. "If there was something wrong with it, you should be speaking to them."

"Oh, we have," Martón said brightly. "We still are."

"Then they'll tell you I have nothing to do with this."

"Well, no," said Martón. "That's not what they're telling us at all."

"I can't help you, then."

Martón regarded her sadly. "This is not a game of chicken," he told her. "I am not going to blink first."

She shrugged.

Martón sighed. "You may need some time to think about the situation," he said. He took out his phone, speed-dialled a number, spoke quietly to the person who answered, and hung up. He blinked at her.

A moment later, the undertaker opened the door. Carey stood up, and he took hold of her arm again. It felt as if his fingertips fitted into grooves they had previously made there. He led her towards the door.

"We will speak again, Ms Tews," said Martón.

The undertaker led her back down the corridor to the stairwell, and down the stairs to the courtyard. A small, scruffy car was waiting, its driver perched on the bonnet smoking a cigar and chatting to another man. The undertaker and the driver took out their phones and swapped data. They both checked their screens, nodded to each other, then the undertaker put Carey into the back seat. The car smelled of tobacco and fried food. The driver got in, and the other man got in the back with Carey, and they drove off, pausing only to wait for a tall wooden gate at the courtyard entrance to roll out of the way.

They turned left into traffic. The man sitting with Carey said, "Anyone?"

The driver checked his mirror. "No."

The man turned to Carey. He was tall and bulky, dressed in jeans and a sweatshirt and an American-style pea jacket. "My name is Balász," he told her. "Were you mistreated?"

"I beg your pardon?"

"Did they hurt you?"

"No."

"Good."

She sat thinking for a while. She said, "You're not the police, are you."

Balász chuckled. "Oh my word no."

"Not the authorities at all."

Balász smiled happily and shook his head. "The people who were supposed to be transporting you to detention had a little mishap," he said. "We're their replacements, aren't we, Levente?" The driver grunted.

Carey looked out of the passenger window at the unfamiliar streets. She noted that the door on her side was locked. "What town is this?"

"Kaposvár," said Balász.

"Where are we going?"

"To see my boss." Balász looked at her. "Perhaps we should stop along the way and get you a change of clothes."

THEY DROVE FOR about three hours. Balász and the driver seemed genial enough company, but neither was a sparkling conversationalist, and she was mostly left alone with her thoughts.

"Am I being kidnapped?" she asked, an hour or so into the journey.

"No, you're being *stolen*," Balász said, and he and the driver laughed.

For a while, the road ran along the banks of Lake Balaton, and from the road signs she thought they must be heading for Budapest, but the road turned north fifteen or twenty kilometres from the capital.

They stopped at a little out-of-town mall and Balász went shopping with her. She selected jeans, underwear, a T-shirt and a hoodie, and he paid for them. She had as good a wash as she could manage in one of the mall's public restrooms, and changed her clothes, and afterward she and Balász visited a fast-food outlet and bought a bucket of fried chicken. They sat in the car, out in the vast car park, and ate the chicken. It was the first halfway decent meal Carey had had since leaving Szolnok about a thousand years ago, and she had to fight the urge to just eat her way to the bottom of the bucket without leaving anything for the others.

It was starting to get dark when they arrived in Esztergom, and it occurred to Carey that she had seen quite enough of Hungary to last her a lifetime, thank you very much, and if she managed to get out of this nightmare with her wits intact she was never coming back.

They drove through an historic district of the town, with a castle high on a hill to their left, then turned down a side street and parked outside a high-end leather goods shop, its window full of handbags and shoulderbags and expensive jackets. Balász led her through the shop to a flight of stairs at the back – none of the shop assistants batted an eyelid at the newcomers – and up to what seemed to be a staff refreshment area. Here were some worn but comfy-looking chairs, a low table with a scatter of magazine printouts, a coffee machine, a cork noticeboard on the wall, and a very large blond gentleman in an exquisite suit approaching her with his hand outstretched.

"Ms Tews," he said, shaking her hand. "May I be the first to apologise for your treatment at the hands of our frankly psychopathic authorities. I hope they didn't harm you?"

Carey blinked at him.

"I am László Viktor," the large man told her. "It was my merchandise that you were transporting."

Carey felt as if she might very well be on the verge of overload. She said, "Oh?"

"Do you dance?" Mr Viktor said. "I dance. It's good exercise."

"What?"

"Have you ever," asked Mr Viktor, "danced the Argentinian tango?"

"No," said Carey. "I have not. And if you're asking, my dancing days are far behind me."

Mr Viktor smiled. "It takes a lot of... *intuition*. One must read the body language of one's partner, almost on a subconscious level. They move, you move. There's no time to think, or the music will lose you – it only takes one misstep. It's very rigorous. The moves themselves are simple to learn, but the *relationship* between partners can take a lifetime."

Carey sighed. "I'm really too old to be impressed by a cute metaphor, Mr Viktor. I'm grateful to you for getting me away from the authorities, but say your piece and I'm out of here."

"You have no money, no resources. Where would you go?"

"I can take care of myself, thank you."

Mr Viktor sat down in one of the comfy chairs and clasped his hands across his stomach. He looked like a particularly contented blond bear. "You lost my merchandise," he said. "It was unique, irreplaceable, and now the authorities have it."

"We don't give any guarantees," she told him. "Jumping stuff across borders is tricky, you know that."

"I want it back," said Mr Viktor.

"I don't have it."

"I want you to get it."

She stared at him. "I beg your pardon?"

Mr Viktor gazed at the Coureur serenely. "It was your responsibility to take my merchandise to its destination, and you failed in that. I don't think it's unreasonable of me to expect you to return it to me."

"I think you're confusing us with UPS, Mr Viktor."

He chuckled, a deep, happy sound. "You get my merchandise back and return it to me. Then maybe I'll send it UPS."

"You can't make me do that."

"Well, no," said the Hungarian. "Obviously I can't *make* you. I can, though, *help* you." He nodded to Balász, who had been waiting patiently on the other side of the room. Balász trotted down the stairs to the shop, and returned a few seconds later with another man. This one was young and lithe, with a rodent look to him.

"This is Benedek," said Mr Viktor. "Benedek will do anything you tell him."

Carey looked at Benedek and said, "Fuck off." Benedek stood where he was.

"Well, *almost* anything," said Mr Viktor. He became serious. "Ms Tews, to my mind this is a matter of trust. I trusted your organisation to transport my merchandise to its destination, and you not only failed but you lost the merchandise. Not only did you lose my merchandise, you delivered it into the hands of the people I was trying to keep it away from. Surely you can see my point."

Carey had had about enough of this bullshit. "They knew I was coming," she told him. "They knew where I was going to cross the border, and they knew there was something in the car. *I* didn't tell them any of those things."

"Nor did I," Mr Viktor said equably. "Chiefly because I didn't know."

"*Nobody* knew," she said. "The mechanic who put the Package in the car knew it was there, but he didn't know where I was going. The only way anyone could have known where I was leaving Hungary would have been to follow me, and *nobody followed me.*"

"Are you sure?"

"*Yes.*"

"Hertz tags all its vehicles," Mr Viktor said. "Someone could have hacked into their location system."

"My mechanic took the tag out."

"Are you sure?"

Carey opened her mouth. Closed it.

Mr Viktor rubbed his eyes. "You should tell us who this mechanic is," he rumbled. "Then maybe Balász can go and have a quiet word."

Carey looked at Mr Viktor, at Balász, at Benedek.

"This is all quite fascinating," said Mr Viktor, "but it doesn't get my merchandise back, does it."

"I can't help you," Carey said again, but this time her voice sounded tired.

"Oh, of course you can," Mr Viktor said happily. "You just need a little time to work out how." He stood up and placed his huge hands on her shoulders. "I have a place near here," he told her, beaming. "Why don't you go there, have a shower, have a proper sleep, a decent meal, and think about the situation. We can talk tomorrow and you can tell me what your plan is."

Carey looked at the three men again. Like her dancing days, her brawling days were long behind her; she wasn't going to be able to fight her way out of this. She needed help, and for that she needed some way of contacting the outside world. She was on her own for the moment. And to be honest, the prospect of a shower was very tempting.

"Okay," she said. It was not remotely okay, but she was aware that it was the closest she was going to get for the moment.

THE EVENING STREETS of Esztergom were bustling with people who all looked prosperous and well-dressed and well-fed and well-rested, and Carey felt out of place and weary. She considered making a run for it, losing herself in the crowds; there was a callbox routine she had memorised for emergencies which would theoretically summon some kind of support, but she was just too tired.

Benedek walked beside her, not too close, not too far away, with an almost balletic grace that under other circumstances she might have found quite attractive. Right now, she just wanted to rabbit-punch him.

They were standing at a pedestrian crossing, waiting for the light to turn green with a crowd of shoppers and office workers on their way home, when Benedek fell over. One moment he was standing there, hands at his side, looking alert and capable, the next Carey was aware of an absence at her side and when she looked down he was lying in a heap on the pavement, twitching. Some of the people around him moved away. The light changed and the crowd in front of her began to surge across the street.

While she was trying to work out what had happened, someone put their arm around her waist and urged her forward. "Walk," a woman's voice said quietly in English, close to her side. "Walk. Don't run, don't look back."

Utterly confused, for a moment she resisted. Then she let herself be guided across the road. Behind her, she heard raised voices. Then she was across the road and walking at quite a smart pace, the woman beside her.

"Don't look back," the woman said again. "Just keep going."

Carey turned her head and found herself looking at a brunette woman in her mid-thirties, well-dressed and with a pretty, intelligent face. "Who are you?"

"My name's Laura. I'm here to help."

"Who sent you?"

"I'm local. There's been an utter fuck-up, okay?"

"You're telling *me* there's been an utter fuck-up. Do you know what happened?"

"No talking now," said Laura, letting go of Carey's waist. "Walk. We'll talk in a minute."

They walked on with the crowds for a few minutes. It was chilly now, and Carey imagined she could smell the Danube, just a few streets away, the border between Hungary and Slovakia. Years of experience seemed to be calving off her like icebergs; everything was confusing, nothing made sense. Every face in the crowd seemed to be turned accusingly towards her, every car that passed was an unmarked police vehicle. She fought to regain some kind of composure and professionalism, was only partly successful.

Abruptly, Laura made a left turn through an archway between two shops, taking Carey with her. She stopped and turned just inside the archway.

"Right," she said calmly but urgently. "Here's what I know. Your Situation was compromised; the mechanic you used to plant the Package in your car didn't remove the car's locator tag and the authorities hacked into it."

"I'd figured that out," said Carey, but Laura raised a hand to silence her.

"Just listen, please. I don't know who gave you up to the authorities – it might have been the mechanic, it might not, I can't find him to ask because he's gone, his business is closed. The man you were with earlier is a mid-level thug; I've never had dealings with him but he doesn't have a very good reputation and you need to stay out of his way as much as you need to stay out of the way of the authorities." She took a phone from her pocket and held it out. "There's a local ID and five grand Swiss on here," she said. "I'm sorry it's not more but it was all I could lay my hands on in a hurry."

Carey looked at the phone. "How did you know about this?"

"An interpreter at the Ministry of Justice sat in on a call to the Texan Embassy yesterday morning and contacted me. I got out to Kaposvár in time to see you driving off with that bastard Balász and I knew he was bringing you here; Viktor's an Esztergom boy and he loves doing his business in that fucking shop."

Somehow, all of this made as much sense as anything else that had happened to Carey. Still she didn't take the phone.

"I'm only a stringer," Laura told her. "I don't have the resources to find you a safe house or new papers or get you across the river; you'll have to make a crash call and sort all that out for yourself."

Carey thought about it. She reached out, took the phone, slipped it into a pocket of her hoodie. "Thank you," she said. She felt a little resentful that the Englishwoman wasn't offering her sanctuary in her own home.

"The phone's clean, so it won't leave a trail, but you should take out a chunk of cash as soon as you can and pay for everything with paper." Laura looked back through the archway at the street. "I have to go," she said. "Try to keep moving, don't attract attention. Get out of this part of town, if you can. And good luck." And with that she was gone.

In spite of Laura's warning, Carey stood where she was for a while after she'd gone, trying to regain her composure and fit everything together. Bits of it made sense, and bits didn't, but that was life. She wished she'd had the wit to ask if anyone knew what had been in the Package.

She walked down the alley, stopped at the end, glanced right and left down the street, took a breath, and stepped out onto the pavement.

LAURA STOOD AT the window of a shoe shop and watched in the reflection as the American woman left the alleyway across the street and vanished into the crowds. She counted to fifty, then walked along to where a car was parked at the kerb. She got into the passenger seat and the young man at the wheel said, "That seemed to go all right."

"This is horrible," said Gwen. "She's terrified."

"She's a pro, she'll get her bearings soon," Seth told her. "We just want her off-balance."

"I think we managed *that* okay."

"Are you all right?"

To be honest, her heart was pounding in her chest almost hard enough to make the car shake. "Yes, I'm fine."

He grinned. "Your first Situation."

"Is it always like that?"

"No," he said, starting the engine and putting the car in gear. "No, sometimes it's *really* crazy."

2.

CAREY ONLY USED the phone once, and not to make an actual call.

She stopped at a currency kiosk a couple of miles from where she and Laura had parted. She took out half the phone's balance in forints, then she found a public callbox and dialled a number, and when the call was answered she said, "Hi, is my shopping ready for collection?" She listened to the instructions she was given.

She walked for another mile or two – it was getting on for ten o'clock in the evening now and she kept an eye open for budget hotels – to another callbox and dialled another number. This time she said, "My Situation went tits-up; I need support."

"Are you in immediate danger?" asked the vaguely computer-generated voice at the other end.

She looked out of the box. "No, but that could change at any moment."

"Who's involved?"

"State security, local mafia, Christ only knows who else. I've got no papers, no clothes, nothing."

"Do you have the Package with you?"

"No; that's really the whole problem."

"Find somewhere to go to ground. Call this number from there." The voice recited a long international phone number. "You'll be contacted. Stay off public transport."

She hung up and left the phone booth and walked back down the street to a fast food restaurant, where, suddenly a little startled by how hungry she was, she ate two burgers and a large portion of fries and drank a couple of Cokes, all the while keeping an eye on the big window onto the street. All of a sudden, it seemed, her feet hurt.

A few doors down from the burger place was a run-down tourist hotel. The man behind the desk barely bothered to look at her as she checked in. The room was three floors up and it was small and grubby, but it had a bed and a bathroom and an entertainment set. She went back down to the lobby and used one of the public phones to dial the number she had been given. The call was answered, but no one spoke at the other end, and she hung up and returned to her room and sat on the bed.

SOMEONE WAS KNOCKING on the door. Had probably been knocking on the door for a while. Carey opened her eyes slowly and became aware that, instead of going to bed last night, she had simply slumped over on her side fully-clothed at some point. Her eyes were gritty and there was a terrible taste in her mouth and she ached all over and there was a tight feeling on the skin of her cheek which probably meant that she had been drooling at some point during the night.

Never coming back here, she thought.

With a groan, she levered herself into a sitting position and discovered a painful crick in her neck. *Never ever*. She launched herself off the bed and limped over to the door and put her eye to the viewer, was treated to a fish-eye image of a small, dapper, well-dressed man holding a bunch of white roses.

Okay. Man with flowers. Carey looked around the room. The windows opened on short tethers so guests couldn't hurl furniture or each other out into the street, and she was too high to jump anyway. She looked around the room again, looking for possible weapons. There was a rickety-looking chair by the desk in the corner, but it would probably fall to bits even before she hit anyone with it. She looked through the viewer. The little man knocked again. Not urgently, not in an official we-have-come-to-take-you-to-the-gulag kind of way, but in the manner of a gentleman visiting his lady friend with a nice bunch of roses.

She came to a decision, opened the door as far as the chain would let it go, and said, "Yes?"

The little man beamed at her. "Hello," he said in English; English English – he had quite a posh accent. "I'm Bradley."

She looked him up and down. She hadn't been able to see it through the door viewer, but there was a bulging canvas carryall on the floor by his feet. "Yes?"

"There's a small café in Budapest owned by a defrocked Church of England bishop," Bradley said conversationally.

"I hear their coffee's terrible," she answered.

Bradley nodded happily. "Could I...?" he said.

"Sure." She closed the door, unlatched the chain, opened the door again. "Come on in."

He picked up the bag and stepped into the room, and Carey closed the door and stood with her back to it. "You'd better be the real thing, sunshine," she told him. "Otherwise I'm going to completely spoil your day."

Bradley was looking around the room with a faint air of disappointment. He grinned at her and put the bag down by the bed and the flowers on the desk. He took out his phone, thumbed up an app, and started to walk around with it held out in front of him like a charm against some vague and not very awful evil.

"Did you sleep well?" he asked distinctly, all the while keeping an eye on the screen of the phone.

Carey shrugged. "I slept."

"Good, good." Bradley ran the phone along the edge of the desk, crouched down and waved it underneath. "I thought we might take a turn around the Basilica later. It's the biggest church in Hungary, you know."

"I didn't know that." She had no intention of going anywhere in daylight.

Bradley was over by the windows now, holding the phone up high and pointing it at the curtain rod. He looked at the screen, seemed to ponder for a few moments, then held it up and started to move again.

"The Primatial Basilica of the Blessed Virgin Mary Assumed into Heaven and Saint Adalbert," he said in an amused voice. "And if you think *that's* a mouthful you should hear it in Hungarian." He headed across the room, opened the bathroom door, looked inside.

Carey followed, unwilling to let the Englishman out of her sight. He was pointing the phone at the mirror over the sink, the light fitting, the little waste bin, the lavatory, the shower head. He looked at the screen of the phone, nodded to himself, turned it off, and pocketed it. Then he turned on the shower and the taps, closed the lid of the toilet, and sat.

"How are you?" he asked genially, in a voice she could barely hear over the sound of running water.

"I've been better," she said. "Do you know what happened?"

He shook his head. "Not yet, and that's not important at the moment. Could you give me a quick rundown of what's been going on since you arrived in Hungary, please. Just the bullet points; I'll tell you if I need more detail."

Carey went through the Situation and its aftermath, as she understood them. Bradley stopped her a couple of times and asked her to expand on something. It took her almost an hour.

"Could I see the phone this 'Laura' gave you, please?" he asked when she'd finished.

"Sure." The phone had fallen out of her pocket while she slept, and it was on the floor by the bed. She retrieved it and took it back into the bathroom, where Bradley turned it over in his hands. "She said she was a stringer," she told him.

"Hungary's a strange old place," he said, taking out his own phone and scanning hers. "There *are* Coureurs here, but they're a bit of a law unto themselves. I've never met any of them. You said she was English."

"She sounded English."

He nodded and swiped through the phone's screens and menus. "Well," he said, handing it back, "it seems kosher. You should dispose of it, though."

"There's still two and a half thousand Swiss francs on here," she told him.

"Someone's emergency operational funds," he said. "Actually, now I think, let me have it. I'll see they get it back."

Carey gave the phone back and he dropped it in a pocket of his jacket and stood up. "I'm going to have a coffee, I think," he said. "There are clothes and things in the bag. Get yourself cleaned up and changed and I'll be back in, oh, say forty minutes and we'll take it from there. Okay?"

It occurred to Carey that she had not seen Bradley stop smiling once since she had looked at him through the door viewer. "How are you going to get me out of here?" she asked.

"You let me take care of that," he said, going to the door. "Lock up behind me, and I'll see you in a little while." And with that he was gone.

She unzipped the bag and looked inside. A couple of pairs of jeans, some underwear, skirts, T-shirt, blouses, a warm jacket, sensible shoes, two fleeces, cosmetics, a tube of hair dye, a disposable battery-powered haircutting comb, and three pairs of spectacles with plain lenses. The clothes were all obviously bought by a man, but it was interesting that they were the right sizes.

WHILE THE AMERICAN woman got ready, Bradley went along the street to a rather disreputable café. He bought an Americano and a small glass of brandy and took them both to a booth near the back. He made a couple of phone calls, then he took the phone the American had given him out of his pocket and looked it over. He scanned it again with his phone, went through its menus and settings. There were no numbers in its contacts folder, nor in its call history. He sat for a few moments, considering.

He took the back off, removed its SIM and onboard memory cards, and snapped them in quarters. Then he used a penknife to lever out the phone's battery and as much of its innards as would come out. He swept the bits of the phone into a little pile in the middle of the table and looked at his watch. He decided to give the woman another ten minutes, and sat back to drink his brandy.

It was already too late; as he descended to the lobby in the lift, the phone had briefly woken itself up and scanned the immediate area for other communications devices. The only other device it found was Bradley's phone, which was in the same pocket. The phone sent Bradley's phone what appeared to be a text message. The message unpacked itself in a fraction of a second, took over Bradley's phone, and then deleted itself. Every hour thereafter, his phone emitted a compressed and encrypted burst of data comprising GPS coordinates of everywhere it had been, everyone it had been connected to, and every conversation it had been privy to.

"HERE," SAID THE cobbler, holding out a hideous black and green sweater. "Put this on."

"You're kidding, right?" Carey said.

"You present yourself at the border wearing the same clothes as you're wearing in your passport photograph, you're asking for trouble," the cobbler told her. "Just put it on over your shirt; you won't have to put up with it for long."

They were in a flat on the eastern side of the city, in a district that seemed to be made up mostly of small garages and workshops and light industrial units wedged in among decaying apartment blocks. The cobbler had been waiting for them, a big beefy man with the face of an unsuccessful boxer and an attaché case full of anonymous tech.

She looked over at Bradley, who was sitting in a threadbare armchair near the window, and he nodded, so she pulled the sweater over her head. She'd opted for a skirt and a blouse over a plain black T-shirt. Smoothing the sweater down with one hand, she ran the other through her newly-cut and newly-auburn hair. She'd run the comb's battery out cutting her hair down to about two inches in length; it was harder to do than it looked in the movies and it didn't make her look all that different, if she was going to be honest, but with the dye job and a pair of spectacles she looked different enough not to attract second glances from anyone who might be looking for her.

The cobbler posed her against the wall and took a couple of photos with his phone, then went back to doing cobbler stuff with the gear in his case. Carey took off the sweater and put her jacket back on and went over to stand beside Bradley.

"Languages?" the cobbler asked, his back turned to them.

"English and French," Bradley said before Carey could speak up.

"She doesn't look French," the cobbler grumbled.

"Who does?" Bradley said cheerfully. Carey looked down at him, and he smiled at her.

"I'm not going to make you English," the cobbler said. "The English passport is an absolute bastard; it'd take me a week to make it convincing. How do you feel about being a New Zealander?"

"I have an American accent," Carey said.

"Can you talk like a South African?" the cobbler said, still fiddling about with something in the case open on the table in front of him. "*Sarf Iffrican*? It's like that."

"No it isn't," Bradley murmured.

"Why don't you just make me South African?" asked Carey.

"Do you speak Afrikaans?" said the cobbler. When there was no answer, he said, "Well, then."

"This is silly," Carey told Bradley.

"Just pretend to be English," he said. "Nobody will be able to tell."

The cobbler turned from the table with a passport in either hand. They were both plastic cards a little smaller than an old-style credit card and they both had her photo and some printing on them. One was blue, the other a pale salmon pink.

"One to get in, one to get out," said the cobbler. He handed the cards to Carey; they were still warm. "Photos, biometric data, legends." He gave her a couple of sheets of paper fresh out of the printer in his case. "These are your legends. Try to remember which goes with which passport." And he burst out laughing, revealing a mouthful of broken teeth.

IN THE END it was ridiculously easy. Bradley simply drove her out to Komárom and put her on a coach and the coach took her across the bridge and the border guards on either side barely glanced at her New Zealand passport and then she was in Slovakia. Two days later, travelling on the French passport, she was getting off a flight in Houston. It was some time before she returned to Europe, and she never again set foot in Hungary.

SURSTROMMING

1.

"THEY'RE LATE," SAID Andreas.

Yngvar looked at his watch. "Only five minutes later than the last time you said that," he said.

"Ah, fuck it," Andreas muttered. They'd been sitting here in the car, parked beside the road in Østfold, a few kilometres from the border with Sweden, for almost two hours. It was cold outside, and Yngvar, who did not smoke, refused to let him roll down a window so he could have a cigarette. "Are you sure we're in the right place?"

Yngvar sighed and pulled up the GPS on his phone and held it up so Andreas could see the screen. "Look," he said. "Can you see the coordinates here? Can you? Hm? And don't you dare ask if I'm sure we have the right day."

"This is fucking ridiculous," Andreas muttered.

No traffic passed them on the road. A few kilometres further back, the Norwegian authorities had closed it by the simple expedient of bringing in a maintenance crew to dig up the carriageways under the pretence of emergency repairs. On the other side of the border, the Swedes had opted for something more showy, staging a chemical tanker crash. Between these two pieces of pantomime, the road and the old Svinesund Bridge were empty.

"I need a piss," Andreas grumbled. He got out of the car and did up his coat, looked along the line of other cars parked along the side of the road. He waved to the nearest, got an answering wave from within, and walked into the trees.

He found himself a spot, unzipped, and began to relieve himself against a tree, but he'd hardly started when he heard undergrowth crunching under a number of feet. He sighed. Typical. He finished hurriedly, zipped up, and made himself presentable just as eight soldiers in vaguely old-fashioned uniform stepped out of the forest. They were carrying modern European automatic rifles, and behind them were half a dozen men and women wearing formal clothes and carrying document cases, their breath pluming in the cold air.

The soldiers reached him and stopped. One of them saluted.

"You're late," Andreas told him.

One of the diplomats, a tall man in late middle age, stepped forward. "You'll have to speak English, I'm afraid," he said affably. "None of us speaks Norwegian."

Andreas regarded him levelly. "Very well," he said in English. He waved behind him, towards the road. "We make the exchange over here."

"Lead on then, please," said the diplomat.

They walked back to the road, where there was a sudden flurry of activity, people getting out of the cars. Yngvar shot Andreas a sour look as he went by, but Andreas just shrugged.

Without having to be told, the civilians drew themselves up into two lines. From the cars there were diplomatic representatives of the largest European nations, as well as a bureaucrat from what still fancied itself to be the European Union. Facing them were the Community delegation. To one side, the soldiers and Andreas and the other members of Norwegian state security tried to make each other blink first.

"Please accept our apologies for our late arrival," the Community diplomat who had spoken to Andreas told the Europeans. He didn't seem particularly apologetic. "We had some travelling difficulties; I'm sure you'll understand."

The Europeans seemed jumpy, excited. Andreas had decided that their seniority among their respective nations' diplomatic corps could not be very high; they were basically hostages, expendable. And more to the point, they were symbolic – their countries already had ambassadors in the Community. They stepped forward, a little hesitantly at first, and shook hands with their Community opposite numbers, and in a few moments the two groups had changed places.

Yngvar came over and stood beside Andreas and they watched the Community delegation climb into the cars, along with four of their soldiers. The other soldiers, along with the Europeans and several of the Norwegian security officers, turned and walked back into the trees. In a few moments, they were gone.

Andreas looked at his watch. Almost two and a half hours late. Yngvar made a brief phone call. Then they stood looking at each other.

"Head Office says this is the last time we get ourselves involved in something like this," Yngvar said.

"No shit," said Andreas.

Yngvar walked around to the driver's side of the car and opened the door. "They didn't word it quite like that, of course. There was swearing."

ON THE FACE of it, the Union, the patchwork of treaties and agreements between the Community and the many nations of Europe, was a triumph. This was a shining new age of fraternity and mutual benefit. European firms opened offices in the Community, Community firms opened offices in Europe. There were university exchange programmes and film and television co-productions, fashion shows, cultural festivals and merchandising licences. Embassies and consulates popped up everywhere. Everyone was happy.

On a more pragmatic level, it was a nightmare. The fact that the Community was a nuclear superpower was not widely known; even less widely known was that its previous ruling faction had contemplated using biological warfare against their European neighbours and had – however accidentally – gone on to release the Xian Flu. From Europe's point of view, the Community was spectacularly dangerous. There was no way to defend against an enemy who could walk across invisible borders anywhere on your territory whenever they wanted, while you were quite unable to retaliate.

It was also spectacularly rich, in natural resources and markets and plain old cash. It was, quite simply, irresistible. Better, on balance, to have it as a friend than an enemy, and – at the very highest, most secret levels of the four or five nations where these things were known – to set the Xian Flu aside in the name of the greater good. The secret would come out one day, because secrets always did, particularly secrets as monumental as this one, but the Europeans who entered into it calculated that History would at least understand what they had done, and they looked at their burgeoning bank balances and feathered nests and were comforted.

For the Presiding Authority of the Community, Europe was full of nothing but win. They suddenly had access to all manner of technology which had previously been unknown – medical technology, in particular – and they looked at their burgeoning bank balances and feathered nests and they, too, were comforted.

Even before its official launch, the Union had been impossibly complex; it had taken more than five years of secret negotiations to get as far as a public announcement. Five years further on, even more layers of complexity had settled upon it, much of it quietly and well out of sight.

A lot of that complexity came from meetings like this one, off-the-books conferences attended not by heads of state or even their ministers but by anonymous bureaucrats, meetings where hostages were politely exchanged for the duration and no official minutes were ever published.

The *Nasjonal sikkerhetsmyndighet*, Norway's National Security Authority, had become involved in this particular meeting because the Community delegation had chosen to enter Europe via a border crossing on Norwegian territory. Thus, it had fallen to the NSM to organise transport and the hostage exchange, and incidentally to stooge around in the cold waiting for the Community's representatives to turn up.

The little convoy of cars drove the short distance to the border between Norway and Sweden, which here ran along the Svinesund, a narrow strait that opened into the Skaggerak at one end and the Iddefjord at the other. Sweden had been a popular shopping destination for generations of Norwegians, and a large out-of-town shopping mall had gradually accreted at the far end of the Old Bridge. Today, however, it was empty, evacuated due to the 'tanker accident'.

There were more cars waiting for them on the Swedish side of the bridge. The convoy stopped and Yngvar and Andreas got out and walked over to their opposite numbers from Säpo, Sweden's Security Service.

"You're late," said Agathe when hands had been shaken.

"Blame them," Andreas told her, indicating the Norwegian cars. "Transport difficulties, they say."

Agathe snorted. She and Andreas knew each other from numerous joint security operations, but this one was a first for them both. "Did the handover go smoothly, at least?"

"Yes." Andreas lit a cigarette and looked around at the deserted buildings of the shopping mall. "This is good work," he said appreciatively.

"Yes, well it won't last forever. We're diverting traffic across the New Bridge but there's about a thousand journalists just down the road shouting about their right to film the accident."

"You should just have brought someone in to dig the road up," Yngvar said. "Nobody ever wants to film that."

Agathe chuckled. "Not so much fun, though. Shall we get our guests to their destination? Then we can have a drink."

"That sounds good," Andreas agreed. "I could use a drink."

THE HOUSE CHOSEN for the conference was some kilometres from the bridge, a High Baroque country seat with salmon-pink walls sitting in the middle of an estate of many hectares of forest. A group of European dignitaries had gathered outside to greet the Community delegation, but it began to spit with rain as the convoy arrived, and the diplomatic niceties were curtailed. Andreas, Yngvar, Agathe and their colleagues followed the diplomats inside, and then all of a sudden their job was over. What happened after that, until it was time for the Community representatives to go home, was a mystery to them.

For the visitors there were coffee and pastries and smalltalk in one of the house's many splendid receiving rooms before being called into the ballroom, where a conference table had been set up. The doors were closed, electronic bafflers switched on, and the two groups settled down to try to avert a war.

LUNCH WAS SERVED in the smaller of the house's two dining rooms. The larger could accommodate banquets several hundred strong, which was deemed a little too grand for what was supposed to be a serious and intimate gathering. The Swedish hosts had provided a range of *husmanskost*, local dishes including pork, salmon and herring. For the adventurous there was *Surströmming* – fermented herring – and for those with delicate sensibilities there were sweet rolls and coffee, served by a small group of waiting staff provided by the independent contractors who were handling the house's security for the duration.

"Do people really eat *Surströmming*?" one of the Community delegation asked the waiter who was refilling his coffee cup. "It smells dreadful."

"I understand it's an acquired taste, sir," the waiter told him. "They have to open the tins outside. I haven't tried it."

"That's a shame. It seems... intriguing." The Community delegate put his cup and saucer on a side table. "I wonder, could you direct me to the lavatory?"

"Certainly, sir," said the waiter. "If you'd like to follow me..."

They left the dining room, the waiter putting his coffee flask and napkin on a table by the door. The Community delegate, whose name was Michael, nodded pleasantly to the security staff in the hallway and, instead of making for the downstairs bathrooms, turned for the main doors. The waiter followed, half a step behind.

Outside, the drizzle had stopped, but there was a sharp chill in the air and the waiter, who was wearing a shirt and tie and waistcoat and an apron, felt it cut right through him. Michael seemed not to notice. He walked away from the house at a brisk pace, smiling to himself.

When they had gone a few hundred metres, Michael said, "Well, this is a pleasant surprise."

"Hello," said Rupert. "I'm armed."

"Well, of course you are." Michael was languid almost to the point of feyness. He was wearing a three-piece suit that could only have come from Saville Row, the sharply-ironed points of a handkerchief protruding from the breast pocket. "All the waiting staff are. I presume you're working for the firm providing security."

Rupert looked out across the lawn in front of the house. A couple of security men were patrolling. One had a large and dangerous-looking dog. The security men were wearing combat gear and windbreakers with *Arabesque Security* lettered across the shoulders in green.

"The salary is pathetic, if you want to know," he said.

"That's a pity," Michael said. "It's hard to make a decent living these days. It's rather brave of you to come, you know. Lion's den, and all that."

"Oh, do stop patronising me," Rupert told him. "I had enough of that before."

Michael glanced at him. "I thought we were friends."

"I can't imagine what gave you that idea," said Rupert.

Michael beamed. "There," he said. "That's better. Shall we walk?"

"Won't they miss you in there?"

"I can't think why. The Europeans will probably be glad to see the back of me; I have the impression I'm starting to annoy them. I know *they're* starting to annoy *me*."

They walked away from the house. The gardens tipped steeply down towards a screen of trees, and Michael had to walk carefully because his leather-soled shoes kept slipping on the wet grass.

"It's good to see you, actually," he said. "We've been trying to contact you, but you never answer."

"Is Molson here?"

"Andrew goes wherever the wind blows him." Michael looked at him. "Which I regret to say is not here, for the moment." He almost lost his footing, recovered himself. "How are you enjoying Europe, by the way? The food's wonderful, isn't it?"

They walked into the trees, and Michael stopped for a few moments as if trying to get his bearings before setting out again along a path between dense, bushy foliage. "How did you find out about this *soiree*?" he asked.

"We've been keeping an eye on Arabesque," said Rupert. "They have a security contract in Luxembourg which we're quite interested in."

Michael nodded. "Yes. In fact, that's one of the things we've been discussing today, Luxembourg. Very perplexing."

"They call it the Realm," Rupert said. "The Europeans."

Michael laughed. "I know. Bless them. We're actually very angry about it. But so are they. Nobody seems to know who's responsible."

"Or nobody wants to admit it."

"All we want is the return of our citizens," said Michael. "The Europeans want to give them back – I think they find the whole thing quite embarrassing, really – but they won't do anything until they receive assurances that we won't do it again. Which we can't give them, because we didn't do it in the first place. As I said, perplexing."

The path dipped down slightly and turned to follow a little stream through the trees. Michael strode across it and Rupert followed. On the other side, the ground rose again, and all of a sudden they stepped out of the woodland and two Community soldiers with European rifles slung across their chests were standing there.

Michael stopped and showed the soldiers some documents. "This gentleman will catch his death if he's not careful," he told them, indicating Rupert, and one of the soldiers took off his combat jacket and held it out. Rupert put it on and looked about him. The estate was gone, the house was gone, Sweden was gone, Europe was gone. There was just a bleak expanse of moorland rising gently towards a screen of hills. There was a road in the middle distance, and parked on it were a number of electric cars, guarded by more soldiers. Rupert sighed. He had sworn to himself that he would never come back here.

2.

THE WHITTON-WHYTES, THE creators of the Community, had started modestly. They had, bit by bit, built themselves a county just to the west of London. When this was successful, they had extended their creation until it occupied an expanse of territory from the Iberian Peninsula to a little east of Moscow, an invisible Continent. They, and their descendants, had then gone on to conquer it.

At its most basic, the Community was a beautiful thing, an artifact like the gardens of an English country house. Its geography was roughly similar to that of Europe, but its landscape was not. A tributary of the River Trent had run through the Campus, Rupert's lost home, but it had been ringed by mountains modelled on the Alps. The landscape Rupert could see through the windows of the car was not very like the landscape of southern Norway; it looked, he thought, more like the North York Moors, where he had spent a pleasant week or so two years before. The Whitton-Whytes, it occurred to him, had mapped England across the whole of Europe, with a few pleasing embellishments stolen from other countries.

There was a wicker basket on the floor at the back of the car. It contained plates and cutlery and glasses and little jars of jam and tins of *foie gras* and caviar and packets of wafer biscuits and bars of expensive chocolate and small bottles of wine and champagne. Michael had a fondness for Fortnum & Mason picnic hampers. For less refined tastes there was a thermos of milky tea and a paper-wrapped package of ham sandwiches made with doorsteps of white bread. Rupert declined both.

"So," Michael said. "Shall we clear the air a little first, or do you want to plunge right in?" When Rupert didn't reply immediately, he asked, "How's the girl, by the way? The one you took over the border with you?"

"She died," said Rupert.

"And they couldn't help her in Europe?" Michael sounded shocked.

Rupert thought of Patricia's final days, in a private nursing home in Berne that had seemed more like a very expensive hotel than a clinic. None of it had done any good, in the end. They'd had a little over eighteen months; sometimes, in dark moments, he thought it had been the treatments that had killed her, not the cancer.

"How are things here?" he asked.

"Here?" Michael had lifted the lid of the hamper and was rummaging about inside. "Oh, we keep rubbing along, you know." He sat up holding a bottle of red wine in one hand and a tin of paté in the other. "Are you sure you won't...? No." He put the bottle and tin on the floor, bent over again for a glass and a butterknife and a packet of biscuits. "We live in interesting times," he said.

"Not least because someone stole part of the Community."

Michael nodded. "Perplexing. Have you, perhaps, heard anything...?"

"It's as much a mystery to us as it is to you. No one seems to have been hurt, if that's any help."

"Yes, the Europeans tell us that. It's a village called Angworth, by the way. The whole village, all its people, just... transposed."

"Which makes everyone nervous."

"It's certainly concentrated minds." Michael sat up, closed the lid of the hamper, and began setting out his snack on top. "They sent us the Squire back," he said, picking with his fingernails at the packaging around the biscuits. "As a token of their goodwill. *He's* pretty cheesed off, as you can imagine."

"Are you also," Rupert asked, "discussing the Ufa explosion?"

Michael had managed to open the biscuits. He put a finger through the ring-pull of the tin and opened it with one smooth motion. "Why ever would we do that?" he asked.

"You see," Rupert said, "from a certain point of view – and this is entirely hypothetical – it seems as if there's *tit-for-tat* going on."

Michael twisted the cap off the bottle, poured a little wine into the glass, held it to his nose, and inhaled. "This is excellent, you know," he said. "Has it ever occurred to you to wonder why we don't make wine as good as this?"

"No."

"Well, for one thing it's cultural, of course. We're English. Beer drinkers to a man, none of that foreign muck. We don't have much of a tradition of winemaking." He poured more wine in his glass, set it on top of the hamper, took a biscuit out of the packet. "But there's another reason. The soil's wrong. Oh, we can grow grapes easily enough, and we can make a *type* of wine, but the soil's not right. And it's not right because the Whitton-Whytes didn't think about that when they created the Community. They provided us with a cornucopia of other natural resources – coal, iron ore and so on – but it never occurred to them to set the right conditions for wine-making." He trowelled a knifeload of paté onto a biscuit, picked up his glass, and sat back in his seat.

Rupert looked out of the window. The soldiers were patrolling slowly up and down the line of cars. "Who are you at war with?"

"Us?" Michael asked in surprise. "Nobody. We're everybody's friend."

"Amanda and Kenneth Pennington," said Rupert.

Michael thought about it, shook his head. "I don't recognise the names."

Rupert sighed. "Something is happening. In Europe. We don't know what it is but we'd like it to stop."

"*We* being you and him. The Coureur." Michael took a bite of his biscuit and shook his head again.

"*We* know about Mundt," said Rupert. "He was killed by a former English soldier. Whether the English were actually involved, we don't know. There's a process they call 'brainwashing,' like hypnosis with flashing lights and drugs. It looks as if he wasn't aware of what he was doing. I don't understand it, but that's how it was explained to me."

Michael sipped some wine. "I don't recall you being this candid," he said. "Where is he? This soldier?"

"The European police have him."

"Hm. They didn't tell us that. Thank you." He popped the remains of his biscuit in his mouth, chewed, swallowed. "There was a joint decision, by ourselves and the Europeans, not to publicise the killing. There's a lot of anti-Community sentiment in Europe at the moment – demonstrations, denunciations in some of the wilder little parliaments and assemblies – we didn't want to inflame that."

"What was he doing there?"

"Mundt?" Michael shrugged. "You spent time with him; you know what he was like. Civil engineering was a passion. The government of the polity invited a delegation to have a look around, and he decided he wanted to go." He drank some more wine.

"And you had access to all his research by then and there was no reason not to let him go."

"Oh, we were keeping a close eye on him. The trouble is, we were expecting him to try to run away, not to get himself killed." Michael sighed at how wonderful the world would be, if only one could truly take into account all eventualities.

"And you have no idea who killed him."

Michael shook his head. "We've been making our own inquiries, of course. Informally."

"Our friend thinks you may believe he was involved somehow."

Michael raised his eyebrows. "Why would he think that?"

"He thinks there's evidence connecting him to the killer."

Michael thought about that for a while. "That's interesting, of course," he said finally. "He really didn't figure in our assessments, but that is interesting. I presume you're here to intercede on his behalf, assure me that he wasn't involved."

"Did you try to have him killed?"

"Has someone tried to kill him?" Michael shook his head. "No, that wasn't us. There have been times when I would have throttled him myself, but life's too short. It would be impractical to kill *everyone* who ever annoyed me; one has to stop somewhere."

There was silence in the car for some minutes. Michael ate a couple more biscuits. Rupert looked out of the window. It began to drizzle outside. The soldiers kept patrolling.

Finally, he said, "I think we can agree that anything which destabilises the relationship between Europe and the Community would not be a good thing."

Michael nodded. "Not a good thing. For anyone. Nobody would want that."

Rupert looked at the Head of the Directorate. He could count the number of times he and Michael had been honest with each other on the fingers of one hand, with some fingers left over. He said, "Do the Europeans know this border crossing exists?"

"Oh my word no," Michael said. "Just as we don't know that they have a couple of assault helicopters hanging around off the coast in case of emergencies."

"You could," Rupert said, "just try *trusting* each other."

"Well, *that* would never do." Michael brushed crumbs from the lapel of his jacket and chuckled. "It really was very brave of you to come here," he said again, half to himself. "Now," he said briskly. "Is there some pressing reason why I shouldn't have you arrested?"

Rupert looked at him. "If you wanted to arrest me you could have done it right away and gone back to the conference," he said wearily.

Michael beamed at him. "It's been good to see you again. It really has."

*   *   *

TWO OF THE soldiers followed them at a respectful distance. Michael put up an umbrella to keep off the drizzle. Rupert thought about a couple he had once known, who had lived in one of the fishing villages on the coast, just a few miles west of here. He remembered how he had played a part in betraying them, on behalf of the man walking beside him, in order to infiltrate the Directorate on behalf of the English Security Services, which had in their turn been infiltrated by operatives of the Directorate. And so it went on, round and round and round.

"Do you think our friend could see his way clear to letting us have one of those invisibility suits he seems to have an inexhaustible supply of?" Michael asked.

"You'll have to keep on making do with low cunning," Rupert told him.

Michael laughed. "When you see him, tell him his sins haven't been forgiven, but we didn't try to kill him."

"That'll help him sleep at night," Rupert said, turning the collar of his borrowed combat jacket up against the drizzle. He put his hands in the pockets, found a roll of mints in one and a chunky penknife in the other. He took them out, looked at them, put them back.

Michael glanced at him, stubbed his toe on a wet hummock of grass, and almost fell over. Rupert caught him by the elbow and stopped him crashing full-length to the ground. This brought the soldiers running towards them, weapons raised and shouting warnings. Michael regained his balance and waved them back.

"You see?" he said. "You see?" His face was flushed and angry; Rupert had never seen him lose his temper like this, not even during the brief counter-coup which had put him in the top job in the Directorate. "All it takes is one slip, one misstep, and people start shooting. Do you think I want that?"

"I don't think anyone wants that," Rupert said, letting go of his arm.

Michael's composure returned. He sighed. "Was there anything else?"

"No," Rupert said. "No, that's it."

"All right. You can go back across the border; nobody will stop you. But you'll have to find your own way out of the conference security cordon. I want to finish my lunch."

Then they just stood there awkwardly for a few moments. Handshakes did not seem remotely appropriate. Finally, fed up of standing in the rain, Rupert just stomped off across the moorland on his own. He had made his way back through the wood into Sweden before it occurred to him that he was still wearing the soldier's combat jacket. He took it off and hung it on a tree and started to walk away. Then he stopped, turned back, took the penknife and the mints from the jacket, and set off toward the house. In a couple of hours the staff would be getting ready for dinner.

3.

THERE WAS A Starbucks on the Market Square in Władysław. It faced a Caffè Nero on the other side. They were both staffed by eager young baristas and they both looked as if they had been dropped here by a fleet of invading alien spacecraft. Which, Gwen thought, wasn't too far from the truth.

Hal wanted to go to Starbucks, but there was a little restaurant Gwen liked just off the square, so they went there instead. It was the day after Market Day, and the restaurant was quiet. They took a table at the back and ordered a pot of tea and a plate of scones.

"This place is changing," Hal said when the waitress had brought their order. "A lot of people don't think it's for the better, either."

Gwen liked the Community. It was her third visit this year, the first time on her own – Rudi had come with her the previous two times. There was something calm and quiet about the place which appealed to her. The countryside around the capital was beautiful and everyone was polite. Of course, the sexism here was breathtaking – there wasn't a single woman on the Presiding Authority – and the last time she was here she'd overheard a shopkeeper quite openly referring to a visiting group of South African agricultural engineers as 'niggers', so there was that.

"They're a conservative people," Rudi said when she told him about it. "The only African people they know about are in books."

"They need their fucking heads banging together," she said.

"Next time you're in the countryside, stop and listen," he told her. "No aeroplanes, no helicopters, no internal combustion. They still have steam trains. And they like it that way; it's what they've been defending all these years."

"So why open the borders?"

He shrugged. "I don't know."

"That's what you get," Gwen told Hal while she poured tea for them both. "You deal with the devil, you get burger franchises."

He watched her. He was an unexceptional-looking man in his mid-fifties, with thinning hair and a neat grey beard. He wore a three-piece suit and a knitted tie. His shoes were beautifully handmade. "I haven't visited Europe," he said.

"Well, you're missing some stuff and not missing some other stuff," she said. "I think you'd enjoy it."

"Where are you from?"

"I'm from *him*," she said. "And that's all you need to know."

He nodded. Gwen had no idea what Rudi's relationship was with Hal; for operational reasons, she had no clear idea who Hal was. She had just been told to meet him on the steps of the Cathedral at a certain time and collect whatever he had for her. It was, Rudi had told her, a milk-run of a Situation, any stringer could handle it, although of course no stringer would ever be allowed near raw intelligence. She had a sneaking suspicion he wanted her out of Europe for the moment, while whatever was happening settled down, which was kind of annoying, but at least she was doing something useful instead of waitressing in that fucking restaurant, and it was kind of exciting, espionage stuff. As on her previous visits, she was in local mufti, a skirt and jacket in heavy scratchy tweedy material over a starched white blouse and thick stockings, and a ridiculous little hat perched on top of her head and secured with hair grips. On the way to the meet, she had stopped off at a little stationers, bought a postcard depicting a village green in Ernshire – like a location for an old Miss Marple film – written a cheery 'wish you were here' on the back, and posted it to Lewis. Then she had headed to the Cathedral with a lightness in her heart.

"How is he, by the way?" asked Hal.

"He's just fine and dandy," she said, taking a scone from the plate in the middle of the table and slicing it neatly through the middle. "He sends his regards." Hal had approached her outside the Cathedral exactly at the appointed time and identified himself by asking for a cigarette, to which she had replied that she no longer smoked. Rudi had called this a *contact string*, and she thought it was a bit silly, but he'd assured her that it was not, it was deadly serious.

Hal took a scone for himself, cut it in half, buttered one of the halves, added jam and cream. He said, "I wasn't able to photograph the documents; there was no time."

"Well, *that's* not very good, Hal," she said amiably.

"I did manage to read them," he said. "I can tell you what you want to know."

"I'm supposed to have documentary evidence, Hal," she said, smearing butter on half of her scone. "You telling me stuff, well, that's just you *telling* me stuff, isn't it. You could be making it all up, for all I know." She was also not supposed to know what intelligence she was being given; in a worst-case scenario, it could allow the Directorate to identify Hal.

"I've never let him down yet," Hal protested.

"I never said you had," she told him. She lowered her voice. "Look, if you think I'm going to debrief you in a *tea shop* you've got another think coming, mate." Although she had a device in her tiny ugly excuse for a handbag, disguised as a fountain pen, which Rudi had told her would scramble any bugs the Directorate might have planted in the restaurant as part of the Community's patient, plodding mass surveillance on its own people. "I just came here for a handover."

"You'll have to leave here empty-handed, then," he said. He looked utterly pathetic, sitting there with half a scone in his hand. "There's no way I can photograph those records."

"Hal," she said, "we're not at home to *no way* today, are we?"

"What?"

She sighed. "Never mind. Look, I'm not allowed to know what you've got, all right? Because if I know that and the Directorate arrest me and *torture* me and I tell them everything – because I *will*, I'm no hero – they'll say, 'Well, there's only one chap who could have told her *that*, it's our old mate Hal,' and then you'll be in a lot of trouble, won't you."

He stared at her. "It's not possible," he said.

Gwen thought about it. "Okay," she said finally. "Just give me the bullet points." Hal looked lost again. "The gist. As vague as possible. Yes?"

Hal, it occurred to her, had never been spoken to like this by a woman before, bless him. He needed a few moments to gather his thoughts. "There were two of them," he said. "In the 1980s, in the place he told me to look for. They lived here for a while, but we sent them back." He paused. "Is that vague enough?"

She shrugged. "Works for me." She took a bite of scone, washed it down with a sip of tea, dabbed her lips with her napkin. "Okay," she said. "I'm going to visit the ladies', and while I'm gone I want you to leave. Go home, go back to work, I don't care. Try not to attract attention. We'll be in touch."

He blinked at her. "What about my..."

"What? Oh. Sorry. Almost forgot." She opened her handbag and took out a small brown envelope. She had no idea what it contained. She slid it across the table, slipped it under his plate. "There you go. Enjoy." She got up and left the table without looking back.

One of the reasons she liked this restaurant was the corridor at the back which led to the lavatories. At the end of the corridor, past the doors to the toilets, was another door, which opened directly into an alleyway at the rear of the building. She opened the door, poked her head out, glanced quickly left and right, then stepped into the alley and walked confidently away from the restaurant.

The alley opened onto a busy shopping street off the Market Square. She crossed the street, walked a hundred metres or so, and entered a shop which seemed to sell nothing but ladies' gloves. Through the shop to the back, where another door gave access to another alley. This one led to a maze of little alleyways, some of them cobbled, some of them not. She muttered the memorised route under her breath, "Left and *right* and *right* and left and *forward* and *left*," and after fifteen minutes or so she stepped out onto a street full of motor cars and shops with Czech signs.

"Right on time," Seth said, stepping up beside her and slipping his arm through hers. They started to walk. "How did it go?"

"Tell you later," she said. "I've got to change these fucking clothes. I look like an extra from *Brief Encounter*."

4.

"We never thought we would actually be visited by one of the trustees," said Mr Coltrane. "For years the trust has taken care of itself, with occasional minor adjustments."

"Is it a problem?" asked his visitor. "My being here?"

"No, not at all," Mr Coltrane reassured him. He looked at the sheaf of documents on his desk. "Everything's in order. We were notified of the death of the previous signatory, of course."

"May I ask by whom?"

Mr Coltrane consulted his pad. "A Mr Salumäe."

"Ah." The visitor nodded. "Of course." The visitor was well-dressed but indefinably tired and careworn. He walked with a cane and he had a very faint accent. Mr Coltrane fancied himself a student of accents, but he couldn't place this one.

"The gentleman's authentications were correct," said Mr Coltrane, suddenly concerned that something was amiss.

"I'm sure they were," said the visitor. He reached into his jacket pocket and took out a plastic card. "As, I hope, these will be."

They spent five minutes matching random groups of letters and numbers from the visitor's card with another which Mr Coltrane had taken from the office safe. There were signatures and countersignatures to be taken, terms to be read out loud, more signatures, then an exchange of encryption keys.

When everything seemed to have been completed to the solicitor's satisfaction, the visitor said, "You'll appreciate that I'm new to this matter; perhaps it would help if you could provide me with an overview of the trust and its disbursements, so I can get up to speed."

"Certainly." Mr Coltrane went back to the safe, returned with a red cardboard folder, which he laid on the desk in front of the visitor. "I have some business I need to take care of," he said. "Perhaps you'd like to stay here and read in private...?"

"That would be very kind," said the visitor. "Thank you."

Rudi waited until the solicitor had left the office, then he got up and went to the window. The firm of Leonidas & Parr, Solicitors

And Commissioners for Oaths (est. 1893) occupied the top three floors above a laundrette in Tilbury in Essex, the final and rather humble stop on a month-long odyssey of safety deposit firms, lawyers and banks which had taken him halfway across Europe and back. At each stop there had been instructions for how to find the next, and keys or authentication codes to release the information held there. And at each stop there had been details of some kind of financial instrument or account involving a very large sum of money. Rudi, who had been keeping a running count in his head as he travelled, believed the sums amounted to a little less than a billion dollars. The money was in continuous motion across Europe and several offshore accounts in the Caribbean, sloshing back and forth like water in the bottom of a rowing boat as if afraid it would be found if it stayed still for too long. Every month, a tiny fraction of it was transferred into a bank in Southend, and from there it was paid out again by Leonidas & Parr, who believed they were acting on behalf of a trust fund amounting to no more than a few hundreds of thousands of pounds.

He watched the solicitor leave the building and cross the street to a little café, then he went back to the desk and opened the red folder.

There were half a dozen sheets of paper in the folder, some of them clearly very old. They were all covered in columns of five-figure groups. The decryption key, which he was clearly expected to have to hand, had not been in the chocolate box, or any of the safety deposit boxes he had visited. Suspecting one final betrayal by either his father or Juhan, Rudi sighed and took out his phone and quickly photographed the sheets, then he dialled a number.

"You should have told me about Mundt," Lev said.

"You didn't need to know," Rudi said. "And hello to you, too."

"I have *petabytes* of data from the prediction engine, some of it involving a *very* exotic form of topology. The Community Man mentioned Mundt. You should have briefed me."

"Professor Mundt is dead," said Rudi. "He's not going to be bothering us again."

"Maybe not, but whoever has his research is going to be able to cause untold *bother*. Do you know what he was doing?"

"I know what people were afraid he could do." Rudi looked

down at the encrypted sheets of paper. "Can you make any sense of what he was up to?"

"It's not my area of mathematics," said Lev. "I can barely skim the surface; I don't even know whether we have all of it. We need to show it to someone who understands this stuff."

Rudi shook his head. "No. Not unless we absolutely have to. Listen, I'm going to send you some images; I need to know if you can decrypt what's on them, okay?"

"Sure, I can do that."

"Good. What about the other thing?" Lev was winnowing the mass of data which had been transmitted by Bradley's phone over the three days before it had fallen silent. Presumably the Englishman had, for routine operational reasons, destroyed it and replaced it with a new one. There was a surprising amount of data, and a lot of it was deeply encrypted; Bradley was obviously a busy man.

"Nothing about the person you're looking for yet, but I picked up a job request you might be interested in."

"I'm a bit too busy to take on a Situation, Lev."

"This one's a request from a government."

"*Les Coureurs* don't work for governments."

"I know, that's why I'm telling you. It's the Japanese."

Rudi looked around the office, thinking. Japanese? Why not? "All right, send me what you've got. Let me know when you know something about the decrypts."

He sent the images, then hung up and picked up the sheets of paper, trying to put all the pieces together in his head, the Ufa explosion, the Realm, the Community, his father's involvement in a billion-dollar trust fund, Mundt's murder. If none of it made sense, perhaps it was because none of it fitted together and he was chasing ghosts. Here he was, sitting in an office in a run-down little town in England, his hands on a quite colossal amount of money. He could just take that money and use it for... something. The problem was, it was already being used for something, something his father had been involved with for a very long time.

Rudi slipped the sheets of paper back into the folder and closed the flap. He went back to the window and looked down on the sparse traffic going along the street. On the other side of the road, the solicitor was just emerging from the café. For almost a century money had been trickling down from the trust fund and his firm had been administering the disbursements quietly, calmly, efficiently, with English discretion. The whole edifice ran like clockwork; there was no need for anyone to intervene. What it was for, what it was *doing*, Rudi had no idea.

His phone buzzed. He read the message Lev had sent him, details of the job the data-scraping operation had picked up, and he rubbed his eyes.

THE PINK PALACE

1.

IT WAS THE first Monday of the month again, and Forsyth went down to the post office to collect his parcel from home.

Leon wasn't doing anything that morning, so they drove down in his van, possibly the only right-hand-drive Ford Transit in the city, certainly the only one with scenes from *Battleship Potemkin* airbrushed on the sides, the pram bouncing forever down the steps on the pavement side to give pedestrians a really good chance to become incensed at the scenes of Bolshevik victory.

The whole inside of the van was lined with fur. The Poles had never quite got the hang of the Western anti-fur movement, declaiming that it was all right for the inhabitants of countries whose Winter temperatures rarely dipped below minus ten to protest against fur coats, but let them get a taste of *real* cold and they'd soon change their tune. Fake fur was still a novelty in Warsaw, and Forsyth was never quite sure about the lining of Leon's van. The interior looked as if he had simply skinned some huge creature and stuck its fur up whole, and there was a faint, disturbing animal smell you noticed when you got in but stopped noticing after a while. Especially when Leon was driving.

"Pedestrian," Forsyth said.

"Where?" Leon tapped the accelerator and the van zipped through an intersection as the lights were changing.

"Somewhere back there."

"Points?" Leon loved *Death Race 2000*.

"We were going too fast to see."

"Bastard." The van almost tipped over on two wheels as it took a corner.

"Doesn't matter," Forsyth said, knuckles popping as he gripped the sissy bar bolted onto the dash. "You missed her anyway."

"Music." Leon punched at the music centre. The van began to thud as if someone was hitting it very hard and very rapidly with a huge rubber mallet. Leon had a directness of spirit that was unusual in contemporary Poles. He loved movies, acceleration, alcohol, loud music, and women, preferably all at once.

Leon liked to introduce himself to people as a political film-maker, but he and his partner made bloodbath movies and hardcore porno remakes of classics. They had one proper Hollywood structure, a late-period Bogart programmed from home-ciné footage taken near the end of the actor's life. Leon had to code everything else himself, from the Lucille Ball they'd used in *Drink My Blood, Vampire Motherfucker*, to the Pola Negri who had appeared in everything from *The Erotic Life of Catherine the Great*, to *Jan Sobieski*, the one straight historical drama they had ever attempted, which had been a resounding flop.

"Post office!" he announced, and stood on the brake. The van left two long stripes of rubber on the asphalt and bounced to a halt.

"Keep the motor running," Forsyth advised, opening the door and jumping out.

Leon gunned the engine. "Never take me alive, old boy," he said in heavily-accented English.

Entering the post office was like coming to a complete stop after travelling at the speed of light. Long queues at all the counters. Marble on the walls. Long dusty slants of sunlight from the windows. Old people everywhere. Only old people ever seemed to use the post office. Old people and him.

As he stood there waiting he began to think that all those old people were watching him. He hadn't done any drugs this morning... well, maybe a spliff or two after breakfast, but that was the only way to survive being driven anywhere by Leon... but it was like these old people all *knew*, like it was tattooed on his face or something, like he was incandescing from all that poor Belarusian grass. Shit. A minor paranoid episode and he hadn't even picked up his parcel yet.

He felt the stares all the way to the poste restante window. The girl behind the counter stared at him too. He handed over his ID and she went away to the big room at the back with all the shelves, and came back with the familiar fat yellow padded envelope. This time, there were also two flimsy blue email forms. Forsyth signed for everything, paid for the emails, and almost ran back out into the sunshine.

"They were all watching me," he said, climbing back into the van.

"Hardly surprising," Leon said. "You're not wearing shoes."

"Bollocks." Forsyth looked down into the footwell and wiggled his toes. "Bollocks. I've been living with you too long." In Autumn, too. You could maybe understand it at the height of Summer, when the city baked in a kind of relentless dusty heat, but in Autumn...?

"*I* didn't make you come out without them," Leon said, affronted. "English bastard."

"*Scottish* bastard," Forsyth corrected absently, tugging at the envelope's tear-strip.

Leon thumped his foot onto the accelerator and the van leaped out into the traffic to a fanfare of horns. "So. What has Big Sister sent this month?"

The strip finally came off and the envelope everted two packages into his lap. One was a kilo-bag of pear drops. Decades of Democracy, and you still couldn't get pear drops anywhere in Poland. Forsyth used to get his monthly ration sent to the block where he lived, but then some lunatic started coming in and setting the communal post-boxes alight, and one morning he came down to find nothing in his box but a fist-sized lump of burnt sugar and charred packaging that stank of lighter fluid, and he'd got his sister to send any future mail poste restante.

The second item was enclosed in that new packaging he'd been reading about, a sort of plastic bag with hollow ribs crisscrossing the outside. You put your fragiles inside, sealed the mouth of the bag with some heat-sealing gadget, and then used a little hand-pump to evacuate the air. As you squeezed the handle some of the air was diverted to inflate the hollow ribs, and what you wound up with was a vacuum-sealed package as rigid as a brick. Forsyth had seen it on a German satellite channel. They'd packed a crystal vase in the stuff and driven a bus over it with no ill-effects.

He held the package up. Inside were six sausage rolls. He smiled. You couldn't get proper sausage rolls in Poland, either; if you could get them at all they were made with frankfurters and short-crust pastry, which wasn't right. He turned the package over. There was supposed to be a little button you pressed to release the vacuum, but you had to be careful because...

There was a pop and the sensation of hundreds of tiny things falling on his head and shoulders.

"Jesus *Maria*!" Leon yelled, and almost crashed the van into a tram.

FORSYTH AND LEON shared a flat in the block that Kieślowski had made famous in *Dekalog*. It had been fashionable, back in the days when Poland was a Slavic Tiger, but it had slowly gone downhill ever since, just like everything else. The lifts never worked and the corridors were covered with derivative graffiti in half a dozen Continental and two African languages. A Ukrainian ragga band calling themselves the Enzyme Kings had taken over the flat next door. Leon loved ragga. The Enzyme Kings' amplifiers didn't have enough volume stops to suit him.

Entering the lobby, Forsyth could hear The Enzyme Kings rehearsing, ten floors above him. The vibrations grew worse as he made his way slowly up the stairs, clutching his bag of pear drops and the remains of the envelope; there was usually a letter inside but he didn't like to read it until he'd had at least one drink.

By the time Forsyth reached his floor, the vibrations of the band were so strong he could feel them in the pit of his stomach. One of the other residents came down the corridor, wagging a finger and talking to him in a presumably angry voice, but Forsyth couldn't hear what she was saying, and he mimed a helpless shrug as they passed. Ukrainians. I mean, who knows?

As he reached his flat, one of those strange moments of synchronicity occurred. The music suddenly cut off, and at that very moment he noticed his front door was open. It was all terribly sinister. He poked his head through the doorway.

"Thought I'd missed you," said Crispin.

"And we couldn't have that, could we," Forsyth said, propping himself against the doorframe and crossing his arms.

Crispin was busy with a game on the coffee table which resembled *Go* but involved arranging numerous tiny coloured spheres, ovals, octagons and assorted 'hedrons on the tabletop. He wasn't doing very well because every time he got a pleasing pattern he popped one of the shapes in his mouth, spoiled the pattern, and had to start over again.

"You started dyeing your dandruff or something?" he asked, looking up and frowning.

Forsyth brushed flakes of puff pastry off his shoulders. "You wouldn't believe me."

Crispin shrugged. "*You* say so."

"So. They let you back into the country, eh?"

"I have to go down the hole, man," Crispin said, going back to his game.

"They'll never let you," said Forsyth. "They've got your eyes recorded on every security system on every building site between here and the Tatras."

Crispin shook his head. "I have to, man." He selected a red sphere, put it in his mouth, and crunched down. "Real important."

"I hear the Ivans are extending the Moscow Metro," Forsyth suggested.

Crispin made a sour face. "Moscow Metro. Shit, man. Been there. Chandeliers." He looked up. "I mean, *chandeliers*?"

Forsyth shrugged.

"*This* is good," Crispin said, poking a yellow rectangle out of the pattern he was making. "I *like* this one."

Forsyth walked over to the sofa and sat down beside Crispin. "What does it do?"

"Can't remember."

Forsyth sat back with his pear drops in his lap. "How did you get in here?"

"Mister Bones let me in." Crispin took from the back pocket of his jeans a little leather case and unzipped it to let Forsyth see the skeleton keys and lockpicks inside. "Say hello to Mister Bones."

"What about the alarm?"

"Ah, shit, man." Crispin reached into a pocket of his greasy combat jacket and took out something that looked a little like an old-fashioned electric shaver, with two long wires terminating in tiny complicated-looking silver plugs dangling from it. "Say hello to Ol' Sparky."

Forsyth took Ol' Sparky and turned it over in his hands. "Have you been mixing with criminal elements?"

Crispin grinned a grin that was more gold than enamel. "Chechens. Technical boys."

"Violent boys."

Still engrossed in his game, Crispin waved a hand.

"Well." Forsyth put the alarm-jumper on the table. "It sounds as if your travels have been more interesting than mine, anyway."

Crispin nodded. His auburn hair had grown down to his shoulders and it didn't look as if he'd washed it in months. He had the calm, trusting, unworried face of a child, and the eyes of a maniac. "Still living with the pornographer?"

"Political film maker."

"Yeah, that." Crispin thought about it. "This his place, yeah?"

"Yes."

Crispin shook his head. "It's not right. Man needs a place of his own. *Landlords*. I mean…"

"Leon's been really good to me," Forsyth told him, as if Crispin didn't know already.

"Whatever." Crispin waved his hand again. "*Try* this, man." He pointed at the yellow rectangle.

Forsyth picked up the pill and put it in his mouth. "What will it do to me?"

Crispin shook his head emphatically. "Can't remember. But I *like* it."

Forsyth swallowed and sat waiting for something to happen. All of a sudden the Enzyme Kings started up again. Against Leon's protests, Forsyth had installed soundproofing, on the grounds that he needed to sleep occasionally, so the Ukrainians' racket was reduced to a manageable level, but the first beat still knocked a print off the wall and made Crispin sit bolt upright, staring wildly about him.

"Jesus *fuck*, I've been hearing that all *afternoon*!" he shouted.

"Neighbours," Forsyth said, feeling himself starting to sink through the substance of the sofa.

"Oh wow," Crispin said, relaxing. "I thought it was *me*..."

Forsyth felt himself smile lazily, felt the sofa gently enfolding him, felt his molecules slipping into the spaces between the sofa's molecules.

"Hey." Crispin jumped to his feet. "Hey, man. Did I show you this?"

"What?" Forsyth asked, still smiling.

Crispin was grinning maniacally. "You'll love this. Just look what I learned to do." He went over to the wall, put out his hand, and pressed the palm against the faded wallpaper.

"Love it," Forsyth giggled.

"Not *that*," Crispin said testily. "*This*." And his arm sank into the wall up to the elbow.

"Oh, shit," murmured Forsyth, and the sofa took him far far away.

IT WAS ONLY slightly harder to get into the site office than it was to get into the country. Fifteen floors up in the Pink Palace, the office was reached by a single private lift, the door in the foyer guarded by two large security men and a retinal reader and the entrance on the fifteenth floor guarded by two more large security men and an electronic door. The site office had seen some interesting times, before the security was put in.

Forsyth showed his pass, bent down and stared unblinking into the reader's cup until the machine gave a little bleep, smiled at the security boys, and went up.

"Whatever you want, I can't give it to you," said Jespersen.

"I don't want anything," Forsyth said.

"All right. I can give you *that*. Have a seat. You look terrible; have you been eating properly?"

Forsyth shrugged. "I've been *eating*."

Jespersen snorted. "Chemicals. Processed food. *Fried* food."

"I like fried food."

"You've come to the right country then." Jespersen pushed with the heel of his hand at the control stick and his wheelchair hummed across the office. "Sometimes I think the Poles would fry salad if it occurred to them."

"I detect negative thoughts."

The wheelchair jerked to a stop by the window. Beyond the glass, Warsaw was spread out like a toy, fading away into flatlands that went all the way to the horizon and then on into Ukraine and Belarus, all fuzzed by the hydrocarbon haze.

"I hate this view," Jespersen muttered.

"I always rather liked it."

"Hah." The chair wheeled round. "You only see it when you visit. I get it every day, when the Reps leave me alone. That's all I get all day, the view and Reps wanting to know when work's starting again."

"Well, now you mention it..."

Jespersen waved his permanently-clubbed fist at Forsyth. "I knew it. And I thought this time you might just want to see how I am."

"You brought the subject up, not me."

"Ah, shit," Jespersen murmured, craning his head to look at the view again. "This fucking thing will never be finished."

"You're too pessimistic, Jens," Forsyth told him.

"I could have dug this system quicker with a soup spoon," said Jespersen. "The Poles don't want a Metro; they just want to annoy the world's tunnel engineers."

"I also want to use your terminal for a few minutes."

Jespersen sighed. "What for?"

"I put out a contact string for some of my boys. I do that now and again, just to keep tabs on where they are, you know?"

Jespersen nodded impatiently. "Yes, yes."

"Well I got a couple of notes yesterday. Do you remember Jonny Gee and Chris Harper?"

"Chris? Jonny? Of course! Great guys! We were always out partying." Jespersen drove the chair forward half a metre, then back again. "How many fucking people do you think are involved in this project? Do you think I'm a personal friend of all of them?"

Forsyth smiled. It was too easy to annoy Jespersen; he really shouldn't do it. He said, "Jonny's wife hasn't heard from him for five months. And Chris's son hasn't heard from him for almost a year."

"This is not the International Red Cross," Jespersen warned in a strangled voice. "Terminal time costs money. I can't just let you use it to reunite errant husbands and fathers with their families."

"The last I heard, they'd taken up a contract on the Line," Forsyth continued patiently. Jespersen nodded wearily; they'd lost hundreds of men to the Line over the years. "And what with the explosion and everything..."

Jespersen sighed. "There are days," he confided, "when I truly wish I was dead."

"More negative thoughts. I expected better from the site manager."

Jespersen glared at him and steered the chair around behind his desk, punched clumsily with his thumb at the tapboard of his desktop, glared at the display. "There is a rumour that the Transport Ministry will grant us some funds to finish the station refurb at Mokotów."

"No good to me," said Forsyth. "The platforms are finished at Mokotów. You need tilers, electricians, people like that. You need Kwak-Kwak's boys."

Jespersen poked the tapboard one more time. "Doesn't matter anyway; nobody knows when we'll get the money. Could be this year, could be next. Probably will be never." He sat back and looked at Forsyth. "Have you any idea how hard this job is?"

"You've always described it very well."

"I must be the only site manager in Europe with eighty percent of his workforce scattered across a dozen countries at any one time. And of course they're all just sitting on their hands waiting for one of the Reps to call and ask them to come back so they can stick up a few tiles or put in a metre or so of wiring before the Government decides it's all costing too much and calls a halt to it again." He glanced at the window as if he suspected the view was mocking him.

"That reminds me. I saw Crispin a couple of nights ago."

Jespersen seemed to sag deeper into his chair. "Where is he?"

"I don't know; I woke up the next morning and he was gone."

"All I needed to make my day complete was to know that maniac is wandering about the city again."

"He says he wants to work."

"No." Jespersen shook his head emphatically. "Absolutely not. If you see him again, you tell him from me that if he goes within a hundred metres of any of the sites I'll have him arrested."

"I told him that, more or less."

"Where's he been, for heaven's sake?"

"We may have discussed that, but I lost track of the conversation."

Jespersen pulled a face. It made his whole head look like a wizened old cider apple. "And if I hear from any of the Reps that their men have been getting drugs from Crispin, I'll have him deported. *And* them."

"I'm sure he realises that, Jens."

"Well just make it very clear to him. Oh, fuck." Jespersen thumped the desktop. "What the fuck does it matter? Let him deal his dope. Let him go back underground. I don't care. I'll die and the fucking thing still won't be finished." He looked at Forsyth. "And you. Stupid Scotchman. Why do you stay in this godforsaken city?"

"I like it here," Forsyth said, and it was only the bald, honest truth. "Now, can I use your terminal?"

CRISPIN CONTENDED THAT the Warsaw Metro was actually a diagram of Polish history. There had been plans for a Metro system as far back as 1918, but after some preliminary excavation work the Great Depression had come along and the project was shelved. The plans were resurrected in 1934, preliminary work began in 1938, the following year the Nazis invaded Poland, and that was that for quite some time.

A number of Metro projects were started and promptly abandoned during the Cold War years, and it wasn't until 1984 that work proper began, although technical difficulties and lack of funds meant that the tunnels crept along at no more than a couple of metres a day and it wasn't until 1995 that the first section of the M1 line, between Kabaty and Politechnika, had opened.

And so it went, year after year. Varsovians loved their slowly-evolving Metro, never suspecting that a storm of new lines, new stations and refurbished old stations lay just a few years in their future, an act of ambition Forsyth thought only Poles could be capable of.

It had been heralded as the biggest civil engineering project in Europe since the Line, which was admittedly quite a high bar to clear. The new government had given it a blaze of publicity, a blizzard of advertising. Venture capital came in from all over the Continent. The virtual reality models were state-of-the-art or better, cutting edge stuff that cost millions to produce, a cats-cradle of multi-coloured lines rotating until they settled beneath the city then exploding outward to reveal a post-post-modern architect's wet dream of stations. It was the most beautiful thing Forsyth had ever seen.

The adverts had brought tunnel men in from all over the world; grizzled veterans who had in their youth worked on the final stages of the Honshu-Hokkaido tunnel, youngsters who had cut their teeth on the Straits Link. Older stations were refitted, new tunnels dug. Eighteen months later the Government changed, the money dried up, and the Metro ground to a halt. The private money disappeared into a fogbank of litigation over broken Government contracts.

Most of the workforce evaporated to other projects, but some stayed. Forsyth found he liked Poland. He was married by then, to a Warsaw girl, and Tomasz, his son, was two months old. He stuck it out, and a year later the Government changed again, suddenly there was money to break ground in Powiśle, and the private investors came out of hiding. Because he had remained in Poland, and kept up a more or less unbroken relationship with the permanent site office, Forsyth found himself promoted to the position of Rep, which meant that when new money was found to start work on the Metro again it was his job to track down the workers for it, wherever they happened to be. He turned out to be rather good at it, and it was better than running a loader fifty metres underground.

Ground was broken in Powiśle, and the Government resigned three months later and the new Government decided it had better things to spend its money on than the Metro.

So it went. The tunnels extended metre by metre, year after year, station by station, Government by Government. By the time Forsyth's marriage had been annulled he realised that Crispin might actually be right. Maybe he *was* involved in writing a secret history of a typically Polish political lunacy. Perhaps, drawn beneath the ground, there really was a secret symbol.

Of course, Crispin also believed that when the Metro was finished the world would end...

LEON CRUISED THE city endlessly, looking for faces. He went out in the early early morning, examining the heaps of rags and humanity huddled in doorways in the New Town, handing out packets of cigarettes and airline miniatures of vodka stolen for him by his cousin's husband, who worked at Okęcie. He walked through the Old Town, snapping tourists with his little Taiwanese digital camera, an antique he'd found at a flea market in front of the Palace of Culture. He was obsessed with finding the perfect face, some distillation of the Polish experience, but he had no clear idea what that would look like. He was so obsessed that he even thought he could find its reflection in the faces of the Japanese tourists who rampaged in crowds through the old Market Square, photographing everything and arguing with the taxi drivers.

He was entirely shameless. Once, half-dozing in front of a film at home, a joint burning down to his knuckles, Forsyth had been jerked back to attention by the face of a ravaged old beggar in the act of hurling a dustbin through a shop window in an unexplained act of vandalism. *His* face. Just what you need to see at half past two in the morning when you're stoned out of your head...

That particular masterpiece, sneaking into the flat on a pirate feed based, as far as they could establish later, in Greater Germany, had been called *Taste The Blood Of Wałęsa*. Leon said it was a political satire and was affronted that the Germans had aired it without paying for the rights. Forsyth took his word for it and threatened to smash his camera if Leon took any more pictures of him.

The new project, as yet unnamed, was ostensibly a life of Stanisław August. The rushes Forsyth had seen were heavily pornographic, and Leon's latest victim was an aged man with long filthy grey hair. He stood on the stage at the far end of Atelier Dudek and watched the camera click from position to position around him on its computerised arm.

"Stand still, fuck you!" Leon yelled, typing furiously behind a bank of tapboards and monitors.

The old man slowly took out a Golden American and lit it. Then he cursed Leon in an dialect so strong Forsyth could only pick out two or three words, none of them nice.

"Actors, eh?" Forsyth said.

"Some people have no gratitude," Leon said. "I've given him a carton of cigarettes, a bottle of Wyborowa and a hundred euros, and he thinks he's Laurence fucking Olivier. Stop doing that."

On the monitor in front of Forsyth, Bogart was doing handstands. Forsyth took his hands off the tapboard. "Sorry."

Leon brushed his fingertips across the editing space on his desk and the camera clicked a fraction of a centimetre to a new position. An image of the old man appeared on the screen, a fully-animated composite of hundreds of images taken over what must have been several sessions. "What about the face, though? What about the face?"

Forsyth squinted down the room. The old man's face was almost hidden by a huge untended explosion of beard. "Nice eyes."

Leon snorted. "You just don't look. Here." He air-typed a couple of short strings of commands and the beard vanished from the screen. Without it, the old man seemed much younger. He had a high-cheekboned, long-nosed face that would have been almost noble if he hadn't looked so tired.

"Nice eyes," Forsyth said again.

"Philistine." The camera moved to a new position. "Just a few more!" Leon called down the studio. "Did you find your missing men?"

Forsyth scratched his head, thinking about his afternoon trawl through the Line's online presence. "It's very odd," he said.

Leon glanced at him. "No luck?"

Forsyth shook his head. "There's no record of them ever going out there. You have to become a citizen to work on the Line, otherwise they won't let you near it."

"So what are you going to do now?"

"I suppose I'll have to go over to Poznań and check the Consulate in person. I can't see what else I can do." He shrugged.

"I thought all the Consulates and Embassies had closed."

"They reopened ages ago. Don't you watch the news?"

"Trains." Leon shrugged.

"Actually," Forsyth said, trying to load his voice with just the right degree of innocent nonchalance, "I popped round to see if you had any spare cash."

Leon sighed, stopped typing and laid his hands in his lap. "Why?" he asked with exaggerated calm.

"I'll need the fare to Poznań."

"Now?" Leon said in a loud voice. "*Right* now?" At the far end of the studio, the old man had started to shuffle off the stage. "Stay *there*!" Leon shouted at him. The old man swore, but he stayed where he was.

"It's my job," Forsyth said. "I'm supposed to look after my men."

"Yeah. But someone else is supposed to be paying you to do it," Leon said briskly, starting to type again. "Not me."

"I'll claim it as expenses when I get back," Forsyth said amiably. "It's just a loan."

"Just like last time?"

Forsyth couldn't remember the last time he'd borrowed money from Leon. Or rather, he couldn't remember one single specific time. They all sort of ran into each other.

"Just like last time," he agreed, not wanting to argue too much with someone he was trying to borrow money from.

Leon nodded. "Right. And last time I waited six weeks to get my money back."

Forsyth remembered the occasion now. He smiled at the old man, who was fidgeting uncomfortably on the stage. Eventually, all the images of him would be combined into a single programmable structure, infinitely manipulable, a virtual actor. It was possible, albeit trickier, to do the same thing with old film footage, but Leon said that involved hours of nitpicking coding and lacked subtlety anyway. Forsyth couldn't tell the difference.

Leon sighed, stopped typing, and pulled out his wallet. "Here," he said, handing over a wad of euro notes. "How much is that?"

Forsyth counted the money. "Four hundred."

"And I want it all back." Leon started to type again. The robot arm suddenly clicked to life once more, making the old man jump. Leon shook his head.

"Thanks." Forsyth put the money in his pocket.

"So, I gather we can't expect any rent from you this month," Leon said after a while.

"Jespersen says not."

"Jespersen says not. Terrific."

Forsyth looked at the screen in front of him. Relieved of input, Bogart was sitting in a cane chair in a large airy room. He was wearing pyjamas and a dressing gown. Atelier Dudek's Bogart had been structured from private footage of the actor near the end of his life, already very ill. Leon had bought it a year or so ago from a man he had met in a bar in Hindenberg. It must have been a pirate; nobody would allow something like this to be released commercially.

"Don't blame me," said Forsyth. "Write to the Transport Ministry."

"You're full of shit. Just like everything in this country."

Forsyth shrugged. "So go and work in Hollywood." It was an old argument; they'd been having it almost as long as Forsyth had been living with Leon. "Crispin's back."

"Oh fuck." Leon rested his fingertips on the tapboard and looked at Forsyth. "When?"

"A couple of days ago. When we went to the post office. He was in the flat when I got home. Didn't you see him?"

Leon looked disgusted. "When I got back that night you were mumbling something about being half-man, half-sofa?"

Forsyth grinned.

Leon shook his head. "You were the only form of life in the flat. And I use the word 'life' in its loosest possible sense."

Forsyth looked down the studio at the old man and the clicking, whirring arm of the camera. "He said he had to go back underground."

"*You* have to go back underground," Leon said without looking at him. "Or at least some of the men you represent."

Forsyth shook his head. "It wasn't work. It sounded more important."

"God damn you, stand *still*!" Leon yelled.

*　　*　　*

2.

ALMOST THREE YEARS after the Ufa explosion, the Line was finally running a more or less normal service in western Europe, across territories which had finally accepted that the incident had been a terrorist attack and that Line trains were as safe as human ingenuity could make them. East of the Urals, though, service was patchy.

Not that Europe as a whole paid much attention. The blast had rendered the countryside uninhabitable for a hundred kilometres in every direction, but the news cycle was always hungry and nothing was happening there now the humanitarian effort in the area had bedded in.

Nobody had ever expected the Line to become a reality. Its partisans boosted it as a project greater even than the railroads that had been driven across America in the nineteenth century, a true post-Millennial undertaking, a great adventure, but when it came to actually building the thing a post-Millennial hangover set in. It had been fine in theory, erstwhile supporters whined, it was a wonderful dream, a marvellous thought-experiment. But nothing more.

Somehow, though, it did become reality. There was a TransEurope Rail Company. Later, when anyone thought about it, it seemed that there had *always* been a TransEurope Rail Company, but nobody could quite remember when it had appeared or where it had come from. It just seemed to spring into existence, fully-formed and ready to lay track, and that was what it proceeded to do.

The Line crept along, year after year. Six of the Company's Chairmen were the victims of assassins, and four more met with accidents that might really have *been* accidents, if you were in a forgiving frame of mind. One vanished without trace on the journey between his home in Madrid and his office five minutes' drive away. According to one online wag, the last public works project to have resulted in such loss of life was the Pyramids.

FLURRIES OF SNOW were dancing in the air when Forsyth got off the train in Poznań. He took a taxi from the station to the Poznaśki, a little hotel just off the Market Square, went up to his room, and stood at the window watching the snow drift down. Winter was early; in a few days most Polish cities would be at least ankle-deep in polluted snow and filthy slush and the populace would be in the process of decamping to the ski-slopes of Zakopane and Szczyrk. Leon called it *snow-frenzy* and was proud to boast that he had never allowed his feet anywhere near a pair of ski-bindings.

Snow-frenzy. Forsyth smiled, went over to the phone on the bedside table, and dialled.

"What."

"It's me."

"Oh, well, hello me," Leon said in a bantering tone of voice. "Are we enjoying our holiday?"

"It's snowing."

"Don't move, damn you!" Leon yelled. "Sorry," he said in a quieter voice. "Not you."

"Am I interrupting something important?" Forsyth asked, grinning.

"I've found this wonderful face; too good to lose. I might be able to recast Sobieski."

Forsyth carried the phone back to the window and looked down into the street. A tram was just pulling into the stop across the road. The doors opened and disgorged figures with their shoulders hunched up against the snow and wind. The snow was making fuzzy haloes around the streetlights.

"Crispin came round this morning," said Leon. "Just after you left."

"What did he want?"

"Well... hard to tell," Leon said. "He wasn't speaking any language I've ever heard before."

Forsyth laughed.

"It's okay for you to laugh, you bastard," Leon said. "You didn't have to try and make sense of what he was saying. I mean, we *talked* to each other, but I think we were having two entirely separate conversations."

"I'll see him when I get back. Anything else?"

"Ewa phoned."

Oh dear. "Is she back?"

"She's back and she wants to know why you weren't waiting at Gdańska with your tongue hanging out when her train came in."

"She didn't tell me when she was due back."

"Well, maybe if you had a *phone* like everyone else she'd have been able to let you know she was coming."

"You know how I feel about phones," Forsyth said.

"Fucking dinosaur."

"Was she very angry?"

"I learned some new swearwords," said Leon.

Oh well. "I'll see her when I get back, too."

Silence, at the other end of the line.

"I've got a job to do, Leon," Forsyth said after a while. "Don't give me a hard time."

"Oh, stop whining," Leon said, and hung up.

OFFICIALLY, MOST EUROPEAN governments affected an air of enlightened bemusement when it came to matters pertaining to the Line. It seemed to serve no rational purpose; it carried freight but hardly enough to pay its operating costs, and passengers had to take out citizenship before they could even set foot on a platform. It was just *there*, nobody knew why.

Unofficially, there was a certain cachet involved in having a Line station on your territory. It was irrational, if you thought about it, but there was something about the Line which made it seem important. Most countries had at least two Line Consulates. Some polities had three. Poland had one.

Polish television still had the charming habit of broadcasting debates from the Sejm, and in his long hours of inactivity Forsyth had become something of a student of them. While nothing was ever said straight out – which was unusual in itself in Poland – it was obvious to him that it annoyed Poles to have only one Line Consulate – and that not in the capital. It was, he thought, regarded as something of an insult, as if the Line saw Poland as just a couple of borders to be crossed on the way from Greater Germany to Ukraine and points east, and the Consulate in Poznań little more than a necessity, unpalatable but unavoidable.

As if determined to rub it in, the Line hadn't even bothered to be subtle about its incursion into Poznań; they had just bought one of the old inner-metropolitan stations and a couple of hundred hectares of land around it, demolished most of the surrounding buildings, thrown several tens of kilometres of smartwire around the whole thing, and declared it sovereign territory. Forsyth sometimes wondered if the Line's rulers occasionally tuned in to the Polish version of *Today In Parliament*, and if they chuckled to themselves when they did.

Apart from Hindenberg, the ethnic Silesian homeland in Upper Silesia, and the Pomeranian Republic, there were no polities on Poland's territory. Poland's borders had been going backward and forward for hundreds of years. For quite a large part of its history, the country hadn't existed at all as a geographical entity, and Poles liked to remind everyone that it was here to stay now and ready to take its rightful place in Europe. They also took a certain delight in the irony that, just as Poland consolidated its nationhood after so many years, Europe was fracturing around it. The media liked to gesture casually but with no small smugness at Greater Germany, which was a continually-simmering landscape of volatile little nations.

To the Polish Government, the Line was an abomination, a foreign country that had come here in the guise of a railway track, literally laid across their territory sleeper by sleeper and rail by rail. And the continuing diplomatic snubs only made matters worse.

Forsyth had a sneaking admiration for the Line. It was, when you boiled off all the diplomatic bollocks, an astounding work of civil engineering, a Grand Gesture from a continent which seemed to be putting most of its energies these days into subdividing itself into progressively smaller and smaller states. He thought that one day the Line might be the only thing holding all those little states together, like the cord running through a string of pearls.

"No," SAID THE official.

"Beg pardon?" asked Forsyth.

The official, a little Iberian with a cast in his left eye and an expensive wool-knit suit, looked up from the pad on his desk. "No," he said again.

"I don't understand."

The Iberian sighed patiently. "We have no record of these men," he explained.

Forsyth thought about it. He'd been kicking his heels for three days at the Poznaśki, waiting for someone from the Line to see him, and while Poznań was a nice enough town and the food at the hotel was excellent, he was running out of money.

"They told their families they were enrolling for work on the Line," he said finally.

The Iberian gave a little wince. "The records of the TransEurope Rail Route," he said, emphasising the name for Forsyth's benefit, "show no mention of these men." The Line actually existed as two entities. One, the sovereign nation, was the Independent Trans-European Republic; the other, the TransEurope Rail Route, was the infrastructure, the tracks themselves. It was sometimes easy to mix them up.

Forsyth rubbed his face. The room they were sitting in was small and modern and unfashionably bare. Its only furniture was a desk and two upright chairs. He had the impression it wasn't used very often. Through the window behind the Iberian, he could see a seething curtain of windblown snow that occasionally drew aside to reveal another building across a dreary courtyard, all net-curtained windows and dreary balconies.

"Why would they tell their families that they were going to work on the TransEurope Rail Route if they weren't?" he asked.

The Iberian shrugged and spread his hands.

"They were going to work on the extension in Magadan," Forsyth ventured. "It's a long way away. A bit wild."

The Iberian nodded sadly, as if disappointed to find a suspected character flaw in the man sitting opposite him. "You must appreciate, Mister Forsyth, that a project on the scale of the TransEurope Rail Route could not hope to continue if its farthest-flung sites were hopelessly out of contact with its central authority." He clasped his hands on top of his pad. "We are aware of every citizen working for the Company." He lifted his clasped fists and lowered them slowly back onto the pad. "And these two men are not among them."

Forsyth sat where he was on the uncomfortable chair.

The Iberian unclasped his hands and twitched one shirt cuff

to reveal a silver Piaget. "I am sorry we could not be of more assistance," he said, squinting at the watch. "And I am afraid I have another meeting scheduled."

"I know these two men," Forsyth said, leaning across the desk, tapping the pad, and enjoying the Iberian's unexpressed displeasure. "They're reliable, hard-working men. If they said they were working on the Line, that's where they were."

The Iberian stood. "Mister Forsyth," he said stiffly, "the citizenship list of the TransEurope Rail Route is a matter of public record." This was not entirely true. If you looked closely enough at the citizenship list, and were prepared to do some intensive cross-referencing, many of the names turned out to be sockpuppets and aliases. The Line welcomed the wealthy and hard-working, and was sometimes not too fussy about their pasts. "If your missing gentlemen are not included in it, they were never citizens. And if they were never citizens, they never worked for us."

"Surely it's better to let their families know what's happened. That would be the most important thing. In the case of compensation, I'm sure we could reach an understanding."

The Iberian shook his head and scooped the pad up from the desk. "Understanding." He dropped the pad into a jacket pocket. "These men were never citizens of the TransEurope Rail Route, Mister Forsyth. We do not know who they are or where they are. I suggest you consult their families and their creditors for possible reasons for their disappearance." He walked to the door and opened it. "It has been our experience that many people who wish to escape their familial and financial responsibilities give us as their last address." He favoured Forsyth with a frosty little smile. "It seems that we have become, in the popular imagination at least, a modern Foreign Legion, a place where people go to forget, or at least to become forgotten. It is rather tiresome, if I may be frank with you." He consulted his watch again. "And it takes up more of our time than we can spare."

Forsyth sat where he was. He was a tall man with hunched shoulders and a full head of prematurely-white hair. He had found that sometimes his physical presence could be intimidating if he remained still and looked determined.

The Iberian said, "It cannot have escaped your attention that the Independent Trans-European Republic is experiencing a period of flux."

That much was an understatement. "I'm grateful for your time, if that's what you mean," said Forsyth.

"There is no work in Magadan at the moment," the Iberian continued. "Our citizens there have been redeployed to carry out routine maintenance in other parts of the Republic while this situation continues. If your missing men were ever in Magadan, they are not there now."

"If they have been redeployed, there must be records."

"There are," said the Iberian. "And their names are not among them."

Forsyth got up from his chair. "I didn't get your name," he said.

"Perfectly true," said the Iberian.

3.

THE ENGLISH PUB on Senatorska had draught Guinness and seventeen different brands of vodka. Marek, the owner, had spent a year behind the bar of a pub in Darlington. He had returned with a shining vision of what an English pub should be like, but he'd been unable to get hold of most of the requisite fixtures and fittings. The seating was upholstered in an awful scarlet velour and there was a dart board, but he'd had to take the darts away after one particularly horrific brawl. He'd wanted a pool table, but the nearest one was in Frankfurt-an-der-Oder and would have cost half his annual income.

"Why do we always come here?" asked Ewa.

"Reminds me of home," Forsyth said.

"You told me you hated your home."

"That's what I meant."

Ewa was Forsyth's occasional girlfriend. She painted huge abstracts on panels of plasterboard in an abandoned flat in the east of the city, and sold them for unlikely amounts in the galleries on

Nowy Świat. She was just back from an exhibition in Berlin, and as usual when she returned home she was full of loathing for Poland.

Not that it was difficult to loathe Poland, sitting in the English Pub. The place was full of the usual career drinkers, a few sharp-suited young entrepreneurs, a couple of tourists who had taken a wrong turn or got on the wrong tram and were sitting wondering where they were and what the hell they were doing there. Over in a corner, a little group of Georgians, with wan, hard faces and huge moustaches, was drinking for free. Marek paid them a tenth of his monthly takings and as much free vodka as they could drink, in return for them not making his elbows bend in the wrong direction.

"Stop staring at them," Ewa said. "They'll come over."

"I'm not staring." Forsyth said, but he'd been watching the Georgians almost all night, because the only one of the little group without a moustache was Crispin.

"I hate that man," said Ewa.

"Mm," Forsyth replied. "Pardon?"

Ewa snorted. She downed her glass of Wyborowa in one swallow and glared at him. She had been glaring at him ever since he got back from Poznań. Ewa liked to be met at the station or the airport when she returned from her foreign trips.

"I already told you I was sorry," Forsyth reminded her.

"Yes," she said, unimpressed. "And stop watching that horrible man, or I will leave."

Crispin was laughing and shouting, completely relaxed. He was pouring drinks, joining in jokes. Now he got up. One of the Georgians got up too. They hugged. They kissed. Crispin came over to Forsyth and Ewa's table and pulled up one of the velour-covered stools.

"Hey, Ewa," he said. "How they hanging?"

"I'm going home," Ewa announced, standing up.

"Um," said Forsyth.

Ewa looked down at him. "Well?"

Forsyth looked from Ewa to Crispin, back to Ewa. "I need to talk to Crispin."

"Fine." Ewa grabbed her shoulder bag and stormed out, shoving aside one particularly amorous drunk as she made her way to the door.

Crispin beamed beatifically and waggled his fingers at her. "'Bye, Ewa."

"Thanks for that, Crispin," Forsyth said. "Why couldn't you have stayed over there with your mates, eh?"

Crispin looked over his shoulder. The Georgians were drinking and shouting again. "Good ol' boys," he said, almost nostalgically.

"Crispin, what do you want?"

"Been looking for you," Crispin said, waving to the Georgians.

"I've been in Poznań."

"Yeah?"

"Yeah."

Crispin turned to look at him, his expression suddenly serious. "Ever hear of Babykiller?"

Forsyth put his hand to his face and said, "Oh."

"It's his stash, man," he heard Crispin say. "I put it down the hole last year. I have to get it back."

Forsyth looked up, suddenly tired. "You decided to get involved with Babykiller?"

Crispin made a sour face. "I never expected the fucking government to resign, man."

"You should always expect the government to resign, Crispin."

"Ah," Crispin waved a hand dismissively, "I thought they were there another eight, ten months at least. I had the stuff, I stashed it, then the government went tits-up and we were pulled out of the hole. I never got the chance to bring it up."

"Well, at least it's *safe*," Forsyth mused.

Crispin gave Forsyth his hard stare. It made him look vaguely myopic. "Will you help me or will I have to do it myself?"

"You'll get yourself arrested."

"So help me."

Forsyth sighed. "How long do you have?"

"Tomorrow morning. Then I'm hamburger."

"Well thanks for giving me so much time to get ready," Forsyth said.

"But you'll help, right?"

Forsyth looked at his watch. "Where is it?"

* * *

"JESPERSEN SAYS HE'LL have you arrested if you go near any of the sites," Forsyth said, his breath wisping in the air in front of his lips.

"Fuck him," Crispin muttered, each word a distinct little cloud of fog.

Behind them, somebody laughed drunkenly. Forsyth looked round, but the street was too badly-lit to make out who had made the noise.

"You're some kind of fucking nutcase to get involved with Babykiller, Crispin."

Crispin grunted. "Not that you're being judgemental or anything."

During its various travails, Poland had always thrown up dark legends, and Babykiller was the latest and possibly greatest of them all. Shadowy, vague, seemingly unarrestable. Possibly one man, possibly a collective of underworld masterminds, possibly neither. One story said he was a Lapp, from up North of Rovaniemi. Older Poles, who had never trusted their leaders no matter who those leaders happened to be, contended that Babykiller was government-sponsored, but did not specify which government in particular. Crispin was the only person Forsyth had ever encountered who claimed to have had personal dealings with Poland's demon mastermind.

"It was a dead drop," Crispin muttered. "The stuff was left in a luggage locker at Centralna. I never met him. What, you think he's stupid? You think *I'm* stupid?"

"I don't know about him," Forsyth said. "You already know what I think about *you*."

"To see Babykiller is to die," Crispin said stoically.

"Must be tough on his barber."

"You're so fucking funny."

"I'm also fucking helping you out of the kindness of my fucking heart, and don't you fucking forget it."

"Yeah, all right, man," Crispin said, all contrition. "I'm wound up, yeah? Got a lot riding on this deal, okay?"

"Not least the continued custody of your balls."

Crispin laughed nervously. "Yeah. Right. See, the deal's like this. Babykiller lets me have the stuff on account and I offload it on somebody. I got to offload it for a certain figure, right? But anything over that I get to keep. Can't fail."

Forsyth could think of any number of ways it could fail. He said, "You've sold it to the Georgians, haven't you."

Crispin smiled.

Forsyth stopped on the darkened street and stared at Crispin. "How many times have I told you?" he shouted. "Russians, Chechens, Ingush, Georgians. They're all the same. You can't trust any of them."

"I think you're a bigot, you know?" Crispin said calmly.

"At least I'm not wandering around Warsaw in fear for my life from Babykiller and the Georgians. Oh Christ." Something had just occurred to Forsyth. "Not a fucking war."

Crispin shrugged. "Dunno if you could call it a *war.*"

"Well what in Christ's name *would* you call it?"

Another shrug. "I guess they have a lot of old scores to settle. Hey, I only sell the stuff. If they sell it on and use the proceeds to buy weapons of mass destruction, that's their business. I don't get involved with the end-user thing."

Forsyth raised his hands in surrender. "Sorry, Crispin. I'm not getting involved in financing a ruddy war."

"Oh man," Crispin said sadly. "They don't like the fucking Russians. I don't like the fucking Russians. *You* don't like the fucking Russians, as I recall."

Forsyth remembered a long couple of months working on the Moscow Metro extension. Chandeliers and all. He stood listening to the night.

"I know you loved the Moscow Metro, man," Crispin said, "but this is business."

"You can't trust the Georgians, Crispin," Forsyth said. "All they want to do is kill Russians."

"I'm not going to blame them for that," Crispin sniffed. "Evil empire and etcetera, right? Just doing my bit for the Cold War a few years too late, right?"

If anything was guaranteed to piss Forsyth off, it was people trying to play Central European politics. He had hated that sort of thing even before he had come to Poland. He said, "Nobody wins in a situation like this, Crispin."

Crispin laughed. "You poor sap, Snowy. Everybody wins. Babykiller gets his money and is happy, I get my money and am happy, the Georgians get their guns and get to kill Russians and are happy."

"You're just spreading sunshine around Central Europe, in other words," Forsyth said.

"This is a complicated region," Crispin allowed sagely.

"Well, thank you, AJP Taylor."

"Don't try to talk me out of this, Snowy," Crispin said seriously. "I'm in too deep."

"And stop calling me Snowy. You know I hate that."

STARE MIASTO, THE Old Town Station, had turned out to be the most contentious of the stations in the Metro project. In 1944, after the Uprising, the Germans had taken their anger out on the Old Town and completely rubbled it. When the War was over, the Poles had rebuilt the Old Town. The original plans had been destroyed, the story had it, so they did it from Canaletto paintings. Poles could work miracles when they put their minds to it, although the reconstruction was undertaken using cheap materials and the area was starting to take on a rather shabby look. Still, hundreds of thousands of tourists still came each year, took their photos, and left again, believing they had been looking at the original buildings.

Varsovians tended to be protective of the Old Town, and hands were flung in the air when the plans for Stare Miasto Station were produced. The original plans had called for extensive excavation and selective demolition, and a ghastly faux-mediaeval edifice to house the station concourse. Escalators. Beltways. Forsyth couldn't remember who the architects were – some Swedish firm, he thought – but he thought the place should have won them some kind of award for the collision of kitsch with state-of-the-art transport technology.

After a number of rowdy public meetings and demonstrations, the Swedes had had the contract taken away from them. A new firm – Forsyth didn't have a clue who they were – came in with a huge amount of capital and produced plans which involved the minimum of disturbance. Everything underground; discreet entrances; no beltways. Work was begun – got quite a long way, relatively speaking – and then the Government changed, and after a few weeks the workers Forsyth represented began to drift away across Europe to other projects.

Forsyth and Crispin walked across the Square to one of the station entrances. The entrance was covered with a small, notionally temporary, concrete blockhouse, its sides decorated with brightly-coloured but unimaginative graffiti and peeling flyposters advertising films and rock bands Forsyth had never heard of.

There was a box mounted on one wall of the blockhouse at about head height. Forsyth checked the lock's slot to make sure nobody had poured superglue into it, then swiped his key-card through it.

"High tech, man," Crispin murmured. "Fucking love it."

"Shut up, Crispin," Forsyth said. The front of the box hinged down, exposing a keypad, half a dozen or so little black cubes and the grey rubber cup of a retinal reader. Forsyth typed his security code into the keypad and put his eye to the cup. There was the customary flash of blood-red light that left him blinking away afterimages. After a moment there was a snap of magnetic locks and a little door popped open low on the side of the blockhouse.

"Open sesame," Crispin said triumphantly. "Fuckin' A, Snowy."

"I told you, don't call me that." He unplugged one of the little black memory modules and pocketed it. "Come on."

They ducked through the doorway and Forsyth pulled the door shut behind them while Crispin took a heavy rubberised torch from the charging rack on the wall. "Down here," he said, waving the beam of the torch towards the escalators.

"Just a second." Forsyth popped the cover off the alarm box and switched the system off. "Okay."

They walked down the escalators to the big drum-shaped concourse. The torchlight shone on bright white tile.

"Nice work," Crispin said, looking about him. "Kwak-Kwak's boys do this?"

Forsyth nodded. "Some of them. He lost a lot of them to the Denver Metro."

Crispin snorted. "Yeah, well, at least that had a fifty-fifty chance of getting finished, didn't it."

"Why didn't you go back for that one?"

"Ah." Crispin, his face cast in planes of light and shadow by the torch, looked sad. "Persona non grata back home."

"Oh."

"Not that I'd want to go back. I mean, who wants to go to *Colorado*?" He gestured in the direction of the escalators grouped in the middle of the booking hall. "Down there. Eastbound platform."

"I didn't think you ever got this far into town," Forsyth said as they went deeper into the station.

"I didn't," said Crispin. "I was two stations up the line, got in on one late shift and walked down the tunnel."

Forsyth thought about it. "That's, what, two kilometres?"

"Almost three. I figured if anybody ever found the stuff they'd never be able to connect it to me. Nobody would be crazy enough to walk that far just to stash something."

"It's a long walk," Forsyth agreed. The tunnels were full of machinery and equipment and usually ankle-deep in water until the walls had been properly sealed. A six klick round-trip under those conditions would have taken most of the night.

"Well, a man's gotta do, et cetera." Crispin shone the torch on the white-tiled curve of the escalator shaft. "That really is a lovely shape," he said. "Who got the design contract in the end?"

"No idea."

"The Swedes got shafted, yeah?"

Forsyth nodded.

"I met one of their guys once, when they were surveying." Crispin shook his head. "Fucking spooky, man. So fucking *clean*, you know what I mean?"

"I never met any of them."

"Wow." Crispin's eyes widened at the memory. "Everything was *ironed*. I never saw so many sharp edges on a man. It wasn't natural."

They were at the bottom of the escalators now. A series of low, arched tunnel entrances fanned out along a lovely curved wall of white tile. Forsyth gestured towards the one that led to the Eastbound platform and they walked through it.

He'd only been here a couple of times before, and he still hadn't quite managed to work out how the unknown architects had achieved this little miracle here under the streets of Old Warsaw. All the foot tunnels leading off from the bottom of the escalators were exactly the same length. They led away from each other in absolutely straight lines, neither rising nor falling, at roughly thirty-degree intervals. And each one ended in a different Metro platform. Forsyth had seen the design drawings, and it still seemed to him that by rights all four foot tunnels should emerge on the same platform. He couldn't work it out.

Sometimes, when he thought about it, he remembered the first time he ever went underground, digging the London Underground extension out to Reading, and that solid dread of working with hundreds of tonnes of earth between him and sunlight. The foot tunnels at Stare Miasto made him feel the same way, as if he was in an alien environment.

"Why did you up and leave like that, by the way?" he asked.

"Weird shit," Crispin muttered, which was his shorthand for anything he didn't like. "Really weird shit."

"Oh."

"I was out at Mokotów one shift and the place was full of cammo dudes."

Forsyth stopped. "Beg pardon?"

"Cammo dudes," Crispin said. More shorthand. He sighed. "Uniformed men with weapons," he translated for Forsyth's benefit.

"Oh, come on," Forsyth said, suspecting a heavily chemically-promoted hallucination.

"I'm telling you. I saw these guys down in the tunnel at Mokotów and I thought the Poles had brought the Army in to clean the place up."

Forsyth laughed.

"You may think it's funny, man," Crispin said. "I thought the bastards were coming for me. You know that Mankind's sixth sense is self-preservation? Well I exercised it. Goodbye, au 'voir, etcetera."

"What did they look like?" Forsyth asked. "Yellow? Lots of feathers?" Crispin had once confided that he had seen Big Bird in one of the unfinished stations out in Skorosze. Although, as Leon had later pointed out, that was at a time when you were more likely to see Big Bird than a Metro train out there.

"Black cammo suits," Crispin said in a serious voice. "Those little fucking machine pistols that can turn a car into a colander."

Forsyth shook his head. The Metro wasn't organised to have a standing staff of security guards; it relied on electronic security, which was considerably cheaper and never slept. The idea of armed men wandering around in the tunnels was hilarious. He remembered a previous paranoid episode of Crispin's, which had involved an absolute certainty that Wolfgang Amadeus Mozart had come to Warsaw to assassinate him.

"I have no idea why you're still my friend," he said to the figure walking in front of him, remembering other paranoid moments, other early-morning excursions for vaguely-explained purposes.

"You collect strays," Crispin said, which was not the answer Forsyth had been expecting.

"I'm sorry?"

"You collect strays. That's why you became a Rep. You like to look after people who have nowhere else to go." He said it with such certainty that Forsyth didn't know how to respond. "This way," said Crispin, turning right when they reached the Eastbound platform.

Forsyth paused at the entrance and watched the bobbing light of the torch silhouette Crispin. He looked around the platform. Crispin was right, Kwak-Kwak's gang of itinerant Japanese tilers and platform men had done good work here. Kwak-Kwak's boys were real artisans. Tiling work had some sort of Zen significance for them. You couldn't hurry them, but they always came in under budget and ahead of schedule, and they came out of the hole at the end of every shift smiling secret little smiles, as if they had just solved some intensely personal puzzle.

"Hey."

Forsyth looked along the platform, suddenly aware that he was in almost total darkness. At the far end, the light of Crispin's torch lit a circle of tile and track and the black throat of the Metro tunnel.

"Are you playing with yourself or something back there?" Crispin called irritably.

"No," Forsyth said, and his voice echoed along the platform.

"I mean," Crispin said, turning away and shining his torch

into the Metro tunnel, "I thought we came here for a purpose or something."

Forsyth wandered along the platform until he was standing just behind Crispin. "Will this take long?"

Crispin shook his head.

"Only I've got a hot date with Ewa. Or I did until you turned up."

"Your problem, Snowy," Crispin said, hopping down off the platform and onto the trackbed, "is that you think with your dick."

"That's not true."

"Oh yes it is." Crispin shone the torch up at him. "Remember that girl over in Wola? What was her name?"

"Agatka."

"Yeah. Agatka." Crispin swung the torch down and shone it directly into the tunnel. The light picked out stacks of rail, piles of concrete sleepers, equipment lockers. "You nearly lost your head over that one, remember?"

"No I didn't." Forsyth jumped down beside Crispin.

Crispin said, "Hah!" and his voice echoed dully along the empty station. "Her daddy was some bigwig at Ursus and there was this job going and you were going to take it and spend the rest of your life making fucking tractors, man, I remember. Tractors! Take more than *love* to make *me* do that."

Forsyth shrugged. "You never met her."

"Good thing, too. I'd have read her the Riot Act." Crispin set off into the tunnel. "Trying to take a man out of the hole and put him onto a production line. Jesus."

"It was a managerial job," Forsyth said. "I wouldn't have been on the production line."

"Whatever."

"You'd have tried to sleep with her," Forsyth said, following him. "You always try to sleep with my girlfriends."

"No," Crispin said, shaking his head. "Don't remember that one, Snowy."

They walked for some minutes, picking their way past parked tunnel tractors and redundant pumps. A fat cable ran along the ceiling, supported by staples driven into the tunnel segments. It carried a line of daylight-emulation lamps but there was no power down here at the moment to light them. The only illumination came from the bobbing light of the torch as Crispin swung it left and right and up and down, seemingly at random.

"You tried to sleep with Magda," Forsyth said.

"No I didn't."

"Yes you did. After we got married she said you'd tried to talk her into bed, you bastard."

"Here," Crispin said, shining the torch on the side of the tunnel.

"Don't deny it," Forsyth said. "You tried to get Magda into bed, didn't you?"

"Snowy," Crispin said with an irritable sideways glance. "Let's keep our minds on the matter in hand, yeah?"

"You dragged me down here," Forsyth muttered. "I don't see why you should have a good time."

Crispin stepped over to the wall of the tunnel, took a multitool from his pocket, and used one of its driver bits to start loosening an inspection panel from a utilities conduit. "I'm not having a good time."

"Did you ever try it on with Ewa?"

Crispin laughed and carried on unscrewing the panel.

Forsyth put his hands in his pockets and looked first one way then the other along the tunnel. The ribbed walls vanished into the darkness on either side. He whistled a few flat notes.

Crispin lowered the inspection panel to the trackbed and reconfigured the tool as a wrench. He reached inside the inspection hatch and started to unbolt something.

"How did you get into this, anyway?" Forsyth asked.

"Get into what?"

"Mixed up with Babykiller. The Georgians."

"These things just happen, Snowy." Crispin gave a little grunt and Forsyth heard something fall and rattle inside the conduit. "Shit."

"How do you mean?"

"What?"

"How do 'these things just happen'?"

"Oh, I dunno." Crispin was up on tiptoes now, both arms and his head and shoulders inside the inspection hatch. He had the torch inside as well, and his body was blocking most of the light. His voice sounded flat and dull inside the conduit. "Word gets about, the stuff comes down to me, I find a buyer, the money goes back up to Babykiller. That's how *these things* just happen."

Forsyth looked at his watch, pushed the light button. He had to tilt it to make out the digits. "It's getting late, Crispin."

"Are you charging me by the hour?"

"Very funny." Forsyth tapped his toes and whistled another couple of notes. "It's taking a bloody long time, though."

"Jesus Christ, Snowy," Crispin sighed from inside the conduit. "I think I preferred it when you were bitching about your women."

Forsyth went for a little walk. Half a dozen paces out, half a dozen paces back. "Did I tell you I saw Jens the other day?"

"Yeah, I think so. How is the old bastard?"

"Same as ever." How much longer was this going to take?

"Ever worry that it might happen to you?"

"What might happen to me?"

By the sound of his voice, Crispin was at full stretch inside the conduit. Occasionally there was a metallic rattle as something fell. "One day you're working your happy little heart out, the next there's some snafu and if you're *lucky* you wind up in a wheelchair behind a desk."

Jespersen had had the misfortune to be working on Copenhagen's metro when the belt of a spoil conveyor tore and one end whistled up the tunnel and broke his back. "Can't say I ever thought very much about it," Forsyth said.

"Yeah. Well that's always been your problem."

"I thought my problem was that I think with my dick."

"That too." The light inside the conduit became stronger and stronger, and Crispin emerged from the hatch. In one hand he held the multitool and the torch. In the other was a small opaque plastic envelope. He grinned triumphantly.

"Excuse me for saying so, but that doesn't look like an awfully large amount of drugs," Forsyth observed.

"Who mentioned drugs?" said Crispin. "Did I mention drugs?"

"Well, no. I just sort of –"

"You just sort of assumed, Snowy." Crispin waved the torch at him. "You just sort of assumed that because Good Old Crispin was involved it had to be drugs."

"It seemed a pretty safe bet," Forsyth agreed.

"Well," Crispin said, and then Forsyth was lying on the trackbed, his ears ringing, with no clear memory of how he had got there.

He swallowed a couple of times to try and clear his ears, and the ringing diminished slightly. He lay very still, feeling bruised places on his back and legs. The torch was lying a few metres away, and in its beam he could see the plastic envelope wedged under the wheels of a loader. Crispin was gone.

Forsyth sat up very slowly, completely at a loss. One moment Crispin had been talking to him, the next he was lying on the ground. His head and chest hurt and he could taste blood in his mouth, and there was a wet, earthy smell in the air that hadn't been there earlier.

He got up and went over and picked up the torch. He shone it around, but there was no sign of Crispin, though there were some fresh-looking marks on some of the tunnel lining. He retrieved the envelope and stuffed it in a pocket.

"Crispin?" he called. A bolt of pain went up one side of his neck, making him wince, but he called Crispin's name again. "You utter *bastard*!" he shouted, but no reply came. "Crispin!"

He listened, and this time he thought he heard someone moving in the stationward section of tunnel.

"You fucker, Crispin," he muttered, starting to walk towards the noise. It was then that he happened to glance down and saw a tiny ruby-red dot dancing on his chest. He was so puzzled by this that he didn't watch his footing, and he tripped over something and went headlong onto the trackbed, and at the same moment the tunnel exploded with hammering noise and light.

"Fuck!" Forsyth screamed, and rolled behind a skip. "Fuck!" The tunnel was full of ricocheting fragments of concrete and metal, and Forsyth tried to curl himself into a ball of zero size and mass.

At length, the storm abated and silence fell again on the tunnel, though Forsyth's ears had begun to ring once more. Very slowly, he put his head around one side of the skip, and in the gap between it and the tunnel wall he could see the bobbing light of torches back towards the station. Very carefully, trying not to make any noise and at the same time trying to keep the skip between himself and whoever was in the station, he began to move back down the tunnel. He couldn't stop thinking about Crispin's story of the cammo dudes, men with little guns that could perforate a motor car like a teabag.

At first he moved on hands and knees, but that wasn't anything like quick enough to suit him, so he got up in a kind of crouching run, checking frequently for any more of those red dots of light on his body. The tunnel curved twenty metres or so outside the station, and when he had the bulk of the tunnel wall between him and whoever was back there he got up from the crouch and started to run. Very quietly.

Stare Miasto was an interchange station between the east-west and north-south lines. There were utilities tunnels every hundred and fifty metres, connections between the east-west and north-south main tunnels in case of fire or some other disaster. Forsyth ducked into one of them, switched off the torch, and pressed himself up against the wall, listening. No sound behind him, no light in the main tunnel.

He picked his way carefully down the cross-tunnel, checking each step before he put his foot down. Once he thought he heard a sound behind him, and froze against the curving wall. He waited for a very long time, trying to control his panting breath, but there were no more noises, and he set out again, feeling each step with his toes for obstructions.

His hand encountered a gap in the tunnel wall, and he felt a breath of cold damp air on his face from somewhere down below. This was one of the connections between the four tunnels, a ramp down to the north-south tracks. He stepped through the entrance. The ramp was a spiral, broad enough to allow purpose-designed emergency vehicles to go up or down with casualties or emergency workers. He went down the ramp, listening all the time for sounds behind him.

Whatever had happened, whoever was in the east-west part of the station, he seemed to have left them behind. No sounds except for his ragged breathing. He stopped for a moment and his knees suddenly refused to respond to conscious commands and he slid down onto the tunnel floor. All of a sudden he was exhausted. It was all he could do to keep his head from nodding and his chin from sinking down onto his chest. What he wanted, most of all, at a truly fundamental level far far below conscious thought, was to go to sleep and wake up tomorrow in his own humble but warm and secure bed and know that this whole evening was a nightmare...

A noise lifted him out of his faint, so suddenly that he jerked his head back and banged it against the tunnel wall. It was such a familiar noise that if some remote corner of his mind hadn't been keeping track of where he was he might have ignored it altogether. It was the sound of an underground train, coming up the ramp from below. Except, as that remote corner of his mind reminded him, there were no underground trains on this stretch of line.

He struggled to his feet and carried on down the ramp. He had been walking for a couple of minutes before he realised he could see the walls of the ramp; there seemed to be a faint, lambent glow somewhere ahead, and the sound of another train, and voices...

At the bottom of the ramp he stepped out into warm yellow light, and heard an amplified voice speaking in Russian, and he lost his mind for a moment. Or for a minute. Or for an hour, he was never able to be sure afterwards. All he could be certain of was that he had ceased to be rational for some period of time, and when that period of time came to an end he was on his hands and knees on Juliana Bruna Street, down in Mokotów, being sick onto the pavement and trying to scream at the same time while someone shouted at him to be quiet from one of the flats along the street. He remembered that he had hallucinated someone speaking urgently to him in Russian, then he toppled over on his side and passed out.

"NO," SAID THE speaker grille of the security lock.

"I need your help, Ewa," Forsyth gasped, trying to crush himself out of sight in the doorway.

"You should have fucking thought about that earlier, when you went off with that fucking degenerate." The speaker system reduced Ewa's voice to something that George Lucas might have used for those charming robots in the *Star Wars* films.

"Ewa," Forsyth said, desperately summoning what small reserves of macho remained to him, "let me in."

"Fuck off."

Forsyth looked out of the doorway. Ewa lived in a pretty nice, quiet street, a place the city's recent epidemic of muggers and car thieves had so far overlooked, but suddenly every tree and waste-bin and doorway seemed to have too many shadows. Forsyth pressed Ewa's button again and again, but she refused to answer. He saw a tram trundling along the main street, and began to run towards the stop.

"GRANT, GRANT," MAGDA said, shaking her head.

"I need a place to stay," Forsyth said, sitting forwards on the edge of the sofa and clasping his hands between his knees.

Magda smiled. She was tall and black-haired, with high, Slavic cheekbones and a nose that had been broken as a child when, just to feel the breeze across the spokes, she had put her face too close to a rotating bicycle wheel that her father had been repairing.

"You have no right to do this," said Wojtek, Magda's husband.

"I know," Forsyth said. "I know. But I'm desperate. I think I'm in a lot of trouble."

Wojtek was tall and blond and broad-shouldered. He was smoking a gorgeous Meerschaum pipe and regarding Forsyth like a scientist looking at a particularly disgusting tissue culture. "If you're in trouble we want nothing to do with you," he said. "This is a law-abiding household."

"It always was," Forsyth said, annoyed. "What do you think it was like when I was living here?"

"I didn't mean that," Wojtek said equably. Forsyth thought that Magda could have done worse in her choice of second husband. Wojtek was an architect, and one of the most reasonable men Forsyth had ever met. He was so reasonable he made Forsyth feel nauseous.

"Well what the fuck *did* you mean?" he demanded.

Magda sighed. "Grant, please."

Warsaw, more than most cities and polities of the Continent, was a place of taxis. It seemed that as soon as they were old enough to drive and managed to accumulate enough money to bribe the driving instructors, Varsovians passed their test, installed an antique two-way radio in their cars, and called themselves taxi drivers.

Forsyth had ignored all those taxis, on the grounds that he felt safer with lots of members of the public around him, and the bus ride out to Magda and Wojtek's flat in Ursynów had still been a nightmare. He thought perhaps he was starting to come out of the shock a little, finally beginning to think a little more clearly, but alarmingly it didn't seem to be helping his situation at all.

"I just need a place to stay tonight," he said, and he heard himself begging, the imperfect ex-husband. "I need to sit and think for a while."

Wojtek looked at Magda, and then at Forsyth. "You can have an hour. Then we want you out of here."

Forsyth glared at him, but there was no force behind it. It was impossible to hate Wojtek. He had made Magda happy, had become Tomasz's father in a way that Forsyth had never been. On the few previous occasions that they had met, Forsyth had wanted to hit him.

Magda said, "Grant, you can't stay here. You have to leave."

"Please, Magda." He started to think about the long, long bus journey back into the centre of Warsaw and his very last hope.

"I don't know what trouble you've got yourself into, but we don't want any part of it. And don't shout."

"I wasn't shouting."

THE PINK PALACE had not always been the Pink Palace. Once upon a time it had been Pałac Kultury, the Palace of Culture, a gift to the workers of Poland from the workers of the Soviet Union. Forsyth, who had seen a lot of ugly buildings in his travels, thought that on the evidence of the Palace of Culture the workers of the Soviet Union must have really hated the workers of Poland.

After the collapse of the Communist government in Poland, and the subsequent fragmentation of the Soviet Union, Varsovians had been faced with the dilemma of what to do with the immense Stalinist-Baroque monolith that had been landed on their city like a chunky *Amazing Stories* spacecraft. Should they demolish it? Should they build a pleasing façade over the hateful Soviet one? Competitions were held, to try and find a solution, but without success. The one good thing, the people of Warsaw said, about the Palace of Culture was that you could see it from more or less everywhere in the city, rendering it almost impossible to get lost.

The debate went on beyond the Millennium, and might have meandered on, in the manner of Polish debate, for decades, had the Pink Pilot not taken the initiative, fitted a Heath Robinson paint-spraying rig to a stolen Russian helicopter, flown it low over central Warsaw one night, and ended the debate for ever.

Forsyth thought it was a typically Polish gesture, wild and romantic and expensive and completely futile, but in the days following the Palace of Culture's unscheduled paint-job the Pink Pilot became a national hero. *Nie* ran a straw poll which suggested that the Pilot would wipe the board if he (or she, Political Correctness having taken some small root in Poland by then) chose to run for President. The news networks ran endless items theorising on the Pilot's origins and suggesting a certain amount of official collusion because of the apparent failure of Warsaw's Air Traffic Control to spot the maverick aircraft. Others dredged up the story of Matthias Rust, who flew a Cessna right into Red Square, to demonstrate that such things were not only possible but had a precedent.

Forsyth, kicking his heels that Autumn while the Government argued over the construction of the termini out in Wola, had sat in the flat and watched all the news programmes and thought he could feel the whole city – the whole country – breathe a sigh of relief.

The relief was so tangible that protest marches were mounted when attempts were made to remove the pink paint. When the city authorities tried to repaint the Palace in battleship grey there was a riot. The Pink Palace became a symbol of everything Polish, of the final humiliation of the Soviet enemy. Forsyth thought the whole business was stupid and he found his admiration for the Poles increasing every time he happened to look up while wandering around town and saw the pink edifice.

At any rate, he used to. He could see the Palace from the windows of Atelier Dudek, all lit up and pink, and all of a sudden it seemed sinister and hot, diseased somehow. He shuddered and drank some more vodka.

"Careful with that," Leon said.

"Do me a favour," Forsyth muttered, screwing the top off another airline miniature of Wyborowa and emptying it into his glass.

Without taking his feet down off the mixing desk, Leon looked over his shoulder at the closed-circuit monitors along the opposite wall. They showed various surrealistically-tilted panes of grey-scaled urban landscape around the building, but no people.

"Show me," he said.

Forsyth took the plastic envelope from his pocket and tossed it across. Leon caught it and made a face. "Is this blood here?"

"I think so." Forsyth drained his glass and opened another miniature. The ride from Ursynów into the centre of town had totally unnerved him, on top of everything else that had unnerved him tonight. The one good thing that had happened to him in the last six hours was finding Leon still at the workshop and willing to let him in.

"Shit," said Leon nervily, wiping his hand on the knee of his jeans. He held the envelope up to the light and shook it so the dark object inside jiggled about. "I thought Crispin dealt in drugs."

"Me too." Forsyth jerked his chin towards the envelope. "What is it?"

"I haven't looked, but I've got an idea" Leon said. "You think he was killed for this?"

Forsyth rubbed his eyes. "I don't know that he's dead, Leon. I don't know what the fuck happened."

"But?"

"But I think the Georgians tried to rip him off."

Leon nodded. "Sounds about right. Well." He pinched the edge of the envelope between the nails of his thumb and index finger and tore the plastic. "I should tell you to take this thing that belongs to Babykiller, and which the Georgians want but don't want to pay for, and go away and never come back." He tipped the envelope and the dark object fell out into his palm, a rectangle of black plastic a few millimetres thick and about half the size of a packet of cigarettes, featureless except for a narrow green stripe around one end and a line of tiny gold dots along one of the short edges. An external hard drive. "However," Leon went on, "what kind of friend would that make me?"

"It would make you the kind of friend who didn't care about the rent I owe you," said Forsyth.

Leon smiled and looked at him. "Everybody in this fucking country is a mercenary, my friend, you must have noticed. If I forget about the money you owe me, where else am I going to get it from?"

"I came here for help, Leon. Not to get involved in another money-making scheme."

Leon was examining the drive, holding it delicately between his fingertips under an articulated desklamp. "No serial number, but that doesn't mean anything. Just standard storage."

"I'm going to take it to the police," Forsyth said.

Leon's fist closed gently around the drive. "Just a moment."

"Give it back, Leon."

"Think about it," Leon said smoothly. "You went down into the Metro. Okay, you might be able to explain that because you represent tunnel workers, even though you chose an unusual time of the day to do it. But you took an unauthorised person down there with you." He shook his fist gently. "An unauthorised person who was a known drugs dealer. And you took him down there so he could retrieve some kind of contraband."

Forsyth closed his eyes and groaned.

"And that's just the beginning," Leon continued. "Let's assume you explain all that away. Crispin has probably been murdered. Did you go straight to the police to report it? No, you came here. You behave like a criminal yourself, and go running to your old friend Leon."

Forsyth put his hand to his face.

"And anyway, the chances are that if you go to the police this thing will wind up in the Georgians' hands in a couple of hours and you'll be lying in some basement with your throat cut and your nuts in your mouth. No." Leon stood up. "Let's not go to the police."

Forsyth took his hand from his face and opened his eyes. "Can you find out what's on that thing?"

Leon's eyebrows went up in surprise. "Sure," he said. "That's not even difficult." He flipped open a little door in the front of one of his computers, revealing a row of various-sized slots. He pushed the drive into one of them, tapped a couple of commands, and the monitor in front of him filled with a diagram of the Warsaw Metro.

There was a moment's silence. Forsyth said, "So?"

"So what?"

"Is that it?"

Leon clicked his way through two or three menus, read the results. "That's it," he said. He blinked at Forsyth. "Can you think of a good suggestion why Crispin would want to hide this in the Metro? Or why somebody might want to kill him for it?"

"No." Forsyth rolled his chair closer to the monitor. The diagram was just the standard one from the original design drawings, the one that was in all the brochures. It showed not just the Metro lines but every tunnel and underground space involved in the project. For that reason it was immensely complicated, and it had been stuck away on the inside back page of the brochures because investors tend to find very complicated diagrams rather dull.

"Okay," said Leon. "So maybe there's something encrypted within the picture."

"Like what?"

Leon shrugged. "Don't know."

"Well can you find out?"

"There's no need to shout."

Forsyth thought there was *every* need to shout, but he fought himself calm by an effort of what will he had left. "I'm sorry," he said. "Can you find out?"

Leon scratched his head. "I can look for the more obvious things, but you really need a specialist." He smiled. "Fortunately, I know a specialist."

"Well... *good*," Forsyth said.

"In fact, so do you."

They looked at each other for a few moments, until it dawned on Forsyth who Leon was talking about. "Oh, for heaven's sake," he said.

4.

FORSYTH HAD MET Leon's friend Chudy a couple of times before, and had dismissed him as just another computer-mad kid who wanted to break into the movies. He kept coming round to the workshop with weird structures he'd programmed himself, bizarre confections constructed from bits and pieces of half a dozen different actors and actresses, up to and including an outrageous *thing* – Forsyth couldn't think of any other way to describe it – with Tom Selleck's head, Chesty Morgan's breasts, the body of the Mighty Joe Young, the penis of John Holmes and the legs of Betty Grable. That this mess of bits and pieces worked at all spoke of some degree of skill on Chudy's part, but Forsyth still thought the kid needed psychiatric help.

"You never used that structure I brought you last month," Chudy said, gently rocking himself from side to side on his swivel chair.

"I keep telling you," Leon said equably, "I'm looking for the right property to put it into."

"You never use any of my structures."

Leon gave a great graphic shrug meant to illustrate how hard it was to find high-quality properties these days. He smiled.

Chudy pouted. 'Chudy' was Polish for 'thin,' or 'skinny'; Forsyth assumed the nickname was meant to be ironic, because Chudy was almost spherical, a short, fat, petulant teenager with greasy hair and spots. It was unusual to find this kind of kid in Poland these days, in spite of all the fried food. Poles, Forsyth thought, just had too much nervous energy to be fat.

"So," Chudy said, casting a sly eye around his bedroom, "you need my help, do you?"

Forsyth got up off the bed. "I've had enough of this."

Leon took hold of his arm and pulled him back. "Sit down. Chudy and I are just negotiating. Isn't that right, Chudy? Just like film men all over the world."

This was a compliment which clearly struck home with Chudy. He ran his fingers through his hair and grinned. "Yeah," he said. "Negotiating."

"Good God," Forsyth muttered.

Chudy lived with his parents in a flat in Wola, a district of monolithic high-rise blocks, poor sandy soil and scrubby pollution-stricken trees out on the northwestern edge of the city. The door of his bedroom was plastered with adolescent notices of the 'Keep Out, Genius At Work' variety, and it was clear to Forsyth that his parents heeded them because the room was a disaster area. The walls and ceiling were entirely covered with posters, in places stuck haphazardly one on top of the other two or three deep, a mural of rock groups and centrefolds and fast cars and aircraft, occasionally all on the same poster. The floor was a sort of archaeological treasure-trove of discarded clothing, training shoes, magazine printouts, pens, sheets of paper, little plastic boxes, wrapping materials, ancient paperback software manuals, food-encrusted plates, items of cutlery, mugs, glasses, antique audio and computer CDs and DVDs and their boxes, suspiciously stiff twists of Kleenex, stuffed toys with the stuffing bulging in a sinister fashion out of missing arms and legs. Forsyth had found himself having to walk on tiptoe to reach the bed and sit down, although sitting down on the bed involved sweeping more bits of detritus onto the floor and rearranging the smelly duvet that had been stuffed down between the bed and the wall.

"So how about it?" Leon asked.

"How about what?" Chudy said with the sly look he clearly now associated with negotiation.

Leon shrugged. "You help me out, I help you out. That's how these things work, isn't it?"

Chudy affected to look more sly. Forsyth thought it made him look simple-minded, but he didn't say anything.

The bits of Chudy's room that weren't given over to apocalyptic mess and piles of pornographic magazines comprised the reason for Forsyth and Leon's presence here: a row of four impressive-looking computer systems along one wall, sitting on little folding wooden picnic tables, each with its own printer and three or four different drive formats. Chudy had card drives, old read/write optical disc drives, three sizes of antique floppy drives, external hard drives stacked one on top of the other. One of the monitors was running a scene from *Debbie Does Dallas*, except it appeared to involve Louise Brooks, Brad Pitt and the golden robot from *Star Wars* whose name Forsyth could never remember. He was finding it distracting, so he got up and tiptoed across to the window while Leon buffed up Chudy's vanity.

Chudy's parents' flat was up on the eleventh floor of one of Wola's blocks. His bedroom window looked out on a misty distance of factories and scrubby waste ground and the faraway skyline of central Warsaw. Forsyth could remember much the same view from Agatka's flat, the girl he had very nearly married and whose father had wanted him to work at the Ursus tractor factory. She had lived somewhere around here. He wondered if she was somewhere close by, in one of the other huge blocks. He wondered if his life would have been any different if he had married her and not Magda. Right on the horizon, between two buildings, he thought he could detect a speck of hot pink, like a street sign pointing at just how different his life would have been. All of a sudden, he found himself wanting to scream.

"Okay," he heard Chudy say, "let's see."

Forsyth turned from the window and saw Leon hand over the hard drive, and it struck him how cosmologically stupid he was. He should never have gone to Leon. He should have got out of town, out of the country, and off of Continental Europe, as quickly as he could manage. He said, "I don't think this is a very good idea."

Leon and Chudy both looked at him as if surprised to find another person in the room with them. "Don't you want to know what's on this?" Leon asked.

Forsyth thought about it. "No," he said after a moment or so. "I just want to be out of here."

"So go."

"Oh no, Leon. Not without that thing." He nodded at the drive lying on Chudy's plump palm. "You're crazy if you think I'm leaving that with you."

"Knowledge is power," Chudy said, holding up the drive, and Forsyth instantly wanted to punch him. "This is just hardware; it's what's on it that's important." Leon was nodding agreement, and Forsyth wanted to punch him as well. Chudy said, "You can erase a drive like this, but if you know what's on it you can't erase it from your brain."

Forsyth and Leon had both agreed not to mention Crispin or the Georgians or Babykiller, or even the possibly-mythical cammo dudes, but he still felt tempted to tell the kid that you could erase a person's brain perfectly well with a hollow-point bullet. He leaned back against the windowsill and looked at the two Poles. *A friend of mine was probably murdered last night*, he told them silently, *and all you two can do is behave like you've dropped into some bad cyberpunk miniseries. Well fuck you.*

He said, "All right. Let's see what all this is about."

Chudy grinned triumphantly and slid the drive into a slot in the computer. He typed a few commands and a monitor filled with the Metro diagram. Forsyth went over, feeling untold years of unwashed underwear under his feet, and looked at the screen.

"Well, there's obviously something embedded in the picture," Chudy said, seeing the look on his face.

"Oh," Forsyth said, looking down at the kid. "Obviously."

Chudy typed some more commands. Nothing happened. He said, "Hm, *okay...*" and typed some more. The diagram stayed on the screen. Chudy pulled down some menus, loaded some programs, did some more typing. More menus appeared, full of lines of code. Chudy squinted at them, began to hum tunelessly. Forsyth looked over at Leon, who shrugged.

Chudy worked on the file for two hours. Forsyth had no idea what he was doing, but the kid became gradually more and more frustrated, typing like a maniac, checking every few moments to see if the diagram had magically unfolded to reveal a secret message. The only thing that happened was that it changed colour at one point.

Finally he sat back in his chair and said, "There's nothing there."

"You're sure?" asked Leon.

"It's a vanilla image," said Chudy. He looked exhausted. "There's nothing else on the drive. There's *never* been anything else on the drive. I tried everything."

"Something new," Leon suggested. "I heard the NSA have been –"

"I tried *everything*," Chudy insisted. Forsyth thought the boy was close to tears.

"Okay," Leon said calmly, going over and taking the drive from its slot. The monitor filled with warnings about not closing the media down properly, but Leon and Chudy ignored them. Leon popped the drive into a pocket of his combat jacket and said, "Well."

"What about my stuff?" Chudy demanded, half-rising from his typing chair. "You promised."

Leon was already halfway to the door, and Forsyth had only just started to follow. "You'll get your chance, Chudy," Leon said.

"Bring your three favourite structures over to the workshop on Tuesday and you can watch me programming them in."

"Hey." The look of delight on Chudy's face had clearly erased the puzzling hard drive from his mind. "That's great. I'll see you on Tuesday then."

"I'll look forward to it," Leon said, but by then he and Forsyth were out of the bedroom and nodding goodbye to Chudy's perfectly ordinary but slightly harassed-looking parents.

FORSYTH DIDN'T SAY anything for quite a while after they got back to the van and Leon began to drive, uncharacteristically carefully, back towards the centre of town.

Finally, he said, "Well?"

"It's a puzzle," Leon admitted.

Forsyth waited, but apparently no more information was forthcoming, so he said, "Leon, you may have overlooked this, but this whole thing is rather more than an academic exercise to me."

"Oh, I know," Leon said. "I know."

"So what are we going to do?"

Leon looked out through the windscreen. "Let's go home," he said.

Home. Forsyth sagged back in his seat. "All right," he said. "Why not?"

5.

PRAGA, ACROSS THE Vistula from the Old Town, had gone through something of a hipster revival in the early years of the century, but the hipsters had moved on to pastures new and it had returned to its former scruffy self, a run-down district of garages and battered housing blocks and little factories. It was grey and dirty and rubbish blew down the streets on the gritty breeze. It had also been, for many years now, the heartland of Warsaw's mafia gangs, all of whom would be affiliated in some way to Babykiller and his organisation. Who knew, Babykiller himself might live there.

So it was, Forsyth supposed, a stroke of genius of a particularly warped and illogical kind to hide him here, right in the middle of what he presumed was Babykiller's home territory.

Not that that made him feel at all secure. The thing that had happened to the Georgians had made sure of that.

The evening that he and Leon had visited Chudy, four bodies had been dragged from the river down near Wilanów. When they got back to the flat the news was full of it. The police had confirmed that the bodies were of Georgian citizens, and implied that they were presumed to have been in the city on some kind of criminal business. There was, of course, no way of knowing for sure whether they were the same Georgians who had been doing business with Crispin – Georgians being universally presumed to be both omnipresent and criminal to a man – but to Forsyth the connection seemed obvious.

Leon watched the news item and seemed to go into a trance for a while. Forsyth, student of drugs as he was, watched with a certain academic alarm as his one ally in the whole country appeared to lose his mind for a few moments. Then Leon snapped out of it and started to make phone calls, one of which resulted in Forsyth being deposited, about twenty hours after escaping from the Metro, in this smelly, greasy flat.

The flat belonged to an immensely fat Ukrainian who introduced himself as 'Fox.' Fox smoked all the time, lighting one cigarette from the stub of the last, and sat in front of his malfunctioning entertainment set wearing jeans and a filthy singlet and guzzling bottle after bottle of Okocim beer.

"It'll be okay," Leon assured Forsyth. "Trust me."

"This is madness, Leon," Forsyth said, looking around the flat. "I can't stay here."

"It'll be all right until I can find out what the fuck's going on," his flatmate said. "I promise."

"I've got to get out of the city, Leon. I've got to get out of the *country*."

Leon nodded and patted Forsyth on the shoulder. "I'll try to get something organised. Don't worry. I'll be in touch."

And that had been three days ago.

*   *   *

FOX HAD A running conversation with the media which appeared to have been going on for some considerable time. He sat in his worn-out armchair, chugging Okocim and belching and talking back to the newsreaders and the adverts and characters in films. He passed coarse-sounding comments on news reports about the activities of politicians, shouted warnings to the heroes of action movies, made rude noises when someone in a series had a love scene.

He only spoke a couple of words of Polish, and refused to speak Russian. Forsyth had picked up a few phrases of Ukrainian from some of his fellow-workers when he was working the Moscow Metro, but his pronunciation was so bad that he couldn't get Fox to understand them, so the two of them wandered about in a fog of mutual incomprehension, which seemed to suit Fox all right because he hardly took any notice of his lodger apart from putting huge greasy fried meals on the table at irregular hours of the day and night. Fox took his own meals in front of the entertainment set, and when he was finished he put his plate on the floor. He only seemed to do the washing-up at long intervals: there was always a stack of plates beside his chair, crusted with dried food and congealed grease.

The room Forsyth had been given was full of mismatched furniture: chairs, tables, a sofa, all piled haphazardly one on top of the other. Occasionally Fox would go out and return with another chair or a table and dump it on the stack. What this was all about, Forsyth could only guess, but he had managed to clear a kind of nest for himself amongst all the rubbish, on the floor under a table. He'd padded the floor with three or four big thick blankets, and used his rolled-up jacket as a pillow. Fox liked to keep the heating turned up to equatorial levels, which more or less did away with the need for sheets but subtly enhanced the general miasm of rotting food which filled the flat.

Unable to sleep at night, Forsyth lay on his back staring up at the underside of the tabletop, going over and over the events of that night in the Metro. He still couldn't work out what had happened. One moment Crispin had been there, chiding him for just assuming he was involved in some kind of drug deal. The next moment,

Crispin was gone and Forsyth was lying on the trackbed. Between those two memories, something pretty major had obviously taken place, but Forsyth had no idea what it might have been. He couldn't even work out how long he'd been lying there insensible.

Nor could he force himself to remember how he'd finally managed to get out of the Metro, or how he had got as far as Mokotów. Or too many things. What he could remember, like that Russian-speaking voice, could only have been some kind of hallucination, there was no other way to explain it.

On the fourth day, the doorbell rang. The doorbell was broken; the only sound it made was a sort of dull dry clicking, but by now Forsyth was in such a state of hypersensitivity from hours wandering back and forth around the flat that when he heard the clicking he had to restrain himself from diving screaming out of the nearest window.

Instead, he settled for retreating into his room and curling up under the table, watching the door and resolving to sell his life dearly, leaving aside the fact that he probably wouldn't ever know what he was selling it for.

The door opened, and an eye-hurtingly neat young Japanese man stepped into the doorway, as alien a presence in this messy flat as it was possible to be. He looked around the room for a moment. Then he spotted Forsyth under the table, and he bent down and smiled.

"Forsyth-san," said Kwak-Kwak. "*Konichi-wa.*"

"ONE HAS TO wonder why you did not come to us straight away," said Kwak-Kwak.

"Leon was making all the decisions," Forsyth muttered, scrunching himself up in the Nissan's passenger seat and trying to compress his body below the level of the window.

Kwak-Kwak nodded. "An interesting chap, your flatmate. He tells me he is a director."

"Political film-maker."

"Very interesting." Kwak-Kwak made a right-turn. "He claims to have an impressive collection of *anime*. Would this be true?"

"I wouldn't know."

"He said he would show me when the present situation was resolved." Kwak-Kwak's accent was purest Oxbridge, but he talked like nobody else Forsyth had ever met. "He showed some wisdom in approaching us."

"Leon's good at wisdom," Forsyth said, watching from his scrunched-up position as the streetlights sailed by overhead. "Where are we going?"

"Somewhere safe," said Kwak-Kwak, "until we can decide what to do with you."

"Leon said I *was* somewhere safe."

The Japanese laughed. "Safe? In *Praga*? Please."

"What's been happening?"

"Mister Jespersen is very keen to get in touch with you. The police also are very keen to get in touch with you because there was an explosion in your flat two nights ago."

"What?" Forsyth almost sat up in the seat, but remembered he was supposed to be trying to hide.

"Your downstairs neighbours were killed, unfortunately. As were a number of individuals in the flat next door. Ukrainian nationals."

"The Enzyme Kings." Shit, *shit*. "What about Leon?"

"Leon was not at home at the time. We're not at all certain *where* Leon is at the moment, although it seems unlikely that he was a casualty."

Kwak-Kwak was, of course, far too polite to ask what the hell was going on. Forsyth sighed. "Has anybody been talking about Crispin?"

Kwak-Kwak overtook a couple of parked cars and shook his head. "Is Crispin back?"

"He was," Forsyth said miserably.

"None of my boys has seen him, and no one seems to be talking about him."

"Kwak-Kwak?"

"Yes?"

"Why are you helping me?"

"You appear to have encountered a situation which is beyond your ability to resolve," Kwak-Kwak said, as if it was obvious.

Forsyth thought about that. And, yes, it was obvious. He'd

encountered a situation which was beyond his ability to resolve. It was obvious to anybody with half a brain cell. He closed his eyes.

"Almost home now," said Kwak-Kwak.

"Kwak-Kwak?"

"Yes?"

"Thanks."

"No need."

KWAK-KWAK AND THE workers he represented lived in a walled enclave not too far from the centre of town, next door to what had once been the British Embassy. It was, to all intents and purposes, a polity, sovereign territory guarded by strong silent men with the odd missing finger and torsos that were solid panels of tattooing. Nobody had ever tried to break into the Japanese enclave. Not twice, anyway.

Forsyth woke feeling calm and refreshed and – more importantly – clean. His new room, compared with Fox's flat, was as aseptic as the hotel room in *2001* and considerably less cluttered. There was a futon in the middle of the spotless white floor, tatami mats, and a soft white light hanging from the centre of the ceiling. The walls were paper screens mounted on wooden lathing, and some of them slid aside to reveal cupboards, the en suite bathroom, the doorway.

He lay on the futon for some time, luxuriating in the touch of the cotton sheets and the faint smell of peach-blossom in the air, feeling properly safe for the first time in days.

There was a discreet knock, and after a suitable interval part of the wall slid to one side and Kwak-Kwak was standing there wearing work-boots and neat, clean orange overalls. In his hand was a hard-hat with KAWASAKI spray-stencilled on the front.

"Work?" Forsyth said, sitting up and automatically thinking that he should contact some of the tunnel men he represented if work was going on somewhere in the city. Then he remembered that he was probably never ever going to be able to do that again.

"A safety check only," said Kwak-Kwak. "I have to certify the safety equipment at Mokotów Station before my men can work down there."

Forsyth lay back on the bed, thinking of his conversation with Jespersen earlier in the week. It felt like a thousand years ago. He still couldn't remember how he had got past the security gates at Mokotów. He sighed.

"You have a visitor," Kwak-Kwak said, and moved to one side to let Leon step into the doorway. Leon was carrying a huge overfilled ex-Army rucksack and wearing one of the shapeless patchwork leather hats Forsyth was always seeing on older Poles. They looked at each other and nodded hello.

"I must go," Kwak-Kwak said. To Leon he said, "We will speak later about your *anime*, Grzybowski-san."

"Any time you're ready, Hiroshi," Leon said. When Kwak-Kwak had gone, Leon said, "I haven't the heart to tell him all my discs went up with the flat." He looked at Forsyth. "So. How are you?"

"I'm all right." Forsyth sat up and clasped his knees to his chest. "What the fucking hell has been going on, Leon?"

Leon looked around the bedroom for something to sit on, but the futon was the only furniture, so he sat on the rucksack, put his hands on his knees, and said, "Did Hiroshi tell you about the flat?"

Forsyth nodded.

"A gas explosion, according to the police." Leon tipped his head to one side. "A not totally implausible explanation, considering the state of the water heater."

"I kept telling you to fix that fucking thing," Forsyth said.

"I bumped into Anatoli yesterday. You know, the Kings' lead guitarist? He'd just got out of hospital. He said he thought it was something to do with the decorators."

Forsyth thought about this. Then he said, "What decorators?"

Leon pointed a finger at Forsyth as if the Scotsman had just won a major prize in a game-show. "My point exactly!" he cried. "*What* decorators. The two workmen Anatoli saw letting themselves into the flat on the morning of the explosion with tins of paint and brushes and dust-sheets and all that stuff, *that's* what decorators."

Forsyth closed his eyes.

"Pretty fucking amateur," Leon said, "since the only people they actually managed to kill were two Ukrainian musicians and old Mr and Mrs Dobrowolski downstairs."

"Well," Forsyth said. He opened his eyes and blinked at Leon. "We're homeless then."

"Oh no." Leon shook his head. "*You* were homeless already."

"If Crispin isn't dead, I'll kill him myself," Forsyth said, getting up from the futon and going over to the wardrobe.

"Is it safe to talk in here?" said Leon.

"Probably." Forsyth started to get dressed. Kwak-Kwak had had his clothes laundered during the night, but there was still an unidentified stain on the right knee of his jeans as a souvenir of his stay with Fox.

"I've been going over and over it in my head." Leon shifted his weight, trying to make himself more comfortable on the rucksack. "Crispin gets involved in some mad scheme to sell... *something* to the Georgians on Babykiller's behalf. Crispin hides the drive in the Metro, then has to leave because all work's suspended. Then Crispin has to leave the country – you never told me why he did that."

Forsyth shook his head. "Crispin never said. He was in a hurry, though. I remember that."

Leon shrugged. "Five months later, Crispin comes back. You help him retrieve the drive. Crispin gets killed."

Struggling within the depths of his sweater, Forsyth said, "We don't know that. I didn't see his body. I didn't see *what* happened to him."

"Okay, okay. Something happens to Crispin and he's not there any more, is that better?"

"It's more accurate." Forsyth's head popped through the neck of his sweater. "Although the daft wee sod probably *is* dead."

Leon waved his hand to shut Forsyth up. "Probably. Yes. All right. So the day after Crispin disappears, a bunch of Georgians washes up in the Wisła, and two days after that our flat blows up."

Forsyth found his boots in the bottom of the wardrobe and carried them back to the futon. He sat down and stuffed his foot into one of the boots.

"You didn't actually see who else was down there with you, did you," Leon said.

"It was the Georgians." Forsyth put on his other boot and started to lace it up. "Who else could it have been?"

"I've been wondering about that," Leon said. He took the hard drive from his pocket and held it up. "We've been working on the assumption that whoever it was wanted this, yes?"

"The Georgians," Forsyth said. "Because they didn't want to pay for it."

"But why would they have to?" asked Leon. "There's only a map of the Warsaw Metro on here, and they can get one of those anywhere."

"It's the complete civil engineering schematic, not the tourist map," Forsyth said. "But yes, you're right. It wouldn't be hard to get hold of."

"In which case," Leon said, "either the Georgians were expecting something else to be on here – nuclear launch codes or something, say – and this harmless map was substituted for them, *or* this harmless map is not as harmless as it seems."

Forsyth looked at the hard drive. "Why would it not be harmless?"

"Because," said a voice behind Leon, "there are places where maps are uniquely powerful." A man edged into view in the doorway. He had a young face but grey in his hair, and he walked with a cane.

Forsyth looked from him to Leon, then back again. Then back again. "Are there not enough people mixed up in this mess already?" he asked.

"It's possible," said the man with the cane, "that you have stumbled on something quite significant, and I would like to buy it from you."

"You can take it, and good luck to you," said Forsyth. "As far as I'm concerned, it's not worth anything."

Leon pulled a face.

"In addition," the man with the cane continued, "I can offer you safe passage out of Poland and a new identity in any nation, polity or sovereign entity in Europe."

"There now," Leon said to Forsyth. "*Now* do we have your attention?"

6.

"HAVE YOU EVER," asked Rudi, "tried to tie up some of your life's loose ends?"

"I've thought about it," Forsyth said. "Now and again."

"A bit of advice. Don't. Some loose ends are better off left untied. I tried that."

From the tone of his voice, it seemed to Forsyth that his unlikely rescuer had found the exercise ill-advised at best.

"Did you know, for example, that the people who built Dresden-Neustadt were also involved in building the Line?" Rudi asked. "And that some of *them* – quite possibly *all* of them – are involved in building Stare Miasto station?" He thought about it. "Actually, they've been involved in the whole Metro project, right from the beginning. The joint-venture scheme the Polish government runs is quite unusual; I have a suspicion the funding structure wasn't wholly their idea, but you can't tell with governments here. It's difficult to work out who the private investors are; they seem to come and go, individually or collectively, down the years."

Forsyth shrugged. "They're expensive projects; there can't be that many organisations who can afford to do that."

"Very true. The question I've been asking myself is *why*. Why are these very rich people sinking so much money into civil engineering projects? Has it ever occurred to you, for instance, to wonder *why* anyone would want to rebuild what was already a perfectly good Metro system?"

"It's what happens with Metro systems. They always need upgrading and extending."

"On this scale?"

"The Poles want the best Metro in the world. It's like having the tallest building in the world; it gives you bragging rights."

Rudi rubbed his eyes. "I've been looking at this all wrong," he said. "It's not about trains, it's about *tunnels*."

They were a long way from Warsaw, in a resort hotel just west of Sopot, a glowering Brutalist structure like a Mayan pyramid faced with hundreds of balconies, where one could, if one wrapped up warmly, stand and gaze out towards the Winter-whipped Baltic a kilometre or so away. The place was almost empty; the season was late and the Christmas and New Year guests wouldn't be arriving for another month or so. Even after all these years, Forsyth couldn't work out what would possess Poles to want to spend Christmas in a place like this.

"Your friend mentioned something about Russians," Rudi mused, looking around the cavernous dining room on the hotel's third floor. There was enough glass in the backward-sloping floor-to-ceiling windows to cover a football pitch, but the view they looked out on was a vista of sand dunes and hardy grass and sleet; the weather was so bad today that the sea was barely visible.

"You mean the Georgians?"

"No. When you were in the Metro tunnels. He said you heard Russians."

"I was scared out of my wits," Forsyth told him. "I don't know what I heard."

Rudi smiled and leaned forward a little and put his elbows on the table on either side of his soup bowl. "But you do," he said. "You do know what you heard, don't you."

Forsyth looked at him. "There was a train," he said finally. "The ramp I was on led down to another platform. There were lots of people there, and there was a train."

Rudi raised an eyebrow.

Forsyth sighed. "Before I became a Rep, I did a lot of work at Old Town Station," he explained. "I know that place really well. And there *isn't* a platform there. And even if there *was*, there was no power to run a train and the lights. It was as if..." He shook his head.

"It was as if you weren't in Old Town Station any more," Rudi suggested. "As if you weren't in the Warsaw Metro at all."

Forsyth looked blankly at him.

"Have you ever heard of Stendhal Syndrome?"

"What?"

Rudi looked up at the many hundreds of lights hanging far up on the dining room's ceiling. "There are documented occurrences of people visiting the Uffizi in Florence and becoming... overwhelmed by the beauty of the place. Dizziness, fainting. Stendhal Syndrome.

"Anyway, there was a man – I never met him, but I know someone who did, which is how I know this particular story – who was interested in Stendhal Syndrome. He found examples of similar symptoms in other places – the Maine coast, parts of Cornwall – and he started to wonder if there was something about the topographical structure of these places that was making people unwell. Fortunately, he had access to a *fabulous* amount of computing power and quite a lot of time on his hands, and eventually he came to the conclusion that there are some places where the landscape is just the wrong shape, simply too *intense* for human perceptions.

"This man – his name was Mundt, by the way; does that sound familiar? No? Well, Mundt made something of a conceptual leap. His research led him to a way of manipulating landscape in a way which connected two distant points. Which suddenly made him interesting to a *lot* of people."

Forsyth shrugged. "So?"

"Herr Professor Mundt was very interested in tunnels," Rudi said. "And he lived in Dresden-Neustadt."

"The owners of which are rebuilding the Warsaw Metro. Which is mostly tunnels."

Rudi nodded. "Just so."

Forsyth thought about it. "So what are you saying? That the Warsaw Metro comes out in Moscow?" A few years ago, it would have sounded ridiculous. These days, with people taking weekend breaks in the Community, it actually didn't sound unreasonable.

"That would be something worth killing to protect, wouldn't it?" Rudi said. He looked over Forsyth's shoulder. In the far distance, one of the waiting staff was making the long, long journey towards their table. "If it were true."

"IT'S AN INTERESTING situation, when you sit down and think about it," Rudi said, picking his way delicately between piles of equipment and building material.

Forsyth stopped and miserably shone the beam of his torch on the tunnel walls, the roof, the trackbed. He wished Rudi would shut up. He wished he was somewhere else.

"Why, for instance, would Crispin hide a map of the Warsaw Metro *in* the Warsaw Metro?" Rudi went on. "Apart from the poetic resonance, of course."

Forsythe glowered at him.

"I'm not the person who was supposed to come and help you, you know," said Rudi. "Leon got the Japanese government to contact *Les*

Coureurs on your behalf; I'm running a data scraping operation at the moment, and that intercepted the job request."

"A what?" Forsyth couldn't believe they were having this conversation.

"Data scraping. I'm trying to locate Coureur Central; I have some questions I want to ask them."

"Aren't you a Coureur? Don't you know where it is?"

"No, nobody knows where it is. Or who it is. And yes, I am a Coureur." Rudi smiled at him. "If you think that sounds confusing, you ought to spend half an hour as me."

They started walking again. They'd entered the Metro two stations up the east-west line from Stare Miasto. Forsyth, already petrified to be back in Warsaw, had thought their excursion would come to a premature end at the station's security measures, but the system had let them through unchallenged, and that was when Rudi had launched into a seemingly endless and random musing about... well, Forsyth kept losing track, so he wasn't entirely sure *what* it was about any more.

"The question is why a commercially-available map of the Warsaw Metro should be so important to so many people," Rudi said. "And I don't buy the idea that Crispin told his Georgian friends the hard drive contained nuclear launch codes, by the way; that would just be suicidal."

"You don't know Crispin."

"True. But I'm making an assumption that he's not stark raving mad."

Forsyth shook his head. "We should try not to make so much noise," he said.

"So if there's nothing illegal or even faintly *unusual* on that hard drive," Rudi went on as if he hadn't heard, "why bother hiding it down here? Why bother hiding it at all?"

"We're going to get killed," Forsyth said.

Rudi thought about it. "No," he said finally. "No, we're not." But he did at least shut up for a while.

It was a long, difficult walk to Stare Miasto; Forsyth had forgotten just how tiring it could be walking along the unfinished tunnels. It was almost four in the morning before they reached the complex of ramps and cross-tunnels outside the Old Town station.

Rudi wandered about the tunnel, shining his torch here and there. "You said they fired on you?" he asked.

"Yes."

"A lot?"

Forsyth, on the other side of the tunnel, glared at him.

"Hm," said Rudi. "Okay. Show me this phantom platform, please."

Forsyth led the way to the down ramp. The floor underfoot was gritty. They passed the opening which led to the north-south tunnel and the spiral of the ramp kept going down for another couple of turns and opened into a narrow, straight corridor. There was light at the far end. Rudi stopped, then walked back up the ramp to the north-south exit, shining his torch on the walls, then came back down to stand beside Forsyth.

"And this shouldn't be here?" he said.

"I keep saying," Forsyth murmured.

"Okay." Rudi turned off his torch and set off down the tunnel towards the light. After a few moments, muttering under his breath, Forsyth did the same.

The light brightened as they approached the end of the tunnel, and then all of a sudden they were standing on a broad, deserted Metro platform. Rudi stood looking about him. He looked at the tracks, the walls. He stepped between a line of pillars and found himself in a long arch-roofed hallway. There was a sign on one of the pillars in Cyrillic.

"Kitay-Gorod," he read. His voice echoed down the empty hallway.

"Now do you believe me?" Forsyth asked in a strained whisper.

Rudi walked across the hall, between another set of pillars, and out onto the opposite platform. "I've never been to Moscow before," he said.

"Can we go now, please?"

"Hm? Oh. Yes, of course."

Walking back up the tunnel – the entrance seemed to Forsyth to be concealed by some kind of optical illusion – Rudi said, "Do you remember I was telling you about Professor Mundt?"

"Yes."

"He modified one of the sewer tunnels under Dresden so that it connected with the Vienna sewers," said Rudi. "I didn't see that, but I understand it was quite straightforward – no vast expenditure of energy, no massive earthmoving project, no flashing lights or sound effects. Something deceptively modest. The borders with the Community are like that; half the time you're not even aware you've crossed over." They reached the bottom of the emergency ramp and started to walk up to the east-west main tunnel again. "Thank you for this, by the way."

"You're welcome," Forsyth said through gritted teeth.

TWO HOURS LATER, they were back on the surface. They emerged from the station entrance to find early-morning traffic on the streets and crowds of people hurrying to work through blowing snow. No one paid them any attention. Instead of leaving, however, Rudi took out a phone and dialled a number.

"Hello," he said. He listened. "Yes." He listened again. "Well, *that's* real enough." He looked over at Forsyth, who was debating whether or not to flee and take his chances on his own. "Either I can walk into it with my eyes open, or run away and never know what's going on." He shrugged. "Really? Where?" He listened for a long time. "Okay. Tell him to send me the details." He looked at Forsyth again. "No, I'll take him with me; we can find somewhere for him when I'm done. I don't think he's in any danger at all, but it's not his fault he's mixed up in this. Yes, all right." He hung up.

They stood looking at each other through the snow. Finally Forsyth said, "*Well*?"

Rudi put his hands in his pockets and walked over until they were standing almost toe to toe. "Well," he said, "what you saw is real enough, although I can't think of any rational reason why anyone should do it. The rest of it... I'm not so sure. I think you've been the victim of a rather elaborate con. To what purpose, I don't know. It's interesting, though."

Forsyth looked helplessly around him. "*What*?"

"I'm not going to abandon you," Rudi promised. "There will be money and I will get you out of here. But you're going to have to put up with Poland for a little while longer. There's someone here I need to speak with."

THE LAST OF THE
UMBRELLA MEN

1.

ANIA'S ALARM WENT off at half past four in the morning. Long habit made her reach out and switch it off before she was properly awake and before it could disturb her husband, Lech.

Without turning on the light, she slipped out of bed. She used the bathroom, walked down the corridor to the kitchen, closed the door, turned on the extractor hood and the light over the cooker, and lit a cigarette while she switched on the coffeemaker – loaded and filled with water the night before so she didn't have to mess around with spoons and containers and taps while she was still half asleep.

She took butter and trays of sliced meats from the fridge, put them on the kitchen table with a plate and a knife and some scraps of cheese. From the breadbin she took the remains of yesterday's loaf and cut a couple of slices, put them on the plate and buttered them. The coffeemaker sputtered; she put a mug under the spout and pressed the button.

Sitting at the table, she piled meat and cheese onto the slices of bread and ate slowly, washing the food down with swallows of coffee while she looked at her reflection in the darkened window. Sometimes she thought she had been watching the passing of the years while looking at that reflection, a young woman who had slowly grown middle-aged and tired. A couple of years ago she had realised that what she was waiting for was to see resentment in her eyes.

Breakfast over, she put the plate and knife in the dishwasher, returned the food to the fridge, and stood at the window with a second mug of coffee, smoking another cigarette. The flat was near the top of one of the old Soviet-era blocks in Skorosze, a couple of kilometres from the centre of Warsaw. The heating was a bit hit-and-miss these days, and last year someone had managed to get through the security doors and light a fire in the lift, but it was all she and Lech could afford. All they had ever been able to afford. Looking down from the window, she saw early-morning traffic at the big road junction, one of the first trams of the day rattling along its tracks into town, a group of drunks sitting quietly on a bench in the little park between the block and the street. It could have been any day, any year. Only the drunks changed, as they either dried out or died and someone new took their place.

Her clothes, washed yesterday, were hanging on a drier in the living room. She dressed quickly in bra and pants and uniform, examined a pair of tights for runs before she put them on, slipped into a pair of comfortable flat-soled shoes, grabbed her bag and coat from the rack in the hall, and left the flat.

Outside, there was still an early-morning smell of coal smoke on the air. There was frost underfoot, and it crunched as she walked around the back of the block to the garages. Approaching one of the rank of doors, she took a key fob from her bag and clicked it. There was an answering pinpoint blink of International Klein Blue from a little box near an upper corner of the door. After the flat, the garage's defence system was the most expensive thing she and Lech had ever bought. It was more expensive than the car it was meant to protect, but without the car she wouldn't be able to work. The system involved a number of sentry guns firing darts tipped with a neurotoxin which the security firm promised was nonlethal. The ammunition had to be swapped out every two months because the poison degraded, although Lech grumbled that it was just the firm's way of continuing to charge them.

The car was a hydrogen-cell Audi, five years old, the subject of many fierce arguments and much simmering anger. Their previous car had simply died of old age; there were so many things wrong with it, a local mechanic had opined at an annual service, that it was kinder to just sell it for scrap rather than keep replacing things. So they had done that, and gathered together what money they could and borrowed the rest from friends and family, and Lech had gone to a second-hand dealer and come back with the Audi. Ania had loved it at first sight.

It was an easy half-hour's drive past Okęcie – locals still hadn't got around to calling it Warsaw-Chopin Airport, even after all this time – and down the E30 and 721 to Konstancin. Turning east at Piaseczno, Ania could see a bruised-looking lightening of the sky ahead of her, and the lights of aircraft turning for their final approach to the airport hanging in the air.

By the time she reached Konstancin it was light enough for her to see the pines crowding the sides of the road and some of the old dilapidated buildings of the spa, their grubby stucco coming up out of the dimness. By virtue of its hot springs, Konstancin had been a spa for a couple of hundred years, a destination for the genteelly ill from many kilometres around. Many of the old houses built here by the wealthy of the nineteenth and early twentieth centuries had been abandoned and fallen into ruin, but there were newer structures here, built by the freshly-wealthy from the days when Poland had been a Slavic Tiger. The road took her past the old hospital in the growing daylight, and another kilometre or so brought her to the gates of the rest home.

Although in truth, it was just another hospital, albeit one specialising in the elderly and infirm. Elderly and infirm and well-off – it cost a small fortune every year for someone to stay here – and the fact that there were so many permanent residents either spoke for the number of rich people in Poland, or the number of people desperate to dump their aged relatives on someone else. Sometimes that made Ania angry, but then she remembered her father's stubborn insistence on looking after his ancient and demented mother at home and she saw the point.

She parked at the side of the main building and walked round to the front entrance. The hospital looked like an old workers' hotel from the Martial Law era; a long building five storeys tall, its flat roof festooned with satellite dishes and its face lined with walkways and doors and windows, its pale orange walls just starting to flush with the dawn.

The lobby looked as if it belonged in a utilitarian hotel, too. It was big and airy, with twin staircases doglegging up from either side of a reception desk, behind which sat a smiling young woman in a smart suit. To one side there was a little fountain with a baffling post-modern sculpture standing in it, and to the other were the big double doors to the dining room, from which came the sounds of staff setting tables for breakfast for the residents who were capable of coming down and eating for themselves.

Ania nodded hello to the girl at the desk and pushed through a door at the back of the lobby which opened onto a long tiled corridor. In the staff room at the end, she docked her phone so it could upload her day's duties from the hospital's expert system, and went to get a coffee from the machine in the corner. A few of the other day staff were already there, bitching about husbands, partners, children, money. Ania exchanged a few words, took her coffee out to the loading area at the back of the hospital to have her last cigarette before her midmorning break. Looking out into the forest beyond the fence, she watched a wild boar sow and half a dozen piglets rummaging unhurriedly through the ground litter. She'd lost count of how many generations of wild boars she'd watched from here, down the years.

Back in the staff room, she pitched her cup into the waste bin and checked her phone's downloads. An itinerary popped up; she gave it a quick once-over on her way back up the corridor to the pharmacy, where she docked the phone again to check out a trolley and the requisite morning medications. She wheeled the trolley down a side corridor to the service lift, pushed the button, and when the door slid open she took a deep breath and pushed the trolley inside to begin her day.

2.

THEY COULDN'T PRONOUNCE his name properly, so they called him 'Johnny'. He habitually woke before dawn, no matter what time of year it was, wheeled his chair into the bathroom and had a shower, then sat watching the news until one of the nurses came with his pills. He was, according to his records, in his early nineties, but he presented as a well-preserved eighty, and until a couple of years ago he would even have passed as 'sprightly,' but his legs had started to go and now he found it difficult to get very far on his own without medication to alleviate the pain. The doctor who visited every day had said something about neurotransmitters and myelin sheaths and other things he didn't understand. The doctor looked about twelve years old.

This morning it was the chubby nurse, the one with 'Ania' on her nametag. She wasn't as bad as some of them; at least she knocked before she came in, rather than just barging into the apartment.

"Good morning, Johnny," she said cheerfully, pushing the trolley over the threshold. "How are we today?"

"We are very well, thank you, nurse," he replied politely, as always.

"And we've had our shower? That's very good."

"I do wish you wouldn't talk to me as if I was a child," he told her.

She was sorting out his medication, doublechecking its tags with the information on her phone. "I'm sorry?"

He shook his head. "Doesn't matter. Give me the pills."

There were two pills, both of them small and round. One was blue, one was beige. He had no idea what they were. Ania gave him a little cup of water to wash them down with, then she busied herself tidying up the bathroom while they took effect. When she came out, stripping off her surgical gloves, he was already standing by the bed, waiting for her to help him dress. The pills helped him stand and walk about, but he was still stiff and awkward in the morning. He was just too damned old. It was embarrassing.

When he was dressed and his hair – at least he still had all his own hair and most of his teeth – was combed, he took up his cane and embarked on the long, slow trek along the walkway to the lift at the end. It was always a bit of an adventure early in the morning, but if he didn't get down to the restaurant in fairly short order all the freshly-cooked food would be gone and he'd be left with stuff that had been sitting under heat lamps and he'd rather starve than eat that. He still had some standards.

He had to admit, grudgingly, that the food wasn't bad. He was constantly plagued by nutritionists and well-meaning doctors wanting to get his cholesterol down, but within those parameters he actually ate quite well. He'd been quite plump when he first came here, but now his weight was down to a rangy sixty-five kilos and he couldn't deny that it made getting about somewhat easier, even if the sight of his bony knees in the morning did annoy him out of all proportion.

There was a rack of communal pads by the entrance to the restaurant. He grabbed one as he went past and sat at his usual table, in a corner by one of the windows, far from the other early morning residents gumming their way through their cereal. One of the serving staff came to his table and he waved his phone so it could transmit his ID and dietary requirements.

When the waiter had departed, Johnny activated the pad and called up a menu of news sites. There were many things he hated about the modern world, but the internet was not among them. The communal pads had restrictions to stop the residents looking for porn, narcotics or firearms – all of which had caused problems in the past, some of the residents were pretty feisty – but the news wasn't obviously censored. He was reading a piece about the Community's delegation taking their seat at the United Nations when his breakfast arrived. Grapefruit, orange juice, a cup of coffee, rasher of grilled bacon, a grilled sausage, a small portion of scrambled eggs – obviously today was a day for lifting the foot off the anti-cholesterol pedal. The bacon wasn't bad.

After breakfast, he returned to his apartment for his coat and scarf and went for a walk in the grounds of the hospital. It was a bright, chilly day, and his breath plumed in the cool air as he did a couple of circuits of the building. The grounds weren't very large, and several other of the more ambulatory residents were also taking morning constitutionals in the hour or so before the wheelchair-bound started to emerge from the building and race each other awkwardly along the paths.

After his walk was an hour's physio, which was... well, it passed the time, if nothing else.

He usually had a nap after physio. He found himself napping a lot, these days, which was irritating. He remembered a time when he could work all day and far into the night and wake up the next morning clear-headed and ready to start work again. These days he was lucky if he could make it to lunch without nodding off.

This morning, though, he had barely settled down when there was a knock on the door. When he answered it he found Ania standing outside with two men he had never seen before, and his heart thudded in his chest so hard that he thought for a moment that it was finally going to stop.

"You've got visitors, Johnny," Ania told him. "From your lawyers."

He looked at them. One was nondescript and had a cane; the other had prematurely-white hair and a hunted expression. They were both wearing expensive suits and carrying briefcases, but they were the least likely-looking lawyers he had ever seen.

"Sir," the one with the cane said briskly in French, presumably hoping that Ania would not be able to follow, "my name is Smith, and this is my colleague, Mr Jones. We represent Leonidas & Parr of Tilbury, Essex. Please accept our identification." And he took from his jacket pocket a small black and white photograph and held it out. Jean-Yves took it, and even now, after all these years, his eye first sought out not Woodrow Wilson and Lloyd-George and the other world leaders, but Roland's face, in the background, stern and purposeful. He felt a great tiredness, like the shadow of a cloud.

"You'd better come in, then," he said.

3.

THE FIRST THING he said, when Ania had gone and the two men were sitting on the sofa in his apartment, was, "You're no more lawyers than I am."

"No," the one with the cane admitted. "No, we're not. We're not here to harm you, though, I assure you of that. My father was sole trustee of your fund."

Jean-Yves tipped his head to one side and looked at the younger man's face. "Yes," he said. "I remember him. You look almost nothing like him, you know. I presume your presence here means he's dead."

"About eighteen months ago," said Rudi. He paused, somewhat awkwardly. "There are some questions I must ask you, the first of which is, which one are you? Sarkisian, Tremblay, or Charpentier?"

Jean-Yves glowered at him. "You don't know?"

Rudi shook his head. "There are just the details of payments. And they were not easy to come by."

"I am Charpentier," said Jean-Yves. "How did you find me?"

"My father left me some... items," Rudi said. "They led me to a trust fund of some nine hundred and seventy million dollars. I can only assume my father intended me to take his place as trustee."

"How did you find me?" Jean-Yves asked again. "No one was supposed to be able to find me."

"Well, I had a head start, with the details of the trust fund," Rudi said reasonably. "It wasn't easy, if that's any consolation; my father laid quite a paper trail."

"Yes," said Jean-Yves. "Yes, I remember. Evil little bastard. I always said we shouldn't have trusted him."

"To be fair, you may have been the only people in my father's life who *were* justified in trusting him. In his very long life."

Jean-Yves looked at the two men. "And what about you?" he asked the white-haired one.

"Me?" said Forsyth in surprise.

"Yes, you. Is *your* father mixed up in this catastrophe somehow?"

"This man is under my protection," said Rudi. "And when did this become a catastrophe, precisely?"

"When you turned up at my front door," Jean-Yves said angrily. "No one was supposed to visit me in person. Ever. I'm supposed to be *dead*, for Christ's sake."

"Yes, since 1978," said Rudi. "I read your obituary. That was one of the questions I was going to ask you."

The Frenchman rubbed his eyes. "You have no idea what you've done, coming here like this." He stood up. "You have to get me out of here. Right now."

"Now wait a moment," said Rudi.

"No." Jean-Yves stomped over and poked Rudi in the chest. "I've spent *decades* hiding from them. And you just come waltzing in here with Christ only knows who following you. This is your responsibility."

This was not going quite the way Rudi had envisaged it. He said. "I can relocate you, certainly, but not on the hoof. It'll take time."

"I don't *have* any time. We have to go *now*."

Rudi looked at Forsyth, who was following the conversation with a baffled expression. He said to the Frenchman, "But how can you trust us? I could have come into possession of these bona fides by any number of routes."

Jean-Yves stomped across the room to the coat rack and grabbed his jacket. "Because if you have control of the money you wouldn't be here asking me questions; you'd have killed me on the spot. Now let's go."

FORSYTH DROVE. RUDI told him to head in the direction of Radom, and then busied himself with his phone for an hour or so while the Frenchman sat beside him in the back of the car, fuming gently and occasionally shaking his head and uttering swear words in four different European languages.

"How old are you?" Rudi asked at one point, between flurries of texts and emails.

"I'm ninety-two years old this year, fuck you," Jean-Yves said.

"Your obituary says you were born in 1895. You were photographed at the Treaty of Versailles. You are not ninety-two years old. Look at me, please." He took a photograph of the Frenchman with his phone. "Thank you."

Jean-Yves snorted and crossed his arms and stared pointedly out of the window at the passing scenery while Rudi went back to sending and receiving messages.

It took them an hour and a half to reach Radom, and when they got there Rudi told Forsyth to turn west towards Częstochowa.

"How much do you know?" Jean-Yves asked.

"I know the Sarkisian Collective was a group of mathematicians and topologists and cartographers, which in certain circles is very significant," Rudi told him. "I know you're a lot older than you look, and that makes me suspect that you and your colleagues spent a long time in the Community. I know you have a lot of money, and I know you employed my father to look after it. I know you're afraid of *someone*."

The Frenchman sighed. "Did you find the others?"

"I found details of two other sets of disbursements, both of them discontinued."

"So they're both dead."

"I don't know. One of the disbursements was to a bank in Cannes, the other to a firm of attorneys in Montreal."

"Roland," said Jean-Yves. "Roland always said he wanted to visit Canada."

"What I *don't* know, Professor, is what you've done," Rudi said.

"I don't have to tell you that."

"You do if you don't want us to stop the car and leave you at the side of the road," Rudi told him. "I have control of your money, Professor. What are you going to do without that?"

Jean-Yves rubbed his face. "I was born in Avignon," he said. "My father was a *pâtissier*, my mother a seamstress. My mother was also a genius; if she'd been given the chance she would have been one of the most naturally talented mathematicians in Europe. I think she wanted to live the career she never had through me; she would have beaten me black and blue if I had wound up as a small-town pastry chef."

"There are worse things," Rudi opined resuming thumb-typing on his phone. "It takes a rare kind of patience to be a *pâtissier*. Or at least to be any good at it."

The Frenchman looked at him. Then he shrugged. "Whatever," he said. "My father was *adequate*. It was my mother who introduced me to mathematics, who taught me things I wasn't being taught at school, who prepared me for university."

"Your mother," Rudi said, "wasn't *English*, by any chance, was she?"

Jean-Yves chuckled. "No. But I see where your mind's going. *His* mother was English. Sarkisian."

"*Le Parapluie.*"

"Roland," said Jean-Yves. "At university everyone called him *Le Parapluie* because he always carried an umbrella. We all started doing it; it was our trademark."

"The Sarkisian Collective."

Jean-Yves waved the name away.

"How did you meet?"

"In Paris, at university. Although we weren't there long, because of the War. We met again afterward."

Rudi glanced at the old Frenchman and wondered what lay in the gap between '... because of the War' and 'We met again afterward.'

"I was in Caen by then," Jean-Yves went on. "He wrote to me. I have no idea how he found me; my parents were dead by then, no one from university knew where I was. Roland said he wanted me to join a group of friends – mathematicians and cartographers – who were studying a particularly interesting question of topology. There was a patron who would fund our work. He told me to meet him at Versailles."

"His mother's maiden name was Whitton-Whyte, wasn't it."

"White. He said her name was White. He had some papers she'd left him, things she'd inherited from some distant relative. Maps and things."

Rudi paused, just momentarily, in his texting.

"There was a... treatise," Jean-Yves went on. "Among the papers. It was really *very* strange work; I hadn't seen anything like it before." He paused. "You already know what it was, don't you."

"The holy grail. The creation myth."

Jean-Yves nodded. "Just so. It wasn't the work of one person. It was a bundle of papers, oh, so thick." He indicated by holding his thumb and forefinger about three centimetres apart. "It was written in perhaps a dozen different hands, in different inks. Some of it was very old. There were many annotations and crossings-out. It was actually quite a mess. Roland wanted us to work on it, refine it, try to understand it."

"Which you did, in the end."

"Ah," Jean-Yves looked sad. "I'm not sure we ever *understood* it. But we learned how to use it, eventually, which was sufficient for the purposes of our patrons."

"Your patrons being...?"

Jean-Yves ignored the question. "We worked for *years*. This was no simple problem, it was..." he searched for the words. "It was *all-consuming*. Even with the treatise, we were working in completely unknown territory. Our patrons looked after us, took care of our every need." He paused and looked out of the window again. "We were prisoners, of course. But we became so absorbed in our work that it didn't matter. Only the work mattered. We were like *monks*." He glanced at Rudi. "I suppose you find that absurd."

Still typing, Rudi shook his head.

"We moved, from time to time," Jean-Yves went on. "*Were* moved, I should say. We'd stay in country houses, old hotels, abandoned farms. After a few years, representatives of our patrons would come and we would be told to pack up our work and our belongings and we would be taken somewhere else. We wound up near Auxerre, in a big old house with a vineyard. This was, oh, late 1937, early 1938. Roland saw the way the wind was blowing – we all did, we'd lived through one German invasion – and he said we had to leave in order to protect our work. So we left Auxerre and he led us into the Promised Land."

"The Community."

"No. That was later."

Rudi didn't say anything. He turned his head and looked out of the window.

"It was very isolated," Jean-Yves said. "A house by the sea. We were free to walk anywhere we wanted, but there was nowhere to go. No other habitation, no other people. It was as if we were the only people in the world. And we stayed there while Europe burned and millions died." He sighed.

"Did you see no one else at all?"

"There was a small staff at the house. Half a dozen men and women. They looked after us." He shrugged. "There was a man who used to visit us when we were in France. To visit Roland, really. A quiet man, unassuming, almost apologetic. We called him 'Gaston', but he wasn't French. I got the impression he was Russian. He came and went from the house by the sea. I think he represented our patrons, and he took our work away with him for others to look at."

"How long were you there for?" asked Rudi.

Jean-Yves looked at him. "How familiar are you with the Community?"

"I know there's a time dilation effect, if that's what you mean,"

Rudi said. "Time passes more slowly in the Community. Nobody knows why."

The Frenchman looked smug. "*I* know why."

There was a silence in the car for almost a minute. Then Rudi said, "I presume you're not going to tell us."

Jean-Yves shook his head. "Not even if I thought you stood a chance of understanding it. Which I don't."

Rudi sighed and looked at his phone, thumbed up a text, read it, swiped it away.

"We went to the house by the sea in January 1939," said Jean-Yves. "We stayed there for three years, as far as I could judge. When we came back to Europe it was April 1979."

Rudi stared.

"It was a bit of a shock," Jean-Yves added.

"I can imagine."

"Can you?"

Rudi thought about it. "No," he said finally. "No, I can't. Sorry."

"Most of us wanted to go straight back to the house," Jean-Yves said.

Time passes more slowly in the Community. But not *that* slowly. Rudi tried to think.

"What did you do?" he asked.

"Our lives had ceased to be normal when we went to the house by the sea. We knew we were investigating something... *extraordinary*, but until we came back we didn't realise just how extraordinary it was. We were men out of time. Our patrons had placed fake obituaries in the papers. We were dead. Some of the group wanted to try to find their families; they went away and I never saw them again. I don't know what happened to them.

"One night Roland gathered the rest of us together and told us he believed our patrons would have us killed as soon as they realised that our work was complete. He'd kept the truth from them for some time, but he said they were close to understanding that they didn't need us any more. So he had done a bad thing. At some point, he had come into contact with quite a large amount of our patrons' money, and he had... sequestered it somewhere. He said he'd been in contact with the Community and that they were prepared to grant us asylum. They'd sent him the coordinates of a border crossing in Estonia and were waiting to welcome us with open arms."

Rudi's shoulders sagged. He dropped the phone into his lap and sat back. "And that's when you met my father."

"Your father and another man. They'd been sent to guide us across the border. I didn't find out until later that Roland had also engaged him to take care of the money, and by that time it was too late to do anything about it."

Rudi closed his eyes and swore under his breath. With an effort, he said, "What happened next?"

"Roland was very clever in his negotiations with the Community. He hadn't told them everything we knew, everything we had done. They believed we were mathematicians who had stumbled independently across topologies which would allow us to open their borders from the European side. The world had just passed through two terrible wars; they were terrified that Europe would find a way to invade. It would have been just as easy to have us killed, but instead they put us to work making their borders secure."

Rudi thought about it. Apart from a very brief period in the late nineteenth century, the Presiding Authority had been staunchly isolationist for its entire history, aware of but entirely uninterested in Europe. Only a select few had been allowed to cross the border, in either direction. It would have suited them to seal the place off entirely, but they had already begun to meddle quietly in European affairs and either they had too much time and effort invested in it, or were simply enjoying themselves too much, to stop.

He said, "What went wrong?"

"Nothing," said Jean-Yves. "Nothing earth-shattering, anyway. We were prisoners, that's all. Safe and content, but prisoners again nonetheless. Our social contacts were strictly limited and policed, the Community was *stultifyingly* dull. And the food was terrible. We just decided to leave, so one day we opened the border in Władysław and crossed into Prague. Roland had already contacted your father – I don't know how – and he was waiting for us. And we went to ground. Until today."

"We're here," Forsyth said.

*   *   *

THE COBBLER LOOKED about fourteen years old, a cocky, runty youth in a leather jacket and cowboy boots who carried his gear in an antique calfskin rucksack. From the window of the safe flat, Rudi could see the verdigrised rooftops of Jasna Góra, the monastery which housed the *Czarna Madonna*, a venerated icon ascribed with protecting Jasna Góra from the Swedish invasion in 1655. He didn't like the view. Częstochowa, its bustling streets, its crowds of pilgrims coming to visit the monastery, suddenly seemed dangerous. The whole world suddenly seemed dangerous, far beyond his ability to cope with it.

"The photo you sent me was shit," the cobbler said, handing over the fake passport. "But that's good. Border guards get suspicious if your photo's too good."

It occurred to Rudi that he had had just about enough of cobbler wisdom, which all seemed to boil down to *you don't want to look like your passport photo*. He paid the cobbler and they went back down to the car.

"Where now?" asked Forsyth as they stepped out into the courtyard behind the building, and Rudi felt strong hands grip his arms from behind. At his side, Forsyth and the Frenchman seemed to be struggling with invisible assailants. Rudi didn't struggle. Forsyth was shouting, but no one came to investigate the disturbance. Several patches of air in front of them seemed to boil, and four figures wearing stealth suits appeared. They were all holding automatic rifles.

An SUV with smoked windows drove into the courtyard and pulled up behind the armed men. Three men got out. Two of them were security-guard types in good suits. The third was shorter, slender. He had long auburn hair and he was wearing chinos and a blazer over a dark blue shirt. All of a sudden, Forsyth stopped struggling.

"Hi, Snowy," said the auburn-haired man. "'Sup?"

Forsyth seemed to have been rendered utterly speechless, so the auburn-haired man walked over to Rudi and said, "Hi. Good to meet you. I don't want to hurt anybody. I just want to take what belongs to me and then we'll be gone. Okay?" He had an American accent.

Charpentier began to walk, like someone performing a particularly excruciating mime, towards the SUV.

"And you are...?" asked Rudi.

The auburn-haired man smiled. Behind him, Charpentier seemed to bend himself over and levitate awkwardly into the back of the car. The door closed itself.

"There," said the American. "That didn't hurt at all, did it."

Forsyth suddenly regained the power of speech. "You *cunt*," he said. "I thought you were dead."

The American shook his head. "Nah, not me, Snowy," he said. "Very hard to kill, that's me." He gave Rudi one last look, then he turned and walked back to the car. He and his bodyguards climbed in, the car reversed unhurriedly out of the courtyard, and they heard it drive away. The armed men seemed to *shrug* back into invisibility, and all of a sudden Rudi and Forsyth felt the unseen hands release them. Rudi thought he heard, very faintly, the sound of footsteps on the uneven paving stones of the courtyard. And then they were alone.

4.

SHE WAS SHOPPING in Freňstát when the call came through. It was probably the last free time she would have until the Spring; skiing season was beginning, up in the mountains, and with it the annual flood of tourists who came to try the pistes and the casinos and the spas and generally misbehave.

She took out her phone, saw the ID, and sighed. "Yes?"

"Had a flag go up, boss," said Bruno. "Name of *Laar*. Estonian national."

She looked around the shop. She'd had a vague notion of buying some new clothes, but to be honest this year's fashions seemed ridiculously young to her. She said, "When?"

"Forty minutes ago. He came over the border with another man, Kenneth Paul March. The March passport's an obvious fake; typical Coureur rush-job. The Laar documents seem authentic."

Yes, well, of course they would. "Where are they?"

"The flag said detain at the border," Bruno said. "They're being held there."

The thing was, this was in no way even a surprise. His sidekick, the Englishman she rather fancied, had crossed into the Zone four days ago with a young woman travelling on an Australian passport. Facial recognition had spotted him, although to be fair he wasn't hard to pick out of the crowds of guests; for all its pretence at moneyed cosmopolitanism, the Zone was still largely the playground of wealthy white Eurotrash, not young English people of colour. She'd decided to let the couple be and see what happened, but so far all that had happened was numerous long walks in the late autumn hills, followed by lengthy and openly romantic meals at various restaurants. Didn't matter. The sidekick was a *harbinger*, his way of letting her know he was coming. Just like the stupid business with the Laar identity. It was his idea of professional courtesy; she thought he might even think it was *cute*.

She was tempted to have him thrown into a cell and just leave him there for a couple of days, but she said, "Have them transferred to headquarters, put them in separate interview rooms. I'm on my way."

THE BESKID ECONOMIC Zone was not, technically, a polity. It was more of a theme park, rented from the Czech government by a consortium of corporations and granted a limited form of statehood. A string of resort hotels, most of them of adventurous design, ran along the mountains, and the skiing and the gambling attracted many hundreds of thousands of visitors every year.

Unfortunately, the Zone's general anything-goes reputation also attracted intelligence services from all over Europe, and despite Zone Security's best efforts it only grew worse every year. It was getting like postwar Vienna or Munich; some days it seemed as if she was knee-deep in spies. She had begun to consider early retirement, maybe find herself a little cottage in Wales. She liked Wales. She wondered what she would do there.

The Security building had been designed by a world-famous Chilean architect, who had come up with a structure resembling the lair of a Bond villain, clinging to the vertiginous side of a mountain gorge. The first time she'd seen it, on her first day as an intelligence officer, the view from some of its windows had made her dizzy. Now she hardly noticed.

Her staff had moved the visitors to interview rooms on the third floor. "Has he said anything?" she asked Bruno as they walked down the corridor. "Claimed asylum? Demanded the use of Zone resources to go to war against the Community? Anything like that?"

Bruno glanced at her. "He noticed we'd had the place redecorated."

That made her smile a little as they stopped outside the door. "Okay," she said. "Wait here; I'll do this myself."

"Okay, boss." Bruno opened the door, let her step inside, and closed it behind her.

He was sitting at the table in the middle of the room, smoking a small cigar, his cane propped up against his chair. It had been quite some time since they had last seen each other, and in the way of former lovers they each spent a few moments logging the grey hairs, the new wrinkles, remembering times past, visiting old regrets.

Finally, he smiled bashfully. "Hello," he said.

"Hi," she said, not unkindly.

"I'm trying to stop a war," he said. "And I need your help."

THEY HAD DINNER at a restaurant perched halfway up a sheer mountainside. The spectacular views from the terrace were reflected in the prices, but she had never paid for a meal since she became head of Zone Security. The restaurant was only accessible via a brightly-coloured funicular railway and a carefully-camouflaged access road from the other side of the mountain. After dinner, they went back to the funicular station for the half-hour ride down to the car park. She put her arm through his as they walked. They had the car to themselves, but on the platform at the top she saw the English boy and the girl with the Australian passport among some passengers boarding a few cars back.

She didn't make a big thing of spotting them, but Rudi noticed anyway. He was good at things like that. He said, "Remember him?"

"Who could forget?" She smiled. "Who's the girl?"

"Collateral damage." He looked out of the window; dusk was

falling and the valleys far below were filling with darkness. "Not mine, for once."

She walked to the other side of the car and perched herself on one of the window-seats as the train began to descend smoothly and unhurriedly. "I've been thinking about retiring," she said.

He smiled at her. "You won't."

"I'll *have* to, sooner or later."

"What would you do?"

"I've given some thought to writing my memoirs."

That made him laugh. "Send me a copy."

"I'm not going to say anything about *you*, if that's what you're thinking."

He pouted theatrically. It made him look ridiculously young and vulnerable and she thought back, not for the first time this evening, to the first time they'd met, when he'd been hopelessly naive and useless. Not all changes can be codified by grey hairs and wrinkles.

He put his hands in his pockets and leaned his forehead against the window, looking down into the valley. "I didn't just lead them to Charpentier, I *delivered* him to them. I thought I'd become good at this, but I'd just become *smug*."

"You should stop feeling sorry for yourself and start worrying about what you're going to do about it."

He turned from the window and looked at her. "My *father*," he said. "He really was the fucking Devil."

"No he wasn't," she said. "He was just like us, just getting by the best he could. You can't blame him for that."

"Oh, I can. He's been dead eighteen months and he's still leaving a trail of wreckage. You'd be surprised how much I can blame him."

She tipped her head to one side and looked at him.

"And I'm not helping. I know." He smiled ruefully. "Sorry."

"You've just spent two hours telling me the Community and the Sarkisian Collective's patrons are at war," she said. "You haven't said a single word about how you think you're going to stop it."

"I don't know," he told her. "Any ideas?" When she didn't say anything, he put the heels of his hands to his eyes and rubbed gently. "Do you think," he asked, "Crispin would listen to reason?"

"'Crispin' doesn't exist," she reminded him. She'd used Zone Security's resources to break into the Warsaw Metro's personnel database, pull up Crispin's files, and run a background check. It was so poorly backstopped as to be offensive; Crispin was a legend, a man of fog. "How are you going to find him?"

He smiled ruefully. "I've located a man who can probably put me in touch; I've been running a data-scraping operation to find him." He took his hands from his eyes and shrugged.

"Okay. So this man puts you in contact with Crispin. What are you going to say?"

Rudi looked out of the window again, trying to find a fault in his reasoning. His reflection looked exhausted. He was as certain as he could be, without someone actually showing him documentary evidence, that the Community had bombed the Line. *Why* was a mystery, but that didn't matter right now. What mattered was that the builders of the Line had responded by transposing part of the Community onto Luxembourg, which meant they had access to the Sarkisian Collective's research, which implied that they and the Sarkisians' patrons were one and the same. The implications of *that* were too large to think about at the moment. He had no doubt that if he dug around a bit more he would find other examples of the Community and the Patrons poking and prodding each other like children in a school playground, a clandestine war of tit-for-tat which had only recently broken through into daylight.

"One of them has to stop," he said. "The Community's nervous, they know how easily this could all spill over, but they won't back down. The Patrons..." He shrugged. "I know it sounds utterly extraordinary, but I really think they're running scenarios through the prediction engine in Dresden, over and over again, looking at the ones where they come out on top, manipulating events so that those scenarios come to pass. The world's in the hands of fucking madmen." He didn't mention the growing suspicion that he was part of those scenarios; it seemed absurdly paranoid, even to him.

She sighed. "And you've only just come to this conclusion?"

He turned and looked across the car at her. "You think I shouldn't get involved."

"You're over twenty-one; you're old enough to make your own decisions. I think you're lucky you've not been killed already, for what it's worth."

He thought about it. "*Someone* ought to try," he said. "Otherwise what's the point of anything?"

LEV'S EXPLORATION OF the Patrons' business interests had begun to resemble the exploration of North America. He had begun with a foothold in Dresden-Neustadt and had only slowly come to realise that beyond the trees was a continent which might as well be limitless. Though he had yet to positively identify a single person, he had uncovered many outposts and incursions, and the more he discovered, the more it alarmed Rudi. It was as if there was another structure underlying Europe; like the Community, but this time made of money and influence. Lev was beginning to turn up connections to serious organised crime and national governments. They also owned the Zone.

This had momentarily put Marta – Rudi still thought of her as Marta, she'd never told him her real name and he'd respected that by never trying to find out – in something of a position, which she had resolved by the simple expedient of finding two members of her staff who resembled him and Forsyth and sending them over the border into the Czech Republic using the false passports he'd had made up. It was a fairly ramshackle piece of misdirection, but for the moment, if anyone asked, she could say quite truthfully that according to official records Tonu Laar and his friend were no longer in the Zone.

She dropped him at the hotel – a modest place, by Zone standards, big enough for him and Forsyth to lose themselves among the other guests but not so big that he couldn't scope out any unusual activity – and he went up to his room and locked the door and sat on the bed for a while, staring into space.

He got up and went over to one of the fitted wardrobes and took out an attaché case about the size of an old-style pilots' chart case. He carried it over to the bed and went through the nitpicking sequence of combinations and key-swipes to stop it incinerating its contents, then he opened it and emptied it on the duvet.

Well.

He arranged everything in what appeared to be chronological order, as best he could. Here was the photograph of the Sarkisian Collective at the Versailles peace conference, eight intense-looking young Frenchmen in formal suits, each of them with his umbrella. Rudi couldn't tell which one was Charpentier.

Next, his father's birth certificates, ancient Soviet-era documents marked with official stamps in purple ink. It was by no means impossible to forge documents like this – depending on how picky you were, you could even do it with a printer/scanner and some image-processing software – but why would you forge someone's birth certificate and make them forty years older than they actually were? Five years, maybe ten. But forty?

The two passports. Identical birthdates, identical photos, different birthplaces. In the photos his father, wearing a shirt and tie, was contriving to look serious but only managing to look shifty. Rudi flicked through the little books, looking at the entry and exit stamps. There were, of course, no stamps for the most important border his father had crossed, over and over again. He must have spent quite a lot of time in the Community, off and on, for forty-odd years to have passed in Europe. Rudi supposed it all added up. The one thing it explained – and it was really of no earthly interest to anyone else – was his father's stubborn refusal to give up Lahemaa. Although that made Rudi wonder why he had moved the family there when he did; had there been another operation going on? Infiltration and exfiltration from the Community?

He presumed Juhan's birth certificate had a similar birthdate on it, unless his source in the Community was wrong or someone *else* had been working with his father for the Directorate. Which begged the question of why Juhan had told him the story of the Frenchmen, and why he had handed over the chocolate box when he presumably had some inkling what it contained. Rudi didn't want to think about it too much, because he'd only start breaking things. He laid the passports down beside the birth certificates.

He stood looking down at the documents, turning the hard drive over in his hands. Lev had been quite impressed by the level of encryption used on the files it contained; it had taken him several days to crack them and access the first steps in the paper trail which had finally led Rudi to the quite fantastic sum of money Roland Sarkisian had stolen from his patrons, and then on to Charpentier. He'd also been impressed by how well Toomas had dispersed and hidden the money, although Rudi wasn't remotely surprised; his father's nature harboured depths of deviousness which would have startled a Borgia. What did surprise him was that Toomas hadn't stolen the money from the Collective.

Crispin hadn't wanted the money. Even in these autumnal days a billion dollars was a significant amount, but Crispin hadn't mentioned the money. All he had wanted was Charpentier, because Charpentier had something that was worth more than all the money in the world.

The problem with the Community and the Patrons was that they weren't children. The Patrons, whoever they were, were vastly powerful and wealthy, and the Community was a nuclear superpower which had already – albeit accidentally – released a flu pandemic in Europe. And now the Patrons had Charpentier, the last person left alive who could make sense of the Sarkisians' research. The last person left alive who knew how to destroy the Community.

ET INARCADIA
EGO

1.

MR HANSEN FLEW in to Stansted on a Thursday morning. He was a tall, distinguished-looking businessman with a confident walk and a very fine suit, and his only luggage was a small overnight bag.

He took a taxi into London. The driver was a young man whose grandparents, when they had only been a little older than him, had made the perilous journey from Syria to Turkey to Greece to Croatia to Austria to Germany to England. It had taken them a long time, and their children, born during their flight, grew up multilingual and stateless, citizens of crisis. With the carelessness of the young, the driver liked to joke that he had borders in his blood, and when he mentioned this to his passenger as they sped down the M11, Mr Hansen expressed the opinion that he understood exactly how that felt.

The taxi dropped him outside a building opposite Liverpool Street station. The ground floor was a coffee shop, but the upper floors comprised suites of serviced apartments, available to rent at short notice for periods of as little as two nights. The entrance, to one side of the coffee shop, led into a lobby with a concierge and two lifts. Mr·Hansen spent five minutes checking in, then continued up to the third floor. Here, at the end of a short corridor, he waved his phone at a door. The lock clicked open and he stepped inside.

Long experience made him pause at the door, looking about him. The apartment was bright and airy and modern. There was a living area, with a sofa and armchairs and a coffee table and an entertainment set, an open-plan kitchenette and dining area off to one side. The apartment had only one bedroom, and from where he stood he could see, through its half-open door, the end of the bed and the door to the ensuite bathroom.

Mr Hansen put his overnight bag down by the door and went over to the windows. Without lifting aside the net curtain, he looked down on the buses and traffic and pedestrians moving along Broadgate. He liked London; there was a sense here, for all its modern buildings, of history. He found it comforting.

"It's a place, not a name," said a voice from the bedroom.

He stood very still, considering the options. While he stood there, the bedroom door swung open and Rudi was standing there, leaning on a cane. His face was still boyish, but the passing years had marked him. He looked tired, worn down. He did not seem to be armed.

"You're not even Lithuanian, I think," he said.

Kaunas shrugged. "A *nom de guerre*. You know how it is. You're looking well."

"That wouldn't be hard; the last time you saw me I'd just been waterboarded by the Line's security men."

"That was regrettable; I'm sorry that happened to you."

"I'll bet."

"I presume there's no Situation here? You sent me that crash message?"

"That was regrettable," Rudi deadpanned. "I'm sorry that happened to you."

"Oh, please," Kaunas said irritably. "Don't be childish."

Rudi walked into the living room. "I need to talk to Crispin," he said.

"Who?"

"Don't," Rudi told him. "Just don't. The people Crispin works for are planning a strike against the Community; I can't stop them by force so I'm going to have to talk them out of it."

Kaunas sighed. There was a part of him, he realised, which had always known this conversation was coming, but it's human nature to avoid awkward conversations, to hope they won't happen, and there was nothing anyone could do about that. "May I sit?" he asked.

Rudi made an *after you* gesture, and Kaunas walked over to the sofa and sat down and clasped his hands across his stomach. "Perhaps," he said, "you could begin by explaining to me why you think I can help you to contact this 'Crispin'."

"Because Central was involved with the Realm."

Kaunas raised an eyebrow.

"I had a contact who was going to sell me information about a Coureur operation in Luxembourg," said Rudi. "He was going to sell someone else information about the Realm. At the time, I thought he was selling two different pieces of information, but he wasn't. It was just different angles on the same thing."

Kaunas nodded. "Yes, we were hired for that Situation. Actually, not even hired. We owed Crispin a favour. Logistical support."

"Who is he?"

Kaunas took a moment to gather his thoughts. "Europe is inherently unstable. It's been in flux for centuries; countries have risen and fallen, borders have ebbed and flowed, governments have come and gone. The Schengen era was just an historical blip, an affectation."

Rudi walked across the room and sat at the dining table.

"Governments, nations, borders, they're all *surface*, they always have been," Kaunas went on. "The real structure underlying it all is money, and the institutions which control it. Finance houses, banks, organised crime; if you drill down deep enough, it's all the same. Money has no nationality, no allegiance. While nations rise and fall, it remains the same. It's the most powerful polity of all."

"And that's a very pretty metaphor, but it doesn't tell me who Crispin is."

"The European Union didn't just go away," Kaunas said. "It splintered, and then it splintered again and again, but a thing like that doesn't just wither and disappear. It's still there. The *institution* still exists, and so does its money."

Rudi remembered something Chief Superintendent Smith had told him, something about the EU having very few members but lots of money. "Are you telling me Crispin works for the *EU*?"

"Crispin *runs* the EU."

"Bullshit."

Kaunas sighed. "I wish it were. I've had dealings with him in the past; he's hardly conventional."

"He's a fucking tunnel worker."

"Well, clearly he is not, is he. I told you; he's not normal."

Rudi scowled.

"Basically, Crispin is a CEO. Or an emperor."

"He seems quite... hands-on," Rudi mused. "For an emperor."

"He does like his little jokes."

Rudi snorted. He was still trying to put together a structure of reasoning where Roland Sarkisian's Patrons mutated into the European Union, and then into the entity which had built the Line, and then selected Crispin as its *capo di tutti capi*.

"I know what you've been doing," Kaunas said. "I've been watching you, and I've really been very impressed. The business in Hungary was quite inventive; it took me a while to work out what you'd done."

"What I was doing was trying to find out what the fuck Coureurs were doing rubbing shoulders with Community intelligence officers in Luxembourg."

"It was... complex. *Les Coureurs* do not take sides; sometimes that leads us into unusual situations."

"I don't care about that any more. We can discuss it later. I need Central to put me in contact with Crispin."

"Well, that's not going to happen," Kaunas told him. "Because Coureur Central doesn't exist."

"Oh, fuck off. I'm tired of this."

"The natural assumption everyone makes about an organisation is that someone is running it," said Kaunas. "But that assumes that there *is* an organisation. *Les Coureurs des Bois* is not an organisation. If you really need a metaphor, I suppose the closest I could come would be to say that *Les Coureurs* are an anarchy. Oh, I don't doubt that once upon a time, back in the misty distance, there was a group of individuals sharing a common aim, but that hasn't been true for many years."

"So who's giving the orders?" asked Rudi.

"Nobody is." Kaunas shrugged. "Or rather, everybody is. Everyone is part of everyone else's operation; the people you employ are part of your operation, you're part of someone else's operation, they're part of someone else's, and so on. It's a perfect, self-sustaining whole, a nation without a figurehead, without borders."

"There's a hierarchy," Rudi insisted.

"No, there isn't."

"What about you? What about Bradley?"

"We have an overview, of sorts. We fight fires. Someone has to. I expect it looks as if we're quite high up in the *hierarchy*, and from time to time it suits us to pretend we are, but really we're not. We just go where we're needed, to keep things running smoothly. We're... diplomats, if you like; a point of contact between *Les Coureurs* and governments."

"Where does the money go? Who does the book-keeping?"

"There are some centralised accounts, and Coureurs assigned to maintain them, but mostly everything runs itself. You'd be surprised. It's quite a sturdy edifice, but massively distributed. The mythology surrounding *Les Coureurs* has become hugely rich and complex; it's impossible to know where it ends and History takes over."

"History," Rudi said, a great bleakness overtaking his heart like an oncoming snowstorm. "That's a grey area."

"It depends who you ask."

"Whose operation am *I* part of?"

"Now, that is the interesting question. May I?" Rudi nodded, and Kaunas stood and went over to a corner table, on which stood several bottles of mineral water and some glasses. He opened one of the bottles. "*Les Coureurs des Bois* are highly compartmentalised. Partly that's for operational security, but mainly it's because that's all there is. Compartments. Doing what they do, which is move things across borders. Everyone's freelance, working only when they have to." He filled a glass with water, recapped the bottle, set it down, turned to face Rudi. "Then you started to use those resources for something else. You started giving orders, started coordinating things. For all practical purposes, *you're* Coureur Central." He took a sip of water.

"Now wait just a moment," Rudi said. Then he couldn't think of anything else to say.

"You could just step down at any time," Kaunas told him. "Everything would simply go back the way it was. But you've given

Les Coureurs a purpose, for the first time in their history, and that has made you relevant to Crispin's interests because quite a large amount of Coureur operational funds come from organised crime."

"*What?*"

"Money has to come from somewhere," Kaunas said. "You'll find, if you look hard enough, that a lot of Europe's mafias – the smaller ones, at any rate – are run as Coureur fundraising operations. It's quite an elegant solution, if you think about it."

Rudi looked about the room, trying to process everything and failing.

"Of course, organised crime in Europe belongs to Crispin as well, and so you and he find yourselves at the heart of a Venn diagram. Which makes you interesting to him." Kaunas drained his glass and put it back on the table and smiled at Rudi. "There," he said. "Happy now?"

Rudi tried to concentrate. "You and I are going to talk about *Les Coureurs* later," he said. "Right now I need to talk to Crispin. One *emperor* to another."

"I really don't see what you could possibly do to stop him doing whatever he wants," Kaunas said.

"Can you contact him or not? Because if you can't you're no use to me."

Kaunas thought about it. "Yes," he said finally. "Yes, I can contact him."

"Then tell him I want to talk. Tell him not to do anything until I've spoken with him, otherwise... oh, I don't know, *threaten* him with something, I don't care what."

Kaunas raised an eyebrow. "He's not going to respond to threats. Would *you*?"

"I don't care," Rudi said angrily, walking over to the door and opening it. "Just contact him. Call me when you've set up a meet. And don't you *dare* go anywhere."

Seth fell into step beside him as he stomped along the corridor towards the lifts. "Well?"

"Don't talk to me," Rudi muttered. "Don't ask questions, don't make jokes, don't talk to me."

Seth, who had seen Rudi angry before but never quite this angry, missed a step. "Okay," he said.

They reached the lifts, none of which appeared to be in any great hurry to stop at their floor. Rudi waved at the call buttons, and when that didn't seem to work he punched them a couple of times. Then he punched them again. He'd lived so long with the image of a faceless Coureur Central as part of the cabal of tormentors who had taken over his life that the discovery that Coureur Central did not exist – or worse, that he *was* Coureur Central – was making his head spin a little.

One of the lifts finally stopped and Rudi marched in, trailed by Seth. He waved for the ground floor and stared at himself in the mirrored wall as the door closed and they started to descend. He looked, he thought, quite deranged, and he wondered how long he had been like that.

On the ground floor, he took off at a fast walk across the foyer, wanting nothing more than to submerge himself in the city, become anonymous, try to work out what to do next, but when he stepped out onto the pavement there was a shiny grey people-carrier pulled up to the kerb, and beside it were two large beefy men in smart suits, and between them, dressed in jeans and a black hoodie and with his hair bound into a ponytail, was Crispin, and all the anger drained straight out of Rudi.

"Hello, Crispin," he said with a sinking heart.

"Is Snowy okay?" Crispin asked.

"He's safe and sound and enjoying a new life," Rudi said.

"Good. I hate collateral damage."

"How's Professor Charpentier?"

Crispin smiled and nodded. "A genuine fucking pain in the ass. Also, you and I are going to have to have a conversation about all that money you keep throwing around."

"Kaunas gave me a précis."

"How do you feel about that?"

"I have no idea."

Crispin nodded. "Get in the car. We're going for a ride."

"No we're fucking not," said Seth.

Crispin looked at him, then at Rudi. "I don't do shoot-outs in the middle of crowded city streets," he said. "Not any more. Messy."

"Collateral damage," Rudi noted.

"Exactly. So you come with me, you don't come with me, it's no skin off my spavined ass. But you might learn something."

Rudi thought about it. He had, he thought, been learning rather too *much* recently. "Get in the car," he told Seth. "Let's hear what he has to say."

THERE WAS, HOWEVER, very little conversation in the car for quite a while. Crispin sat in the front. They sat in the back, sandwiched between the bodyguards. Rudi watched late afternoon London pass by beyond the windows.

At one point, Crispin's phone rang. He took it out, looked at the screen, put it to his ear, and said, "Hi." Pause. "Yes, I know." Longer pause. "Yes, I have." Pause. "Yes, I was." Pause. "No, you can't." Short pause. "And fuck you, too." He hung up and put the phone away. "You guys are just fucking divas, you know that?" he said.

When nobody else in the car responded, Rudi said, "Oh?"

"Fucking Kaunas," Crispin said. "Trying to order me around."

"He told me who you are, by the way," said Rudi.

"I just represent a group of interests," Crispin said without missing a beat. "I'm a CEO."

"That's not what Kaunas says."

Crispin made a rude noise. "*Coureurs*," he said. "You know what *you* are? Really? You started out running Syrians across the Mediterranean in boats I wouldn't have put on the Chicago River. You packed Afghans and Libyans fifty-deep into trucks and drove them out of Izmir headed for the Greek border, and half the time they suffocated before they got there. You're criminals, plain and simple."

"Whereas you are...?"

"All that fucking Cold War romanticism," Crispin went on. "Situations and jump-offs and dead drops and Packages. Doesn't change what you are."

"This may all be true," Rudi said, managing to keep his temper with an effort, "but you'll excuse me if I'm a little affronted to be called a criminal by *you*."

There was a silence at the front of the car. Then Crispin chuckled. "Affronted," he murmured.

"Whatever you're planning to do to the Community, you have to stop," Rudi said.

"Says who?"

"Millions of people are going to die."

Crispin shrugged. "Millions of people are going to die anyway, eventually. Billions. In a hundred years or so everyone on Earth right now will be dead. So it goes."

Rudi said, "Please. Don't do it."

Crispin turned in his seat and looked into the back of the car. "You see, that's one of the reasons I like you," he said appreciatively. "If this was a James Bond movie, you'd kill my two guys here with some lethal gadget disguised as a pen," the two bodyguards looked at Rudi as if daring him to try, "and then you and I would have a climactic battle, at the end of which I'd die horribly and you'd foil my evil plan. But this is real life, and all you've got left is *please*, and you still don't stop."

They had left central London now, making their way down a traffic-choked main road through faceless and mostly blameless suburbs. In the distance to the west, a catenary of lights hung in the early evening sky like a special effect for a 1970s alien encounter film. Aircraft queuing up to land at Heathrow.

"There used to be a village called Heath Row," Crispin said, apropos of nothing, apparently. "It's still somewhere under the airport. Thousands of years from now, people are going to excavate at Heathrow and they'll find this buried village and wonder what the fuck was going through people's minds way back then."

"It was a hamlet," said Seth, who was still annoyed enough to be argumentative. "Not a village."

"Hamlet, schmamlet," said Crispin. "Are you guys listening to me?"

"Bearing in mind we're sitting in the back of a car with two large and presumably heavily-armed men, I think you can safely assume you have our complete attention," Rudi said numbly. The bodyguard to his left sniggered quietly.

"This is where it all started, you know," Crispin said, gesturing out through the windscreen. "Colnbrook, Datchett, Windsor.

Ernshire. You know what the first error was? The first alteration the Whitton-Whytes made to the map?"

"Stanhurst," said Rudi. "They wrote Stanhurst in."

"No, it was a house."

"Oh? And how do you know that?"

"Stanhurst Manor," Crispin went on as if he hadn't heard. "They started small. They created a patch of land, oh, six or seven acres, took a couple dozen workmen across the border, had them build a house. Then they had the workmen build some more houses and go live there. And once they had a foothold they just kept expanding it until they thought it was big enough."

Rudi tried to imagine a pocket universe the size of a market garden. What must it have been like for the first settlers of the Community, watching day by day and year by year as a new landscape appeared before their eyes? The Whitton-Whytes must have wondered, in their private moments, if they hadn't become gods; they wouldn't have been human if it hadn't at least crossed their minds.

"When did your... organisation become interested in what they were doing?" he asked.

Crispin seemed quite pleased by the question. "Quite early on," he said. "We managed to sneak some people in, but they never came back. Went native, I guess."

"Or got whacked," Seth put in.

Crispin thought about it, as if the possibility had never been considered by him and his predecessors. "Nah," he said finally. "The Whitton-Whytes were never into that."

"So, you've been keeping an eye on the Community for, what, more than two hundred years?" Rudi asked.

"About that, yes." Crispin nudged the driver gently and pointed, and the car slowed and made a left turn. In the distance between the houses, Rudi could see the outlying buildings and radar towers of Heathrow. "Mostly it was just a watching brief; we had our own stuff to worry about, and they weren't threatening anybody. We managed to get somebody in in 1889, but they didn't want to talk to us."

"But a year later they wanted to talk to the English."

Crispin nodded. "Summer of 1890, they started putting out feelers to the British government. Fall of 1891, the British started rolling up our operation here, very quietly."

Rudi thought about this. "And the two of you have been at war ever since?"

Crispin put his head back and laughed. "No!" he guffawed. "You think we were worried about the loss of a few networks? Jesus. The Community have *never* understood us. They think we're the Mafia, and we're not. We're Europe. We thought it was *quaint.*" He shook his head. "Nah, we tolerated each other, which was fine by us."

"Until they figured out you were interfering with the Campus."

Crispin sobered. "They can't hurt us, not really."

"If they can't hurt you, don't hurt them," Rudi tried again.

"Oh, I'm not going to hurt them," Crispin said goodnaturedly.

"You're not?"

"Nah. I'm just going to send them a message."

They drove for another few minutes in silence, then the car pulled to a stop and Crispin said, "Well, here we are."

Rudi leaned around the passenger-seat headrest to look out through the windscreen. A few metres ahead, the road simply stopped. In front of the car, for as far as he could see, were fields and hedges and little stands of trees. In the distance, above the trees, a faint twirl of smoke from a chimney.

"*This* is new," Seth said.

"This is not going to be one of those times when the criminal mastermind reveals his master plan and then the plucky heroes use the information to foil his schemes," warned Crispin. "There's nothing you could do, and even if there was, it's way too late for you to do it."

"To be honest, it's unusual for me to have any information at all," Rudi told him sourly. He opened the door and got out of the car and put his hands in his pockets. The road ended in a sharp, straight line, as if God had reached down with an enormous craft knife and severed it. God had then gone on to peel up everything on the other side of the line and replace it with a new landscape, as if he was laying carpet. On this side of the line were the houses of West London – and people were just starting to come out and stand looking in wonder at what had erupted into their lives. On the other side was...

"Impressive," Rudi said to Crispin, who had got out of the car and come over to stand beside him.

"Where's Heathrow gone?" said Seth, walking up to the edge of the new landscape, not quite daring to step over.

"I'm not going to tie up all the loose ends for you," Crispin told Rudi. "You'll have to do that for yourself. I don't even know what all the loose ends are, and frankly I've run out of fucks to give."

Rudi half-turned and looked at him.

"Ho Chi Minh attended the Versailles Peace Conference," Crispin said. "Did you know that?"

"No, I didn't."

"He was there to ask the Great Powers to support an independent Vietnam," Crispin went on. "He had an argument based on the US Declaration of Independence. Imagine that. Nobody paid him any attention. The world would have been a different place if someone had just had the courtesy to listen to him."

Rudi waited.

"The creation of the Community was a family secret," Crispin said. "It got handed down from generation to generation of Whitton-Whytes until about two hundred years ago. I don't know what happened then because there's no predicting what families will do – maybe someone just got fucked-off because they weren't invited to a wedding or something – but at some point there was a failure to *transmit information*. The chain got broken and the family secret wound up leaving the Community and eventually Roland Sarkisian inherited it from his mother."

"The *treatise*."

Crispin nodded. "Sarkisian and his bunch of number crunchers were at Versailles, too," he said. "You've seen the photo. *They* had a proposal for the Great Powers as well, but the difference was that people paid attention. They'd just come through the most terrible war the world had ever seen, and Sarkisian offered to build them a new world, one without nationalities or borders, and they jumped at it."

"Why?" asked Rudi. "Why would the Collective do that?"

"Because Roland Sarkisian was one of the most venal men who ever lived. All he was interested in was money. The Americans didn't want anything to do with it – they thought Sarkisian was crazy – but the Europeans already knew about the Community, so they ponied up an advance and Sarkisian and his boys cooked up a proof of concept for them."

"The House By The Sea," said Rudi. "Where time passes ever so slowly."

"Yeah. That was Phase One. By the time Sarkisian and his guys took off with our money, it was already twice as large as the Community."

"That was over a hundred years ago," Rudi said.

"Yeah." Crispin beamed. "Now it's a whole planet."

Rudi stared out over the fields, the enormity of what the Sarkisians and their patrons had done only now beginning to dawn on him.

"The Machine in Dresden tells us things," Crispin said. "It's been telling us a lot of stuff about the Community."

"Have you ever," Rudi asked, "read *Billion Dollar Brain*?"

Crispin snorted. "It cost a *lot* more than that." He scratched his head. "They've done a deal with the devil," he said. "I don't know what they thought they were going to get out of it, but Europe and the Americans are just going to want more and more of their resources. Eventually the Community are going to put the brakes on, Europe's going to retaliate somehow – probably economically, at first – and what do you think's going to happen then?"

Rudi thought he heard, in the far distance, the faint sound of a church bell.

"The Community's trigger-happy," Crispin went on. "This progressive faction that's running things now is only hanging on by the skin of its teeth. They've got nuclear weapons and they've got the flu virus – which they've both used, if you'll recall. They'll just burst out of there like pus from a boil and there won't be anything anyone can do to stop them but they'll try anyway and things will get utterly fucked up."

"This is the Community, isn't it," Rudi said, waving across the fields. "You've swapped them over, like you did with the Realm."

Crispin looked at him. "You're really quite smart, you know," he said.

"If I was smart I wouldn't have found Charpentier for you."

Crispin beamed. "You knew exactly what you were doing. You figured out that thing in Warsaw, didn't you."

"Sort of," Rudi admitted.

Crispin shook his head. "I'm genuinely sorry I fucked things up for Snowy like that, but I was in a hurry. He's not in any trouble in Poland; I made sure of that."

"Doesn't matter; he's safe now. It might be a good idea never to contact him again, though."

"Hell," said Crispin, "he's never going to see me again. *Nobody's* ever going to see me again."

"What were you doing working in the Warsaw Metro in the first place?"

Crispin shrugged. "Keeping an eye on our investment. Staying busy. Keeps me off the streets, anyway."

Rudi walked forward to the edge of the farmland, reached out, plucked a stem of long grass, twirled it between his fingers, marvelling that not so long ago it had been in another universe. He said, "This is..."

"Pretty cool, huh?" said Crispin, smiling and looking out over the new landscape. "Fuck me but I love it when stuff works."

"And this is your message?"

Crispin nodded proudly. "Think we've got their attention?"

"You could have just sent an email," said Rudi, and Crispin laughed.

"Who elected you King of the World?" Seth called from the edge of the farmland.

"I did," said Crispin. "You have a problem with that?" He said to Rudi, "We're going away. We've made ourselves a place and we're going to see if we can make it work out."

"Sarkisian World?" Rudi said. "Mafia World?"

Crispin took out a packet of cigarettes, lit one, stood with one hand in a pocket of his jeans, gazing out at his creation. "The EU never stood a chance," he said, almost to himself. "Too many borders. We'll do it better, but we want to be left alone. Or we'll do more of..." He gestured out across the fields.

Rudi glanced about him. Quite an appreciable crowd was gathering here at the end of the road. Most of them were filming the scene with their phones. Others were calling friends, family, news outlets. Any moment now there would be police vehicles and army helicopters, but just now it was really quite peaceful. A paused breath at the dawn of the *pax Crispin*.

He said, "Have you run *this* particular scenario through the Neustadt? The one where you cause so much fuss that everyone calms down and has a good think about what they're doing?"

Crispin grunted. "Do I look like I came down with the last fall of snow? Calm never lasts long. A century, maybe two, and Europe and the Community will be at war."

"That's quite a long time. A lot could happen."

"One thing about time," Crispin mused. "You think you have a lot of it, but it runs out real fast."

"Where's Heathrow gone?" Seth asked again, and when Rudi looked at him he saw that the catenary of lights in the sky had begun to break up. Silently and without any apparent fuss they were all beginning to rise into the sky again. The nearest set of lights, though, was continuing to descend, and now he could see the aircraft slung between them. He could just hear the sound of its engines, over the excited chatter of the people around him.

He said, "They weren't after the train, were they. They were after the *tunnel*."

Crispin sighed. "I said I wasn't going to tie up all the loose ends for you."

"Hey," Rudi said. "I'm doing my share of the lifting."

"They were really stupid," said Crispin. "*All* the tunnels on the Line are border crossings. Blowing one of them up barely slowed us down."

"Because of the Campus?"

Crispin pulled a sour face. "They blamed us for what happened to the Campus. *We* weren't dicking around with viruses in there; that was all their own stupid fault. All we were doing was working with the Science Faculty."

"In secret. Behind everyone's backs."

Crispin made a rude noise. "Sometimes that's the only way to get stuff done. It was just the sort of fucking fit of pique you'd expect from them, and *that*'s one of the reasons why they're dangerous. They've got really poor impulse control."

"You didn't try to negotiate? Try to explain?"

"We're the European fucking Union," Crispin said. "We don't *negotiate*." Then he chuckled.

The airliner was much closer now. It was huge, one of the new transcontinental jets, big enough to carry the fuselage of an old-style 747 in its belly. It was still descending, even though it must have been obvious to everyone on the flight deck that Heathrow was no longer there. Rudi wondered what was happening in the Community, the sudden eruption of all those hectares of concrete and buildings and gigantic passenger aircraft into the peace and quiet, and it suddenly occurred to him that Crispin's organisation had just gifted the Community an air force, of sorts. Actually, not just an air force; Europe and the Community would be in the courts for decades, trying to establish who the cornucopia of technology and duty-free and bonded goods and gold bullion at Heathrow belonged to now. Maybe that would keep them too busy to invade each other, maybe it would bring hostilities closer. There was no way to know; if he'd been clairvoyant he wouldn't have got involved in this mess in the first place.

The airliner dipped closer, the sound of its twelve engines drowning out the rising panic of the crowd at the end of the road. It really was colossal; it seemed so utterly *unlikely* to Rudi that it could stay in the air. He pictured the scene in the London Air Traffic control centre in Hampshire. He imagined there was shouting.

It was only a few hundred metres above the treetops when the note of its engines changed; there was a boom of thrust and for a moment it seemed to hang there, suspended in the air above two superimposed worlds. Then it started to climb again, at first imperceptibly, then more quickly. It passed deafeningly overhead and the crowd, almost as one, ducked. A stink of aviation fuel washed down out of the sky. Everyone turned and watched the immense aircraft rise slowly into the east. A small forest of arms went up as everyone lifted their phones to film it.

"That was pretty neat," Crispin said. "You think that was autopilot or someone at the controls?"

"I have no idea," said Rudi, hoping that his heart would one day stop tapdancing in his chest.

"Pretty neat," Crispin said again. His phone rang; he took it out and held it to his ear. "Yeah? That's good." He hung up. "No casualties in the Community, either," he said.

Rudi thought of the end-to-end takeoffs from Heathrow every day. Crispin's timing must have been *exquisite* not to trap at least one jet in the air in the Community. He appreciated that kind of professionalism.

He said, "So, why have I just watched that?"

"You're running things," Crispin said.

"I am *not* running things."

"You're running the Coureurs, whether you meant to or not. And that means you're running a big chunk of the action, one way or another. Of course, a lot of it's *our* action, too, so maybe one day one of our representatives can have a quiet discussion with you about matters of jurisdiction." He shrugged. "Between you and me, you can hand all that stuff over to someone else, or use it to do something useful. Up to you."

"So...?"

"Someone needs to deliver the message," Crispin said. "Someone who can talk to people here and in the Community. People who will listen and not be dicks. Play nice, don't try to find us. Do you think that's too complicated to understand? It's all words of one syllable."

"You're assuming that anyone will listen to me."

"They'll listen. We'll probably have to do this one more time before they get the point, maybe two. But they'll listen."

Now the airliner was gone, some of the braver souls in the crowd had decided to step out into the fields. When they didn't explode or disappear or fall down writhing in agony, others had followed them. Now maybe a hundred people were standing waist-deep in the wheat, chattering excitedly and filming each other and making phone calls. In the distance, Rudi could see figures with torches walking towards them from a line of trees in the growing dusk.

"And for my next trick," Crispin said, half to himself, "I'm going to make a railroad disappear."

From behind them, up the road, Rudi heard approaching sirens. He said, "We'd better make ourselves scarce. We don't want to be here when the authorities arrive."

Crispin seemed completely at ease. Having everything go to plan will have that effect on a person. He grinned and shook his head. "Nah," he said. "Just innocent bystanders, that's us."

*   *   *

BY THE TIME they left the site of the event, the crowd was more than a thousand strong, at least a hundred of them baffled Community citizens. There were police vehicles and fire engines and ambulances and helicopters and journalists and cameramen and no one seemed to have the first idea what to do. It took Crispin's driver almost an hour to back the car down the road to a place where he could turn round. As they drove back towards Central London, a fleet of trucks went by, their loadbeds stacked with fencing.

Crispin chuckled. "Gonna need a *lot* of that."

Rudi found it more interesting that the English had managed to find that much fencing and so many trucks and get them loaded in such a short time, but he said nothing.

Instead of driving into town, the car turned off onto a busy road. Rudi saw a sign that said *Borough Of Ealing* go by, then a big grassy space, then they were dipping down a hill to a frankly insane-looking interchange choked with early-evening traffic.

"Where are we going?" Seth asked.

Crispin didn't answer. He seemed perfectly happy giving the driver directions, even though the driver appeared to know where he was going.

The car negotiated the interchange, then spent forty minutes or so stop-starting at traffic lights. Rudi saw a sign for Wembley Stadium. A branch of IKEA went by. He thought about what must be happening at the moment in the place where Heathrow had once been; it would be interesting to look at social media right now and be one of the few people in the world – in either world – to know what was going on. That would be a considerable novelty for him.

Eventually, after one particularly bad traffic jam, they turned off the busy road. Shortly after that, they made a right turn beside an Underground station. Bounds Green. Rudi, whose knowledge of the geography of Greater London was sketchy at best, was entirely lost, but that didn't matter. For a very long time, it seemed to him, he had felt like a fly who had wandered into a grandfather clock and was gazing in awe at all the cogs without the slightest idea what they were for, just a dim insect sense that everything fitted together somehow. Maybe it was time he stopped, because it hadn't done anyone any good.

They drove a short distance from the Underground station, then the car pulled into a side street and everyone got out. The driver and the bodyguards went to the back of the car and took out a number of bags and suitcases and rucksacks, then they closed and locked the car and Crispin led the way up the street.

After a few metres, he turned in to a narrow path between two houses, and they all followed. The path started out as tarmac underfoot, but as it passed beyond the houses the surface changed and Rudi could feel trodden-down grass and earth beneath his feet. They were walking along a quite narrow strip of wild land – he felt the thorns of an overhanging bramble catch his sleeve and pull away. Through the trees to one side, he could see the lights of houses, and on the other, down what seemed to be quite a steep embankment, more house lights.

"I never met a *deus ex machina* before," Rudi said.

Up ahead, Crispin had taken out a torch to light their way. He guffawed. "*Deus ex Michigan*, maybe."

"Where are we going, by the way?"

"You'll see," Crispin told him. "Got a little surprise for you."

Ahead of them, Rudi saw two figures standing on the path. They were holding little lanterns, the kind you take camping with you and hang up in your tent. Luggage was piled at their feet. He only recognised one of them, but he knew who the other was. It couldn't, he realised, have been anyone else.

"Chief Superintendent," he said.

Smith grinned. "Hello," she said.

He looked at her. "I wish I could think of something cutting or wry to say to you, but I really think I'm all out of smart lines."

"About fucking time," Crispin muttered as he fiddled with a rucksack.

"The people who died on Muhu, they were working for you?"

Smith shook her head. "No. That wasn't supposed to happen," she said. "It was a mess. I'm sorry your friend died."

"What happened?"

"We don't *know* what happened," Crispin said. "We don't know who the other guys were or who they worked for or what they wanted. All we were doing was watching you and waiting for you to lead us to Sarkisian and his boys, we weren't prepared for a fucking bloodbath. By the time the chaos died down, you were gone. So we had to go through that fucking pantomime in Warsaw to smoke you out."

Rudi didn't know what was more disturbing, discovering that Crispin wasn't omnicompetent after all, or discovering that there was yet *another* unknown player out there.

"For what it's worth, I figure it was the Chinese," Crispin said. "Or maybe just some guys who wanted the money."

"Don't *you* want the money?"

Crispin pulled a face and shrugged. "We've managed without it all these years. You keep it. Or give it to charity. Yeah, give it to charity, make some cats and dogs happy."

"It's almost a billion dollars," Rudi protested mildly.

Crispin snorted. "You're such a fucking straight arrow," he said. "Money's not everything."

"No, but you can buy everything with it."

"That fiasco in Estonia wouldn't have happened if it wasn't for the money," Crispin pointed out. "We knew your dad worked for the Community but we didn't know he was mixed up with Sarkisian's bunch until the old guy got in touch."

"My father?"

"The other old guy. The rocker. He tried to sell us the bank codes to our own money, stupid bastard."

Rudi sighed and turned to the other figure. "If you didn't know my father was involved, why did you send me that photograph of the Sarkisians?"

Andrew Molson was tall and fair-haired and handsome in the lantern-light, in a raffish, disreputable sort of way. His handshake was firm. He said, "Nice to meet you finally."

Rudi looked about him at Crispin's little excursion. He looked at Molson, and words failed him. He shook his head.

"You mustn't be too hard on yourself," said Molson. "You weren't to know."

Rudi squinted against the light of the lantern in Molson's hand. "Who *do* you work for, actually?"

"He works for me," said Crispin, slinging the rucksack over his shoulder.

"No I don't," Molson said genially. "You work for me." And Rudi had a dizzying moment when he felt that he was the fly looking at the intelligence which had made the clock.

"Ah, whatever," Crispin said.

"We thought you might help us find the remaining members of the Collective, if we made it an interesting enough problem," Molson told Rudi. "We didn't anticipate that you'd be quite so... intimately involved."

"Well thank Christ you're fallible," Rudi said. "Otherwise I'd be *really* angry about all this."

"I've spent a long time trying to stop my people and your people destroying each other," said Molson.

"Why?"

Molson looked a little surprised by the question. "The Presiding Authority really were going to use the flu virus to depopulate Europe and then come over the border and take over, but it got out before they were ready and your people managed to survive. They would have tried again, if you and I and our friend from the Campus and a lot of other people hadn't stopped them."

"What the hell did I have to do with that?"

"Everyone did their bit."

"Who elected you President of the World?"

Molson chuckled. "It's a dirty job, but someone has to do it. I don't put as much stock in our friend's giant calculating machine as he does; I think there's a chance to avert a war between my people and yours."

Rudi tipped his head to one side.

"The Union gives everyone a breathing space, time to take stock," said Molson. "What we've done," he indicated the little group, "is give Europe and the Community an incentive to work together."

"Or you'll push the button again."

"It's not as easy as that. We'd rather not do it."

Rudi looked around him. Seth and Crispin and Smith were chatting in low voices; the bodyguards and the driver were standing off to one side, attentive but professionally deaf in the way of henchmen down the ages.

"Who killed Mundt?"

Molson looked soberly at him. "We don't actually *know*," he said. "*We* certainly didn't, and neither did the Community. We're working on the assumption that it was the same people who tried to kill you in Estonia. The sniper's mind is completely gone, erased by layers of psychosis; he doesn't even know who he is, let alone who he was working for. I got there too late to stop him."

"But not too late to use him to send a message to me."

Molson beamed happily. "Anyway, the Community have Mundt's research, and much good may it do them; all they can do is open and close borders, and without the Collective's work that's all they'll be *able* to do."

Rudi sighed. "It's still enough to destabilise things, being able to open border crossings any time they want."

"Well, yes," Molson said. "That's why we sent his research to *The Guardian*."

"Oh, you *didn't*," Rudi said, aghast. "Are you insane?"

"It's not Mutually Assured Destruction if only one side has it," Molson said innocently.

"Jesus Maria," Rudi muttered. "Who *are* you?"

In the lamplight, Molson's face took on a sly expression. "Would it help if I told you my name was really Stephen?" He looked at Rudi and grinned. "No? Ah well, maybe you'll work it out eventually."

"Are we done?" asked Crispin.

Rudi looked from one to the other. "I wish you people would stop fucking with my life," he said.

"Hey, it wasn't just us," Crispin grumbled. "To be fair." He looked around the little group. "Let's go, yeah?

The bodyguards and the driver started to pick up bags and suitcases. Rudi looked about him and it suddenly occurred to him that he couldn't see the lights of the houses any more, or hear the distant sound of traffic. He inhaled slowly through his nose, breathed out again. The air smelled of damp soil and foliage and nothing else. He looked up, but there was too much cloud cover to be able to see the stars. He wondered which constellations he would see, if he could.

Molson shouldered his rucksack and nodded to Smith, who gave Rudi a little wave and turned and walked away down the path. The guards and driver followed her.

Crispin held out a set of keys. "Here, have a car," he said. "Or not. Get the Tube, I don't care." Rudi took the keys, and Crispin turned and strode after the others.

"He's actually very charming when you get to know him," Molson said.

"I've done all the getting to know him that I'm going to do," Rudi told him, and Molson laughed. "You might mention to him that this borderless Utopia of his will still have a border with us," Rudi added. "There are always borders."

"And where there are borders there are always Coureurs. Yes, you make a fair point. And I believe one such scenario was war-gamed in Dresden. Your name came up quite a lot in those war-games, actually. He has quite a lot of respect for you."

"He has a funny way of showing it."

Molson smiled. "You're still alive, no? Anyway, best get on. I'll be seeing you."

"You'll have to find me."

"That's never been a problem." Molson turned and followed the others, an agent who had apparently doubled himself so many times that he no longer had a country, finally going home. For a few seconds Rudi and Seth could see the light of his lantern through the overhanging branches and bushes, then it was gone.

"So," Seth said. "What now?"

Rudi sighed. "I need a drink," he said, and he turned and walked back towards Europe.

HIRAETH

1.

AFTERWARD, THEY WENT over to Każimierż for the reading of the will. The notary's office was up eight flights of stairs above a klezmer bar, and the sound of violins and dulcimers and clarinets drifted faintly up from below as the six of them, as per the deceased's instructions, sat crammed into the poky little room.

The notary looked after the legal interests of half the restaurateurs around Floriańska, and as such was the final repository of many secrets. She was a small grey woman in a dandruffy business suit, and she had the annoyed look of someone who cannot be surprised any more but still has to put up with people trying.

There was the familiar Polish ritual of signing and witnessing and stamping of documents – all of them on paper because that was how things were done. There was initialling and checking of identifications, in order to ensure that no interlopers had wandered in on the proceedings. Only when all this was accomplished to her satisfaction did the notary open the threadbare cardboard folder containing the will.

The reading took around forty minutes, during which time Rudi judged that the temperature in the office fell by roughly fifteen degrees. He carefully kept his eyes on the notary the whole time, but he could not fail to notice in his peripheral vision as heads were turned and harsh looks directed at him.

Returning to Floriańska, they found that the street had been taken over by seemingly hundreds of dachshunds and their owners. Many of the dogs were in costume, and so were a lot of the people. Rudi experienced a surreal moment, until he realised it was the annual Jamnik Parade. Poles loved dachshunds, and the parade had been part of Kraków's cultural calendar for almost a century. Rudi had forgotten all about it, but all of a sudden it seemed perfect for the general Kafkaesque tone of the day.

At the restaurant, Max's cousin had brought in a team of outside caterers to provide the meal. Many of the other mourners were already gathered there, and Rudi could actually watch as word of the events at the notary's office passed through the restaurant like a gust of wind through a field of barley.

He decided to concentrate on the food, arrayed on several pushed-together tables at one side of the room. There was barszcz – made up using powder from a sachet, he decided after tasting it. There were various quick and easy salads, cold meats, roasted chicken drumsticks, carp in jelly, sliced baguette going stale in baskets. *Cocktail sausages*. Rudi thought it was disrespectful. Max's current chef was a preternaturally calm woman named Zuza; she and Rudi had exchanged a few words, professional courtesy in the manner of two gunslingers passing each other on the street of a Western town. She seemed more than capable of producing a funeral luncheon.

"She said she didn't want any money spent," she'd told him. "The widow. Cheap as possible, I was told."

"This is a restaurant, for fuck's sake," he'd said. "He deserved better than a *buffet*." All she could do was shrug. Poles had a saying that went something like, 'Not my circus, not my monkeys.'

He leaned on his cane and looked around the restaurant. All of a sudden, it seemed smaller than he remembered, and it needed redecorating. It was crowded with people, all chatting quietly. Some of them were eating, some not, but all of them were drinking. Max's cousin, deep in choleric conversation with several older men and women, seemed to have taken particular advantage of the bottles arrayed on tables around the room. Rudi saw more harsh looks turned in his direction, heads shaken sadly.

At some point, he became aware of a presence beside him. He looked and discovered that Dariusz, Wesoły Ptak's liaison with the restaurateurs of the area, had contrived to materialise soundlessly at his elbow, smoking a cigarette and holding a glass of vodka.

They looked at each other for a while, then Dariusz said amiably, "There was some debate about whether you would turn up, you know."

Wesoły Ptak ran the protection rackets in this part of Kraków, and Dariusz was their representative on Earth, although he also worked as a stringer for *Les Coureurs des Bois*. Rudi had always wondered whether that meant the Coureurs actually ran Wesoły Ptak, or if the little mafioso was just moonlighting. That was one small mystery he didn't have to worry about any more. He wondered among whom the *debate* had taken place.

"I wanted to pay my respects," he said.

"And claim your inheritance," Dariusz added.

Rudi shook his head. "No," he allowed. "No, that was a surprise."

Dariusz looked him up and down. "You seem well."

And *that* statement could be parsed in any number of ways. But it seemed honestly meant, so Rudi decided to be charitable. "Thank you," he said.

Dariusz lowered his voice a fraction. "My masters would like a word," he said.

My masters. Rudi shook his head. Central was a self-fulfilling prophecy, the creation and sum of its citizens. From that perspective, Wesoły Ptak was almost certainly being run as an operation by one or more Coureurs for the purpose of raising funds for other, more unfathomable, operations. And so on, like a Matrioshka doll or the Mandelbrot Set, infinitely recursive. He'd done something similar himself, in the past. If *Les Coureurs* were a nation, as Kaunas had said, they were a nation like Europe. Splintered, Balkanised. *I am a nation,* he thought, and he found it simultaneously scary and empowering.

He wondered what Wesoły Ptak's Coureur creators were up to, and how much trouble he had caused them down the years. He wondered what would happen if he made contact with them. He wondered whether he even wanted to. He said, "I'm done with them."

"But they're not done with you." There was no sense of threat in the statement. Just two old colleagues meeting again after a separation of... how many years had it been?

"How long is it since we last saw each other?" Rudi asked.

Dariusz thought about it. "Fifteen years?" he asked. "Twenty?" He, himself, seemed not to have aged a single day, a testament to the preservative properties of the life of organised crime.

"Surely not twenty."

Dariusz shrugged. "So much has happened in the interim. The world has changed beyond recognition. Perhaps it just seems like a long time."

"A lot has certainly happened," Rudi said. "In the interim." He looked around the room again. From the other side, Seth caught his eye. He shook his head fractionally and Seth went back to letting a plump *babcia* Rudi vaguely recognised practice her English on him. Gwen, standing beside him, waved hello; Rudi waved back.

"I'm to tell you that it's over," Dariusz said, lowering his voice further so that Rudi found it hard to hear him.

"How can this be *over*?" Rudi asked. "It's not a football match. People have died."

"It's certainly not a football match," said Dariusz. "There are no winners and losers, only survivors. You appear to have survived. Congratulations."

Rudi wondered where the decision had come from. The prediction engine in Dresden-Neustadt? It was hard to be certain who was running the world any more, although obviously it wasn't the people who thought they were. "Has there been any word," he asked, "from Crispin?"

Dariusz smiled. "I have no idea who that is."

"Of course not." The initial shock and awe of the Heathrow Event – the authorities hadn't even bothered to try to suppress or conceal it, there was just no point – had settled, as Rudi had suspected, into a prolonged bickering between England and the Community about what to do with the transposed territories and people. A surprising number of people who had been at Heathrow wanted to remain in the Community. The Community didn't want them, they didn't want to leave, there had been a riot. There was talk, according to the media, of the transplanted Heathrow declaring itself an independent nation within the Community. It was problematic.

Even more problematic, but just as hard to suppress, was what had happened to the Line, most of its rolling stock, and all its citizens. Nobody seemed certain whether or not to claim its territory, which was considerable. No one wanted to take up the Line's track, with its peculiarly unhelpful gauge. The consensus seemed to be *wait and see*. There was no percentage in purposely antagonising an organisation which was capable of rewriting worlds. If it was an apocalypse, it was a discreet one. The world went on pretty much as it always had. More than anything, Rudi found himself disappointed. One always wants the great events of one's life to mean something. Certainly something more than very wealthy people doing what very wealthy people always do, which is protect their own interests.

"I would like to see what he's doing over there, though," Rudi added. "One day."

Dariusz drained his glass. "The only thing we can be certain of is that there are trains there." He held out his hand, and after a moment Rudi shook it. "What will you do with the restaurant?"

"I don't know. The news is still... new."

"I'll come round in a week or so, see if you're still here, and we can discuss your subscription."

The *subscription* prevented Wesoły Ptak from torching the restaurant. "Who's paying it at the moment?"

Dariusz made a dismissive gesture. "Call it a payment holiday."

Rudi looked at him, remembering when the little mafioso had seemed powerful and quite scary. "Out of interest," he said, "who told you to recruit me, back then?"

Dariusz smiled. He clapped Rudi on the arm. "We'll talk about the subscription." And he turned and walked away into the crowd of mourners.

After Dariusz had gone, Rupert eased his way over to the table and looked down at the arrayed food. "This is... disappointing," he said.

Rudi sighed. "I know."

"Problems?"

Rudi looked in the direction Dariusz had disappeared in. "Business as usual."

"Problems, then."

Rudi chuckled. "I think we've been parked, for the moment. Eventually someone will decide we're of some use; then they'll be in touch." He picked up a chicken drumstick and bit into it. He scowled and put it back on the serving platter. "This is a disgrace," he muttered.

"The Directorate already want to know what Crispin's up to," Rupert said.

"Of course they do."

Rupert seemed about to try some of the food, then decided against it. Life in Europe had spoiled him; there was a time when he would have made a spirited attempt to clear the table, all on his own. "I was checking my drops in Prague yesterday," he said. "There was a note from Michael. Sorry to bother you, but we were wondering... blah blah blah."

So far, all Rudi – all anyone, as far as he was aware – knew was a name. It was still a shadow, a *possibility*, floating somewhere below the surface of the great lake of rumour and supposition and straight-out bullshit that sloshed back and forth across Europe. The name of a fabled land beyond the sunrise. It was not a name, he knew with some certainty, beyond the capabilities of the Community's intelligence officers to discover.

"Did you reply to their request?" he asked.

"Not yet," Rupert said. "Fuck 'em."

Rudi nodded and sipped his drink. "*Fajnie,*" he murmured. There was a sense he had gained, travelling around Europe for the past few months, of a *pause,* a break while everyone got their breath back and took stock and tried to work out what to do next. As far as he was concerned, that could last as long as it wanted.

"I don't want to add to your problems," Rupert told him, "but that man over there is talking about having you killed."

They both looked over to where Max's cousin was becoming more and more animated, to the point where the people he was ranting at were trying to get him to calm down.

"How do you know what he's saying?" Rudi asked. "You don't speak Polish."

"They're speaking German. I understand enough German to know 'I want that fucker dead' when I hear it."

Rudi sighed. *Hindenbergers.* "It's okay. He'll be fine when he sobers up."

"If you say so."

"I'm in more danger from the food." He looked around the restaurant again. It looked like the setting for a particularly complicated joke. *People of many nationalities walk into a bar...* There were Poles here, Silesians, Kosovars, Italian and French chefs, a Spanish restaurateur, the senior staff from Max's Berlin restaurant, two English people, an Estonian, and the last citizen of the Campus. Michał, the restaurant's former maitre d', had suffered a stroke some years previously, but there he was, supported by a powered exoskeleton and communicating with other mourners by typing his side of the conversation with his one good hand on a pad which spoke out loud for him. His support worker was slumped in a corner, sleeping off the three bottles of Wyborowa on the table in front of him. The wake was a patchwork of poor, dead Europe, all come to mourn poor, dead Max, who had simply dropped in his tracks one day while following his monstrous, manipulative, controlling bully of a wife around the supermarket with a shopping trolley.

Across the room, the widow, Iwona, was talking to a group of people Rudi didn't recognise. She was managing to look at once piously bereaved and carnally available, which he thought was quite a trick. They had never met before; he knew nothing about her apart from Floriańska gossip he'd picked up in the few days he'd been back, but as they left the notary's office she had given him a look of such raw animal anger that he missed a step. It was a look which said *you have the thing I want and I will kill you for it some day.*

Well, it wasn't as if people wanting to kill him was a new thing. Iwona was hardly the only person in Europe to have wanted him dead. She wasn't even the only person in the *room* who wanted him dead. He'd been quite surprised by how one could get used to something like that, if one had to.

He had no idea what had gone on in Max's head in the autumn of his years, but life was like that. It never tied things up neatly; no one ever got to see the whole story, and anyway the stories never ended, just branched off into infinity. You got used to that too, as a Coureur. You jumped a Package from Point A to Point B and you never knew what happened after that. Most of the time you never even knew what you were carrying. It was a bit like being a chef, really. Guests came into the restaurant and you often knew nothing about them – if you didn't actually go out into the restaurant you never even *saw* them. They ate their meals and they went away and maybe they never came back. What were *their* stories?

Rudi shook his head and turned his back on Iwona.

He was not, even after everything, immune to the irony of inheriting the restaurant, the way he seemed to have inherited the Coureurs and the money Roland Sarkisian had stolen from the EU. Life is often absurd; all you can do is keep putting one foot in front of the other, looking for the joke in things – because there is always a joke, even if it's bitter and sour – hoping for the best and trying not to be too broken when it doesn't happen.

THE HUNGARIANS ARRIVED around nine in the evening, five huge men in exquisite suits. They were sober and respectful of demeanour, but the fifteen or so remaining mourners all moved as one out of their way and watched nervously as they sat down at one of the tables in the corner.

Their leader, a man who sometimes called himself Kerenyi and sometimes László Viktor, came over to where Rudi was standing talking to Seth and Rupert and Michał.

"Well," he said as he shook hands. "This is jolly."

"I didn't organise it," Rudi told him.

"One would hope not, obviously. Why is that very drunk man glowering at you?"

Rudi didn't need to look; for the past hour or so Max's cousin had given up making threats in favour of sitting with a couple of his Hindenberger friends and applying himself to becoming insensible.

"He's not a problem," he said.

"You want I should do his knees, just to be sure, actually?" Kerenyi asked with avuncular sincerity.

For just a moment, the thought did appeal, but Rudi shook his head. "I think just seeing you with me will be sufficient, thanks."

Kerenyi shrugged and pulled a sour face. "I remember when this place used to be fun."

"That was when Max was alive."

The Hungarian nodded. Then his face broke into a huge uncomplicated grin. "But hey," he said, "you own this place now, yes?"

Bad news is like entangled atoms; it manifests itself faster than the speed of light, over large distances. Somehow, though, it had needed someone to say it out loud to make it real, rather than using careful allusion. He had, he realised, been hoping he had misheard the notary.

"Yes," he said, with a genuine sense of surprise. "Yes, I do."

"So this place will be fun again?"

Rudi thought about it. "I'm hungry," he said. "Are you hungry?" And he took off his jacket and rolled up his sleeves and pushed through the swing door into the kitchen.

ACKNOWLEDGEMENTS

THIS WAS A tough one to write, at a tough time. That it exists at all is due to Gem, Ross, Liza, Dorian, Leif, Robin, James, Susannah, Suze, Frania, Kath, Pip, all the Helens, Fred, and everyone who put up with my whining and bitching and sent me good wishes while I was working on it.

Liza, Cary and Caroline beta-read the manuscript, and again any and all mistakes are mine, not theirs.

Juhan Habicht not only translated *Europe in Autumn* into Estonian but fixed all the mistakes in the book while he was at it; translators don't get nearly enough recognition and I owe Juhan a huge thank you.

I've always been lucky with my covers, but Clint Langley has done a wonderful thing with the covers of these books, and I owe him my deepest thanks.

I'd also like to thank Jon, Ben, Rob, Dave and Mike at Solaris, and Lydia, who is no longer there but has always been a friend to the books.

Carey Tews, Sarah Smith, Grant Forsyth and Stephen Coltrane are all real people, and they donated money to John Underwood's fund-raising effort for Anthony Nolan, in return for having characters named after them. I tried not to make the characters do anything *too* actionable. If you want to donate at John's JustGiving page, you can do it here: https://www.justgiving.com/John-Underwood-Anthony-Nolan. Alternatively, donate to Delete Blood Cancer at http://www.deletebloodcancer.org.uk/en, or register as a stem-cell donor. I can't promise to name a character after you, but you'll be making a difference all the same.

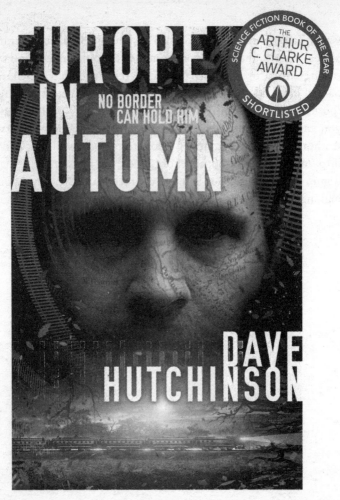

EUROPE IN AUTUMN

NO BORDER CAN HOLD HIM

SCIENCE FICTION BOOK OF THE YEAR
THE ARTHUR C. CLARKE AWARD
SHORTLISTED

DAVE HUTCHINSON

Rudi is a cook in a Kraków restaurant, but when his boss asks Rudi to help a cousin escape from the country he's trapped in, a new career — part spy, part people-smuggler — begins. Following multiple economic crises and a devastating flu pandemic, Europe has fractured into countless tiny nations, duchies, polities and republics. Recruited by the shadowy organisation *Les Coureurs des Bois*, Rudi is schooled in espionage, but when a training mission to The Line, a sovereign nation consisting of a trans-Europe railway line, goes wrong, he is arrested and beaten, and *Coureur* Central must attempt a rescue.

With so many nations to work in, and identities to assume, Rudi is kept busy travelling across Europe. But when he is sent to smuggle someone out of Berlin and finds a severed head inside a locker instead, a conspiracy begins to wind itself around him. With kidnapping, double-crosses and a map that constantly re-draws itself, *Europe in Autumn* is a science fiction thriller like no other.

 WWW.SOLARISBOOKS.COM

Follow us on Twitter! www.twitter.com/solarisbooks

EUROPE AT MIDNIGHT

'SEEMINGLY EFFORTLESS LITERARY FLAIR'
THE GUARDIAN

DAVE HUTCHINSON

THE ARTHUR C. CLARKE AWARD
SCIENCE FICTION BOOK OF THE YEAR
SHORTLISTED

In a fractured Europe, new nations are springing up everywhere, some literally overnight.

For an intelligence officer like Jim, it's a nightmare. Every week or so a friendly power spawns a new and unknown national entity which may or may not be friendly to England's interests. It's hard to keep on top of it all. But things are about to get worse for Jim. A stabbing on a London bus pitches him into a world where his intelligence service is preparing for war with another universe, and a man has come who may hold the key to unlocking Europe's most jealously-guarded secret...

'A work of staggering genius.'
Paul Cornell

'A real feat of the imagination, this is a really exceptional book, unlike anything I've ever read before.'

Chris Beckett
Arthur C. Clarke Award winner

TONY BALLANTYNE
DREAM LONDON

Captain Jim Wedderburn has looks, style and courage. He's adored by women, respected by men and feared by his enemies. He's the man to find out who has twisted London into this strange new world. But in Dream London the city changes a little every night and the people change a little every day. The towers are growing taller, the parks have hidden themselves away and the streets form themselves into strange new patterns. There are people sailing in from new lands down the river, new criminals emerging in the East End and a path spiraling down to another world.

Everyone is changing, no one is who they seem to be.

It is the biggest experiment in history...

Eidolon
LIBBY McGUGAN

...and it must be destroyed

When physicist Robert Strong — newly unemployed and single — is offered a hundred thousand pounds for a week's work, he's understandably sceptical. But Victor Amos, head of the mysterious Observation Research Board, has compelling proof that the next round of experiments at CERN's Large Hadron Collider poses a real threat to the whole world. And he needs Robert to sabotage it.

Robert's life is falling apart. His work at the Dark Matter Research Laboratory in Middlesbrough was taken away from him; his girlfriend, struggling to cope with the loss of her sister, has left. He returns home to Scotland, seeking sanctuary and rest, and instead starts to question his own sanity as the dead begin appearing to him, in dreams and in waking. Accepting Amos's offer, Robert flies to Geneva, but as he infiltrates CERN, everything he once understood about reality and science, about the boundary between life and death, changes forever. Mixing science, philosophy and espionage, Libby McGugan's stunning debut is a thriller like no other.

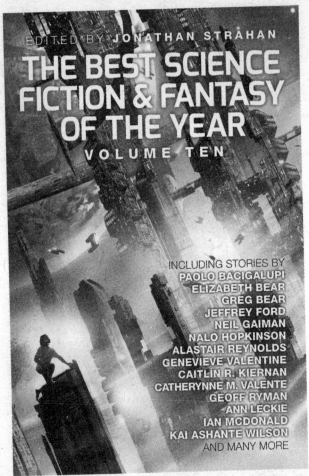

EDITED BY JONATHAN STRAHAN

THE BEST SCIENCE FICTION & FANTASY OF THE YEAR

VOLUME TEN

INCLUDING STORIES BY
PAOLO BACIGALUPI
ELIZABETH BEAR
GREG BEAR
JEFFREY FORD
NEIL GAIMAN
NALO HOPKINSON
ALASTAIR REYNOLDS
GENEVIEVE VALENTINE
CAITLÍN R. KIERNAN
CATHERYNNE M. VALENTE
GEOFF RYMAN
ANN LECKIE
IAN MCDONALD
KAI ASHANTE WILSON
AND MANY MORE

Jonathan Strahan, the award-winning and much lauded editor of many of genre's best known anthologies, is back with his tenth volume in this fascinating series, featuring the best science fiction and fantasy from 2015. With established names and new talent, this diverse and ground-breaking collection will take the reader to the outer reaches of space and the inner realms of humanity with stories of fantastical worlds and worlds that may still come to pass.

Featuring stories by: Neil Gaiman, Elizabeth Bear, Greg Bear, Geoff Ryman, Ann Leckie, Jeffrey Ford, Nalo Hopkinson, Nisi Shawl, Ian McDonald, Paolo Bacigalupi, Alyssa Wong, Kelly Link, Alastair Reynolds, Tamsyn Muir, Simon Ings, Gwyneth Jones, Usman T. MaLik, Nike Sulway, Caitlín R. Kiernan, Robert Reed, Kelly Robson, Catherynne M. Valente, Kim Stanley Robinson, Genevieve Valentine, Vonda N. McIntrye, Sam J. Miller and Kai Ashante Wilson

 WWW.SOLARISBOOKS.COM

Follow us on Twitter! www.twitter.com/solarisbooks

EDITED BY JONATHAN STRAHAN

DROWNED WORLDS

with stories by
Ken Liu
Paul McAuley
James Morrow
Charlie Jane Anders
Kim Stanley Robinson
Kathleen Ann Goonan
Jeffrey Ford
and more

'Books as good as this should be of interest to any admirer of short fiction, regardless of genre.'
The Guardian on The Best Science Fiction and Fantasy of the Year Volume Eight

We stand on the brink of one of the greatest ecological disasters of our time – the world is warming and seas are rising, and yet water is life; it brings change. Where one thing is wiped away, another rises.

Drowned Worlds looks at the future we might have if the oceans rise – good or bad. Here you'll find stories of action, adventure, romance and, yes, warning and apocalypse. Stories inspired by Ballard's *The Drowned World*, Sterling's *Islands in the Net*, and Ryman's *The Child Garden*; stories that allow that things may get worse, but remembers that such times also bring out the best in us all.

Multi-award winning editor Jonathan Strahan has put together fifteen unique tales of deluged worlds and those who fight to survive and strive to live.

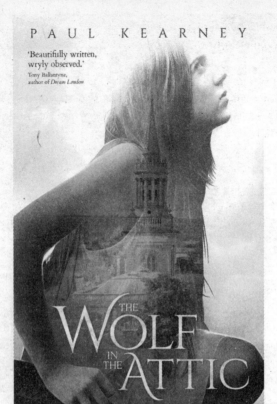